Satan's Silence

Alex Matthews

Intrigue Press

For information, please contact Intrigue Press, P.O. Box 456, Angel Fire, NM 87710, 505-377-3474.

ISBN 0-9643161-5-3
LCCN 96-79331

First Printing 1997

This book is a work of fiction. Although Cassidy McCabe and the author have many circumstances in common, none of the actions or events is based on real events in the author's life. Names, characters, places and incidents either are the product of the author's imagination or are used fictitiously. Any resemblance to actual events or persons living or dead is entirely circumstantial. Although the author and publisher have made every effort to ensure the accuracy and completeness of information contained in this book, we assume no responsibility for errors, inaccuracies, omissions, or any inconsistency herein. Any slights of people, places or organizations are unintentional.

Grateful acknowledgment is made for permission to reprint the following material:

A line from the comic strip *Sylvia* © 1995 by Nicole Hollander. Used by permission. All rights reserved.

For my husband Allen,
Who makes all things possible.

The author wishes to acknowledge the invaluable assistance of Allen Matthews, who tirelessly read revisions and made the computer do what she wanted; Chris Roerden, who provided editing, mentoring, and encouragement; Phyllis Rubin and Sunny Hall, who listened; and Nancy Carleton, Denise Stybr, Jan Fellers, and Carol Houswald, who gave invaluable feedback as critique group members.

1

Missing

Pretty weird stuff, Cassidy McCabe thought as she drove through a warm September storm, the rain-smeared windshield distorting her vision like a funhouse mirror.

Heading across Oak Park, she was on her way home from a training group for therapists which taught a new method of therapy that separated out different parts of the personality. *Some bizarre stories today.* One therapist had presented a case that gave her the willies, made her wonder if working with subpersonalities might be a tad risky. The therapist described a male client, seemed to be a decent sort, who possessed a part that was honest-to-God evil. *Shades of The Exorcist.*

Sure, there are garden-variety sociopaths. On the extreme end, monsters like Dahmer and Bundy. But a down-to-earth family man popping up with a part that wants to poison the kids' pets? C'mon.

Cassidy heard voices chattering inside her head all the time, parts that squabbled, debated, pulled in opposite directions. Identifying these voices as subpersonalities enabled her to better understand the internal workings of people—herself as well as clients. So when she'd first encountered the Subpersonality Model of therapy, it made perfect sense to her. Having joined the training group and attended three monthly meetings, she had so far netted good results using this model, although today's talk of strange parts was unsettling.

Stopping at the Chicago-Ridgeland light, she peered through early evening gloom at a small group huddled against the downpour on the northeast corner. It was the time of day when the sheltered workshop let out, releasing a dozen or so men and women, all with the same innocent, childlike expression. Oak Park, a place for everybody, one of the reasons she loved living here.

A junk car, its grill crushed in like a beer can, barreled through the red light, nearly sideswiping her. A reminder that her social-worker belief in intrinsic human worth was occasionally challenged by some of the types Oak Park made a place for. Turning right, she headed toward her house on the village's eastern edge. She lived a block from Austin Boulevard, the line separating an impoverished, gang-banger jungle on the east from her own zealously active, integrated suburb on the west.

As she drove, her mind slipped into a familiar groove, the two voices in her head bickering in their ongoing quarrel.

He should call more often. Every week it's the same—open-arms Saturday night, bye-toots in the morning. This from the voice that, like her mother, considered having Zach in her life only slightly better than roaches in her kitchen.

The other voice, the one that favored sex and self-indulgence, jumped in instantly. *So what if Saturday nights are all you get? You'd rather stay home with a good book? Zach may not be around as much as you'd like, but when he is, it's fireworks and shooting stars time.*

She arrived at the Hazel-Briar intersection with her cranberry colored two-story standing on the southeast corner. Parked in front of her house was a battered van, psychedelic depictions of naked bodies painted on all sides, the words *Gacy's Boys* scrawled through the middle. She headed south on Hazel, intending to turn around in the cul-de-sac at the end of the block so she could park on her own side of the street. The village had installed cul-de-sacs throughout the east end to discourage Chicago bad guys from cruising Oak Park. Passing the van, she scrutinized the scraggly-haired figure slouched in the driver's seat. *Better not sit there too long—I'll have the police on your butt.*

She circled the cul-de-sac, drove north to the end of the block, then stopped behind the unfamiliar van. Jumping out of her Toyota, she ran through the storm toward her house, the arm she held up to shield her face pelted by wind-driven bullets of rain. She burst onto the enclosed porch, shook out her cinnamon hair, and dropped her wet jacket on the wicker couch. A flier lay just inside the screendoor: "Meet your neighborhood beat officer." *Another crime on the block?*

Mingled with the howl of wind and rain, she heard the thunk of boot leather slapping concrete and whirled to see a chunky male land on her top step. He propped his hands on either side of the door, bringing a scruffy face beneath a backward baseball cap up close to the screen. She momentarily stopped breathing. In her neighborhood stories of midday robberies were not uncommon.

Stepping in front of the screendoor, she shoved her hands against the frame to hold it closed. She asked, voice less than cordial, "What can I do for you?"

"Lookin' for Dana." He yanked his hands away from the house, jammed them onto his hips, then ran fingers through his short, ragged beard. "Friend of mine, he told me she was here." He talked rapidly, words coming in short bursts like rounds of gunfire.

Dana's a client. Why think he'd find her here? Cassidy leaned closer to get a better look. Jumpy, dilated eyes, constant fidgeting. *Must be on something.*

"Dana, you know, Dana Voss. You ask her, we're tight, her and me's like this." He held up two crossed fingers. "She crashin' with you?"

"Wrong address. I don't know anybody by that name."

"C'mon." He softened his voice in a crude attempt at cajolery, then half-heartedly pushed at the door.

Blocking it with her foot, she pressed harder on her side. *V.I. would probably take him out if he gave her any trouble.* But Cassidy, who wore petite sizes and did not lift weights, was not about to try throwing him off her steps.

"Look, this ain't no joke." His voice turned gruff. "I gotta see her. You tell Dana—Curly's gonna look her up, ain't no way she can get out of it. I got business with her—important business. Won't do her no good, trying to hide out."

"Maybe you didn't hear me. Now if you don't mind . . . "

"All right, all right." He raised his hands, palms out, and stumbled backward down the steps. "But you tell her, you hear? Curly's got business with her."

Cassidy watched as he trotted back to the van and drove out of sight. Even if he'd been normal—even if he might actually be a friend—she would never give out information about a client.

This character must be from Dana's past life when she was heavy into drugs, almost three years ago. So why would a sleazy-rocker-head be on her tail after all this time?

Cassidy went inside and started up the L-shaped stairway. She stopped at the landing, suddenly remembering she hadn't seen Starshine since early that morning. The calico had planted herself against the back door and yowled to go out. Knowing the cat did not like rain, Cassidy had tried reasoning, tried ignoring, but finally gave in to her irresistible and ear-splitting demands.

Tiny fingers of panic clutched at her stomach as she did an about-face and sprinted down to the porch. Starshine never stayed away all day. Often, minutes after letting her out, Cassidy would find a pouty cat on the stoop, her attitude seeming to say, *What took you so long?*

So where was she? She should've been waiting at the door. *You forgot about her. Didn't go back right away and let her in like you were supposed to. She gave up on you. Ran away.*

Cassidy stood on the top step, arms wrapped around her midsection, rain hurtling against her. The porch window she left open so Starshine could come and go as she pleased blew back and pounded into the one beside it. She called "Kitty, kitty," but her voice got lost in the whoosh and drumbeat of the storm. Wind chimes jangled furiously. She envisioned a tiny, triangle face, one ear black, one ear orange. A small sodden cat huddled under a bush, ears and whiskers drooping, tail plastered to the ground. Shivering, Cassidy hugged herself tighter.

Why didn't she jump through the open window and wait on the porch, way she usually does?

Cats are inconsistent. Like to keep you off balance—like men.

She plodded back upstairs, telling herself to stop worrying. *Damn cat—never wanted her in the first place.* But despite muggy, end-of-summer heat, she couldn't shake the clammy feeling that had settled over her when she first realized Starshine had gone out that morning and not returned.

≈ ≈ ≈

Trudging into her bedroom at the top of the stairs, she peeled off her rain-dampened jeans and replaced them with the ripped ones lying on the floor. She inhaled deeply. *Starshine missing, this guy Curly after Dana.*

She pictured Dana, her tall, lanky client. Dana and her two-year-old as she'd seen them a month earlier when she stopped at her client's house to drop off Dana's left-behind jacket, mother and daughter rolling together in the grass like two puppies at play. The idea of Creepo Curly coming near either one of them set her teeth on edge.

Need to warn her. She sat at her large executive desk in the corner of the bedroom and picked up the phone.

"Oh Cass, I'm so glad you called. I was thinking of—what I mean is, I thought maybe I'd come in for an extra session. I mean, if it's okay with you."

Tuesday after Labor Day. No clients scheduled. "Sure, I could see you tonight. But what's up?"

"Over this long weekend, I just—I had a hard time, that's all. I'm all—I'm just all stressed out. And now you call, it's sorta like you read my mind."

They scheduled an appointment for seven. Cassidy considered warning her about Curly but decided to wait until Dana arrived. She wanted to watch her reaction.

After hanging up, Cassidy sat, hand on receiver, reviewing Dana's history. Rejecting, critical father, overindulgent mother. Teenage sex and drugs. Psych hospitalization at twenty. Continued drugging after the hospital. Lived with friends, bummed around. Pregnant at twenty-four, quit drugs on the spot. Withdrawal tough but no slips. Started new relationship. Moved into two-flat owned by cousin and cousin's husband. Boyfriend Wayne moved in with her. Began therapy six months ago.

Anybody who's straightened herself up like Dana has deserves a chance. What she does not deserve is the ghost of mistakes past turning up on her doorstep.

ཙ ཙ ཙ

Cassidy, wearing a violet blouse and burgundy pants, led Dana into her office at the rear of the house. Her client settled on a beat-up, black vinyl sofa beneath one of the room's two wide windows. At twenty-seven the young woman was a decade younger than Cassidy, but the gap between them seemed greater, more like the distance between parent and child.

Cassidy said, "Before we get started, there's something I need to ask you about. A guy named Curly came to my door looking for you."

Dana's face paled. "Curly? Why would he show up here?" She shook her head as if puzzled, waved a dismissive hand. "Brains fried, know what I mean? Total waste. I mean, total burn-out. No telling why he does anything."

"What reason would he have for thinking you lived here?"

Spreading her hands palms up, Dana shrugged elaborately.

"But you know who he is?"

"Oh sure." Dana's knee started a jiggly little dance. "One of the dopers, know what I mean, used to hang out in this bar we all went to. Real slimebag. Considered himself a musician—can you believe it? A musician. But he was—he was too fucked to get anywhere. Never had much to do with him myself." Her brown eyes shone with innocence. "Can't imagine why he'd, you know, want to look me up now." She shook her head. "Can't imagine."

First time, ever thought she was lying. "Well," Cassidy said slowly, "if you can't explain about Curly, guess we'll have to put that on hold for now. So, what's got you all stressed?"

"Something happened." Dana's rose-petal face tightened. "Something bad. But I don't want to talk about it, okay?" She pushed unruly, fawn-colored hair back from her cheek. "Anyway, what I've been—what I'm dying to tell you is, I've finally decided about the baptism. I'm gonna, you know, do it. Really do it."

Realizing Dana would get to the "something bad" in her own time, Cassidy said, "You've been agonizing for months. What got you to decide?"

"Josie, she's the one, she talked me into it." Dana's frosted fingernails rolled up the bottom of a grubby, oversized T. "It was Josie."

"So if it doesn't go right, it's Josie's fault?" Cassidy softened her voice to take the sting out. "Must be convenient, living with your boyfriend on the second floor of your cousin's house, having Wayne and Josie make decisions for you."

Dana hunched forward on the shabby vinyl sofa. Propping her right ankle on her left knee, she pulled her leg close to her body. "Guess I'm, you know, trying to avoid responsibility again, huh? How'm I ever—how'm I gonna to be a proper mother for Cypress if I can't grow up myself?"

"I don't know. How are you?"

Laughter burbled up, a clear water stream bumping rocks. "That's what I hate about coming here, know what I mean? You never let me get away with anything."

Smiling fondly, Cassidy leaned back in her director's chair and rested a burgundy pump on the low wicker table separating her from her client. Droopy leaves from a thirsty-looking coleus tickled her foot. "What would you like to get away with?"

"Same game I used to, you know, play with Mom. I'd say something mean about myself, okay? Then she'd—what she'd say is, 'You're the bestest little girl in the world.' "

"You want me to be your mother?"

Wide brown eyes filled. Slender hands wadded the T-shirt. The light from the window behind her head was as dense and heavy as smoke. The interior light from an overhead brass fixture failed to penetrate the corners of the paneled room. Humidity brought an ancient, musty odor up from the carpet.

"What is it you want?" Cassidy slipped into her crooning, you-can-tell-me-anything tone.

"My mother—my mother back, the way she used to be."
Dana's hand darted for the Kleenex box on the wicker table.
Her thickly lashed eyes squeezed shut.

"One part of you wants to be a little kid again and get your
mother to take care of you." *You always talk this way after
your subpersonalities group.*

Wiping the tears, Dana crushed the tissue into a tiny ball
in her right hand. Her mouth twitched down, then instantly
swept back into its usual upward curve. "I've been having
those—those attacks again," she ventured. Worried brown
eyes flitted to Cassidy's face, checking for disapproval. One
hand picked at a square of plastic tape that covered the hole
left by a missing button on the seat of the garage-sale sofa.

"Anxiety attacks?"

Dana lowered her eyes and nodded slightly. "This was, you
know, really weird. We were sitting—I mean, it was Wayne
and me, we were at this bar watching television. Anyway, this
guy on TV, he had a knife, okay? He had this knife in his
hand." Her voice shaking, she gulped in air. "And he—he
raised it way up high like he was gonna, you know, slash
something, and then . . . "

After a long pause, Cassidy said, "Then what?"

"I'm afraid to . . . " Dana pulled her knees up tight to her
chest, stretching the faded T over them. "Afraid you'll think
I'm crazy, okay?"

"What happened?"

"This guy on TV, he was gonna—gonna slash somebody,
and when the knife started—it started comin' down . . . You
gotta understand, I only had just this one beer. I mean, I swear
it was only one. And when the knife started comin' down, I got
this weird feeling, know what I mean? Real scared . . . didn't
know where I was . . . " She paused, mouth open, chest
heaving.

Cassidy said, "That's all right. Just take your time."

"I jumped up from the bar . . . I mean, I knocked over my beer, ran out—out onto the sidewalk. Next thing I know, Wayne's holding my arms, shaking me. Beer all over, screaming—screaming and I couldn't stop." Dana huddled into herself, dropping her head and letting her tousled brown hair fall forward. Ragged, gasping sounds came from within the closed-off curve of hair and body. Wind gusted outside, shaking window panes. A tree branch scraped the soffit above the office.

"Take a deep breath," Cassidy instructed, voice low and soothing. "That's right. It's okay now." She continued until Dana's breathing deepened and her body relaxed. She had worked with Dana like this before, first guiding her into a light trance, then asking a subpersonality to communicate. "Just let your eyes close. That's right. Now see if you can find the scared part, the one that got so frightened by the man on TV."

Dana froze. Her whole body jerked. "No!" she screamed in a small, childlike voice. "Don't!" The back of Cassidy's neck prickled. Dana seemed to crumple, becoming younger and smaller before her eyes. Whispering to herself, Dana started rocking back and forth.

Cassidy leaned forward. *Omigod! What's going on?* Keeping her voice even, she asked, "How old are you?"

"Four." A tiny voice. Eyes scrunched tight, Dana extended one hand to show Cassidy four fingers.

"Where are you, sweetie?"

"Dark." The voice quavered. "Scared. Don't like it here. Wanna go home. Where's Mommy?"

"Tell me where you are."

"Dead peoples. Dead peoples in front of a church. First they put us in a big car and made us all shush, then they drove a long ways. I hadda go tinkle and they told me *shush* and I wet my pants. Daddy's gonna be mad."

"Dead people in front of a church? A cemetery?"

Dana nodded. "Cem'tery. Dead peoples. Don't like it here. They got big tall bear. Waaay big!" She extended a hand upward. "Waaay up in the sky. White. They told us *stand there* and I looked up. Looked at the big white bear. I don't wanna see."

"See what?"

"Nothin'."

"You looked at the white bear so you didn't have to see—?"

Dana put a finger to her lips. "Don't tell!"

"Who said not to tell?"

"Mens did."

"What men?"

"Big tall black mens."

Cassidy nodded encouragingly even though Dana's eyes were still closed. "Black mens?"

"They got black skirts. Long black skirts."

"Do you know who they are? It's okay to tell, sweetheart. You're safe now."

"Don't know." Her voice went shrill with panic.

"What did the men in the black skirts do?"

"Don't tell!" Her voice imperative. *"Same thing happen to you."*

"The same as happened to somebody else? One of your friends?"

Hunching over, Dana stuck her thumb in her mouth.

"Which friend?" Cassidy ran the tip of her tongue across her bottom lip.

"Which one gets it? Him or me? Not me. Him. Do it to him."

"Do what? Tell me what they did."

"They said *look* but I wouldn't. Looked at the bear so I didn't have to see. But I *heard*." Dana clamped her hands over her ears, "Couldn't make it stop."

Cassidy laced her fingers in her lap, hands pressing together so tightly the knuckles went white. "You heard your friend screaming?"

Dana nodded vigorously. "Couldn't make it stop."

"They hurt your friend?"

Dana nodded again.

"Then what happened?"

"Down the hole."

"What hole?"

"White thing on top. Mens moved it off and threw him in. Have to *keep quiet* or they put me down the hole. Daddy's mad. Wet my pants. *Bad girl. How could you be so stupid. Stinky. Go away.*"

Dana's eyes suddenly flew open and flicked around the room. Folding her arms across her stomach, she doubled over, a guttural wail pushing its way through clenched teeth. She slid to the floor between sofa and table and curled into a ball, body shaken by long, wrenching sobs.

2

Drop-in

Pushing back the wicker table, Cassidy knelt beside Dana, breathing in the faint odor emanating from her client's body, a mix of sweat and fear. *What've I done? Full-blown regression. Shouldn't have tried working with parts. She was already scared by the anxiety attack, spooked about Curly.*

Stroking Dana's hair, she made comforting sounds until the sobbing quieted. "C'mon up." She pulled Dana into a sitting position on the floor, back propped against the claw-footed sofa. "Be back in a minute." Cassidy left the office, passed through the waiting room into the kitchen, and returned with a cool washcloth to wipe Dana's face.

Dana grabbed Cassidy's wrist, the long nails pricking her skin. "Not supposed to tell." Her voice was shriller than normal, but at least it sounded adult.

"You're safe here. There's nothing to worry about."

"No, wait, you don't—you just don't get it, do you? I can never, I mean, no matter what, I can't talk about it. Never!"

"No one'll ever know."

Dana covered her face. "You don't understand."

Squeezing Dana's shoulder, Cassidy got to her feet. "I'll just get us some tea." Inside the waiting room was a small counter with a hot water pot and herbal teas. She filled two mugs, then sat back down on the mustard carpet. Handing one to Dana, she said, "Could we talk about what happened?"

"No!" Almost a shriek.

"Okay, but you need to realize it all happened a long time ago. There's no reason for anyone to find out anything."

Dana's wide, milk chocolate eyes stared disbelievingly. Gripping the mug with both hands, she took a tentative sip. "Sure could use something, you know, stronger."

Me too, but I'd never admit it. "Aside from 'something stronger,' what would make you feel better?"

"I need—I mean, I've gotta get home. Right now. If I'm gone too long, Wayne, he'll wanna know, he'll try to find out what happened."

"I can't let you drive like this. Why don't I call Wayne or Josie to come get you?"

"Don't!" The panic was back in her voice. "Please, I don't want them to see me like this. They'd make—they'd try to get me to talk about it." She thumped down the mug and struggled to her feet. "I gotta get outta here."

Cassidy stood also. "You're still upset. I don't want you driving alone."

Dana's liquid brown eyes implored her. "I'll be all right. I promise."

She'll be okay. Oak Park's safe. This from her rose-colored-glasses voice.

You had your purse snatched right outside your own back gate. You're always thinking Oak Park's this ideal community with its racial-peace-and-harmony gig. You're in denial big-time, her gloom-and-doom voice argued back.

Only a few blocks. She's in the car with the door locked, she'll be all right.

ða ða ða

Cassidy stood on her back stoop in the drizzle—all that remained of the storm—and watched Dana drive away in the

14

tiny red Fiesta she'd borrowed from her cousin Josie. A block away on Austin Boulevard sirens howled, building and fading, a sound so familiar she scarcely heard it anymore. She rubbed fine droplets out of her lashes, blinked, and scrutinized her weedy, overgrown yard, awash in yellow street lights. Starshine approved of unmown grass: all the better for stalking. Cassidy called "Kitty, kitty." No response. She locked up and trudged through the house.

Approaching the stairway, she picked up television voices drifting down from above. Zach must have used his key to come in the front door, which she couldn't hear from her office in the back. *Not like him to just drop over.* He'd initiated a relationship three months ago, establishing a routine in which she spent Saturday nights at his Chicago condo and he remained generally incommunicado the rest of the week.

Apparently breaking the pattern tonight—all on his terms, of course. He can show up whenever he damn well pleases, but there's no way he'd let me walk into his bedroom uninvited.

Upstairs she found Zach lounging diagonally across her king-sized bed, remote control in hand. Her jaw tensed as she noticed his dirty socks on the satin comforter her grandmother had given her. *Why so picky? The cat's practically shredded it anyway.*

He glanced up as she crossed the room toward her desk, which faced the wall opposite the television. "Where's Starshine?"

"What're you doing here?" Cassidy slid into her swivel chair and began flipping through a pile of mail, the glossy desktop barely visible under heaped papers. Rainstreaked windows on either side of her massive corner desk reflected dark, scattered images.

"Remember that story I told you about? Cops on the take? I finished it early and thought I'd stop over." Zach's crisp baritone slowed to a burry drawl.

Although he was talking to the back of her head, Cassidy knew from the sound of his voice exactly how he'd look: smoky eyes narrowed and soft; wide mouth relaxed into a half smile; compact body sprawled out in faded jeans and black Heinekin's T-shirt, so old it fit like shrink-wrapped packaging.

"Now that the storm's blown itself out, the forecast is for several days of late summer heat." The peppy voice from the other side of the room grated on her nerves.

"Would it be asking too much to turn off the background noise?" Cassidy went through the pile a second time.

The television droned on. She concentrated on putting junk mail into the trash, bills into the wicker basket.

Zach killed the power. "You want me to leave?"

She rotated her chair halfway around to meet his eyes. He'd turned away from the TV and was facing her direction, pillows plumped behind his back, feet hanging off the side of the bed. His broad face wore its usual look of detached curiosity, as if she were some intriguing anomaly he was trying to understand so he could write it up for the newspaper.

"You come and go whenever you like but I have to walk on eggshells." Crossing her legs, she brushed white cat hair off her burgundy pants. "I don't think you'd be exactly thrilled if I just dropped by your place."

Zach picked up a glass from the nightstand, rattled the ice, and took a swallow, his demeanor unaffected by the scowl that came over her face when she noticed the drink. Jack Daniels and soda, no doubt. Before he came along, she'd never kept anything stronger than wine in the house. Now he just walked in, using the key she'd given him, mixed a drink from the bourbon she'd stocked in hopes of luring him over more often, then wandered up to her bedroom to watch TV.

Cassidy checked her watch. Nearly nine. "You here for the night? I thought you hated sleeping anywhere except your Marina City waterbed."

One shaggy brow rose slightly. "What's eating you, any-way?"

"Nothing." She paced two steps over to the bed, snatched the glass out of his hand, gulped down half the contents, then sank back into her chair. "Starshine's gone and I just had the most grueling session I've ever had in my whole entire life, that's all."

"What do you mean, 'gone?' "

"I let her out this morning and haven't seen her since."

Zach started to get up. "I'll go check."

"I just did." Cassidy's chin dropped. "She ran away because I forgot her."

"Shit."

"The alternative—she isn't here because she can't get here—is worse."

He emptied his glass. "I'll fix you a drink."

And another for yourself. "I don't want a drink."

He raised his stocky, just under six foot body from the bed. "I'm going to call her."

"All right, fix me one too."

Zach returned minutes later. "You wanna talk about your session?" He handed her a glass, then eased down on the bed and took a sip from his own.

"I can't—you know that."

He leaned against the headboard, his steady blue-gray eyes infusing her with his own sense of calm, as though an I.V. line ran between them. "You want me to leave?" he asked again, voice mild.

She swallowed deeply and kicked off her pumps. Propping her heels on the cold radiator, she reclined in her chair and chewed on her bottom lip. The window above the radiator was open, letting in a fresh, damp breeze. Small puddles had formed on the oak windowsill. "I don't know what to make of it," she said, half aloud.

Zach sipped his drink and waited.

She did not intend to tell him, but suddenly the words started pouring out. "This guy named Curly came to the door trying to find Dana, the client I was just with. He was driving a psychedelic van and seemed to be on drugs." *Shouldn't have used her name. Shouldn't have talked at all. Oh shit, why'd I do that?*

Words kept coming; she was powerless to stop them. "When I told Dana, she pretended she didn't know anything about it, but her reaction was obvious. Then later in the session, something really strange happened." Staring into the dark, reflective window, she spoke more to herself than to Zach. "It was all my fault. The leader of this training group I'm in said never to separate personalities unless the client's pretty much centered, which Dana certainly wasn't."

"Separate personalities?" His face turned dubious. "What kind of voodoo you practicing now?"

Her voice sharpened. "This method is very effective. Long as you don't jump in too fast, which is where I went wrong. It's based on the idea that we all have lots of different subpersonalities, each with its own distinct role. A part that wants to do the right thing—sort of like a conscience. A part that wants to feel good. A part that wants to work, another that wants to play."

He raised his glass, tipping it in her direction. "My feelgood part is on the job."

She frowned. "The way this method works is, the therapist locates parts that are creating a problem and helps clients bring them into line. This woman tonight had an anxiety attack a few days ago, so I asked the scared part to show itself. Normally people use imagery and simply visualize their parts. But this time Dana regressed on me. I watched her turn into a four-year-old—a little kid reliving this horrible memory—

right in front of my eyes." Goosebumps broke out on Cassidy's arms.

"Abuse?"

"Sounded like a Satanic cult or something. She talked as if she were a little girl forced to witness the sacrifice of another child. Said these black-robed men took a bunch of kids out to a cemetery and actually killed one of them, then threw the body down a hole with a 'white thing' on top." Cassidy gave her head a vigorous shake. "But it couldn't have been a real memory."

Zach's eyes became more alert. "Why not?"

"Just too spooky. I can't believe things like that really happen." She thought a moment. "No, that's not right. I know a couple of therapists with ritual abuse survivors as clients. In fact, they're suddenly popping up in all the literature—sort of the disease of the week. Which in itself makes me wonder. I guess it's mostly I don't want to believe it." She gave an involuntary shudder. "And the other thing is, what she said doesn't make sense. She kept referring to this big white bear in the middle of a cemetery."

"St. Paul's. The cemetery surrounding that little church in the southwestern forest preserve."

"Huh?" Her forehead creased doubtfully. "What're you talking about?"

"Headstone. This rich guy's old man used to hunt grizzlies, so the guy gave his father a monument in the shape of a fifteen-foot white bear. It was over thirty years ago the bear went up."

"What a fount of trivia. You could make your fortune on game shows, you know that?"

"This's more than the usual stray tidbit." Zach laced his fingers on top of his smooth, dark head. "There're some intense personal memories attached to that bear."

"Let me guess . . . " Cassidy wrinkled her nose. "Is that where you used to hang out with your dopehead friends, back when you were in training to be a dropout?"

"College, summer after my junior year. Met this hot-looking babe—older woman, had ten years on me. Turned out she had a thing for St. Paul's churchyard." His mouth eased into the mock leer he used when he wanted to get a rise out of her. "I gotta tell you, that chick taught me some pretty hot licks rolling around amongst the gravestones."

"Tad ghoulish if you ask me."

"Ungrateful wench. Just think of the benefits that've accrued to you owing to the artistic touches I picked up at the foot of the white bear."

"If it's gratitude we're talking," Cassidy said sweetly, "maybe you ought to write a little thank-you to *my* ex."

Zach gave her a benign smile, the most she was likely to get out of him. "Forgot to tell you," his voice returned to business. "A call came in while you were in session. It's on the machine."

Turning back to her desk, she removed a social work journal from the top of her answering machine, a journal Starshine had knocked down from the shelf above, and punched playback. A woman's voice said, "This is Bobbi Salvino. I'm a volunteer at Parenthesis—you know, the parent-child drop-in center. One of our members heard you speak, and we wondered if you'd be willing to give a talk to our single parents group." She left her number and clicked off.

"Parenthesis?" Zach said. "Another group? Oak Park's got more agencies than Chicago has pols."

"Oh shit." Cassidy buried her face in her hands. "I have to do it. I can't not do something that might bring in more clients. But I'm already so overloaded I can't keep my lawn mowed or the bills paid. Haven't seen the top of my desk in months."

"Right. A complete failure. Here this huge fixer-upper is falling down around you just because you went to grad school, got a divorce, started a practice, and now you're working your ass off to pay down your ex's back taxes. You keep this up, they'll take away your Superwoman cape." He patted the bed. "Stop feeling sorry for yourself and come on over here."

She held her ground a moment, then relented. Resting her cheek against his shoulder, she inhaled the musky, male scent of him. "I miss Starshine."

"Me too."

❧ ❧ ❧

The next morning Cassidy awoke to find the bedroom door open and the window air conditioner, turned on to compensate for the increase in body heat, blasting out coldness. Zach obviously did not share her fanaticism about conserving energy and keeping the electric bill down. She raised up on one elbow. Last night's glass containing half an inch of water stood in front of her digital alarm, obscuring the numbers and creating a new ring on her rosewood nightstand. Yesterday's garments lay heaped on the floor, panties inside out, bra twisted like rope through the armhole of her cotton blouse. *Why can't you hang up your clothes?* her proper behavior voice railed. *It'll be months before you get that blouse ironed again.*

How was it possible for her clothing to get so tangled? Perhaps Zach, who'd been up during the night, did it to confuse her. Rolling over, she lay on her back, hands behind her head, toes curling, as she gazed at the fine webbing of cracks overhead. Closed blinds kept out the light. She had no idea what time it was and no interest in raising her arm to look at her watch. It was far too quiet, all wrong to be so undisturbed when she was used to being pounced on and bitten and chewed. She thought about going downstairs and calling but it seemed useless. If Starshine wanted to come home, if she were able to come home, she would have by now. No use in calling, no use in getting up, no use in anything.

She was considering the possibility of staying in bed until time for her six o'clock client when she heard footsteps on the stairs. She sat bolt upright, covering her breasts with the sheet.

Zach appeared in the doorway with two mugs of coffee.

"I thought you'd gone off to work." Cassidy let the sheet drop. "You left the door open with the air on."

He came in, kicking the door shut behind him, and placed her purple mug adorned with the stylized image of a cat—the mug he'd given her—on the nightstand. "Wanna check out St. Paul's?"

She held the mug in both hands, sipping as Zach raised the blinds to let in a bright stream of light. That first cup of coffee in the morning was better than sex. It restored sanity. It made getting out of bed possible. Her drug of choice.

"Did you get up in the night and tie my clothing into knots?"

Chuckling, he dropped into her desk chair and rolled it over to the bed. "You're not answering my question. How about a field trip to the cemetery?"

"No, I'm serious. Didn't I hear you up last night?"

Setting his jaw, he tried to stare her down. Cassidy called it his Clint Eastwood look, although the comparison was patently absurd, his smooth, oval face bearing no similarity at all to the craggy, movie-star countenance. Nonetheless, she thought of it as an Eastwood look because it was his attempt to stare her into submission, to shut her up when she asked annoying questions. Fortunately, it never worked.

She held his eyes until he gave up and answered. "What difference does it make?"

"You were gone so long. I got that old knot in the stomach, the one I used to get when Kevin'd wander around at night.

Always meant he was brooding over that grudge list he kept against me."

Zach dropped a large hand on her sheet-covered knee. "I'm sure you had it coming. But don't worry, I'm not a brooder."

"So, what were you doing up?"

He gave her his Woman-you-are-a-thorn-in-my-side squint. "Trying to find Starshine."

"You went out hunting for her in the middle of the night?"

He looked embarrassed. "Now that you've pried out my dirty little secret, let's get back to business."

The phone rang, and she scrambled out of bed to dig through the pile on the floor for something to cover her naked body. Now that Zach had raised the blinds, she couldn't get to the phone without parading past the window in full view of the street. She tried to pull her bra through the armhole of her blouse but the hook snagged on a button. The phone hit ring three—one more and the machine would cut in.

"Oh well." She sank back on the bed and continued untangling her bra. "Didn't want to talk to anyone anyway—not unless it's somebody with a runaway calico." She got a sick feeling, guilt over having been too cheap to fork over the seven dollars for a village tag that would've transformed Starshine from illegal alien to naturalized pet.

The machine clicked and a cheery voice came through the box. "This is Dorothy next door. Last night around midnight, Rhonda was putting the car in the garage, and she noticed this tarted-up van sitting across the alley. And the guy in it had a straight bead on your back door. I called the cops, but he got away before they arrived, guess Rhonda spooked him. Your lights were out so I asked the officer not to bother you, told her I'd give you a call in the morning. So, what's the story? Kevin turned hippy and taken to spying on your new boyfriend or what?"

"Jesus!" Dropping the bra, Cassidy flipped bushy, un-combed hair out of her face. "Hope he wasn't in the alley when Dana left."

"You said he was high. Maybe he's her dealer, trying to collect."

"Dana's been clean since she first got pregnant."

Zach's clear, blue-gray eyes appraised her. "How do you know?"

"She told me she quit and I believe her. Her little girl's the most important thing in her life and Dana knows she'd screw the kid up if she were using."

"Lot of people quit for a while," he persisted. "How much experience've you had with heads? Kids get high all the time, their own mothers don't notice."

"Who'd know better than you?"

"I'm talking normal people with real mothers."

"There aren't any normal people." Cassidy combed her hair with her fingers. "Now I realize you were handicapped, growing up in one of those North Oak Park, blue-blooded families the way you did. Which, of course, made it easier for you to get away with drugs, sex, rock and roll. But Dana doesn't have an overbearing, socialite mother who doesn't know she exists—just a cousin who lives in the same house and mother-hens her to death."

"Whatever." He looked at his watch. "You've managed to distract me for almost three minutes. Now let's get on with today's agenda. You and I are going to the forest preserve to check out a big white bear."

"I don't get it. Why would we want to do that?"

He shrugged one shoulder. "Just finished a series and I'm sick of sitting at the computer. It's a pleasant place for wandering. I've got an idea where the kid's body might've been stashed and I want to see if my memory serves correctly."

"I thought you had a real job. You know, where they expect you to appear at nine o'clock and put in your eight hours."

"Nah, I just play around." He scratched his jaw. "John—that's my editor—John and I've been working together so long he's learned to stay out of my hair. Sometimes I run around talking to sources. Sometimes I work at home to avoid interruptions. Sometimes I screw off, don't work at all. I put words in the computer, he's happy." Grabbing her hand, he pulled her out of bed. "C'mon, get your clothes on."

She eyed him with suspicion, afraid he would not stop with a visit to St. Paul's. *Don't you want to visit the cemetery?* a small voice whispered seductively. *See if it matches Dana's memory?*

Therapists do not play detective with their clients, her proper behavior voice cut in.

But he was going to do it anyway, with or without her, and she would feel safer knowing what he was up to. Grudgingly, she pulled a tank top and shorts out of her drawer.

Ʒᴥ Ʒᴥ Ʒᴥ

A short time later they were heading west on the Eisenhower Expressway in Zach's elderly Datsun. Turning south on Mannheim Road, they meandered through a string of old towns intersected with mini-malls and commercial strips. After nearly an hour, they crossed the Des Plaines River, the boundary between suburbia and preserve, and were instantly transported from contemporary ugly to frontier forest. They turned again and continued another fifteen minutes along the western edge of a rolling wooded triangle comprising the enormous southwestern forest preserve.

Arriving at a hilltop cemetery, Zach cut left onto a dead-end road and drove upward to the gate. He parked across the street from St. Paul's, a gray stone church, picture-book quaint, with stained glass windows along the side and a narrow steeple rising from one corner. The building perched on the crown of the hill, the graveyard extending downward on all sides except the front, a towering granite bear glistening in the sun about fifty feet to the west. A fuzzy blanket of heat enveloped them as they left the car and trudged toward the open gate in the wrought iron fence bordering the cemetery. *Not supposed to be this hot in September.*

They followed the cement walkway through the gate, then veered off toward the white bear. Cassidy plodded across dry, close-cropped grass, Zach moving on a parallel course a couple of yards to her right. Stopping directly in front of the bear, she replayed Dana's words in her mind: *dead peoples, big tall mens in long black skirts, looked at the bear so I didn't have to see.* She recalled the TV image that had first triggered Dana's reaction: a raised hand with a knife.

Narrowing her eyes, she tried to envision what might have happened here. She could get an indistinct sense of Dana as a four-year-old amid a small group of children. She could picture a handful of men in hooded black robes herding the preschoolers into a clump in front of the monument. But beyond that, her mind balked. Seeking some kind of altered state that would get her imagination unstuck, she swayed slightly in the intense heat, staring fixedly until her mental image shimmered and blurred.

A hand landed heavily on her shoulder. Her nerves tightened like guitar strings, her whole body jerking.

3

Field Trip

"What is it?" Zach spoke softly in her ear, voice husky with concern. It was this sense that he noticed nuances, that he cared about her feelings, which had attracted her in the first place. But moments like these were so fleeting, she sometimes suspected that what passed for understanding was no more than a reporter's device to make people talk.

"Nothing," she declared, her voice a shade too loud. Turning to face him, she wrapped her hands around his neck, feeling damp and stuck-together where their skin touched, then leaned back to look up at him. "I was just imagining you with your hot mama, rolling around together on the graves."

He grinned and patted her butt.

She disengaged her arms, brushing the back of her hand against chin stubble as she separated herself. Although she kept makeup and a change of underwear in a drawer at his Chicago condo, he'd never so much as left a razor at her place.

They wandered separately over packed earth and yellowing grass for half an hour or so. She peeked through broken glass into the garbage-strewn interior of a small Greek temple, went through the motions of checking out any number of elaborately carved angels and crucifixes, read a boring roll call of Irish names and eighteen-hundred-something dates.

Hot, thirsty and brain-numb, she was ready to hunt up Zach when he rounded a corner of the church and called to her. He led her away from the main portion of the cemetery, stretching across the crest of the hill, to the opposite side of the church, where a steep embankment cut away to an overgrown ledge. This area, which she'd avoided because of the drop-off, was older than the hillside above, and far more unkempt. Thick branches shut out the sunlight from overhead, and the brush-covered graves were sunken, the headstones broken or missing.

Zach stopped in front of a square slab of white concrete.

"What is it?" she asked.

"Old well. They capped them like this when they switched over to city water."

"You think this is what Dana was talking about?"

"Don't you?"

&ﾉ &ﾉ &ﾉ

As they drove back north on Mannheim Road, Cassidy said, "Doesn't mean anything, you know." She cranked the Datsun's air up to max. "She could've seen the bear and the 'white thing' when she was out there with some boyfriend—just like you did—then mixed the images up with scenes from a movie. We've got nothing conclusive here." Lifting her shoulder-length hair, she let cold, tingly air dry the back of her neck.

"So what do you think's going on? False Memory Syndrome?"

"You always surprise me. One minute you're the cowboy-skeptic, next thing I know you're spouting off like an expert."

"Reporters get exposed to all the psychobabble. After interviewing false memory supporters, psychiatrists on the insanity plea, etcetera, etcetera, I've learned the jargon. Just because I speak the language doesn't mean I buy the bullshit."

"To get back to your question, F.M.S.—if there actually is such a thing—results from a therapist or someone else planting suggestions. Certainly not the case here."

"Then why all the doubts?" His voice got clipped, the way he sounded when following a lead. "I thought the deal was, if memories surface spontaneously, therapists are supposed to believe them."

"Not if the client's delusional," she muttered.

"Is she?"

She gazed at the parched, end-of-summer landscape zooming by. "I wasn't seeing any signs. But she did have a psychiatric hospitalization back when she was twenty."

"Schizophrenic?"

"No."

"What then?"

As he surged in front of a truck, Cassidy studied his profile, noting the deep cleft that ran from the base of his hawklike nose down to his jaw. *I'm in trouble here. He gets that look on his face, he won't stop till he digs up everything.* "Before she regressed on me, I figured it for an isolated incident."

"I thought people who went psychotic were basically nuts."

"I used to have the same idea—that a psychotic break meant chronic mental illness. But Dana doesn't fit the picture." Cassidy rattled the vent, adjusting the flow of stinging air away from her bare shoulders and arms. "It's been seven years and she's really straightened out her life. Without meds. So I attributed her break to the drugs."

"Why would a drug related episode seven years ago cast doubt on the experience she had yesterday?"

Cassidy rested one leg on the other knee, gripping her ankle and pulling it up tight on her thigh. "You keep asking why I don't like it. Let me turn it around—how come you're so fired up about a twenty-three year old crime?"

"I dunno." His jaw tightened. "Why do you always have to ask questions like that?"

"Like what?"

"Questions that don't have clear-cut, tangible answers." He flexed his shoulders. "Just because it's an old case doesn't mean it's old news. There's a Chicago cop—leading expert on cults—who quit a few months back because of threats to his family. Dana's story could lead to something hot. And besides, this sort of thing's a turn-on. Most of the stories I do are routine. Investigation's exciting."

She waited to see if there were more.

"Maybe I've got some kind of hidden agenda, wanna do something worthwhile for a change—like busting evil Satanists. Nah, that's probably not it."

"You're right. It'd be totally out of character." They drove several miles in silence, passing an old movie theater with a marquee listing six films; an independent department store—the small-town kind that was nearly extinct; a dilapidated building with a For Sale sign in the window.

Zach accelerated, squeaking through a light just as it turned red. "Dana doesn't sound like your typical client."

"After the hospitalization her parents wanted no part of her, so she bummed around a few years, then moved in with her cousin and the cousin's husband. Cousin Josie. Back in my old life, before I went into the therapy biz, Josie and I were high school teachers together. So when Cousin Josie finally convinced Dana to go into therapy, I was it. Guess she knew me well enough to figure I'd be willing to take on somebody who could barely pay my minimum fee."

"So now you've got a client who's maybe a cult survivor and you're seeing her at what? Thirty dollars an hour?"

"Anyway, before Dana moved in with Josie, she was involved with some jerk who got her pregnant, then ran out when she refused to have an abortion. Soon as she learned about the baby, she stopped drugging and hooked up with Wayne, who seems to be a decent sort. They moved into Josie's two-flat together—before the baby was born—and they've been doing all right since then."

Zach zipped into an opening in the left lane only inches longer than the Datsun. Cassidy shut her eyes and braced her feet against the floorboard. *God, if I tried that, I'd be gulping Xanax for a week.*

"So," Zach drawled, "since you're so iffy about her story, only thing to do is check it out."

"What do you mean?" Cassidy bit off the words, knowing she wouldn't like the answer.

"I'm going back tonight, see what's in that well."

Staring out the side window, Cassidy bit down on her bottom lip. "That's the stupidest idea I've ever heard."

"It probably would've been better if I hadn't told you."

"Probably."

"But you know what you always say about honesty."

Hearing the grin in his voice, she turned back to fasten her eyes on his face, a futile attempt to make him listen. "Zach, please, don't do this. It can't mean anything but trouble. First of all, it's illegal. Think of the hassle if you get arrested."

"I spent a lot of time in that graveyard and never got caught."

"Second, if you come up empty, it won't prove anything. After all these years, the . . . um, evidence is probably long gone."

"Won't be the first time I've chased a wild goose."

"And if you do find something, it'll be even worse. Dana was totally spooked by that flashback. The last thing she needs is for some story about a cult sacrifice to show up in the newspaper. If you do anything to hurt her, I'll never forgive you. Or myself for blabbing."

"That mean you don't want to come along? Actually, now that I think about it, you'd just be in the way."

She lowered her chin and ground her knuckles into her cheek. "I can't talk you out of it?"

The Datsun stopped at the end of the exit ramp leading onto Austin Boulevard, a couple of miles from her house.

"All right, I'll come."

⁓ ⁓ ⁓

The hill, a gentle incline when they drove to the top in daylight, became a treacherous cliff when they tackled it on foot that night. After stopping at the gate, which was padlocked and spotlighted, Zach said they would have to hike in. He parked behind the graveyard at the foot of the hill, and they started up the steep mile of woods separating the road from the cemetery.

Cassidy, who scrambled behind Zach, was nearly ready to quit when she finally saw a break in the trees ahead. Zach stood beyond the treeline, hands on hips, his steady movement finally arrested like the immobilized figure with the non-Duracell battery.

She groped through the last couple of yards, then sagged against his sturdy body. A six-foot, wrought-iron fence rose directly in front of them, a wall to ward off the onslaught of trees, wild creatures, and copulating couples with graveyard fetishes.

She killed the beam of the large flashlight Zach had given her. Although the cobalt sky was much darker in the forest preserve than closer in to the city, an incandescent quarter-moon cast a vapory sheen across the hilltop, illuminating headstones and church. When they had first taken off, the air seemed sharply cold. But after half an hour's climbing, her armpits were soaking, her forehead slick. She wiped a hand across her face and asked, "Now what?"

Zach took the flashlight and set it down, along with the coiled rope and nylon bag he'd been carrying over his shoulder. Making a sling with his hands, he said, "You go first."

She hesitated, then placed her right foot in his hands. He boosted her high enough to insert her left foot between the spikes on top. Grasping the poles, she pulled herself into a squat, then held tight for a wavering moment, head twisted to squint down at Zach.

Love is overrated. You should've listened to your mother.

She lowered herself clumsily to the ground on the other side. Zach handed the gear through the fence, then scrambled over himself.

This guy's far too expert at breaking the law. You promised that after Kevin you'd stay away from men who view rules as a personal challenge.

Zach reached for the rope and bag, then took off toward the well. She shot one look at his retreating figure, another at the fence, then hurried after him across the graveyard, making a brief stop in front of the white bear. As she stared at the ghostly monument, looming even taller in the moonlight, she was able to envision Dana's scenario more clearly.

When she arrived at the well, Zach was setting up a mechanism comprised of pulleys and ropes that he'd removed from the bag. He tied a rope around the concrete slab, then hooked one side of the pulley to a tree and the other to the rope he'd fastened to the slab. When the rig was suspended tautly between tree and slab, he hauled on the rope's loose end, dragging the slab far enough to uncover a circular hole beneath it. Cassidy shone the flashlight down inside.

The hole was about three feet in diameter, its stone walls slimy from ground water oozing through cracks. A faint, sickly-sweet odor rose from the opening. The light rippled over dark water at the bottom, reminding her of Starshine's luminous black eyes when she was in her wild mood, more tiger than pussycat.

Nothing short of torture would induce me to stick even one of my body parts inside that thing. "How deep do you suppose the water is?"

"Don't know." Zach was focused on looping another rope around a nearby tree.

"It stinks." She took a step back, crunching a spiky bush that hooked into her purple sweatshirt. "You can't go down there."

Zach stood on the edge, jerking the rope to make sure the knot held.

She grabbed his arm. "You go down in that hole, you'll never clean up enough to get any woman into your bed again."

"The only woman I want is you." Tossing the rope over his shoulder, he tilted her chin and dropped a kiss on her forehead. "And I don't think you're about to boycott my bed just because of a little aromatic well smell."

I hate that I'm so easy. And I hate even worse that he knows it.

He took the flashlight out of her hand, stuffed it in his pocket, and began lowering himself into the hole. Three feet below the surface he announced that he'd hit bottom. Peering down, all she could see was the top of his head and bobbing patches of light.

"Just a couple inches of water." His voice was muffled. "Quite a grab bag. How the hell do you suppose anybody managed to throw beer cans . . . ?"

Moving back from the edge, she hugged herself tightly, feeling the chill again. *If I were sitting on my own front porch, which is where I oughtta be, probably wouldn't feel cold at all. It's just this place.* At the thought of home, she got even more impatient. "This is impossible! There's no way you'll ever find anything down there."

"What's this? Yuck."

"What is it?"

"At first I thought . . . . Just the remains of some animal."

Several moments passed. Dark, thickly leaved branches formed a claustrophobic arch overhead, irregular splotches of lighter-blue sky showing through. "I've had enough. I want you to give it up and take me home."

Another interminable silence. She wondered how long she'd been waiting, wished she could see her watch. *Seems like hours.* She shifted her weight and chewed on her bottom lip.

"If you don't come up this instant, I'm going to untie this rope and drive off and leave you." *Empty threat. Don't have keys.*

No answer. The silence stretched on. She began to feel like the only living person in the entire, hundred-acre forest preserve. Not a breath of wind. Sounds she had not been aware of before emerged from the unnatural stillness: a twig crackling, cat shrieking in the distance, insects droning like the buzz of an electric wire. Something creaked. The moonlight suddenly dimmed. Gazing up through the branches, she saw that a thick cloud layer had moved in front of the moon.

"Oh shit." Zach's voice, hollow and distant, came from the hole.

4

Consultation

She shivered violently.

A moment later he hauled himself up.

"What?"

"Tell you when we get back to the car." Glancing down at the hole, he muttered, "Sonsovbitches," then hastened to pull the cement cap back over the well and cram his gear into the nylon bag.

"I want to know what you found!" Her voice came out too loud, sounding shrill and unnatural in the quiet forest.

Zach handed her the flashlight, slung the rope and bag over his shoulder, then said, voice tight with anger, "Let's get out of here."

They struggled through the forest, tossed the gear in the back of the wagon, and collapsed into the front seat. In the closed car the stench of decaying vegetation that Zach carried with him from the well nearly gagged her. She opened her window and breathed in sweet woodsy air. Clearing her lungs, she put a hand on his arm. "Sorry I yelled at you up there. Although I have to say, I've had about as much as I can take of this Lone Ranger act of yours. I am not Tonto—get that? Now tell me, what did you find?"

"There's a skull—kid's skull—in the hole."

Her stomach clenched, a lump gathering in the pit. "You can't be sure. How could you be sure? How could you tell it's not some animal skull?"

He looked at her grimly. "You really don't want to believe this, do you?"

❧ ❧ ❧

On the return trip Zach pressed a little too heavily on the accelerator, slammed a little too hard on the brakes. After five minutes of silence, he switched on the radio, cranking up the volume to unleash a thudding blast of rock.

Nerves already jumpy, Cassidy gripped the armrest and huddled back in her seat, feeling physically assaulted. Sound waves pounded her body, driving her deeper and deeper into her corner.

First time he's ever pulled anything like this. Must be the kind of contemptible behavior familiarity breeds. She tolerated it as long as she could—two minutes at most—then snapped off the radio.

Zach waited a beat. "Not your taste in music, huh?"

She started to tell him exactly how not to her taste it was, then clamped her mouth shut.

He's having a hard time. Really bothered.

Good. He should be. This is no summer delight for me either. He should've stayed out of it, should've listened.

Many miles later as Zach drove north on Austin Boulevard she took a good look at him. His jaw was set, his hands white-knuckled on the wheel. She was in for a quick drop-off unless she could stop feeling put-upon and get some communication going. As a therapist, she often made instant switches from being in her own skin to being in the client's, so her personal off-button was in good working order.

When he pulled up at her back door she said, "We've got to talk."

"I'd rather go home."

"Sometimes you have to do what I want. So far, everything's been your way. Now it's my turn."

Trudging up to the stoop with Zach at her side, she glanced around for Starshine. Still no sign of the cat. The lump in her stomach got heavier.

Leaving a trail of dried mud across the linoleum, Zach headed straight for the cabinet where she'd stowed the Jack Daniels. As he mixed two drinks, she gazed through her window into her neighbor's kitchen a couple of yards to the south. A tired looking woman in her early forties was tidying up. Dorothy Stein, the woman who'd called about the van, was mother to a large brood of adopted kids that resembled a mini-version of the U.N.

"C'mon and sit." She dragged him out to the front porch and they plunked down on the wicker couch. Zach hunched forward, one hand circling his glass, the other resting on his knee. She perched sideways to face him. A snappy breeze carrying the muted scent of mums, pansies, and fading marigolds whipped through the three casement windows not painted shut. Unfortunately the flower-perfume was not strong enough to overpower the unpleasant odor still coming from Zach.

She lay her hand on his arm. "Now talk to me. Instead of going home and drinking yourself stupid, talk about it."

"I don't need you to be my shrink." His voice held the dangerous, growly tone that signaled she was on thin ice, one step away from an abrupt walk-out.

"Yes you do. If you won't talk on your own, you need me to beat it out of you." She pounded on his broad, black-shirted chest. The canopy of trees lining the street rustled continuously, a background lullaby punctuated by clanking wind chimes.

"I don't know how to talk. It's not how I handle things." He gulped down half his drink. She lifted his left hand and placed it on her knee, lacing her fingers through his. His husky voice picked up again, grudgingly. "It's just that . . . . Well, when I found the skull, it shook me, that's all. It was so small. I couldn't believe how small it was. I turned the flashlight on it, and it just . . . . It didn't seem like a game anymore. That was a real kid, a kid who got slashed and tossed down a well. What a lousy way for a little kid to end up."

"Yeah, it was." Catching her lower lip between her teeth, she bit down hard. A beat-up car, engine rumbling through a hole in the muffler, raced halfway down the block and slammed to a stop in the middle of the street. A car door banged, followed by the screech of a female voice. "All that money for booze, nothing for child support." The car peeled off.

Zach sighed heavily, finished his drink and thumped the glass down. "Now that you've had your way with me, can I go home?"

She tightened her grip on his hand. "Couple more items on the agenda."

"Didn't anybody ever tell you—you wanna hold on to a man, don't torture him?"

"You going to the police with this?"

"Legally I ought to, but I'm inclined to hold off awhile. If I report it, they'll pressure me for my source, and I'll have to refuse. Case is so old now, they're not likely to put much time into it. So I can't see it buys us anything to go to the police at this point."

"What do you mean, 'at this point?' "

"You know what I mean."

"What exactly do you have in mind?"

"Poke around a little. See what I can find out."

"Why can't you just leave it alone? It happened over twenty years ago. Why drag it up now?"

"Why ask why? Just drink beer."

Yanking her hand away from his, she shook her fist in his face. "You make me so damned mad!"

"Okay, I have to do it for the same reason you have to ask irritating questions and dig into things that are none of your business. Because it's what I do. You get so fucking sanctimonious about your work—like it's some kind of sacred mission. Grant me the same privilege. I believe in mucking around in slime and bringing things to light. Especially things that are disgusting and unwholesome. It's all I believe in. Shining light in places nobody wants to look."

ั้ง ั้ง ั้ง

Midmorning the next day Cassidy, seated in her desk chair, stared through the bedroom window at green maple leaves against a bright blue sky. She mentally reviewed everything she'd heard from the two members of her training group who had ritual abuse clients. One of them, a social worker named Joan, had taken her client in for consultation to a psychologist who specialized in treating cult victims. *God knows, it wouldn't hurt to hear what an expert has to say.* Cassidy tugged at her ear, trying to remember Joan's last name and what she'd done with her number.

She searched her desktop mess for the Rolodex. *Number probably isn't in it anyway.* She'd filled all her Rolodex cards some time ago. Since then numbers tended to end up on scraps of paper or, if they were important, in the back of her calendar where client data was listed. Digging out the Rolodex, she discovered, as expected, that Joan's number was among the missing. *Gotta buy new cards.* She was sorting through her rat's nest of stray notes when her memory clicked in with Joan's last name. After looking up her colleague's number in the phone book, she dialed and got a live-voice answer on the first try. She explained her situation and asked for the consultant's name.

"Dr. Victoria Kramer," Joan said, following up with a phone number. "Office on Michigan Avenue. Her fees are steep but she's worth every penny."

Cassidy jotted down the name and number. "You really needed to see her? I mean, you don't think you could've handled it just as well on your own?"

"God no, she really knows her stuff. Kept me from making all kinds of mistakes."

After hanging up, Cassidy swiveled back to the window, propped her feet on the radiator, and picked up the wine bottle she used for collecting loose change: a savings account for her friend Maggie's birthday dinner. She stared into curved green glass. The bottle was less than half full, not nearly as many dimes and quarters as there should have been. Since Dana was broke and Cassidy would have to pay the consultant's fee herself, she was tempted to use money as a cop-out. But she knew the real reason for wanting to avoid consultation came from her feelings, not her wallet.

What's with you, anyway? You try to do everything yourself and end up falling on your face. Hate people giving advice. Hate Zach taking over. Hate other people knowing more than you do.

Stop being a brat. You can't afford to screw up Dana's therapy just because you don't like asking for help.

Reluctantly, she rotated back to the desk and reached for the phone. Twenty minutes later, she'd wrested a dubious consent from Dana and scheduled an appointment with Dr. Kramer for the following afternoon.

She glanced at the clock. Twelve-thirty. *Almost forgot. I promised to take Mom out for lunch.* She picked Helen up at her apartment, then drove to the parking lot behind the strip of businesses on the corner of Oak Park Avenue and Lake Street, heart of village shopping and eating. Crossing Oak Park Avenue, they stood in line at Erik's, an upscale deli where village trustees and high school drop-outs lunched elbow-to-elbow in a beferned dining room crammed with glossy, blond-wood tables.

They took a window table, thumped down their trays, and waited for their orders to arrive. Helen sipped her Diet Coke and said, "I suppose I ought to be thankful for an occasional lunch, now that you've snagged one of those Lawrence boys." The busboy delivered their plates, Helen's huge beef sandwich, Cassidy's thick quesadillas. "But I miss the old days, when you had time for Wednesday night dinner at my place."

Shifting her gaze to the sunlit sidewalk outside, Cassidy withheld a sigh. "Zach Moran, remember? Not 'one of those Lawrence boys.' " Two teens, black male with dreadlocks, white female with spiky pink hair, strolled by. Arms encircling waists, hips glued together, they puffed cigarettes in unison. The girl fixed her mascara-ringed eyes on Cassidy, sending a telepathic message: "Whadda ya lookin' at?" Oh, to be young again.

Pulling herself back, she regarded her mother's moon face. The heavy makeup Helen wore served only to emphasize the wrinkles in her forehead, the sag in her cheeks. Cassidy made an effort to soften her voice. "I've got three regular Wednesday night clients now. Thank God, my practice is finally increasing, which means no more nights off during the week."

"I can't understand how you get clients to come to your house at all, the way the place looks. Dandelions in the spring, now the weeds. And those sofas in your office."

Cassidy forced herself to take a full thirty seconds before responding. "I can't do everything."

"It's not that I'm blaming you. That house is a full-time job in itself. I know, I know . . . ." She raised her hands to keep Cassidy from interrupting. "Right now your practice has to come first, you'll take care of the rest later. I just think the house is too much for you, that's all."

You, Kevin, and the rest of the world.

Dropping her sandwich on the plate, Helen dabbed at her mouth with a napkin. "You still haven't said when you're going to introduce me to that man of yours."

"Soon as we can work something—"

"Suppose he thinks he's too good for us, that's why he can't be bothered. His name may be 'Moran', but he's Mildred Lawrence's son. Mildred and her Nineteenth Century Women's Club, her North Oak Park mansion, and her cleaning lady. I'll never forget, she was a year ahead of me in high school. A Dooper, you know, Dear Old Oak Parker. Mildred and her crowd, they were always the cheerleaders, in all the right clubs. I never got invited to any of the parties or dances. Not me. I was just one of those south Oak Park kids. I knew all about them, they didn't even know I existed."

Cassidy covered her mother's hand on the table. "You must've hated it."

"And now you're going out with Mildred's son." She sniffed and pulled her hand away. "But I'd be careful if I were you. Anybody who can't be bothered to meet your family—my guess is he's not all that interested."

Meet the family? Let my mother loose on Zach? Cassidy stopped eating, figuring she could make another meal from the remaining half of her quesadillas.

A flock of small children careened into the restaurant, followed by two moms pushing strollers. One small boy, racing ahead of the others, banged into Helen's chair.

"Really," Helen stage-whispered loudly. "Children should be kept at home till they're old enough to mind their manners."

One of the mothers shot her a venomous look. The two women collected their brood and marched off to a table on the other side of the room.

Cassidy squeezed her mother's arm. "I had a bunch of kids, I'd probably take them to Erik's. And you'd be the proudest Grandma in Oak Park."

🙚 🙚 🙚

She let Helen off in front of her apartment, drove home, and parked in her detached garage at the far end of her corner lot. The garage, which faced north on Briar, stood a good ten yards from the house, which faced west on Hazel. Following her chain link fence toward the gate, she remembered with a dull ache the night she'd come home to find a tiny calico staunchly planted on her stoop. Her eyes swept the yards across Briar. No cats. The only animate object in sight was a black boy, looked to be around eight, skateboarding in the middle of the street. She'd seen him all alone out here before. *Why isn't he in school?*

She scanned her own yard, her gaze skimming the overgrown grass, the cement steps, the empty stoop. That was when she saw it. A jagged hole in the window of her back door. She stopped dead. *My God, a break-in!* Racing up to the gate, she stopped again. *What if somebody's still inside?*

She spun around and saw the kid whizzing by. "Hey you," she yelled. "Come over here, will you?"

He turned, making a large sweep, then skated slowly up to the curb. "Whadda ya want?" The high-pitched voice distant and bored.

"You see the guy who broke into my house?"

"Nah." He wagged his head, opaque brown eyes remote. "Saw somebody comin' out, though."

"More than one? Were they carrying anything?"

"Nah." His glance trailed off, and Cassidy was afraid he might drift away before she finished.

"Please, tell me exactly what you saw."

"What I said. Some guy comin' out. Ran off somewhere." He gestured in the direction of the alley.

44

"A man? Just one?"

He nodded.

"White or black?"

"Whitebread."

"Can you tell me what he looked like?"

He shrugged and began to skate away. "Just some honky." He glided off to the intersection, then turned north onto Hazel.

Not still there. I can check it out now, call the cops later. She sprinted to the stoop, pulled a tissue out of her bag, and turned the knob. The door, which she'd locked when she left, grated open over broken glass strewn across her waiting room chairs and floor. She stood on the threshold, teeth clenched, blood pounding in her ears. Nothing out of place except the glass. Picking her way through splinters and shards to the oak room divider, she went around into the kitchen, which was undisturbed.

She moved from room to room, examining every detail, searching for the slightest indication that someone had been inside her house. Nothing. Not a single item out of place or missing. She went through her bedroom and the two second floor junk rooms. She even wandered around the basement, although everything in that unfinished, subterranean space was so jumbled it could've been ransacked and she wouldn't have noticed.

She was sweeping glass when an amiable "Hi" startled her into dropping the broom. Her head snapped up, eyes lighting on a boyish face peering through the hole in the window, a young man with a police cap sitting squarely on his head.

"How'd you get here?" She tiptoed through the broken glass and joined him on the stoop. "I haven't even called yet."

"A jogger stopped me a couple blocks down Briar." He jerked his head in a westerly direction. "Said he saw a broken window, so I rode over to investigate."

She noted the police-uniform shorts, casual blue shirt, and racing bike propped beside the stoop. "You must be our neighborhood beat cop."

"The name's Gary Crider. I live over on Harvey." He perched a buttock on the wrought iron railing. "This a burglary? I called it in already, so six orange-and-whites'll be screeching up any minute now." He removed his cap and scratched his scalp through short, sun-bleached hair. *How can he be a cop? Barely out of high school.* But the gun, radio, and handcuffs strapped to his belt attested that he was.

She explained that, although a white male had been seen exiting and the same male had probably broken the window, as far as she could tell his only activities had been coming in and going out.

"Glad it wasn't any worse." He shook his head, scowling slightly. "I've lived here all my life, hate seeing things like this happen." His face reverted to its natural, sunny expression. "But at least here in Oak Park, the police stay on top of things."

As if to prove his point, two police cars and one unmarked pulled up almost simultaneously. The fresh-faced beat cop ambled over to join the newcomers.

Why break in but not take anything? An image surfaced in her mind: Curly, face close to the screen, voice vaguely threatening, saying he had "business" with Dana. *Curly? Fried brains expecting to find Dana under the bed?* Or was she trying too hard to make all the pieces fit together, cramming things in where they didn't belong? At her location, one block west of Austin, break-ins were almost routine. His not having stolen her costume jewelry didn't mean anything. Burglars were frequently incompetent. They got scared and ran away. *Whatever happened, chances are I'll never know.*

By the time she was ready for bed, the cops had dusted for fingerprints, combed the house, written reports, and departed. The splinters were all removed; new glass was installed in the window. She wanted to tell Zach but had run into his protective side before and knew he would insist on coming over. Since she did not relish being rescued, she did not make the call.

She pulled back the covers and lay down, hating the stillness, wishing for the comfort of a fang embedded in her toe, whiskers prickling her cheek, a soft body rumbling against hers. Starshine had simply vanished. *One more thing I'll never know.*

⁊ ⁊ ⁊

Dana huddled in the Toyota's passenger seat, her back toward Cassidy. "Don't know why I let you talk me into this," she muttered.

"Sure you do," Cassidy responded cheerily. "The part that wants to get healthy is stronger than the part that's afraid."

Dana twisted her head, firing off a surly look. "You're always saying these—I mean, I hate it when you talk that subpersonalities shit."

"You wouldn't like the other answer any better—which is, I need back-up from someone who's experienced in ritual abuse." Cassidy turned onto the ramp leading to the Eisenhower. Early Friday afternoon and already the inbound traffic was heavy. But at least the weather was cooperating, the temperature down from the ninety-degree mark it had been hitting of late, the air so clear and bright it was even possible to forget for the moment that the planet was suffocating in its own poisonous fumes.

Dana said, "You keep talking about—you keep saying it's ritual abuse. I hate it when you do that, okay? I mean, how can you be so sure?"

"You're right, it's awful to think something like that could've happened to you."

"What this's really about is, you think I'm crazy," Dana complained, voice whiny. "That's the reason you're making me

47

do this. 'Cause you think I'm delusional again. It's so, you know, unfair."

"Consultant or psychiatrist, your choice." Cassidy scrutinized the four lanes crawling into the city, trying to decide which was the fastest moving.

"But I shouldn't have to see either one. Not if I don't want to." Dana slumped lower on her spine.

"We talked about this before, remember?"

"It all happened so long ago. Why do we have to—I mean, why can't we just forget this stupid flashback thing and work on the, you know, the other stuff? What's happening *now*— that's what's important, okay?"

Tuning out the fretful voice, Cassidy eased on the brake in the thickening traffic as they neared the Loop.

"Hate psychiatrists! They always want to give you meds that cost—I mean, they cost five dollars a pop and then what they do is, they zombie-out your brain." Dana crossed her arms over her chest. "Did you know psychiatrists put perfectly normal people in hospitals just so they can fill beds? It's a big rip-off, know what I mean?"

"Only if they have insurance." Cassidy checked her watch. Embarrassing to show up late, especially when consulting a prominent psychologist who charged two hundred an hour, money earmarked for her excruciating summer electric bill. Her punishment for pumping out fluorocarbons with her window air conditioner. She aimed the Toyota at a gap in the left lane and sped into it. Only twenty minutes till her appointment, and on Michigan Avenue, the glitziest, high-rent street in Chicago, parking was possible only if you had a first-born son to sell.

Dana squirmed around to face Cassidy. Although wearing the usual fringed cut-offs and sockless sneakers, she'd dressed for the occasion by donning a clean, nearly-new orange tee. In contrast, Cassidy's fuschia blouse and plum skirt represented the opposite end of the spectrum. She grimaced, picturing the two of them side by side, a cartoonish Mutt and Jeff: Dana's long-tall-Sally scruffiness up against her own pint-sized, gypsy-style flash.

Tapping frosted fingernails against a bare thigh, Dana said, "There's something—I wanna ask you something, but I'm not sure ... I mean, it's really hard to get out."

"What?"

"You know how I've been feeling about—about the baptism."

"You must be pretty nervous, I guess."

"Do you know how long it's been since I even, since my mother said one word to me?" Her left knee started up a jiggly little dance.

"About seven years, isn't it?"

"Don't think I'll ever—I mean, I can't even imagine being able to forgive them. Not ever."

Cassidy maneuvered around a truck.

"How could they, you know, stick me in the hospital like that, then just write me off like I never, like I wasn't even their kid?" Dana's voice thickened. "It was the meanest, worst thing ever happened to me in my whole life."

Cassidy glanced over to see Dana wiping a hand across her eye. "That was a terrible time for you."

"Don't know what I would've done—I mean, I couldn't have gotten along without my friends taking me in, then Josie. I might've ended up on the street, mumbling to myself, you know?"

"You would've made it somehow. You're stronger than you think."

"Anyway, what I'm trying to say is, every time I think about seeing Mom and Dad face to face at the baptism, I just—I freak. So what I wanted to ask is ... well, what I'm trying to say is, it'd mean the world if you'd just come along and sort of prop me up."

Attend a baptism? In a church? Church did not bring out the best in her. "I understand why this is so difficult. But Wayne and Josie will both be with you, and they're certainly on your side. Won't that be enough?"

"I know I'm being—well, I'm being a baby, okay?" Dana gazed fixedly out the side window. "But I get so, you know, scared. Every time—when I even imagine introducing Wayne to my parents, I mean, just think what Dad'll say when he gets a load of the ponytail. And Josie knows everybody, so she'll have to spread herself around, talk to all of 'em. But if you were there, you wouldn't have to pay attention to the family. You could just sort of keep your eye on me, make sure I'm okay."

This is not a good idea. Overstepping boundaries. Mixing roles. "Let me think about it."

❦ ❦ ❦

Victoria Kramer withdrew a legal pad from the middle drawer of her sleek walnut desk. Above the desk half a dozen walnut-framed certificates were displayed on a pearl-toned wall.

"You've probably never worked with a consultant before, so I want to assure you that even though your therapist provided me with some initial information, from now on you'll be present for everything I have to say. You don't have to worry that Cassidy and I will be conferring behind your back." The pyschologist's voice was so deep and resonant that any words coming out of her mouth would have carried weight, even if they were merely, "Pass the Kleenex, I feel a sneeze coming on."

Dr. Kramer stepped briskly around her desk, crossed the two yards of intervening space, and slid into a leather arm-chair that right angled the sofa where Cassidy and Dana sat.

Victoria Kramer continued, her tone reassuring. "The first thing we need is an assessment to find out the extent of your cult involvement."

"You think there's more to it than just this one memory?" Cassidy tugged at her plum skirt, which had hiked up on her thigh when she seated herself.

Scrunched deeply into the corner next to the psychologist's chair, Dana mumbled something Cassidy couldn't make out.

Stroking her chin with thumb and forefinger, Dr. Kramer gazed sympathetically at the young woman who so clearly didn't want to be there. The psychologist's handsome face was nearly unlined, her skin supple and clear. What particularly struck Cassidy was that her short, sculpted hair and large, warm eyes were the exact same shade—a rich, caramel-brown—and that somehow she had managed to clothe herself in a gorgeous silk suit that was a perfect match to her hair and eyes. Cassidy, who always felt a slight sense of awe toward anyone capable of attaining such harmony of color, found herself feeling like a Dixieland band in the presence of Orchestra Hall.

Dr. Kramer chose her words carefully. "When cults get access to a group of children, they usually engage in a number of activities, not just a one-time event."

Cassidy opened her mouth to ask what activities, then thought better of it. No point alarming Dana or planting ideas. She laced her hands together in her lap. "Can you do the assessment today?"

"Exactly what I had in mind." Victoria Kramer jotted a note on her pad. "Dana, I know this must be pretty disturbing, but we need to do it. And you could make this whole thing easier if you'd be willing to look at me."

Dana, her eyes fixed on skyscrapers visible through a floor-to-ceiling window, murmured, "I don't wanna talk about it."

Cassidy watched to see how Dr. Kramer would handle a balky client. She wanted the consultant to be good enough to justify the two hundred bucks but not so good that she herself would feel totally outclassed.

As Victoria Kramer talked, reeling Dana in with her marvelous voice, Cassidy made her own assessment of the psychologist. Tall and solidly built. Well-distributed weight. Classic, rounded figure: hourglass, not fashion model. Commanding presence. *Can't imagine anybody talking* her *into graveyard escapades in the middle of the night.* Indeterminate age—somewhere between thirty and sixty-five.

"It's not that I want to cause you further pain. If there were any way to avoid dealing with the past, I'd be happy to do it." Dr. Kramer extended a manicured hand corded with protruding blue veins that pegged her age as somewhere over fifty. Identifying the psychologist as a generation older alleviated some of Cassidy's defensiveness. Easier to accept authority figures who did not turn out to be younger than she.

Dr. Kramer continued to hold out her hand. Finally Dana slid her palm into the consultant's.

"Nobody else can possibly know what it feels like to be you, Dana. But I want you to understand, I've worked with many women who were abused by cults. I have some sense of what you've been through. And I *can* help. Please, let me."

Dana said, the words barely audible, "What're you gonna, I mean, what do you wanna do to me?"

"First I have to find out if you're still connected to the cult."

"What makes you think . . . ?" Dana stammered. "I mean, what're you saying? I wasn't, you know, connected. I was just a little kid who got—I got shanghaied into . . . " Her large brown eyes shut suddenly, then blinked open in a tic-like motion. " . . . into, you know, watching."

"I'm sure that's the truth as you understand it." Dr. Kramer turned toward Cassidy. "Any possibility Dana might have developed . . . other personalities?"

Cassidy cocked her head in surprise. "I don't, um . . . see any evidence of it."

Addressing Dana, the psychologist asked, "Ever have any blank spots in your memory? Even little ones?"

"No!" Dana's voice was edged with panic. "I mean, I can't think of any, okay?" Her hands twisted the bottom of her orange shirt.

"We won't worry about that right now." Dr. Kramer crossed her caramel-heeled feet at the ankles. "What I'd like to do, if it's all right with you, is use hypnosis to find out more about what happened when you were a child."

Dana's eyes darted to Cassidy. "I can't stand, what I mean is, it was just too awful. I can't, you know, go through all that again."

"It'll be different this time," Dr. Kramer said. "You'll be in such a deep trance the only thing you'll be aware of is the sense of relaxation. You won't even remember afterward."

Cassidy felt a pang. *If I'd known what I was doing in the first place, Dana wouldn't have had to go through that awful regression.*

After securing Dana's agreement, the psychologist began speaking in a slow, rhythmic voice, gradually taking her deeper and deeper into trance. As the induction continued, Cassidy struggled to avoid going under herself. She tightened her fist and released it, chewed on her lower lip, glanced around the room. Looking at the certificates again, she focused on reading dates and trying to calculate Kramer's age. The cult specialist had received her bachelor's from Brewster College in '58, her doctorate from the U. of C. in '64. Assuming she graduated college at twenty-two, Cassidy figured she must be around fifty-six now.

When the slackness in Dana's face and body indicated a deep, hypnotic state, Dr. Kramer told her she was going to ask a series of questions and instructed her to signal a "yes" answer by raising her right forefinger.

"Okay, Dana, here's the first question." The psychologist tapped her pencil on the tablet. "I believe you are twenty-seven now, is that correct?"

Dana's finger rose, then dropped, the movement slow and jerky, as if pulled by a string.

"Do you have a three-year-old daughter?"

The finger remained motionless.

"Is your child two?"

The finger moved up and down.

"When you were little, did you see one of your playmates killed in a cemetery?"

The finger moved up and down.

"Were you ever hurt by the same people?"

The finger moved up and down.

"Were you ever sexually abused?"

The finger moved up and down.

"Did you see anyone else killed?"

The finger remained motionless.

"Do you know the names of any of the people who hurt you?"

The finger remained motionless.

"Do you know why you were with those people?"

The finger didn't move.

"Do you remember what group you were in when you were four?"

No motion.

"Do you think they can still hurt you?"

The finger moved up and down.

"How old were you when it stopped?"

The finger moved up and down four times.

Dr. Kramer directed Dana to forget everything that had happened in trance and return to the present, feeling rested and relaxed. A moment passed, then Dana's eyes opened, revealing serene, milk-chocolate irises. She gazed warmly at the psychologist, as if they were old friends.

The psychologist covered Dana's hand with her own. "You have some additional memories. Memories that are not yet ready to come out."

Dana's skin blanched. Deep creases wiped away the peaceful look.

"You've been badly injured," Dr. Kramer continued. "Whenever people have been harmed so severely, they need a lot of help. More than they can get in an hour a week, even with the best of therapists. You want to make sure your baby has a safe, healthy childhood, don't you?"

She nodded.

"Then the best choice would be for you to go in the hospital."

Her face stricken, Dana slid forward and gripped the sofa cushion with both hands, ready for instant flight. "You think I'm crazy. Like this is all—you think I'm hallucinating again, don't you?"

Cassidy placed a steadying hand on Dana's arm. A picture flashed through her mind—dark hole beneath overhanging trees. *It's real, all right. All too real.*

"I believe every word," Dr. Kramer said. "The only reason to go into the hospital is that, when these memories start coming up, there's a possibility you might feel like hurting yourself. Or . . . that something else might happen."

"I'm not going to, you know, kill myself. I can't do that. I've got a baby."

Cassidy's eyes narrowed. "What do you mean, 'something else?' "

5

Baptism

Dr. Kramer shook her head slightly to stop Cassidy's question.

"I won't do it." Dana smacked the arm of the sofa. "I mean, you can't force me—can't make me go in the hospital. Not again."

The psychologist knitted her winged brows. "I can understand your not wanting to go. I only suggested it because you may need a more secure environment." Then, a trace of wistfulness in her voice, "I just want to be sure you're safe."

Dana, face still chalky, managed a tremulous smile.

"You've got a good therapist." Dr. Kramer nodded at Cassidy.

The toe of Cassidy's burgundy pump twitched. *Where's that coming from? I could be a total flake for all she knows.*

"The two of you will just have to continue as is and I'll be available if you need me. Now, is there anything else?"

Cassidy leaned forward. "I've heard about cults setting it up so they have control over children. But it seems so risky. Why're they so eager to get hold of kids?"

"This gets a little ghoulish." Kramer's eyes appraised Dana. "You sure you want to hear it?"

Dana replied. "It's okay. I can take it."

"Well, I've been told there are certain rituals Satanists perform that require virgin blood, so they select particular children—children who are kept sexually pure—and these are the ones they sacrifice. So they can make sure the blood is virginal, you see."

Cassidy's back teeth clenched.

Victoria Kramer continued, "Speaking more generally, Satanists are in rebellion against all that's decent and good, and one way they act it out is by defiling children. They also use children for pornography—a profit motive there. And for sexual gratification. Ritual sacrifice has the dual purpose of appeasing Satan and terrorizing the other children into maintaining silence. Beyond that, there may be an urge to contaminate innocence, to create in their victims a sense of shame and badness which then gets handed down to the next generation."

Cassidy saw Dana shudder at that last remark. She blurted, "How could anyone do such horrible things to children?"

Dr. Kramer rose and crossed the room to stare out the window, then turned toward them again. "In mental health, we're trained to think in terms of chemical imbalance, illness, disorder. When people get destructive or antisocial, we look for inadequate parenting, abuse, organic dysfunction. We're not allowed to even hint at moral judgment."

"Sort of like the No-Bad-Dogs concept applied to people," Cassidy interjected.

"What I'm about to say my peers would consider heresy," Dr. Kramer's voice dropped to a lower pitch. "But after years of working with cult survivors, I've come to think that good and evil actually do exist. In fact, I'd say some human beings are thoroughly evil. At times I'm tempted to believe they're simply born that way."

Before they left, Dr. Kramer wrote her home number on a business card and handed it to Cassidy, instructing her to call if anything further came up.

☙ ☙ ☙

Arriving back in Oak Park after a harrowing drive through rush hour traffic, Cassidy dropped Dana off in front of Josie's two-flat. Dana jumped out, then turned to ask about the baptism again.

"Well . . ." Dana's large, puppy eyes implored her. "Okay, I'll come."

She drove a few more blocks, zigzagging through the four by six mile village, turned east on Briar, and moments later pulled into her own driveway. Cutting the engine, she drummed her fingers against the steering wheel, gaze fixed on the garage door's cracked, peeling paint. *Way over your head here. Need to find Dana another therapist who knows what she's doing, then run like hell.*

She deposited her car in the garage, then trundled down the long stretch of sidewalk toward her back gate, armpits damp from the heat, feet sore from too many hours in heels. *Why do you make these half-hearted attempts to conform? Should've been a sixties' flower child, burned your bra and worn sandals.*

She waved at a family of cyclists pedalling toward her, Mom and Dad each towing a kiddie car with strapped-in toddler, all properly helmeted. As she turned in the gate, her gaze drifted to the stoop. A small calico sat erect on the mat. Cassidy caught her breath, blinked, then dashed forward on a surge of elation.

Starshine eyed her warily, ready to jump out of reach if Cassidy were so precipitous as to make a grab. Using great self restraint, Cassidy unlocked the door, opened the screen, and waited as the cat stepped daintily over the threshold. Once inside, Starshine made straight for the corner next to the refrigerator where her dish was supposed to be, only to find it missing, Cassidy having cleaned up the feline cuisine corner two days ago. After sniffing a large patch of empty floor, the cat sprang to her usual spot on the linoleum countertop, pinned Cassidy with wide, dark eyes, and uttered a recriminating, Mrowr!

"What did you expect? You've been gone for days."

Cassidy moved fast to open a can, dish up food, and set the bowl in its proper place on the floor. Starshine, her sides concave, polished off the bottom before Cassidy could get herself upright.

Jumping back on the counter, the cat licked her chops as her dilated pupils contracted, the amber irises shifting to a warm, glistening green. Cassidy scratched behind her ear and touched noses.

"Thought I'd lost you," she murmured, her face close to fur that had taken on a gray, gritty cast after three days of outdoor living. "Yuck. You need a bath."

The cat rumbled in contentment.

Taking a step back, Cassidy scrutinized the diminutive calico who had first appeared at her door nearly three months earlier. She was still so small Cassidy thought of her as only half-grown, barely out of kittenhood. "What've you been up to, anyway? You couldn't have gone into heat already—could you? You can't be old enough yet."

The cat's eyes squeezed to mere slits, as if to say, "I'll never tell."

A sense of outrage came over her at the thought of tiny Starshine beset by ruffians twice her size. "Don't you know how I feel about teenage pregnancies? Babies having babies! It's disgraceful."

Dismissing her with a blink, Starshine wrapped herself in her tail and proceeded to wash up.

≈ ≈ ≈

"I started this morning." The lively voice coming through the receiver was surprisingly perky for her mother. "At the housing center. A friend of mine said I had to volunteer there 'cause that's what she does. Elaine, she's the girl who supervises the volunteers—a black girl, did I tell you? But actually, she's very nice, didn't seem any different from you or me. She said I picked it up especially fast. Isn't that something? I bet you never thought your mother'd turn out to be a fast learner."

Cassidy gazed out her bedroom window at a jogger in headphones. A gathering of teens in the middle of the street turned and gestured behind the back of the oblivious jogger. Headphones were definitely an asset.

"I always knew you were smart."

"Well, of course you'd say that. But I don't guess you ever thought I'd get out and do anything on my own."

"Volunteering's a great idea. You need something to fill your time, and the center's really important in maintaining integration."

Her mother sighed, triggering the familiar pang. "I always thought I should keep myself available for you and Gran, especially after your divorce, when you didn't have anybody. Seemed like, since you were alone and I was alone, we could . . . . But I finally got it through my thick skull that the truth is, you don't really have time for me." She let out a humorless rasp. "Guess when it comes to my daughter, I'm not a fast learner."

After the conversation was over, Cassidy lingered a moment, her hand on the phone. *Was that my mother? Not a word about Zach. No guilt trips about my not coming to dinner anymore. I oughtta call back, demand to know who that woman is and what she's done with Mom.*

An odd feeling passed through her at the realization that her mother's sniping had seemed no more than a token gesture, almost an automatic reflex instead of the usual heartfelt complaint. Pushing the feeling aside, she returned to the never-ending task of clearing her desk.

❧ ❧ ❧

When Cassidy left her house Saturday morning to drive to the Apple Creek Church, she was already running the usual fifteen minutes behind. She had no Saturday clients at this point, one of the reasons she'd overruled her better judgment and agreed to attend Cypress' baptism. The temperature had shot up again, the humidity making it seem even hotter than indicated by the digital numbers on bank signs—no two alike.

On her way out of Oak Park, she was surprised to notice splashes of yellow on some of the maples. *Trees shouldn't be turning yet. All this heat—still seems like summer. It's always torrid or freezing, nothing in between.*

Following Dana's directions, she headed southwest on I-55, passing from the outer fringe of suburbia into flat farm country, empty except for the remains of dried crops, fence-lines demarking separate parcels of land, and the occasional house, barn and cow. Exiting onto a four-lane road that veered southeast, she drove another twenty minutes before hitting Apple Creek, the small town closest to Dana's family farm. Her map told her that the town lay ten miles south of St. Paul's Cemetery.

A couple of miles past Apple Creek, population 3,500 according to the sign, she spotted Christ's Love Church. The sprawling, white frame building, bell tower rising from the center of a pitched roof, seemed slightly out of focus in the diffuse, grainy light. Turning into the side parking lot, she crunched across gravel toward Josie's red Fiesta. Dana and a young man who must be Wayne stood beside the tiny car. Josie's head poked out the window.

Shouldn't let clients coax me into crossing over into their personal lives. Not good therapy. Besides, getting dressed up and sitting through a church service is not my idea of a fun

Saturday morning. Heat assaulted her the instant she opened her door, the stagnant air held in place by a low, gray flannel sky.

"You're finally here." Wearing a filmy, apple-green dress slightly too big for her lean frame, Dana flounced up to the Toyota.

Wayne tossed his cigarette to the ground and said, "She wouldn't go inside, not till you showed up." Voice slow and easygoing, Wayne seemed the type who never felt hurried or rushed.

Josie hopped out of her car. "No harm done. They're not about to start without us."

Cassidy introduced herself to Wayne, who rubbed a palm against the thigh of his shiny gabardine suit, then shook her hand. "Wayne Farelli. Guess you must know all about me." Smiling shyly, he turned to open the Fiesta's rear door.

Wayne dragged a small girl in a fussy, white dress from the back seat and stood her on her patent leather feet.

Dana scuffed the toe of her white flat in the gravel. "Do we really need—I mean, really have to go through with all this? Couldn't we just, you know, turn around and go back?"

Wayne placed a hand loosely around the back of her neck. "Hey, babe, it's gonna be all right. I won't let anybody give you a hard time." He had long, dishwater-blonde hair pulled back into a stringy ponytail, with wispy strands hanging loose around a delicate face that was almost too pretty for a man.

Josie picked up Cypress, pulling the child's plump fingers out of her mouth. "C'mon gang, let's get this over with." Her voice fairly chirped with good humor, the same voice Cassidy remembered hearing her use to herd students back in their teaching days.

Trooping across the gravel to the church, they entered a dim foyer filled with organ music and continued into the sanctuary, which accommodated two rows of pews separated by a central aisle. Above the altar was a round, stained glass window, with pulpit to the left and organ to the right. As they traipsed toward the front, Cassidy counted five additional heads, which, according to what Dana had told her, belonged to the two grandparents, Josie's mother, and a couple of other relatives. Dana stiffened as an older couple—the parents, Cassidy assumed—turned to stare.

Josie led the group into the second pew. Shortly after they were seated, the organ player, a woman wearing a coral dress whom Cassidy guessed to be the minister's wife, removed her hands from the keyboard, and the music faded in a final wheeze.

A man in a dark suit stepped onto the platform. He had longish, red-brown hair and a neatly trimmed beard. He nodded toward the second pew. "Dana, Cypress, Josie—it's good to have you here. And Dana's two friends." His gaze rested briefly on Cassidy and Wayne, then moved to the five heads seated behind them. "And, of course, the grandparents and other family members." His voice was rich and mellow.

"We're here today to celebrate Cypress' baptism. What that means to me, folks, is recognition of the fact that Cypress, like all other persons young and old, is a child of God."

Cassidy's green-and-purple flowered dress clung to her bare legs. She should have worn a slip and pantyhose but couldn't stand more than the bare minimum of clothing in this sticky, oppressive weather. Shifting on the hard wooden seat, she hoped the preacher would not turn out to be one of those types who could never get enough of his own rhetoric.

"There's no way I can stand before you as a gatekeeper," the minister continued. "I don't hold any keys to the kingdom, and I have no power to decide who gets in and who doesn't."

What about you, kiddo? You in or you out? This from the voice constantly after her to do the right thing.

"So what's the reason for baptizing children? Why do it if you don't receive a gold-plated promise that this sprinkle of water here will guarantee a ticket to open the pearly gates, like those electronic cards people carry nowadays."

Every time a Nixon or Reagan betrays this country, I make sure never to vote for the sonovabitch again. God's screwed-up worse than any politician, so if this is his kingdom we're talking about, why would I want in?

"But even though I can't dispense promises of heavenly salvation—or anything else, for that matter—I think the church is very wise to maintain rituals like this one. As human beings, we need our rituals to remind us of the basic truths— truths we so easily forget. I think the basic truth for today is this: if God can love us all—imperfect, flawed, mean-spirited as we are—we should be able to do a little better at loving each other."

You even believe in God?

On alternate Tuesdays, maybe. Gives me somebody to yell at when shit happens.

"It's our job as parents, grandparents, and members of the community to take responsibility for all children: to make sure each and every one of them receives the protection, nurturing and love they all deserve. Just remember, every child comes into the world trailing clouds of glory."

Clouds of glory, huh? But what if some children are born evil, like Dr. Kramer said?

After the sermon was finished, water sprinkled, and prayers said, the guests were invited to reconvene in the church parlor, coffee and cookies offered up as bait.

Wonderful. Throw the entire family into one room and watch a whole new layer of animosity ooze to the surface, the way a petri dish grows mold.

As everyone shuffled down the hall toward the east end of the building, Dana clutched Cassidy's arm. "Can't talk to them, know what I mean? I'm gonna for sure say the wrong thing."

Cassidy covered Dana's hand with her own. "Would it be so bad, telling them how you feel?"

"You don't know my dad."

They followed the minister and the coral-clad organist into a homey room with wide windows along one wall and clustered seating arrangements composed of mismatched sofas and chairs. As the group fanned out around a long table at the front, Cassidy got her first good look at Dana's parents, the couple who had stared when they walked in.

Dana's mother, Laurel Voss, was medium height, with a narrow face that might have been horsey if not for the pointed chin. Dressed in a stylish silk suit, worn in total disregard of the heat, she was attired more formally than the others. Sidling up to the table, Laurel occupied herself behind the coffee urn, filling her cup, adding cream and sugar, stirring and stirring.

Dana's father, Ernie Voss, whose rangy build shot up well over six feet, looked considerably older than his wife. Positioning himself halfway between table and door, he stood with legs apart, hands crammed in pockets, his weathered face bristling with impatience.

Dana hovered behind Cassidy's left shoulder, Cypress hanging onto one hand, Wayne standing nearby. Glancing around, Cassidy noted that Dana's eyes were glued to her mother. Laurel, her gaze lowered, pretended to study the cookie tray, although her hunched shoulders and frightened face made it clear she had something other than snacks on her mind.

"Aunt Laurel, it's so good to see you." Josie swished around the table, her crisp, sunshine yellow skirt rustling loudly in the too-quiet room.

Laurel turned to her niece with open arms, her whole body expressing relief. "Josie, hon, it's been way too long. But where's Howard? I was hoping he'd be with you."

"His company's had him out in San Francisco for ages, working on some project or other." Josie waved broadly, brushing it off. "Matter of fact, I'll be flying out to see him in just a couple of weeks." Taking Laurel by the arm, she tugged her in Dana's direction. "Now don't you two hang back. Lord knows, it's a crime for mother and daughter to go so long without talking."

Laurel shot a doubtful look back at Ernie, then allowed herself to be dragged along. As she approached, Cassidy picked up a flowery scent of cologne, one she had noticed Dana wearing from time to time.

Cassidy stepped sideways, leaving Dana to face her mother. Cypress hugged Dana's legs. Wayne remained solidly at her side. Cassidy held her breath, waiting for one or the other to speak. Dana finally said, "Hi Mom."

Laurel blinked rapidly. "You've grown up so, I don't hardly know what to say." Her voice was thick. "Josie here tells me you're doin' real good."

"So, what do you think of Cypress?" She hoisted the little girl onto her hip. "Imagine me with a—I mean, a kid of my own. You never thought I'd be able to take care of myself, let alone a two-year-old."

Flicking a glance at Ernie, Laurel brushed her fingers across the child's chubby hand. Cypress pulled away, smiled coyly, and ducked her head into her mother's shoulder. "Whozat?" she whispered.

Laurel gazed raptly at the long-lashed, sky-blue eyes. "She's just so pretty. Reminds me of you, when you were, I don't know, just a tiny little thing. Something I wanted so bad was to get you baptized . . . ." Ernie cleared his throat. She paused, then turned toward him. "Don't you wanna come over here and see your granddaughter, hon?"

Walking stiffly, he moved closer, stopping a couple of feet behind his wife. He towered above the others, even Wayne and Dana, a matched set of Tall Club contenders. His face was elongated, bald on top with a gray, Brillo-pad thatch circling the sides and a coarse mustache sprouting from his upper lip. Slivers of flint peered out of deep-set, narrow sockets. He spread his legs and crossed his arms.

His attitude proved too much even for Laurel, who stood in the middle, husband on one side, daughter on the other, torn between their opposing poles by almost visible lines of tension. "There's nothing Ernie hates so much as giving up a grudge," she snapped.

"I wouldn't call it a grudge exactly." He drawled the words out as if bored, the articulation more professional than Cassidy would have expected. "I just don't much enjoy having to spend time with trash."

6

Broken Date

Hands on hips, Josie pushed in front of him. "Ernie Voss, you should be ashamed, saying such a thing. You're half the problem yourself, the way you've always been so hard on her. Dana deserves some credit considering how far she's come."

"Now honey." He placed a large, knobby hand briefly on her shoulder. "I suppose you mean well, but sometimes I think you traded in your brains for that bleeding heart you got on your sleeve. Are you telling me I should be glad my daughter's got herself a live-in boyfriend and an illegitimate child?" He scratched his chest through his short-sleeved shirt. "But I didn't come here to fight, and I can see Laurel's practically peeing her pants, she's so eager to get her hands on that baby. So I'll shut up and let the two of them get on with it."

In a tic-like motion, Dana squeezed her eyes shut, then opened them instantly. "Gee Dad, thanks." Her voice was loaded with sarcasm. "I always—I mean, I always figured I could count on you." Wayne put a hand on her shoulder. Cypress whimpered sleepily. Dana lifted the child higher and said, speaking directly to her mother, "This kid, she's getting heavy, okay? Let's go sit down if we're really gonna, you know, talk."

Dana and her mother headed for a sofa in the center of the room, Ernie trailing behind to sit in a nearby armchair. Josie sent Wayne a let's-butt-out look, and together they drifted to the far end of the table.

Shifting her weight from one foot to the other, Cassidy decided she would rather stand by herself than chat up Josie. She and Josie had been close during her former life as a teacher, but when Kevin walked out three years ago, Josie had backed off from the friendship as if she considered divorce a contagious disease. Having dropped Josie several notches down on her favorite-people list, Cassidy now had little interest in making small talk. Besides, she needed to remain close enough to Dana to perform a quick prop-up if necessary.

As she waited by the table trying to be watchful but not obvious about it, the organist stepped up beside her. The coral-dressed woman said, "Every time I whip up a batch of that pink crud, I feel this overpowering urge to throw in a bottle of vodka. Unfortunately, I never give in to it." She flashed Cassidy a conspiratorial grin. Her large, uptilted eyes and distinctive cheekbones were reminiscent of Audrey Hepburn in her middle years.

"You play the organ *and* you make the punch?" Cassidy asked. "Then I bet I guessed right—you must be the minister's wife."

"Guilty as charged. I'm Annie Halsey, part of the Denny and Annie team." She swirled the ladle, then licked a drop off her finger and grimaced, her ebony eyes twinkling to show she wasn't serious. "Dennis and I do just about everything around here."

Cassidy dipped punch into a plastic cup and tasted it. "You're right, it does need vodka. Reminds me of PTA meetings I'd rather forget." She wiped the side of her cup with a pink-cherub napkin. "So, you two been here at the church long?"

Annie wrinkled her nose. "Seems like forever. We started right after divinity school, expecting to use it as a springboard.

Thought we'd end up at some urban, liberal-minded church where Dennis could make his mark as an activist minister and I could pursue my own career as a concert pianist." She extended both hands, angling long, slender fingers as if placing them on a keyboard.

"How come you're still here?" She glanced at Dana, who was head-to-head with her mother, a big smile on her face.

"Soon as we arrived, Denny started coming up with all kinds of plans to improve the community. You see, his real passion isn't so much religion as social action. I know, it sounds like something right out of the sixties, but that's when we grew up—what can I say? Anyway, there was so much to do here. And Dennis, God love him, is just about the most involved man I've ever met. I like to complain, but the truth is, I wouldn't want him any other way." She ran her hand through fine, dark hair, fluffing it out around her ear. "Although I have to admit, I'd love to go to U. of C. cocktail parties where we could discuss foreign policy and sniff a line of coke now and then." Annie grinned impishly.

"You'd fit right in." Cassidy leaned one hip against the edge of the table. "But here—how do you get away with being so outrageous?"

"It was rough at the beginning. We were way too progressive for the community, and the congregation almost threw us out a time or two. But it'd taken them a long time to find anybody willing to serve out here. And besides, Dennis has lots of charisma, and he's always there when people need him. So we've been able to sort of nudge and push and pull people along, and most of them've come to accept us. Poor Denny—the hardest part's probably been bailing me out when I say the wrong thing and get people pissed off. But I figure—hey, in the long run, it's cheaper to speak my mind than pay a shrink."

If everybody were this outspoken, I'd be out of business.

Plastic glasses suddenly started to wobble. Wrinkles formed down the length of the white cloth as it jerked toward the far end of the table. "Whoa," Dana yelled, leaping off the sofa and racing toward the end from which the cloth was being pulled. She scooped up the tablecloth-tugger, a two-foot Cypress too small to be seen until she got hauled into her mother's arms. "Wanna cookie?" Dana said. "Let Mommy help." She held the child above the tray. "Show me which one." Moments later, Dana was on her way back to the sofa with Cypress balanced on one hip and her free hand full of cookies. Josie and Wayne had split off in separate directions, Josie near the door with her own mother and the two miscellaneous relatives, and Wayne by the window with the minister.

Taking another sip of punch, Cassidy said, "You've been here so long, you must know Dana's whole history. And her family's."

Annie lowered her voice. "Laurel may've come to church a few times, but according to rumor, Ernie put a stop to it. Evidently he never lets her stray far from home. It kills me when women stay with men like that. I just want to slap them and say, 'Wake up!' The only time Laurel ever broke loose and did anything on her own was when she started a co-op play group so Dana'd have a chance to be with other kids. But Ernie was against it so Laurel had to quit, although I think the group went on for several years without her."

"Did you know Dana at all?"

Annie shook her head. "Like I said, Ernie kept them away from church, and the family in general stayed pretty much to themselves." She reached down the table and pulled the cookie tray closer. "Here, try one of the peanut butters. They're not half bad, if I do say so myself."

Cassidy selected a fat cookie, crosshatch pattern on top. It reminded her of sitting at her grandmother's kitchen table, being very careful to press the fork into the dough exactly as she'd been shown. "Delicious." She brushed cookie crumbs off her chest. "If the Vosses aren't members of the congregation, why do all this?"

"Dennis is such a soft touch." A worried look flitted across her angular face. "Sometimes I wish he didn't work so hard. But anyway, Josie spent summers with the Voss family, and she used to attend our vacation Bible school. So she called Denny about the baptism, and of course we'd all heard talk about the estrangement between Dana and her parents. And it seemed like getting them together . . . ."

"You can't leave now!" Dana's voice, shrill with agitation, stopped the organist in midsentence. Cassidy's eyes whipped toward the Voss family. Ernie had risen and was standing opposite Dana, who perched on the edge of the sofa. Cypress was clutching her mother's skirt. Laurel, sitting next to her daughter, had a look of panic on her face visible even from several yards' distance.

Dana sliced the air with her hand. "This is the first—I mean, the only time you've even talked to me in years. And now you're gonna—you just wanna walk out?"

Ernie took a step back. Dana and Laurel got to their feet. Dennis Halsey crossed the room to position himself between Dana and her parents. Cassidy and Annie hustled over to fill out the circle.

Where're Wayne and Josie? Cassidy scanned the parlor, surprised to discover that no one else was there.

Moving behind Laurel, Ernie gripped her shoulders. "What's the matter with you? There's no point hanging around. She's crazy as ever."

Dana seized her mother's hand. "You gonna let him jerk you around again? You have any idea what it did to me when you—you just stuck me in the hospital, okay? And then you—what you did is, you walked out of my life. You threw me away, for God's sake. Just when I needed you the most."

"She did what she had to," Ernie thundered. "You put yourself in the hospital with your drugging and sleeping around. You made her life a living hell. There wasn't a thing she could do except cut her losses and let you drown in your own shit."

Laurel, her face convulsed, took a half step toward her daughter. "The books, they all talked about letting go. I didn't know . . . . What I did, I honestly thought it was for the best."

Dana yanked her mother's arm. "If it hadn't been for—if Josie hadn't been there, I'd've died."

Cypress, standing with face buried in her mother's skirt, began to wail.

The minister pulled Dana and her mother closer, wrapping an arm around the shoulder of each. He said to Dana, "Don't make this any worse than it is already. It's not the same as before." He turned to Laurel. "You've taken the first step. You just need to make sure the next one comes soon." He stepped back, clasping Laurel's hand in both of his. "Can you promise your daughter a phone call within the next week?"

Laurel nodded. A disgusted snort came from Ernie, who was backing toward the door.

"Now," Dennis dropped Laurel's hand and returned his gaze to Dana, "can you let your mother go?"

Dana covered her face with her hands. The minister pulled her into his arms and she lay her head on his shoulder and wept. His wife picked up the howling child and walked her over toward the window. Ernie dragged Laurel out the door.

Fat lot of good you're doing here. You could be home having a meaningful conversation with your cat.

Josie came bustling in from the direction of the women's room. A minute later Wayne reappeared smelling of cigarettes. Deciding they could handle the mop-up without her, Cassidy whispered goodbye in Dana's ear and took off.

❧ ❧ ❧

She dragged into her stuffy bedroom where Starshine was pawing through a mound of trash falling out of the tall waste basket she had knocked over.

Cassidy flipped on the air conditioner. "You find any secret treasures, I get fifty percent off the top. I own exclusive trash rights around here." Standing the plastic container upright, Cassidy gathered used tissue and junk mail from the floor. Starshine grabbed a champagne cork she had stolen from the waste basket and scuttled out of the room.

Plopping in front of her desk, she checked the answering machine. Two blinks, indicating two messages. She hit playback.

"My name's, uh, Ursula Kronos." Frail, wispy voice. "And I was thinking . . . that is, I'd like to talk to you about possibly making an appointment." A nervous laugh, followed by a phone number.

Beep.

All right! Another client to help pay my summer electric bill. Sounds shaky . . . . Have to be careful how I reel her in.

"Zach here. Bad news about tonight. Something came up—gotta see where it takes me. Sorry to break our date on such short notice but I'll make it up to you."

Beep.

Make it up to me? Her stomach tightened. *Where've I heard that before?* She swiveled her chair to gaze at an arrangement of photos on the wall opposite her bed. Pictures of her mother and grandmother, herself as a child, a wedding shot of her parents, and a large photo of her ex-husband Kevin. He stood on the bow of a sailboat, bronze curls blowing in the wind, an I-love-you-babe grin on his face that could still on occasion make her weak in her knees. She'd taken the photo down when he moved out, then missed it so much she had to put it back. How many times during the course of their twelve-year marriage had the words "I'll make it up to you" come out of his mouth?

Starshine reappeared and leapt onto her desk, sending bills and unopened mail skittering to the floor.

Rotating back, Cassidy propped her chin on her hands. "So, what do you think it means? When we first started, Zach said he was scared of commitment, not sure he'd ever be able stick with anybody. Told me he'd try to make it work but couldn't promise anything. Now we've hit the three-month mark, and he's starting to get weird."

She began rolling a pen between her fingers but the cat grabbed it away and knocked it off the desk. "Maybe he found somebody with drop-dead looks. Or hotter in bed." Cassidy had a trim figure and narrow face with deep set hazel eyes but harbored no illusions that anyone would ever use the word "hot" and her name in the same sentence.

Starshine sat erect, large black pupils regarding her coldly.

"I know, you hate when I act like this. After Kevin and all his women, I vowed to stay away from unavailable men, and here I've gone and done it again. Insecurity always brings out my sappy, lovesick, adolescent mode." She rubbed the chipped corner of the desk, the corner she'd dropped when she and Kevin first struggled to carry it upstairs. It had come to serve as a reminder that men were untrustworthy creatures at heart.

"You notice how evasive he was? 'Something came up.' So now I have to decide—do I demand an explanation or let it go?" She remembered what she'd gone through with Kevin: she had to either keep her mouth shut and silently go crazy, or ask questions and listen to the lies.

Better to leave it alone with Zach, better not to ask. Not unless she was prepared to hear an unpleasant truth, perhaps hear that the "something" that had come up was another woman. One thing she'd learned from experience—her clients' as well as her own—was that you'd better not ask the question unless you were willing to hear the answer. And then to deal with the consequences. And if there *was* another woman—as there had always been with Kevin—she'd have to be willing to deal with a break-up.

She was not ready for that. Breaking up was easier if you inched your way into it. Compiled a list of grievances. Shifted your image of him from good guy to jerk. Learned to enjoy Saturday night TV again.

Starshine yawned elaborately, exhaling cat-food breath and expressing her opinion of lovesick adolescents. As the cat's jaw languidly closed, Cassidy noticed a black dot burrowed into the short hair of her chin. The dot moved, then was gone.

"Yuck." Cassidy sat up straight. "What kind of lowlife have you been consorting with, anyway? And if you've been consorting, then you *are* pregnant."

Eyes slitted, Starshine took on her condescending, Egyptian princess pose.

"You're so pretentious. But the truth is, you're just as susceptible to flea-bitten jerks as the rest of us."

Starshine stretched, raising her rump and extending her forepaws. Eyes taking on a wicked glint, she swiped at Cassidy's dangling earring.

"You brat!" Cassidy dropped her to the floor. "I don't care if you are in a delicate condition. Doesn't give you the right to take advantage of my sickening, lovelorn state."

Reaching briskly for the phone, she returned Ursula Kronos' call and scheduled an appointment for Tuesday. Next she dialed her mother. "I just realized I don't have any plans for tonight and thought maybe we could get together." She braced herself for the usual motherly comeback: What?-Saturday-night-with-no-date? Although Cassidy was careful to make sure her mother never actually met Zach, this in no way prevented her from expressing strong opinions regarding his qualifications as a boyfriend.

"Well, dear," her mother said, "I'm sorry to hear you're stuck with nothing to do. I really wish I didn't, um . . . . As it just so happens, I already promised somebody . . . ." Her voice trailed off.

"Mom, what're you up to?" Cassidy drew sharp, zig-zag lines on the back of her unopened credit card bill.

"Oh, it's just that I met this new friend Elaine—the one I told you about, remember? That black girl. Did I say she's really nice even if . . . I mean, she's awfully nice for . . . ."

Cassidy's jaw tightened. *Will you listen to that patronizing tone? Mom's lucky Elaine puts up with her at all.* She refused to speak, giving her mother the same treatment she used on clients when they tried to squirm out of telling her something.

"So anyway," her mother's voice picked up weakly, "Elaine suggested we go to this very nice lounge she knows."

"Are you telling me you're going *cruising?*" Cassidy's voice rose in disbelief. She had a sudden vision of a smoky dive, her gray-haired mother leaning against the bar in a long slinky dress that outlined her round stomach, the no-nonsense loafers peeking out from under her skirt.

🐸 🐸 🐸

"Well, Ursula, what's going on that made you decide to give me a call?" Seated in her director's chair, legal pad in lap, Cassidy gave the thin woman perched on the vinyl sofa a reassuring smile.

"Well, you see, a few years ago I got the idea to . . . uh, retire early. That is, I'm only sixty-two, and I have this pretty little flower shop . . . I mean, used to have it. Owned it nearly thirty years, I guess. But then I thought it'd be nice to have more time. While I've still got my health, you see. Do a little gardening, maybe travel some." Ursula edged toward the end of the sofa to avoid the bright morning sun that angled through the window behind her head.

Oh, oh. A plant person. She'll notice my coleus, how desperate it is for repotting, report me for cruelty to flora—or is it fauna?—and never be back.

"Any problems with retirement?"

"Actually," the woman leaned forward, her whispery voice taking on a confidential tone, "I kind of like it. Guess I can't imagine why I waited so long." Her face was bony and lined, skin on the sallow side. Shoulder length hair, blonde streaked with gray, hung like frizzed straw, a perm gone bad. Despite the sticky heat outside, she wore a high-necked blouse with sleeves that buttoned at the wrists, perhaps to hide her gaunt frame. Looking closer, Cassidy realized Ursula was beyond thin. Anorexia was rare in women this age, but not impossible.

"How's your appetite?" Cassidy jotted down a couple of descriptive phrases. "Have you been sick recently? Or maybe dieting?"

"You probably asked that because I'm kind of on the thin side," Ursula said, a hint of pride in her spun-glass voice. "But don't worry, I'm not starving myself or anything. It's just that I'm sort of a vegetarian—only natural foods. No alcohol, no preservatives. Totally organic. Keeps the cellulite off. What about you, dear? Do you, uh . . . juice?"

"Not really." Cassidy tilted her head. *What is it she's not telling?* "So, no problems with retirement or health. What is it then?"

"Well, you see . . . " settling back on the sofa, she picked at an edge of the tape Cassidy used to patch holes. "I never married. Not that I didn't have the chance, you understand. Guess there were plenty of boyfriends, but when it came right down to it, I never felt the urge. The other girls, they all got married, but far as I could tell, there wasn't much fun in it. That is, seemed like once the man put a ring on their finger, they sort of had to do what they were told. And if they didn't, the husband—well, from what I could see, he could get kind of mean sometimes. So I always thought . . . ."

"Do you have any regrets about not marrying?" Cassidy crossed one leg over the other. The suspended foot began to jiggle.

"Well, I . . ." Ursula pulled a tissue from the pocket of her long, gauzy skirt, dabbed at her nose, then wrapped the tissue around a scrawny finger. "Guess I'm kind of uncertain. That is, I never wanted some man telling me what to do. But now, sometimes it gets sort of . . . well, it gets a little lonely."

"Is that why you're here? Because you're lonely?"

"Uh, not exactly."

7

Making It Up

At the end of the hour, Ursula handed her a pastel check sprinkled with red rosebuds, gathered her voluminous gray skirt into her lap and said, "I'd sort of like to, uh . . . make another appointment. That is, if it's all right with you."

"Certainly." Cassidy picked up her calendar from the wicker table and they set a time.

On their way out, Ursula placed a weathered hand on Cassidy's arm. "I'm so glad I called, my dear. I can't tell you how much better I feel now that we've . . . uh, talked."

Must've done something right—but I haven't a clue what it was. Don't suppose it'd be proper form to ask: "Was it good for you? Did you come?"

❧ ❧ ❧

After Ursula left, Cassidy took the pad upstairs, intending to record name, number, and address right away on one of the new cards she'd bought for her Rolodex. She pulled out a card, then scanned her desktop clutter for the familiar white plastic frame it fit into.

Shuffling through papers, she moved stacks from one side of her desk to the other. No Rolodex. She stood, hands pressed against the window frame, and stared blindly at a squirrel in her maple tree. *So where is it?*

Could the guy who broke into her house have taken it? There was only one person who might conceivably smash the glass in her back door in full view of all Briar just to steal a Rolodex. And that was Curly. So Curly was the *who*. The remaining questions were *why* and *what*. Why was Curly after Dana? What had he found in the Rolodex?

What Curly found depended on whether or not Cassidy had entered Dana's name. She'd run out of cards months ago, and even before that, she'd been lax about recording new clients. *Can't remember if Dana's in it or not. Probably a good thing I didn't get those new cards sooner. Least there's a chance Curly doesn't have her address.*

But the more interesting question was *why*. It was also the easiest to answer, assuming she could pressure Dana into telling the truth. Cassidy flipped to the back of her calendar where client numbers were meticulously listed. *Probably buried on my desk when he was here—he didn't even see it.* Reaching for the phone, she punched numbers.

Three rings. Dana was usually home. When Wayne offered to support her, she'd jumped at the chance to stop waiting tables and become a full-time mom. Five rings. The phone was picked up and a breathless "Hello" came over the line.

"This is Cassidy." She swung around to rest her heels on the radiator. "I had a break-in and I'm fairly certain it was Curly. I think he stole my Rolodex to get hold of your address."

"Ohshit!" A one-word gasp.

"You need to tell me what this is about." Cassidy kept her voice mild, not allowing any of her anger to leak out.

"Jesus, Cass, I'm really sorry, okay? I mean, I never would've . . . I never thought . . . . It just never entered my mind, know what I mean? All I can say is, I'm really, really sorry." The words tumbled out all in a rush.

"Why is Curly trying to find you?" Cassidy came down hard on each word. There was a long pause, during which she heard a clatter of cat footsteps trotting up the oak staircase. Amazing how cats, with their reputation for stealth, could make such a racket. Starshine hit the top stair, bounded across the bedroom, then skidded onto her desk, sending a flutter of paper to the floor.

Dana asked, her voice small and scared, "So now he knows where I am?"

Cassidy explained the maybe-he-does, maybe-he-doesn't theory. Then, her tone slightly tougher, she said, "You've got to tell me about Curly."

"Curly's just some guy, um . . . some guy, you know, I borrowed money from."

"The truth."

A deep sigh on the other end. Starshine prodded Cassidy with her nose. Juggling the receiver, she twisted toward the desk to scrape a fingernail along the side of the cat's triangular face.

At last Dana said, "He's Cypress' father."

Cassidy sat forward and grabbed the chair arm with the hand that had been scratching Starshine's cheek. "You said he bolted. Didn't want any part of you or the baby."

"I didn't wanna tell you."

"Tell me what?" Cassidy released the arm and made herself lean back. Outside the window the squirrel bounced from limb to limb in her tree.

Another deep sigh. "That I spent four years with an asshole—what I mean is, four years with somebody who used me for a punching bag."

Offended at Cassidy's failure to attend to her needs, Starshine jumped onto the windowsill. Dana said, "What I did is, I moved in with Curly when I got out of the, you know, hospital. A real creepo, okay? Like he kept me in this basement apartment, wouldn't let me talk to my friends. Reason I didn't tell you is, I was—I was just so ashamed. I mean, what kind of girl lets a guy do that, you know? I s'pose it was mostly the drugs. He was a dealer, kept me supplied, okay? And me, half the time I was so wasted I didn't know what I was doin'."

Cassidy's stomach knotted. She hated men like Curly, could understand Dana's not wanting to admit having been with him. "You told me you crashed with friends after the hospital. So if asshole Curly had you locked in the basement, how'd you get away from him and into Josie's two-flat?"

"I wanted out but he always said he'd kill me—I mean, really kill me—if I left. So mostly I just did what I was told, okay? Except when he was gone, sometimes I'd sneak out to see my girlfriends. That's how I met Wayne. He was real good to me, always sayin' how I should leave Curly, sayin' he'd help. But I couldn't. I mean, I was just too scared. Then I got pregnant, and I knew I had to stop the drugs and get out. For the first time I had a reason, know what I mean? A real reason."

Starshine's ears pricked, her tail twitched. The squirrel, which had jumped from the tree to the porch roof, skittered in front of the window.

Dana continued, "Josie, she said I could come live with her. So one time, when Curly was playing a gig, Wayne packed up his stuff and mine and hauled us over to her place. Since Curly was down in Oak Lawn, I didn't think—I mean, it seemed like he wouldn't be able to track me all the way up here to Oak Park. But I felt bad, know what I mean? Putting Josie in danger like that. Curly, he told me about an old girlfriend who tried to get away and how he burned down her house. So I gave Josie some story about why I had to move, okay? Never told her 'bout Curly. Just made up some story."

"What other stories have you made up?" Cassidy scratched the back of her hand, which had suddenly started to itch. As she dug into the skin, she felt a cluster of tiny bumps.

"That's all. I mean, the only one. When I started therapy, I knew I had to tell you 'bout the rest of it—the drugs, the hospital, my parents. But I figured not talkin' about Curly wouldn't hurt anything, know what I mean? I felt so bad, so shitty after tellin' all that other stuff . . . . What I mean is, I just couldn't stand having to say one more bad thing about myself. And since you and Josie are friends, and she didn't know . . . . Well, I just didn't wanna talk about it."

"Therapy's confidential. I'd never tell Josie." Remembering what she had told Zach, her face burned. She suddenly had a visceral understanding of Dana's sense of shame.

"I know that now." A tinge of remorse in her voice.

The squirrel raced up to the window and stood on its haunches, taunting Starshine. The cat clicked her teeth, a strange, instinctive behavior Cassidy had never witnessed before. Cassidy said, "You still haven't explained why Curly showed up at my house."

Dana's voice picked up speed. "He followed us there. Wayne and me, we went to Fitzgerald's that Sunday night— Sunday before Labor Day, okay? You know Fitzgerald's, don't you, Cass?"

"Sure." Fitzgerald's was a popular, live music roadhouse on Roosevelt Road just south of Oak Park.

"We were sitting there around midnight, you know, just sitting, when who should come sailing through the door?"

"Curly."

"Well, I nearly fell off my chair. I mean, I was so surprised. I never thought—well, anyway, I told Wayne we had to get out. Even though it was a big crowd and it seemed like maybe he hadn't seen us, I just wanted to run out the door. I mean, we didn't run—what we did was, we put our heads down and kind of snuck away. So anyway, we got outside and jumped into Wayne's pickup, and then he blasted—what I mean is, he took off like a rocket out of that parking lot. Me, I was turned all the way around, staring out the rear window. And then, just when we were heading onto Oak Park Avenue, I saw that beat up old van tearing along after us."

"So he did see you." Cassidy patted her chest, trying to coax Starshine into more lap time. But the cat, still fixated on the squirrel, failed to respond.

"Curly chased us all over the village, okay? Wayne, he kept turning corners but he couldn't—he just couldn't shake the jagoff. All I could think of was—I kept thinking we had to keep him away from Josie's. And then I remembered your porch and how dark it gets at night. So I had Wayne turn into your alley and park a couple of houses down. Then we hustled through your backyard around to the porch, and what we did is, we hid out there."

"He must've assumed you went inside. That you lived here."

"I guess. But I never thought—what I mean is, we saw him drive around the block a few times, then he parked in front and finally he just drove off. So I figured it was over, okay? I mean, seemed to me he'd just . . . he'd go away. I never thought he'd come by your place. Never thought of it."

Okay for him to burn down my house, so long as he doesn't bother Josie.

"Cass? What's the matter? You're not mad or anything, are you?"

"I know you didn't mean any harm." *Wheedling—it works every time.*

"Now that I've told you . . . well, there's one other thing, all right?"

"What?" Starshine dropped to the floor and sauntered out of the room, not deigning to toss a single glance in Cassidy's direction. It was her pretend-the-human-doesn't-exist act.

"That night when Curly was chasing us, well, what I want to tell you is, Wayne said all kinds of crazy things. I mean, really crazy. I hate to admit it but . . . I'm scared of what he might do, know what I mean?"

"You have any reason to think it was more than just talk?"

"Well . . . ."

"What is it?" Scratching again, she wondered about the bumps, then remembered the moving black dot on Starshine's chin.

"I don't wanna tell you." The little kid voice was back. Cassidy waited. "I found a gun in Wayne's bottom drawer, okay? We had this big fight about it. I don't, you know, want guns anywhere near Cypress. But he wouldn't get rid of it. A big fight, know what I mean?"

"He knows guns are illegal in Oak Park?"

"Yeah, he knows." She paused, then continued. "And there's—well, there's something else. I found this letter in his wallet. Letter from his mother, okay? She mentioned something 'bout him being in trouble back when he was—when he lived in New York. I asked him what, but he wouldn't, you know, he wouldn't tell me."

Apparently the sanitized version of Wayne Dana presented in therapy's not the whole truth.

Cassidy finished the conversation by getting Dana's permission to report Curly, a.k.a. Eddie Salaski, to the village police. She repeated Dana's story to a detective who assured her that he would discuss the matter of an Oak Park break-in with Mr. Salaski, and would also drop a hint that the Gacy Boys van would henceforth be *vehicula non grata* in the village.

❧ ❧ ❧

Cassidy and Zach sat on the porch watching a raspberry-sherbet sunset gradually turn to dusk. The enclosed air baked with the magnified heat of a greenhouse, the row of casement windows having captured and intensified the afternoon sun.

The three not-painted-shut windows stood open, but the outside air scarcely moved. Despite the heat, she preferred sitting where they could see the sunset and hear the trees rustle rather than in her stuffy living room or the air conditioned bedroom, which would have moved the evening along faster than she intended.

Zach filled her fluted glass, then crunched the black Freixenet bottle down into the ice bucket. Smiling lazily, he clinked his glass against hers. "Here's to 'making it up.' "

She heard Kevin's voice again: *Hey, babe, I'll make it up to you.* "So, what do you have in mind? Don't forget, I get to torture you if it's not good enough."

Zach had switched gears on her, offering to spend Friday night at her house instead of having her spend Saturday at his. After last weekend's broken date, she figured she better take what she could get for now, and work herself up to a showdown later. She also had decided not to question his vague something-came-up excuse, hoping he would tell her himself—which he didn't. Instead of fighting over where he'd spent last weekend, she would conserve her resources for the bigger fight: where they were headed in the future.

The sweaty champagne glass felt cool in her hand. She took a large sip and held it in her mouth. Shimmery silk. The sound of a power mower reminded her that her grass had grown another inch in the past week.

He pulled her under his arm. It was too hot to cuddle. Leaning against him made her feel sticky and lumpish, but she needed the contact, skin against skin. His fingertips slipped beneath the waistband of her magenta shorts. His voice whispered huskily in her ear. "How's this for making it up? We could go upstairs to your bedroom, pretend it's a graveyard, and teach each other everything we know."

His fingers inched their way down, giving her hot shivers. Reluctantly she extracted his hand. "No way am I playing stand-in. Especially not for any hot-mamas out of your past."

"Well then," he placed outspread fingers lightly on her thigh. "If you're not in a heavy-breathing mood, let's talk about Dana's mother."

"Oh no you don't!" She jabbed him in the ribs, then furtively scratched the back of her hand. "I get to torture you, remember? Let's talk relationship. Let's talk commitment. Or, better yet," Cassidy swallowed a mouthful of champagne, "let's talk you moving in." From the steps outside Starshine jumped onto the sill of the window Cassidy kept open for her. The cat gazed warmly at Zach who was in particularly high regard after having complimented her extravagantly on her cleverness in coming home.

Zach took a handful of red pistachios out of his jeans pocket and dumped it on the paint-chipped picnic bench. "What's with all the hand scratching? Anything contagious?"

"Stop changing the subject."

Zach tossed Starshine a pistachio but she ignored it, grabbing instead a wadded paper napkin left from lunch. Prize clamped in her jaw, she pranced inside.

"Looks like that lost weekend of hers didn't affect her klepto urges any," Zach observed. "You ever find her stash of hot champagne corks?"

"Nary a trace. She's usually doing me a favor—cleaning up behind me like she did just now. But sometimes she crosses the line. The worst was when she stole one of the earrings my grandmother gave me."

Zach patted her knee. "But you forgave her."

She stiffened. *Code for: I can be any kind of jerk I want. You'll always take me back.*

He refilled their glasses, stuck a pistachio in her mouth, and said, "We've got to get hold of Dana's mother. Find out what kind of group the kid was in 'round age four."

Cassidy reared back. "I'm Dana's therapist—I can't do that." She jabbed him again. "And you can't either because you wouldn't know a thing about it if I hadn't temporarily flipped out and blabbed stuff I'm not allowed to say. Since I can't discuss clients, you don't know anything. End of story. Now let's get back to the real issue, which is where this relationship is going."

Starshine reappeared, leapt onto the rim of the wicker couch, and nuzzled Zach's neck. He said, "I need to talk to Dana's mother. I want to get her on the phone tonight. But don't worry, I'll use a cover. Nobody'll ever know about your moment of insanity."

"No. N-O. Uh uh. Absolutely not." She chugged some champagne.

Using both hands, Zach maneuvered her back under his arm. She leaned into him and curled up on the seat. "Cassidy," his voice dropped, becoming unaccustomedly somber, "Satanists are very bad people. They do things that would make your skin crawl. Steal children. Mutilate infants and animals. They've even been known to sacrifice cats. Are you willing to ignore the fact that a child was murdered? That there are parents somewhere whose kid disappeared and they never even knew what happened to him?"

"Shit," Cassidy muttered. "I hate when you do that."

"What?"

"Prey on my moral sensibilities." Starshine bit her hair, then gave it a yank. Hauling her down, Cassidy tried to hold onto her but she squirmed away and nestled in Zach's lap instead.

"I know how bad Satanists are." Her voice resigned. "That's one of the reasons I wanted to stay out of it. Those two therapists I mentioned, the ones with ritual abuse clients? They've had all kinds of scary things happen."

Starshine rumbled loudly as Zach scratched her cheek, demonstrating how sweet she could be when treated properly. He said, "Look, all you have to do is give me her parents' names. I'll handle the rest. You can even listen in on the extension."

"She'll hear me pick up the phone."

"Don't worry, I'll take care of it."

"Okay, one phone call." She nibbled her bottom lip, considering whether to pass along the new information about Curly.

Telling him anything was a complete screw-up—now you want to tell him more?

Need someone to talk to. Too scary keeping all this stuff to myself. Besides, he's right about that kid who got killed. We can't just pretend it never happened.

She said, "Long as I'm in this deep, I might as well tell you the rest," and proceeded to bring him up to date about Cypress' father.

They finished the champagne and went upstairs to use the bedroom phone. Cassidy provided the parents' name and town, and Zach got the number from directory assistance.

"This Mrs. Voss?" A short pause. "My name's Zach Moran, reporter for the *Chicago Post*. We're doing a feature on Apple Creek, past and present, and the librarian said you've lived in the area a long time. Anyway, the reason I'm calling is, I'd like to do a brief telephone interview, just a few questions to get a slant on the way things used to be." Another pause. "I know it's Friday night, but reporters work all kinds of crazy hours. If you'd rather I call back some other time . . . ."

He gave Cassidy a nod and she scurried downstairs to pick up the kitchen phone on the wall next to the dining room doorway. Starshine zipped ahead to inspect her dish in the corner across the room. One quick sniff and she sprang onto the counter, flattening her ears and twitching the tip of her tail, a feline scowl to protest the sorry state of her food bowl.

"What's that?" Zach's voice, clipped and businesslike. "Somebody pick up the extension on your end?"

"We don't have an extension," Laurel sounded apologetic, as if possessing only one phone were a sign of inadequacy.

Zach responded, "Oh, well, who knows? Ever since the breakup, Ma Bell's been a little nutso. I understand from the librarian that you've got grown children and you haven't worked outside the home."

"Only one, a daughter. She's got a little girl herself so actually I'm a grandmother."

"As a stay-at-home mother, you had the kind of traditional lifestyle that's rapidly disappearing, which is one of the reasons I wanted to talk to you. Nowadays, even in a place like Apple Creek, most of the mothers work and have to find some kind of child care. Do you live in the town itself or out on a farm?"

"Just a small farm, I don't know, a couple of miles from town."

"Must've been hard to find other kids for your daughter to play with, living outside of town like that. What kind of preschool groups did they have back then?"

8

Cousins

"I can't say for sure, Mr. Moran. Apple Creek's a pretty small town. I don't know, there's never been much for kids around here."

Starshine jumped down, trotted across to the doorway where Cassidy was leaning against the frame, and nipped her knee, a further sign of displeasure at Cassidy's poor performance in the catfood department.

"What about Sunday School? Indian Guides? Any daycare or play groups?"

"Sunday School, of course, although Dana never got a chance to go. Seems like some lady from out of town . . . . But I don't know, I really can't recall."

Minister's wife said Laurel started a play group. She can't have forgotten that.

"One thing I do remember, when Dana was three and a half or four . . . ." Cassidy heard the faint sound of a door banging shut. Laurel's voice resumed, whispery and rushed, "There wasn't anything. She didn't belong to any groups. Now, please, don't call again."

The slam of the phone loud in her ear. Footsteps overhead, Zach on his way down. She stared at a yellowed Sylvia cartoon, one of dozens taped to the fridge. "Food never spoils in the refrigerator of the woman who eats out."

What's Laurel afraid of? And why'd she need to lie?

ða ða ða

Saturday morning they shared the shower, dried each other's backs, then returned to bed to get all hot and sweaty again. By noon they were ready to abandon the damp, twisted sheets and put on clothes. Zach sported a new black T bearing the words: Will work for beer.

Claiming that sex burned at least five hundred calories, Zach insisted on refueling at Honey and Thyme, a neighborhood cafe that served good, homemade food and was not, miraculously, part of a chain. After a stupefying breakfast of bacon, eggs and pancakes, Zach dropped her off with a quick kiss. "Call you during the week."

She climbed the steps to her back stoop. *Trouble with love, no matter how much I get, I always want more. One good, hot rush, then six days of withdrawal.*

A high-pitched giggle from the Stein yard next door broke through her fog. Her stoop, attached near the southeast corner of the house, stood six feet from the fence between her property and her neighbor's. She glanced down into the next yard where Dorothy, her husband Paul, and their brood of adopted kids, complexions ranging from ebony to wheat, were busy weeding. Dorothy, kneeling beside the fence directly opposite the stoop, looked up at her. "Meet the new neighbors yet?"

"New neighbors?" Cassidy furrowed her brow, feeling dumb that she hadn't noticed.

Dorothy pitched her voice so it wouldn't carry. "I'm so glad to have a black family right next door." She tilted her head, jostling a light brown, Orphan-Annie mass of curls, in the direction of the house to the south of the Stein's. "Moved in last month. Be great for my kids to have someone else around who's not all pale and pasty like us."

Gripping the stoop's wrought iron railing, Cassidy peered into the yard on the other side of the Steins'. A black man was rolling fresh paint onto the garage, assisted by two small children who dipped brushes into the bucket, liberally splashing themselves, the ground and the siding. Midway between house and garage, Mom squatted next to an even smaller munchkin, evidently trying to keep the child out of flying-paint range. A white dust-mop dog ran in circles around the humans, barking joyfully.

Cassidy's gaze returned to Dorothy, her back bent to pull a waist-high weed out by the roots. "Good thing you update me now and again. Otherwise, I'd be completely out of touch. So, what's the scoop?"

Dorothy straightened and removed her gloves, looking pleased at the opportunity to play neighborhood switchboard. "Seems like a great new family. Darnella told me—Darnella and Cal Roberts, those are the names—she told me they picked a place cheap enough to get by on one income so she could stay home with the kids." Wiping a hand across her forehead, Dorothy flipped loose, sandy curls back from her face. "Even though I have to work myself, I think it's cool when moms can stay home. He's an investment banker—three-piece suit, the works. She's got her master's in English, but right now about all she has time to read is Dr. Seuss. They've got girls three and six, a four-year-old boy in the middle."

"Off to a good start, already painting the garage." Cassidy wrinkled her nose, aware of a nasty little sense of resentment. *Makes mine look even worse by comparison.* Scratching idly at the tiny bumps on her hand, she said, "Well, thanks for the info. Your yard's looking terrific. When you finish, you can send that team of ants over here."

Chuckling, Dorothy bent down to tackle the next weed.

Cassidy turned on her heel and headed toward her garage, more aware of chipped paint than ever. Driving to a nearby pet store, she returned with a proprietor-recommended flea collar tucked in her bag. Inside she discovered Starshine to be conspicuously absent from her usual, waiting-to-bitch-her-out post on the chair beside the door.

Swear she reads my mind. Cassidy rounded the oak cabinet that separated the client waiting room from the rest of the house, then halted abruptly as the kitchen came into view. Dried-dirt cat prints circled the entire room, from the dining room doorway across to the counter, down the length of the linoleum countertop, over the stove, and back out the door into the nether regions of the house. "At least she should be easy to track."

A crystal vase filled with mums that Zach had brought as part of his making-it-up campaign had been knocked off the countertop, resulting in a wide puddle on the floor. Within the puddle's circumference were chunks of broken glass, a dozen wilting mums, Starshine's upside down bowl, and clumps of cat food sitting like Lilliputian islands in a tiny sea. At the opposite end of the counter a stack of *Family Circle* magazines lay strewn across the green linoleum.

That's it. She's crossed the line. It's capital punishment time—or at least banishment into the basement for the entire night.

She hid the flea collar in the cupboard with the cat food, mopped up the floor, then restacked the magazines. *Family Circle* was a far cry from Cassidy's usual choice in reading material, but her mother had pushed them off on her, despite considerable evidence that the implied maternal message was a complete waste. *She must've figured out by now, nothing's going to transform me from my own froggy self into her version of a princess.* The magazines had sat untouched on her porch for months. Then, when Zach started joining her on the wicker couch, she'd moved them inside, embarrassed that he might think she actually read them. They now resided in her kitchen, awaiting a phone call to find out whether or not the village wanted them in the blue recyclables tub.

After cleaning the kitchen, she followed the paw prints to a wilted geranium in the living room. An acrid smell rose from the planter; dirt lay scattered around it. Guilt hitting her, Cassidy realized she'd been too distracted of late to remember the litter box, which had gone unchanged for more than a week. *Guess she's telling me something. Maybe the death penalty's overdoing it a tad.*

The tracks, which had faded out to small splotches resembling coffee spills, continued across the living room and up the staircase. Peering at the evidence, she also noticed clumps of cat fur drifting like tumbleweeds over the hardwood floor. The fur, she realized, was routine: not part of the crime scene, just a detail that seldom penetrated her acquired blindness to dirt. She followed the trail to the staircase, where bite-sized pieces of toilet paper, like Hansel and Gretel crumbs, led upward. At the top of the stairs, she gazed across a short hallway into the bathroom, the setting for Starshine's *pièce de résistance*.

The narrow room, festooned with toilet paper, featured a white strip running from far wall to sink spigot, from sink to tub faucet, from tub to laundry basket. Cassidy ripped her way through to the roll on the opposite wall, where deep fang marks punctured the remaining inch of paper.

She stepped to the bathroom closet to fetch a new roll. The remains of a four-roll package lay on the closet floor, a cushiony circle of shredded paper and celophane.

Cassidy stared at the cat's handiwork. *A nest. She's made herself a nest and at the same time given me an emphatic message: If her bathroom's not fit to use, mine won't be either.*

૨૭ ૨૭ ૨૭

Starshine did not step forward to claim credit for her accomplishments and Cassidy wasted no time looking for her, having long since learned that cats can never be found unless they want to be. Many hours later, Cassidy's stomach reminded her that breakfast, no matter how heavily overdone, would not last indefinitely. Her mood lightened by having done the penance of housework for her multiple inadequacies, she headed for the newly cleaned kitchen. She opened the refrigerator, hoping her last shopping trip had been more recent than her last litter box change.

A furry body wound through her legs.

"Aha!" She closed the refrigerator. "Knew you couldn't hold out past dinnertime."

Starshine bounced onto the counter and gave her a self-satisfied smirk.

"My turn now." Cassidy opened the cupboard, wrapped her left hand around the flea collar, and slowly moved her right hand toward the cat's neck.

Starshine's black pupils widened in suspicion.

As the cat tried to jump down, Cassidy lunged, grabbing a handful of scruff and encircling the thrashing hindquarters with her other arm. She spent the next five minutes trying to hold the cat in place, twist the collar around her neck, and buckle it. Once the collar was fastened, she released Starshine and leapt out of claws' reach.

Mrowrrr! Starshine uttered a plaintive, betrayal-filled howl.

"It's only a collar. And anyway, it's for your own good." *Who said that—your mother?* "You don't really want to provide living quarters for *fleas,* do you? I mean, only peasants have fleas. And you . . . you're so upper crust, so regal."

Starshine's ears pricked, her wild black eyes narrowed.

"And pink's so good on you—brings out the green in your eyes."

Ever so slightly, the cat's chin lifted.

"Pink's definitely your color. And besides, your new collar makes you look so elegant—even more distinguished than before."

༂ ༂ ༂

Late Sunday afternoon shadows were lengthening in her backyard as she wrestled with bushy, three-foot weeds growing around the foundation of her house. Hearing the phone, she raced into the kitchen, wiped gritty hands on her shorts, and grabbed the receiver.

"Hey, babe." Kevin's voice, as rich and full-bodied as good burgundy, poured across the line. "Time to check in, don't you think? We haven't talked since I dropped off that little gift back in June."

Her breath caught. *Three years after trading me in for a newer model and he still can get to me.* "Right. The pendant you boosted from your girlfriend. I wear it every day, next to my heart." She stretched the cord across the kitchen to wash her hands at the sink.

"Where's the new guy, darlin'? He around? Or can we take a little nostalgia time here?"

"Oh, you want to reminisce, do you? Shall we talk about the chlamydia I caught 'cause of that bimbo of yours who was doing a little night work? Or maybe you'd rather discuss the time you nearly got arrested for selling phony securities?"

"So, the boyfriend's not there, huh? Thought you were gonna pick somebody who'd stay on the leash next time."

"Okay, 'fess up. What kind of trouble you got yourself into now?" She dried her hands, wiped her sweaty forehead with the towel.

"I was thinking about the Labor Day weekend we went to that Springfield motel the year before we got married. We spent half the day in bed, lived on bagels and brie. Then at night we'd go for long walks around the lake. That one time we found an isolated beach and went skinny dipping. I still have this vivid image—you looked like a mermaid, moonlight rippling across your skin."

His words brought up a matching picture deeply etched into her own memory. She envisioned him standing waist-deep in water, body muscular and trim, carved face reminding her of pictures of Greek gods with long, tousled curls. She could hear his voice, unusually solemn: "I've never seen anyone so beautiful."

Stop this right now. Every time she allowed Kevin to beguile her, she ended up regretting it. Pushing the picture away, she clinked ice cubes into a glass, fished one out, and rubbed it against her forehead. "So, what's happening? Your new girlfriend getting ready to dump you? You trying to line up a fallback?"

Several minutes later, after finally getting rid of him, she filled her glass with water and stared through her kitchen window into the new family's backyard, two houses down. The sprinkler was running and a gaggle of pint-sized, black and white bodies splashed through it, the little dust mop dog darting in and out. Mom sat at the picnic table handing out something, popsicles maybe. *This is what Oak Park's all about.* She wanted to freeze frame the picture, save it in her memory.

Although she'd never subscribed to her mother's *Family Circle* fantasy, at one point during her pre-awareness stage with Kevin she'd dreamed of giving out popsicles to kids of her own. *If a fairy godmother tapped me on the shoulder, would I still want that now? Who knows?*

That's what talking to Kevin did: It made her all sappy and maudlin. Every time he popped up, she spent the next few hours remembering, wondering, playing what-if. She was embarrassed to admit that the attraction still lingered, even though the therapist in her head knew precisely where the magnetism lay. What drew her most were his worst qualities, the traits she most deeply hated: his damn-the-torpedoes, thrill-seeking side that brought out the parts of herself she constantly tried to deny.

And why for God's sake did he have to ask about Zach? She already had to exert full mental powers to keep from obsessing over Zach's change of pattern—no explanation given, thank you—leaving her with Saturday night and all day Sunday suddenly empty, far too much time to wonder what the hell he was up to.

"Ouch!" Cassidy felt a soft thud against her upper back, claws hooking into her shoulders. Twisting frantically, she tried to yank the cat loose, but the harder she pulled, the tighter Starshine dug herself in. Several agonizing moments passed, then she stopped struggling and dropped to her knees. The cat bounced daintily to the floor.

"You are such a bitch." Cassidy stood up, rubbing bloody claw wounds under her shirt.

The cat looked pointedly at her empty dish.

"There are subtler ways to get my attention." She opened a can. "Besides, I just fed you an hour ago. How many you eating for, anyway?"

Cassidy filled the bowl and the cat attacked her food.

"Zach says I should take you to the vet. Apply a final solution."

Mrowr! The cat leapt to the counter.

"Abortion—that's all I meant. It'd save a lot of trouble in the long run."

The cat began her ablutions, refusing to grant Cassidy any further acknowledgement.

"Even waiters—world experts on the subtle art of ignoring—could learn a thing or two from cats." But regardless of Starshine's clearcut indifference, Cassidy persisted with her one-way conversation. "Maggie's expecting me tonight for a barbecue. But the more I think about it, the more I don't want to go."

The cat interrupted her washing to give Cassidy a long stare ending in a bored blink.

"Everybody else'll be a couple, straight or gay. Maggie and Susie don't get along that well, but at least they're together. Maggie's sure to ask about Zach. Then I'll have to explain that he stayed over Friday night, disappeared afterward, and won't be seen again till he's damned good and ready. And if I say the words out loud, I'll have to think about what I said, and there won't be any way to avoid asking myself why I put up with it."

She called Maggie to beg off, inventing an illness for her mother as an excuse. *Probably figures I'm lying.* Her friend had chastised her often enough for keeping problems to herself. *Maggie's right, I oughta open up more.* But she knew the only way she'd lay out all her troubles was if someone pried it out of her. The part that needed to be strong and struggle through on her own had been in control far too long to allow it.

Having escaped the barbecue, she suddenly realized she did not in fact relish the idea of another Saturday night alone. She tried her mother and then her grandmother, neither of whom answered. No surprise where her grandmother was concerned. Gran was the most active, fun-loving person she knew. But it made her wonder about her usually stay-at-home mother, who, now that she thought about it, hadn't called to nag in over a week.

The only thing she could think to do was get on her bike and ride out her frustration. Loping toward her garage, she tried not to notice how high the grass had grown. *Yard's putting on its abandoned-lot act.*

Kevin had bought a top-of-the-line Toro mower shortly before he left, overriding her protests that, first, they couldn't afford it, and second, a simpler model would hold up better. "We go first class, babe," he'd said. "Nothing but the best."

After conking out at the end of summer, "the best" was now taking up space in her overcrowded garage, while she—too besotted by love and distracted by crises—could not get herself together to trade it in on a basic, less temperamental model. Meanwhile, the grass kept growing. *Crazy to keep the house. I'm the kind of inept, unhandy, yardwork-hating individual who should be forever condemned to apartment living.*

Hauling up the garage door, she backed her bicycle out past hoses, tools, and lumber piled along the wall. The bike, an ancient rattletrap that had started out as a three-speeder, currently had only one working gear. So she now rode permanently in low, medium or high, she wasn't sure which.

As she closed the garage door, a dark red sedan rumbled toward her down the alley that ran behind her lot and emptied onto Briar. It rolled to a stop a few feet from where she stood. Ursula, looking through the driver's side window, smiled brightly and fluttered her skinny fingers in a little wave. The frizzled head, neck stretching to peer through the windshield, seemed almost dwarfish all alone in the big car. Ursula gunned the motor and cut a sharp left.

What's she doing here? Watching as the vehicle trundled a little too speedily past her house, Cassidy spotted a shiny, gold-leaf insignia in the back, then dropped her eyes to the vanity plate: GTSHED. *A Cadillac? And what's GTSHED?*

Pedalling along in the same direction, Cassidy saw the red Cadillac turn left three blocks ahead. *Sightseeing Oak Park alleys? And who'd ever have imagined Ursula in a Cadillac? But then, who'd have imagined me in a marriage with Kevin? Or, a nondomestic-type like myself with this big house and yard?*

The dusky, blue-shadowed evening was mild. She biked beneath a leaf canopy of towering elms that had somehow managed to survive the plague of Dutch elm disease. The smaller trees, maples she thought, showed green leaves brightly laced with gold. Many of the yards and parkway corners blazed with feathery, blood-red salvia, yellow mums, and violet pansies, all carefully groomed. *People who do that kind of gardening must have more hours in their day.* She meandered through a block party, smiling to herself at a mob of kids, various colors and sizes, grappling beneath the parachute the park district used for children's games. *If only it could be like this— all the time, everywhere.*

When she'd ridden long enough to push both Zach and Kevin into a back corner of her mind, she stopped in front of a two-story gray stucco with double, side-by-side doors. Although her bike seemed too far gone to be stealable, she locked up anyway, abiding by the Oak Park myth that anything not nailed down would be walked off with. For Oak Parkers, a favorite pastime was telling can-you-top-this stories about bizarre items that had disappeared from yards and garages.

She rang the bell labeled "Howard and Josie Crandel," and Josie answered. They exchanged the usual greetings, Cassidy claiming to have just dropped by and Josie pretending to be pleased. Accepting an invitation for iced tea, Cassidy followed her hostess through a room overflowing with collectibles: a plumed hat, bird's nest, and framed display of old door keys graced one wall; a boxed arrangement of antique door knobs sat on a coffeetable; rag dolls lined a shelf. Any space not taken up by inanimate objects sprouted, sprayed or drooped living green ones. The overall effect might have been stifling but instead was whimsical and fresh. *I tried decorating like that, it'd be a disaster.* As she crossed the living room, Cassidy caught a whiff of cigarette smoke, the one discordant note in the entire fanciful scene.

Josie led her into the kitchen, which boasted more of the same. A twiggy plant, mostly bare branches with a few pasty leaves, sat in a plastic tub on a round oak table.

"My basil's dying," Josie lamented. "I got the book out," she pointed to a botanical text laying open beside the planter, "but it's no help. Lord, I hate to lose it—I use the leaves all the time in cooking."

Cassidy shrugged. "Only plants I have any luck with are the species plasticus."

As Josie filled tall glasses, Cassidy dropped into a straight-backed chair at the table. Josie joined her, moving the plant aside to avoid peering through moribund branches.

"Well . . . " Cassidy took a deep breath. "That baptism was really something, wasn't it?" *Watch your step. Josie for sure knows the rules of confidentiality.* "How'd it go afterward?"

"Dana did a little drinking," Josie admitted, her perky voice making light of it. "And some talking . . . ." Her eyes shifted away from Cassidy's. "But I can't say I blame her. That Ernie—he's such an old goat. Sometimes he seems the epitome of . . . of an unregenerate, redneck Republican." She smoothed her hair, dark brown threaded with gray. The same simple, curled-under style that had framed her face for the entire ten years Cassidy had known her.

"Ernie does seem a mite controlling," Cassidy commented.

"To put it mildly." Josie's wide mouth puckered wryly. "He practically won't let Aunt Laurel out of his sight." Her lips slipped back into their determined smile, her usual let-me-cheer-you-up expression. Her fine-featured face, unretouched by make-up, might have been pretty if she hadn't so clearly gone for plain. She wore an orange, puff-sleeved blouse and denim skirt: except for the orange, she could have passed for Amish.

"Dana's mother ever work?"

"Ernie wouldn't allow it. He's got a home office, so naturally he wants Laurel constantly available to run and fetch— sort of a surrogate Rover. He's some kind of computer whiz. It never ceases to amaze me how a person can be practically a genius in one area and a total idiot in another."

"Idiot, as in husband and father?" Cassidy tasted the strong, acrid tea. She preferred it sweet but did not want to interrupt the flow. Besides, Josie probably disapproved of sugar and Cassidy wouldn't want it to get out that she was an unregenerate, death-by-chocolate sweet-freak.

Josie shook her head, puzzled. "I've always wondered. Does Laurel tolerate it because she wants to? Or because she's financially dependent and thinks she has to? I guess that's what life was like for prefeminist women."

"Yeah, and now we're liberated. Which gives husbands the right to abandon their wives and skip out on child support." The words came out sounding more bitter than she'd intended.

Pushing her chair back, Josie stood abruptly. "Don't mind me." She laughed nervously. "I just remembered I've got to make the salad for the Head Start fundraiser tomorrow."

She embarrassed 'cause I still sound hostile about divorce? Fits with the way she got suddenly unavailable when I went through mine. Cassidy's teeth clenched. *Probably one of those Norman-Vincent-Peale types who gets nutso when everything isn't sweetness and light.*

Josie measured brown rice and water into a casserole dish.

Cassidy sipped her iced tea, ignoring Josie's signal that it was time to leave. "Minister's wife told me Laurel started a co-op play group but Ernie made her quit."

"Oh that Annie." Josie put the casserole in the microwave and punched a pad to start it humming. "As the minister's wife, she ought to keep her mouth shut because everything she says comes back to haunt her. Here she knocks herself out doing good for folks in the community, then ruins it all by gossiping. Sometimes I think she just gets bored and wants to stir things up."

"I'm amazed how much you know about Apple Creek."

Josie leaned against the counter, a knife in one hand. "Mom forced me to spend summers out there till I was sixteen. She had to work, you see, and wanted to get me away from the concrete and the drug dealers. Lord, how I hated those long, boring summers. But now I look back and figure a taste of country living was probably good for me. Anyway, I used to hang out mostly with my aunt because Dana was so much younger and Laurel needed somebody to talk to." She took a chunk of turkey out of the refrigerator and began slicing. "This salad's great—you should try it. Turkey, brown rice and walnuts. Just wish I had some basil to throw in."

Cassidy considered the age difference between Josie, who was thirty-five, and Dana, who was twenty-seven. A twelve-year-old would probably remember what was going on in her four-year-old cousin's life. "Sooo . . . " Cassidy drew the word out, searching for a lead-in to her real agenda. "If Ernie wouldn't let Dana be in the play group, did she ever get the chance to join anything else?"

Turning back around, Josie gave her a long, measured look. When she spoke, her voice was flat and decidedly unchirpy. "Why do you ask?"

9

Forest Preserve

"Well, uh . . . Dana doesn't remember much about her early years, but she thinks something might've happened. Maybe in a preschool group, some kind of group or other, and I was just wondering . . . ."

After a long silence Josie finally spoke, her tone low-pitched and grim. "The night of the baptism, when Dana was drinking, she talked about what happened in the cemetery."

"Why didn't you tell me? Here I've been tap dancing all around it."

Josie put a hand to her throat. "Oh Lord, I don't know. Dana's all upset about you not believing her or wanting to put her in the hospital or some such. I was afraid if I told you about it, I'd be getting in the middle. I didn't want to interfere with what's going on between the two of you."

She's right. Shouldn't be talking to Josie. This is triangulation. "I can see your point. And of course I'd never discuss anything that happened in a session. That wasn't what I had in mind at all." *Shut up. You always overdo it.*

"So—why *are* you asking?" Josie's level gray eyes met hers.

"Well, the whole thing was just so weird. I wanted to have some kind of context, um . . . . I mean, it seemed like if I knew which group it actually was . . . ." She realized she was headed for trouble.

"You don't believe her."

Cassidy's eyes narrowed. "You sound so certain. You ever run into anyone else with a similar experience?"

"If she says it happened, it happened."

"It's not that I don't believe her." *That's for sure.* "It's just . . . I'd like to get some idea how it happened. I need to know how she ended up in a situation where she was so vulnerable. It'll help the therapy." Cassidy sucked in her cheek, waiting to see if Josie would buy it. *Thank God for the therapy mystique. Since nobody really understands it, they'll accept almost anything.*

Josie's face softened. "There's not much I can tell you. Dana was always right there underfoot. Seemed like Laurel never got a break."

"There was the play group—the one Laurel started. You ever hear anything about that?"

Josie shrugged. "I don't think so. But that doesn't mean anything. I was only around three months out of the year so there was a lot I didn't know about. One thing I do remember is hearing Laurel and Ernie arguing once. About Dana. The only time I ever heard them exchange a harsh word, and they were really going at it. It was about daycare—whether or not to put her in it."

"One wanted her in, the other didn't?"

Josie nodded. "Only I can't remember which was which. And I don't know if she ever went."

"You used to attend vacation Bible school, didn't you? She ever go with you?"

"Lord no. Ernie had no use for religion. One of the things Laurel talked about was how she wished she could go to church but Ernie wouldn't let her."

Cassidy tried a few more questions that went nowhere, then said, "I'd better let you get on with your salad." She deposited her half-empty glass in the sink and started to leave.

Following her to the door, Josie ventured, "There's something I've been meaning to ask. I suppose you know Howard's been working in San Francisco for months now. And way before all this trouble started, I bought a ticket to fly out for the weekend. But with Dana so unsettled, I'm nervous about leaving."

Cassidy turned, her hand on the doorknob. "How's she been since the baptism?"

"Except for getting drunk right afterward, she's been better than I expected. Probably relieved it's over."

"Well, Wayne'll be here. I get the impression he's really good with her."

Josie's eyes flickered. "Heavens, yes." A short laugh. "He's a godsend."

"She can always call me if she needs to, but I don't think there's anything to worry about. She's stronger than you realize."

As Cassidy unlocked her bike, a suspicious voice piped up in her head: *What is it she's not telling me?*

ﻬ ﻬ ﻬ

When Zach left after breakfast on Saturday, Cassidy did not expect to see him again until the next weekend, or possibly even longer, now that their regular Saturday night pattern had mysteriously slipped away. But he surprised her by calling on Monday.

"I've got an appointment Wednesday afternoon with a park district supervisor, name of Roger Korsac, who lives in the southwestern forest preserve. He's agreed to talk to me about Satanism in the area surrounding St. Paul's. Want to come along?"

She had one session on her calendar for that time but it was a client with a flexible schedule. She said yes.

109

Zach picked her up after lunch on Wednesday and they retraced the first leg of the route they had driven two weeks previously on their original expedition to see the tall white bear. Headed south through slow-moving traffic on Mannheim Road, Cassidy stared blindly at a seemingly endless strip of malls and fast food joints as she half listened to a WBEZ debate over federal taxes, which failed to interest her.

Snapping off the radio, she asked, "Why does he live way out in the forest preserve?"

Zach frowned at her having turned off the public radio station he listened to incessantly. "If you read the newspaper, you'd understand why some supervisors live in remote areas. When the district first bought up the land, they acquired these empty farmhouses which they handed out as free housing. Reporters occasionally sniff around the forest preserve district to see who's giving what to whom, so every now and then another free housing exposé lands in the paper."

"Why should I waste my time reading sensationalistic news stories when you can tell me all I need to know in two minutes? Actually, you usually tell me more. But that's okay, I don't mind being informed. Just so long as I don't have to wade through sex-and-violence bullshit to do it."

They crossed the Des Plaines River and entered the forest preserve, but this time, instead of angling along the western edge toward St. Paul's, they turned east and followed a curving two-lane road deeper into the woods. On their last trip, the trees and underbrush had all sported varying shades of green. Now she saw distinct splashes of red and gold, the fall colors rendered especially vivid by a flood of bright sunshine. Cassidy rolled down her window, discovered the rays held almost no heat, then put it up again. The temperature had finally dropped for the first time in two weeks.

"So," she continued, "this supervisor, Roger Korsac, he's been living in the woods for what, twenty-five years? And our plan is to find out what goes on out there at night—other than screwing on graves, that is. Since you told Korsac this is part of a newspaper investigation, how'll you explain bringing me along?"

"Thought I'd introduce you as an intern reporter."

"Hey, that puts me in a one-down position, sort of like Roz Russell in *His Girl Friday*. I don't like being cast as the female who fetches coffee."

"Okay, you be the reporter and I'll be the intern." He cut left onto a narrow road. A thick wall of trees shot straight up at the edges, giving Cassidy the sense of driving at the bottom of a shadowy canyon.

Zach glanced over at her. "Why'd you decide to come along, anyway? I thought you wanted to keep your distance from this whole investigation."

She looked straight ahead. "I can't stand not knowing what you're up to."

"I could report in when I got back."

Her conscience prickled. *Report in, as in tell him what you've been doing.* "Guess you should know I took a shot at Josie. She had one interesting tidbit, a memory of Ernie and Laurel arguing about whether to put Dana into some kind of daycare. So far, the only two possibilities seem to be Laurel's play group and this unspecified daycare center."

Zach said, "Arguing . . . maybe that's why Laurel got off the phone so fast when we heard the door slam. Probably Ernie arriving on the scene. We definitely need to find out who did daycare back then."

The Datsun turned into a wide gravel drive and continued another half mile to the farmhouse. They stopped next to a green pickup inscribed with the forest preserve insignia, then mounted sturdy porch steps fronting the frame house. The trim was freshly painted. A tidy patch of lawn separated the yard from the surrounding forest.

Cassidy adjusted Zach's collar, which had turned up in back. *Amazing. The man actually owns a shirt with buttons.* Dressed in sport coat, dress shirt, and jeans—no tie, a tie would be going too far—Zach looked exactly the way she thought a reporter should. Cassidy had made a similar stab at achieving a professional image, having selected her favorite outfit, the one she reserved for first sessions with new clients: a purple silk blouse and black wool skirt crisscrossed with white cat fur. Considering she didn't own a jacket, it was the best she could do.

No one answered their knock, so they followed a trail of smoke around to the back. A scattering of dry leaves crinkled underfoot, the first she'd noticed on the ground. As they rounded the corner, she saw a small, wiry man in a brown ranger uniform stirring the contents of a cauldron that hung over an open fire. He waved them over to join him at the rear of the shallow lot.

"Bubble, bubble, toil and trouble," he intoned in a false baritone. Then, reverting to his own sprightly voice, he said, "In case you're wondering, this is not a witch's brew. What I'm doing here is practicing a recipe that dates back to one of the earliest settlements in the territory. I put on demonstrations down at the nature center, so I have to be sure I've got it right. It's not that easy when you can't control the temperature and have to guess at the cooking time. Doing these demos really makes me appreciate what the early settlers went through."

About eye level with Cassidy, bristling with energy, he had dark eyes reminiscent of well-worn, patent-leather shoes, the gleam faded but not entirely gone. His head, capped with tightly curled gray hair, nodded briskly.

Moving up-wind to avoid gray billows that stung her eyes and tickled her nose, Cassidy peered into the cauldron at undefined chunks floating in brown goo. "What's in it?"

"Tell you what." He rocked forward on the balls of his feet. "First you taste, then I'll explain."

"Taste?" she repeated doubtfully.

He captured a chunk with his long wooden spoon and poked it in her direction. She reared back. Sniffing warily, she gradually approached and tongued it into her mouth. She bit into tough, stringy meat that had a pungent, wild taste to it. "Interesting," she commented, attempting a Spockian neutrality.

"Good for you." His apple-cheeked face broke into a huge grin. "You're a trooper, you are. Squirrel, that's what. Not exactly to our modern taste, but a delicacy to early folk who lived off the land."

If it's roadkill, I don't want to know.

The ranger turned toward Zach. "You must be that fella from the *Post*. I'm Roger Korsac. And this gal here . . . ?" He tilted his head in Cassidy's direction.

"Cassidy McCabe," she jumped in. "His girl Friday."

Korsac let out a brief cackle, then his jovial face darkened. "When you called, you said you wanted to know about cult activity in the forest preserve." His tone became all business, words clicking like typewriter keys. "Well, sir, before I start, I need your guarantee I won't open the *Post* and see my name in print."

"Strictly on background," Zach said. "You have my word."

"All right, I'll tell you what I can. I've never talked about any of this before, but now . . . I guess it's time. There've been rumors around the district as far back as I can remember. Rumors about Satanic rituals performed in the woods and even sometimes in the cemetery—up there at St. Paul's. The guy who had this post before me, I guess he was here only about three years. Well, this guy was a real go-getter—real by-the-book kind of ranger—and this fella, he reported seeing torches at night, evidence of some sort of rituals, stuff like that. Then his dogs started dying. One by one, they died. Poisoned, they were." Korsac stared off into the trees, stirring the pot thoughtfully.

Zach asked, "They ever find out who did it?"

"No sir, not even a suspicion. Well, what happened next was, this guy ahead of me just seemed to go downhill. Fell to pieces, he did, and had to leave the service. So they offered the post to me."

Legs burning from the heat of the fire, Cassidy took a step back. "Did you want it? After what happened to your predecessor, I mean."

"You have to understand, I had a wife back then—she's gone now—and three kids and not a lot of money. So the idea of a free house wasn't all bad. Anyway, long story short, after we'd been here a few months I saw torches for the first time. Halloween night, it was. Best night of the year to bring out the crazies. So the next day I went and prowled around."

Hearing a screech overhead, Cassidy raised her eyes to see a large black crow glide down and settle on a tree next to the house.

"Pesky crows. I put birdseed out in the evening but the crows chase the songbirds away. Anyway, in the thickest part of the woods I found a clearing with a heap of ashes and charred wood where they'd had a big bonfire. Around the edge of the clearing they'd scratched out a line of earth, roughly the shape of a pentagram, it was. In front of the fire, right in the center of the pentagram, was this big boulder with dark stains on it. And I found a few bones in amongst the ashes. Animal bones, I'd guess, or . . . maybe not."

The back of Cassidy's neck tingled.

"When I stepped inside that pentagram, it seemed like the woods went dead quiet. Now, I know that couldn't really have been true. There's noise all the time—birds, insects, and such. So I guess it must've just been my imagination. But that's how

I remember it. Dead silence and a feeling I've never had before or after." He passed a gnarled hand over nubby gray hair. "Don't know how to describe it exactly. Oppressive, suffocating. Like I couldn't breathe. The only word I can think of—I know this sounds melodramatic but I can't think of any other way to say it—the only word is 'evil.' "

Zach's eyes narrowed. Korsac rocked slowly forward, then dropped his heels to the ground. Cassidy swallowed, trying to bring some moisture into her mouth.

"You never told anyone?" Zach asked.

"I thought about those dogs, I thought about my kids, and I walked away and never went back."

❧ ❧ ❧

Thursday afternoon Cassidy was sitting at her desk, bills piled in front of her, when the phone rang. She picked up, happy for the interruption.

Dana's voice sounded indistinct, as if she were not speaking directly into the receiver. "You know what's happened? What's happened is, I'm gonna be alone this whole weekend. All alone."

"Josie's trip to San Francisco, you mean? But won't Wayne be there?"

"He just got a call from his sister, okay? His mother went into the hospital, something about her heart—can't remember what. Anyway, his sister, she told him to get his butt home right away. So he's—what he's doing is, he's flying out tonight. And Josie, she's taking off in the morning. Then Cypress and me, we'll be all alone till Sunday night. I told them I'd be fine 'cause I didn't wanna be a burden, you understand? But I'm not fine. I can't stand being alone, know what I mean?"

"What is it about being alone you can't stand?" Starshine jumped into her lap. Whenever she was on the phone, the cat demanded attention.

"What it's like is, I always feel like something's going to happen. And I get those—I mean, I have those attacks. Can't breathe, can't sit still. Pains in my chest, okay? And I get to thinking I'm gonna, you know, gonna die."

"Panic attacks are really bad." *Should've insisted she see a psychiatrist for meds.* "Maybe your mother could stay with you."

"No way. Dad'd never let her go. I don't even want to ask 'cause then I'd feel like shit when she said no."

"Are you worried about Curly? Has he been around?"

"No sign of him. Guess you were right 'bout the police keeping him away."

"Would it help if you came in for a session tomorrow evening?" Starshine stood on hind legs and rubbed her face against Cassidy's cheek, trying to push the receiver away.

"I don't—what I mean is, my purse got stolen and I don't have any money," Dana said, voice low and miserable. "Felt really stupid, know what I mean? I wasn't looking, somebody just grabbed it out of the grocery cart."

"Don't worry about paying tomorrow. You can catch up later." *Such a fun game, catch-up. I know it well.*

"I do need to see you, okay? Been having these, you know, dreams. I wake up feeling worse than a hangover. One of those memories trying to come back, seems like."

They set an appointment. After she hung up, Starshine nuzzled even closer, poking her nose into Cassidy's face, neck and ear. "I notice you're developing these intense affectional needs. Could it be your maternal instinct kicking in?"

The cat nipped her chin.

"I take it you don't like my playing shrink any better than Zach does."

Swiveling around to prop up her feet, she settled herself for a long cuddle-in, an activity she much preferred to bill paying. "Panic attacks. Memories resurfacing. What if she does get suicidal?" She scratched the cat's cheek. "I shouldn't be trying to handle this without psychiatric back-up."

At the end of the day when she'd finished with all her clients, she went upstairs to find one message on the machine. She punched the button and listened to Zach's voice: "I think you better watch the ten o'clock news."

Beep.

10

Night Call

At ten-fifteen Cassidy was sitting up in bed, remote control in hand, when the screen flashed to a male reporter standing in front of a burned-out building. "Forest preserve supervisor Roger Korsac died last night in a four alarm fire." *Shit, oh shit, oh shit.* "The house where Korsac has lived for the past twenty-five years was completely destroyed." The scene switched to paramedics lugging a body bag out of the rubble. "Investigation is underway to determine the cause of the fire." The picture shifted again and cartoon fruit-figures on the screen began jiggling to a bouncy tune. Cassidy cut the power.

She grabbed the phone and called Zach. "What could've happened? It wasn't because of us, was it? Tell me it isn't what I think it is."

"I don't much believe in coincidence."

"But coincidences do happen. I mean, sometimes two things can occur at the same time and they're not connected. And anyway, how could anybody know he talked to us?"

"I should've watched to see if we were followed. Should've fucking thought of it."

☙　☙　☙

The following evening Cassidy was at her desk trying to catch up on paperwork when the doorbell rang. She scooted downstairs and opened her front door. Gazing across the enclosed porch, she saw three children standing on the steps.

She crossed the painted wood floor and peered down at the small bodies on the other side of the screen door. "Hi kids. What can I do for you?"

"I'm Carrie," the black girl said. "An' this's my brother Chip." She indicated the smallest of the three, a boy whose hand she held. "An' my friend Janey." The white girl standing beside her. "We wanted to ask if we could climb your tree." She jerked her head toward the maple near the corner of the house, its leaves entirely gold now.

"You have much experience climbing trees?"

"Yep. Climb 'em all the time. We're good at climbin'." Small, tight braids surrounded the girl's head, the pulled-back hair emphasizing her large almond eyes and fine facial bones. She wore an immaculate yellow sweater, Gap jeans and clean Nikes.

"What about your brother here? He looks awfully small for such a big tree."

"Nah, he can do it. He's a little monkey, that's what Mama always says. She says he can get on top of anything." A row of tiny teeth grinned up out of the boy's round face, his dark hair topped by a Cubs baseball cap, bill pointed backward.

"Your mother know you're out climbing trees?"

The other girl, a delicate blonde, replied, "Carrie's mom says it's okay, long as she's there to watch." Janey pointed down the block toward Darnella Roberts, who stood on the sidewalk in front of her own house, youngest on hip, watching the transaction. Cassidy waved at the other woman and said, "Okay, kids. Go to it." *Insurance agent'd kill me.*

She ambled back to the piles on her desk. *Amazing. Kids who ask permission instead of just doing and taking whatever they want. And a mother who watches over them.*

ᐥ ᐥ ᐥ

Dana arrived at six o'clock, Cypress in her arms. "Didn't have anybody to leave her with, okay?" Face pinched, voice shaky.

"Shouldn't be a problem." Cassidy grasped a small hand, the child's chubby fingers curling over hers. Breathing in fresh, sweet, baby-scent, stroking a rosy cheek, she felt an old familiar tug, the urge for a child of her own that occasionally surfaced when she was confronted with other people's children. She pulled her hand away and stepped back in an effort to cut off her sense of unfulfilled longing.

She offered Dana tea, filled her own purple mug, then ushered mother and child into the office. Dana perched on the edge of the sofa. Cypress stood next to her, head on her mother's lap, thumb in mouth. Cassidy sat in her director's chair on the other side of the wicker table. Grimy twilight filtered into the room through the two wide windows.

Dana dropped her head, looking up from under her brow. "Had another of those, you know, memories. But I dunno if I should tell. Just dunno."

"Why not?" Pushing aside a coleus stem, Cassidy set her mug on the wicker table.

"Not supposed to." Dana's voice creaked unsteadily.

"What do you think would be best?"

"I gotta talk or I'll go crazy. Only, I'm . . . I get really scared. But I gotta talk."

"Scared of what?"

"I'm scared—what I'm scared of is . . . punishment." Jittery brown eyes flicked over Cassidy's face.

Cassidy kept her expression neutral. She said softly, "Go on."

A long pause. "I woke up this morning, it was after one of those dreams and the whole thing came back to me. The whole thing. This time I was in a room. It was dark, kind of spooky, and those same people—guys in long robes, I mean—they were there. And the same bunch of kids. We were—what we were doing is, playing on the floor with this puppy. Cutest darned puppy—big soft eyes, long floppy ears. Then one of those robes, he grabbed the puppy and held it down on some kind—I think it was a table or something with a cloth on it." Dana's brown eyes stared into middle space, gazing into that long ago room. Her lips were parted; she was mouth-breathing in short gasps.

"Take a deep breath." Cassidy spoke slowly, using her low-pitched, trancy voice. "Breathe deeply, that's right."

Twisting her fingers in Cypress' hair, Dana said, "The robes, they were standing in a circle and they kept on chanting, the chanting kept going on. And that poor little puppy, yipping and crying." She gulped air, startling Cypress, who raised her head and blinked. "And then, what they did was, they cut up the puppy and caught the blood in a bowl. And then they—they made us drink it. And what they said was—they said, 'Now you belong to Satan.' "

Cassidy's mouth was dry, her throat so constricted it was hard to swallow. She lifted her mug with both hands and took a sip of the tepid tea.

Dana suddenly hauled Cypress up to her chest, wrapped both arms around her, and squeezed hard. "Mommy, no!" The child struggled to get away. "Lemme go. Mom-mee!" Dana abruptly released her hold, dropping Cypress back on her feet. Clutching a handful of Dana's oversized T-shirt, Cypress buried her face in it and whimpered.

"That's okay, honey." Dana stroked the amber head. "Mommy won't hurt you. Wouldn't think of hurting you." Her red-rimmed, haunted eyes fastened on Cassidy. "They said we'd be all right. They said, long as we kept our mouths shut, okay? But if we ever . . . if we ever talked, Satan would know and we'd be punished."

🐸 🐸 🐸

A sharp wind clattered the chimes and whipped through the three open windows on the porch. Friday night, nearly midnight. The house lights were off, leaving the porch in darkness so thick Cassidy could barely see Zach's hand resting on her thigh.

She nestled deeper into his shoulder and continued telling him about her session with Dana. "Something else she just remembered. Before she went in the hospital—way back when she was twenty—she got drunk and told her boyfriend about her cult experiences. So she's convinced the psychotic break was her punishment. Satanic retaliation for loose lips."

"And now she's blabbed again—I suppose that means she's expecting another breakdown."

Cassidy smoothed her hand down the arm Zach had draped across her body. "Not bad for a psychological heretic."

"You'll make a believer of me yet."

"Anyway, I tried to get her to check herself into the hospital, but she refused. Kept saying she wasn't crazy, Satan knows all, he'll get her for talking."

"Not much more you can do, is there?" He removed his arm and refilled their glasses from the jug of Carlo Rossi on the picnic bench, disturbing Starshine, who'd curled herself into the tiny crevice between them.

Mrow! She shot Zach an indignant look, then circled three times and settled back into the same spot, her motor revving up to full throttle.

Cassidy said, "I've been thinking about Roger Korsac and I'm pretty sure now I understand why it happened. At first it didn't make sense. Why him instead of us? Then I got it. If somebody followed us to his place, hitting him was an obvious way to get the message to us. Living alone out there, he was an easy target. We would've been a lot riskier. Two people in densely populated areas—not that simple. So instead, they went after Korsac, knowing the implication would be clear: butt out before anybody else gets hurt."

"But they misjudged us."

"Zach! It's killing me, knowing Korsac died because of what we did."

"You've got that backward. Korsac died because the Satanists are still in business and we're breathing down their necks. We're the good guys, remember? Their burning Korsac out should make us even more determined."

"How can we go on putting other people in danger? It's one thing, taking risks ourselves. But we've got no right doing it to anybody else."

"We'll just have to be more careful."

"You're not going to quit?" She felt his body tighten.

"What do you think?"

Jerking around to face him, she said, "Don't give me any of that therapist bullshit. Just answer the question." Wind howled through the trees. A siren wailed past on Austin Boulevard.

He gulped half his wine, then reached for her hand. "If anybody should understand about not letting go, it ought to be you. You said they were sending a message. Well, whatever we do, we're sending one back. You want it to be: you win because you killed an innocent person?"

She yanked her hand away and stared at the black silhouette of trees thrashing in the wind, the trees mirroring the feelings that were thrashing inside of her. As her feelings gradually settled, she realized he was right. They couldn't cave in to murder. She slipped her hand back into his. "Another person who'd be good to talk to is that minister—Dennis Halsey, I think his name is."

"I'll get on it, see if I can set up a time for Tuesday."

Tuesday? Her subpersonalities group was Tuesday. But after what had happened with Dana, she wasn't sure she wanted to continue.

He lay an arm across her shoulder. "When we talked about my staying over tonight, we didn't say anything about tomorrow. The way it looks now, tomorrow night won't work for me."

Three Saturdays in a row? Talk about sending a message.

ॐ ॐ ॐ

Starshine gazed down from the refrigerator, her almond eyes moist with concern. As Cassidy stared into those deep green eyes, she received a telepathic message: Roger Korsac's locked in the tower, about to be set on fire. You have to rescue him.

She snagged Zach and they raced upstairs. Her staircase had become a tower with endless metal stairs winding upward. Panting heavily, she suddenly realized the air was filled with smoke.

She started choking, couldn't stop. Turning to tell Zach they had to abandon Korsac to the fire, she discovered that he was gone and the stairs beneath her had vanished. As she clung to the metal railing, the smoke thickened.

The telephone rang and she sat bolt upright. Leaping across to the desk, she grabbed the receiver. "What is it?"

Dana's little-girl voice on the other end. "I shouldn't have, you know, called." A muffled sob. "I didn't—God Cass, I just didn't know what else to do."

Cassidy pressed her free hand against her stomach. "Now take a deep breath and tell me what's happening."

"Cypress isn't . . . I mean, Cypress is gone."

"Are you sure?"

"I woke up, okay? And I knew, I just knew something was wrong. And I went into her room and," she sobbed again, "she wasn't, what I'm trying to say is, she wasn't in her crib. I looked everywhere, absolutely everywhere. And she's gone."

"Have you called the police?"

"No, I can't, okay? And don't you call 'em either."

"We may have to."

"You can't!" Dana screamed. "No! No! No!"

Gotta call the police.

Maybe Dana just woke up from a nightmare, Cypress isn't really gone. Maybe she climbed out of her crib, fell asleep somewhere.

"Dana, stop that right now!" The line went suddenly silent. "I won't call the police just yet if you'll be quiet."

"Okay."

"Be at your door in fifteen minutes."

Her watch said nearly four as she raced toward the garage, nerves so tight she ran stiff-legged. Birds were staging a high volume concert in the veiled pallor just before sunrise. Minutes later, she stood on the porch of the gray stucco ringing the bell. Dana, her face tear-streaked and ashen, answered instantly.

She led Cassidy up a narrow staircase to the second floor. "This is a big mistake, okay? I shouldn't have—I never should have called. It's just that I got drunk last night, and what happened is, when I woke up I was so hung over I couldn't remember how it all went down." They proceeded into the living room. "So I thought Cypress was, you know, gone. Well, she is gone, but I know where—what I mean is, I know who's got her."

A shabby, overstuffed sofa and chair were angled to form a vee on one side. With a large-screen television in the opposite corner and a playpen in the middle, the room was overcrowded. The stink of cigarettes and dirty diapers seeped from the apartment's pores.

Dana flopped on the sofa and Cassidy sat in the armchair. "So what's the deal?" Cassidy asked. A bracket shelf displaying photos of Cypress, the flimsy metal frames neatly aligned, hung on the wall behind Dana. A beer can lay amid the toys in the playpen.

"Started drinking last night." Dana ducked her head, puffy brown eyes darting a guilty look at Cassidy. "I tried calling—tried Wayne at his sister's. But he wasn't there. And I was so uptight, couldn't stand it, know what I mean? So I got blitzed, okay? And then around midnight the doorbell rang, and it—it was Curly. I shouldn't've opened the door but I was too drunk—I mean, so drunk I couldn't think straight. He sort of shoved the door open, backed me upstairs, and pushed his way in." Dana wrapped her hands in the bottom of her T-shirt. Her eyes flitted to Cassidy's face.

She checking to see if I'm gonna buy it?

"Said he wanted to see his kid. Then he just picked her up, know what I mean? And he took her. I tried to stop him but I was—I was so wasted. After that, I must've passed out or something." Pulling her knees up tight against her chest, she stretched her T-shirt over her legs and dropped her forehead, thick hair tumbling forward, closing herself up like a clam.

If Curly grabbed Cypress, wouldn't she have fought back? Wouldn't it look like there was some kind of struggle no matter how drunk she was?

"Dana," she said gently, "the police can help."

Dana's head snapped up. "I told you, no police, okay?" Her mouth twisted sideways. "He said . . . what he said is, he'd disappear and . . . " her reddened eyes filled, "I'd never get her back. If I called the cops on him." She covered her face. Soft, hiccupping noises came from behind her hands.

An end table beside the chair held a porcelain lamp and an overflowing, toilet-shaped ashtray. Cassidy picked up a butt that had spilled out and placed it carefully on top of the heap. *This doesn't feel right. What I should be feeling is empathic, protective. But what's coming up instead is—scared for Cypress . . . iffy about Dana. Wary almost.* A dark idea started to take shape in her mind but she pushed it away.

Cassidy asked, "What can I do to help?"

"I just gotta wait it out, wait till he brings her back. Sorry I dragged you out for no reason."

"I think . . . I need to call the police." Cassidy had to force the words out.

"Oh please, oh God, you can't!" Dana's voice turned hysterical. She jumped to her feet, started pacing frantically. "I wouldn't have called, never would've told you if I thought . . . Don't you get it? If the police are involved, I'll never see her again. Never."

"I don't believe he'd ever get away with it."

Dana shot her a venomous look. "I do."

"Well, we don't have to decide right this minute. The first thing we need to do is get your anxiety down. When you've had some rest—real sleep, not passing out sleep—we can talk about it. You have anything to help you relax?"

"Xanax, okay?" The guilty look again. "Got 'em from Josie." She stopped pacing but continued to fidget. One leg jiggled; her hands twisted her shirt.

Great. Drug problems and Josie gives her Xanax. Not a word to me.

Dana disappeared into the bathroom, returning with a prescription bottle and a glass of water. "But you gotta promise, I mean really promise. No cops, okay?" The panic was back in her voice.

Cassidy sighed. "Why not just let me use my own judgment?"

"You gotta promise. Look, Cassy, this is really, really important. More important than anything I ever asked before." Her eyelid twitched. "There's no way I'm gonna, you know, just go to sleep unless you absolutely promise." She grabbed fistfulls of hair in both hands and started pulling.

Child's disappeared—can't just ignore it.

But Dana's falling apart, headed for a full-blown break if I don't get her calmed down.

Cassidy observed her closely: jittery arms and legs, accelerated breathing, agitated eye movement. "All right, I promise."

After gulping two Xanax, she gradually quieted and a short time later Cassidy was able to get her into bed. Dana's breathing deepened; her eyes rolled up in her head, lids slowly closing. Cassidy gazed down at the pallid face, softening now in sleep, becoming younger and more childlike as she relaxed: a face not nearly mature or strong enough to cope with this industrial-strength crisis life had thrown at her. The dark thought Cassidy had pushed out earlier bobbed toward the surface again, but a wave of protectiveness swept it away. She tiptoed out of the bedroom.

Now what? Cassidy looked longingly toward the door. *She wakes up, somebody's gotta be here.*

Who should be here is her mother. Real mother, not therapist-surrogate.

She'd promised not to call the police. No promises regarding anyone else. Only five a.m. *Too bad, toots. It's your turn now.* She found a wall phone in the kitchen, punched numbers, and leaned against a counter facing the refrigerator. Laurel answered after half a dozen rings, sounding reasonably alert. Cassidy explained the circumstances. "When Dana comes around, you need to be here."

"Her baby's gone? Omigod! This can't be happening. Not again." Laurel's voice broke.

Again? What's this again?

Laurel continued, "Ernie's gonna . . . he'll have a conniption." A pause. "Oh, who the fuck cares? I'll be there inside of an hour."

Not as scared of him as she seems. Maybe she just lets him think he's in control. Cassidy dropped into the armchair, planning to wait until Laurel appeared, then get the hell out. She picked a longish butt out of the pile in the ashtray, tore off the paper, and rubbed tobacco between her fingers, letting shreds fall onto the end table's scarred mahogany surface.

Remember all the mistakes with Ryan? Didn't do everything you could and your client ended up dead. After all the heartache on that one, you promised yourself you'd start doing things right. And that means—admitting when you need backup and getting it.

What can backup do I haven't done already? Dana refused to see a psychiatrist, refused to call the cops. What else is there?

She didn't refuse to see the consultant. Kramer told you to call. If there ever was a situation where acting like a lone gun was a bad idea, this is it.

She fished Dr. Kramer's card out of her wallet and called the psychologist at home. A resonant, wide-awake voice answered.

How is it that these other people sound so alert at this hour of the day? I never sound awake before ten—even when I am.

Cassidy told her what had happened.

"You realize, of course," Dr. Kramer said, "we can't rule out the possibility that she's harmed her child."

11

Cut Off

Cassidy swallowed hard. "Couldn't it be the way she said? I mean, Curly might've gotten her address from the Rolodex. And he has threatened her before." She gazed at the collection of clippings and photos attached to the refrigerator with happy-face magnets.

"What do you think?"

She ran her tongue around the inside of her mouth. "I think she's lying."

Victoria Kramer made a soft, clicking sound. "It's such a shame." Her voice tinged with sadness. "The damage done to these women. Anybody who treats children like that . . . . Well, that's not our current problem. Are you aware that Satanists often implant unconscious commands in children which can lead to suicidal or homicidal behavior later in life?"

"You think Dana might've been acting on a command someone embedded when she was four? How could they've guessed way back then that she'd end up with a baby?" Her fingers straightened a clipping, a recipe for play dough.

"I've known of similar situations. The woman's given a command in childhood, then later, when she's an adult with a baby of her own, she receives an anonymous call, hears the password, and the command's activated. It's a method the cult uses to pull people back after they've managed to escape. Either that, or to silence them if they've started talking."

Jesus—and I thought Dana was overreacting when she talked about punishment.

"We don't know that's what happened." Cassidy's mouth was so dry the words came out in a scratchy whisper.

"No, of course not," Dr. Kramer said briskly. "And it's not our job to find out. The police are the ones who need to do that."

"But—I promised."

"Do you really think you can *not* call?"

Maybe I could wait, get Dana's permission. Maybe Laurel'll do it. Maybe Curly'll come waltzing through the door, Cypress in his arms. She sighed. "You're right. I have to do it."

She had just finished talking to the police when it hit her. The gun. Wayne kept a gun in his drawer. All guns were illegal in Oak Park, and this one was probably unregistered as well. Was that the reason Dana'd been so adamant about the police? Was she afraid of what a computer check would turn up on Wayne?

You could take the gun. Then she'd be breaking the law too. She could be arrested. What right did she have to interfere? *Right to protect Dana.* If Wayne's wanted in New York, if he gets arrested, Dana will lose her primary source of support. Just when she needs it the most. She's already on the edge—one more thing could push her over. *And it'll be your fault. For breaking your promise.*

Which was worse: breaking a promise, breaking the law, breaking a client? *And you yelled at God for screwing up.*

Cassidy glanced out the window at a glimmer of light showing above the rooftops. Police would arrive any minute. As quietly as possible, she opened the bedroom door, the hallway fixture providing enough visibility that she could find her way around. Dana lay on her side in the double bed. She moaned and uttered a couple of garbled words, but her eyes remained closed. A low chest of drawers piled with comb, underwear, jewelry and scarves stood against one wall; a taller bureau piled with jeans, belts, and dirty socks against another.

Cassidy squatted in front of the bureau and tugged at the bottom drawer, which gave way with a squawk, creaking forward in uneven jerks. Probing beneath a jumble of sweat-suits, shorts and sweaters, she felt around the bottom until her fingers touched metal, then pulled out a dark, blue-black revolver.

Closing everything up, she returned to the living room and held the gun under the lamp to examine it. With its curved chamber, it reminded her of cowboy movies. But this gun, up close, was uglier than anything she'd ever seen in a movie. *What am I doing? I do more ranting about gun control than anybody.*

She hated guns, hated having to touch this one, hated protecting Wayne from the trouble he had brought on himself by stashing an illegal weapon under his shorts. But anything to keep Dana from coming completely apart.

She stuffed the revolver into the bottom of her handbag and sat down to wait for the police.

❧ ❧ ❧

In less than five minutes Detectives Manny Perez and Lou Waicek were standing at the door. Perez was in his midforties, tall and graceful, cafe-au-lait skin and soulful, black-coffee eyes. Waicek was on the down side of thirty, at least six inches shorter, built like a small refrigerator, sandy skin and impenetrable, granite eyes.

Cassidy recounted what Dana had told her about the abduction.

"So . . . ." Perez rested his hands loosely on his hips, relaxed and confident in his Italian silk suit, displaying a velvet-glove, take-charge kind of style.

"She need to be in the hospital?"

Clutching the top rail of the playpen, Cassidy chewed her bottom lip. *Don't take chances. She'll be safer in the hospital.* They won't commit her unless she's a danger to herself or others. *She could be suicidal.* But if Cassidy tried to put her in the hospital, Dana would think she'd given up on her. She finally said, "Long as her mother's here, I expect she'll be okay."

Following Perez's instructions, she went into the bedroom and awoke her client. As Dana struggled to sit up, Cassidy said, "I'm sorry—I'm so sorry. I couldn't keep my promise. There are two detectives in the other room."

Dana did that tic-like thing with her eyes, squeezing them shut, then instantly popping them open. She shot Cassidy one whipped-puppy gaze, then refused to look at her again. Dana stumbed into the living room and they sat together on the sofa. Perez settled into the armchair; Waicek dragged a kitchen chair into the doorway.

Perez asked questions and Dana provided crumblike answers. She was in the midst of a listless string of one-word responses when Laurel burst in the door. Bolting to her feet, Dana hugged herself tightly. Laurel, face contorted, sidled around the playpen and gathered her daughter into her arms. Cassidy, on the other end of the sofa, got an overdose of the cloying scent wafting around Laurel.

Perez crossed one long leg over the other, his face sympathetic. Waicek shifted restlessly in his straight-backed chair in the doorway.

Thank God, the second shift's here. Cassidy watched mother and daughter clutch at each other as if one of the two were drowning, although from the outside it was impossible to tell who was sinking fastest. She reached for her handbag, removed a business card, and scribbled on the back. After a long stretch of sighs, sniffles, and indistinct words, the huddle broke and Cassidy stepped between them.

Holding out her card, she spoke directly to Laurel. "I'm leaving her in your hands, but she's going to need a lot of help—more than you can give her, probably more than I can. I'd like to keep her out of the hospital, but she's got to see a psychiatrist. I know somebody who's quite good—I've written his name on my card. Will you promise to get her in as soon as possible?" *And keep your promise better than I kept mine?*

Laurel gazed vaguely into her face and took the card, although Cassidy doubted that anything she said had registered. Perez, his black eyes crinkling, gave Cassidy a quick nod. Reading his gesture to mean she was off the hook, she eased around the perimeter of the room, slipped out the door, and started to close it behind her.

A yank from the other side pulled the knob out of her hand. Scrambling down two steps, she leaned against the wall, hoping neither detective had suddenly decided that she was indispensible. This was one time she did not want to know everything that happened, perhaps because she feared that the more she found out, the harder it would be to believe Dana innocent.

As the door opened, Cassidy was surprised to see Laurel coming after her. She placed a tentative hand on Cassidy's arm. "I just had to catch you and thank you. You didn't, I don't know . . . didn't let her down when she needed you. I just feel so bad . . . I know I've made a lot of mistakes, and I wanted to tell you how much it means . . . " her voice caught. "How much it means to get a second chance."

♨ ♨ ♨

A gauzy, tangerine ball was suspended above the Chicago skyline by the time she slumped into her Toyota. She headed straight for a twenty-four-hour Dominick's supermarket to pick up a bag of peanut butter cups, feeling as out of control as a failed cigarette-quitter. Her childhood habit of binging on Reese's had overtaken her last summer when Zach's brother Ryan, her client at the time, ostensibly committed suicide. After the crisis passed, she had once again sworn off. This was her first slip since then.

Waiting for a slow-moving clerk to open the register, Cassidy saw Ursula stroll through the entrance. *Weird how she keeps turning up.* Picturing what she must look like—hair in tangles, face drawn with exhaustion, purple T that belonged in the ragbag—Cassidy turned away, hoping not to be seen.

She watched out of the corner of her eye while her client dithered over the carts, disappeared into produce, then came around into the store's main section. As Ursula wandered toward her, Cassidy shifted in the opposite direction.

"Why, hello there." Coming from behind her head, Ursula's wispy voice sounded surprisingly chipper.

Cassidy swung around and smiled stiffly.

ð   ð   ð

When she finally made it home, morning light streaming through her windows sent a rise-and-shine call in direct opposition to the I've-gotta-sleep command coming from her brain. Her brain won. She did a few minutes of yoga and hit the bed.

Cassidy crashed for a couple of hours, then got herself up, planning to check on Dana and talk to the police. She dialed Dana's number several times but no one answered. She dialed the Voss number once and Ernie picked up, only to tell her in his gruff voice to "get the fuck out of our business." She reached Manny Perez, who said they were talking to everyone concerned but had no leads as yet.

Zach, the only other person who knew as much as she did, was the one she really wanted to talk to. But Zach was a reporter. Even worse, a crime reporter. And Dana's story had just become news.

She paced from one bedroom window to the other. On the street below, a large black woman wearing gold brocade and floppy hat plodded behind a gaggle of kids, girls decked out in frilly dresses, boys in suits and ties. Hard to remember it was Sunday, and there were people actually going through their normal routines.

Doesn't matter whether I call Zach or not. He'd know instantly about the kidnapping—at least, she hoped it was a kidnapping—the way reporters do, as if they had police scanners implanted in their brains. Plunking into her chair, she put her hand on the phone. *What if he's not home? You don't know where he was last night. He's not home, those nasty, old jealous feelings'll get all stirred up again.*

She gritted her teeth and punched numbers. The machine clicked, then he said a groggy hello and turned off the recorder. *Noon, and he's just waking up? Must've been quite a night.*

She pushed the thought out of her mind and told him what had happened. "You won't be writing this up, will you?"

"You know I handle police business."

"But you've got all that inside information. Isn't that conflict of interest or something?"

"Reporters are vultures—you said so yourself. We don't have ethics."

She put a hand to her chest, fingers digging into the base of her throat. "You're not going to use anything I said in confidence, are you?"

"Not to worry. All I'll do is call that detective, what's-his-name Perez, talk to Dana and her parents, then quote what they say. At this point it's strictly routine."

❧ ❧ ❧

The next morning her alarm went off at three a.m. and she jumped out of bed, threw on her clothes, grabbed her heavier-than-usual bag, and dashed out to the car, wishing for once that the Oak Park street lights were less bright than they were. *Two days in a row, up before dawn. Must be some kind of record.*

She drove straight east on Division Street, through one of the worst sections of Chicago. It was the first time she'd ventured into this part of the city after midnight. Every time she crossed Austin Boulevard, she was struck by the difference one street could make, but at this hour of the night the contrast between Oak Park's tidy blocks and Chicago's blasted warzone was even more dramatic: steel bars barricading doors and windows; broken bottles in the street; burned-out, boarded-up buildings; vacant-faced adolescents hanging on corners; drivers from another planet.

She moved steadily east, watching closely on all sides. This would not be a good time for a strange encounter of the drunk-driver kind. After twenty minutes of locked-jaw driving, she stopped in front of the Chicago River Bridge and waited until no other cars were in sight. Pulling up to the middle of the bridge, she put the engine in park, stepped out, and looked down into the black water. She wrapped her hand around curved metal at the bottom of her bag, pulled out the gun, and dropped it into the river.

ॐ ॐ ॐ

Monday afternoon she decided to take out her frustration on the giant weeds growing along the fence next to Briar. Starshine, who liked to assist, pranced outside with her. The sun's slanting rays still held considerable heat, but there was enough shade to work in comfort. She squatted beside the fence and grabbed a thick stem, her hands bare because she couldn't find her gardening gloves. *Least the flea collar's working and they don't itch anymore.* Starshine flattened herself in the overgrown grass and slunk toward her, tail horizontal and twitching. As Cassidy jerked on the weed, the cat flew forward, slashing her hand before she could whip it away.

"Don't act out your predatory fantasies on me." She licked at salty beads seeping through torn flesh. "You're not a jungle cat, just a pregnant, domestic calico."

Starshine, a smug look on her face, scratched her ear.

A rumble of voices from the corner caught her attention and she looked up to see the three-thirty gang sauntering down Briar. Every day after school a loose cluster of about ten black teenagers led by a kid the size of a Bears lineman mosied down the middle of the street toward Austin. From what she could hear, they spoke a special language made up almost entirely of obscenities and insults and characterized by an up-yours defiance. Cassidy figured it to be a developmental stage, the major task of which was to come off menacing, to convince the rest of society, or perhaps themselves, that they were *baad dudes*.

She stood, intending to keep her eyes on them till they'd passed her house. The white woman across the street stopped raking leaves and moved into a watchful position on her Briar-facing front porch. As the kids drifted along, some staring pointedly at Cassidy, she heard her neighbor call out: "I saw you throw that beer can on my lawn. Can't you people show any respect?"

Cassidy tensed, her gaze jumping to the pumped-up kid out in front. He spun on his heel, faster than seemed possible for his bulk, and swaggered over to stand in the woman's yard. "Whadda ya mean, 'you people?' " He ground out the words, a verbal equivalent of spitting in her face.

One more step, I'm calling the police.

"I meant, 'you teenagers.' " Her neighbor's voice was nearly as forceful as his.

The hulk turned slowly, stalking back to his place at the head of the pack, and continued toward Austin.

Cassidy resumed breathing. Moving to the other end of the fence, she started back to work in a patch of sun, needing to recover from the chill that had come over her as she watched the confrontation. Would great little kids like the Roberts' turn into hostile teens, hanging in all-black groups and flipping the finger at whitey? Or would it be possible for these younger kids— color-blind now—to grow up differently?

She thrust her hands into the weeds and Starshine sprang into full stalking mode, her stomach, which was starting to bulge, nearly dragging the ground. Slithering behind a bush, the cat pretended she was invisible.

A red pickup parked at the curb a few feet away, interrupting the game. Cassidy stood and read the words inscribed in curlicue letters on the door, "Class Act Painters." A man wearing paint-splotched overalls got out: Wayne.

She brushed hair out of her eyes with the back of a grubby hand. "How's Dana?"

"Wish I knew." His voice had the slow, melancholy ring of an old ballad. "I can't figure what to make of it."

"Maybe I should go see her."

"That's the thing." He rested his hands on the fence and looked down, pale blue eyes blinking slowly. The thin face with its high cheekbones and soft mouth seemed more suited to a painter of canvases than houses. "She won't let you near her. Anybody even mentions your name, she pitches a fit."

"I shouldn't have promised."

"Josie and me, we understand. What else could you do? But the deal is, we can't get anywhere with her. She's been staying in her room, blinds closed, lights off. Keeps saying it's all her fault 'cause she told."

"She eating? Getting any sleep?" Cassidy grasped the chain link fence, hands about a foot below his.

"Josie was able to get some food down her. And she's sleeping okay."

"Does she seem delusional? Is she talking crazy?"

His long fingers stroked his chin as he considered her question. "Hard to tell. When you figure she really believes this crap, really believes Satan's out to get her, I suppose it makes sense. Who knows? I never was much for religion. But I guess it isn't any crazier, believing in Satan than in astrology or reincarnation."

"Well . . . " Starshine raced across the yard, bit her ankle, then zoomed off. "Doesn't sound like there's much more you can do, other than keep a close watch and get her in to the psychiatrist as soon as possible. You know if Laurel made the appointment?"

He shrugged, indicating that he didn't. His long-lashed eyes meandered over her face. "I only wish Mom'd picked some other weekend to have her stroke. Sure turned out lousy, Josie and me both being gone the same time. That fuckhead Curly. Someday he's gonna push the wrong guy, end up with the few brains he's got left leakin' out a hole in his head."

Cassidy gazed into the gentle, aesthetic face, wondering about the other side of Wayne. Until hearing about the gun and the trouble in New York, she'd accepted the picture Dana presented: easygoing, nurturing, committed to the woman he was living with and the raising of a child he'd taken as his own. *Maybe he's one of those guys, a pussycat at home, tiger on the street.*

"You think Curly took Cypress?"

"S'pose you know the police are lookin' at Dana as a suspect."

Cold needles down Cassidy's spine. "What do you think?" Her voice came out in that scratchy whisper again.

"Nah." Wayne's head shook repeatedly. "She didn't hurt the kid. Dana and me, we met up a couple months before she got pregnant. We actually hung out quite awhile before we started, you know, getting it on. Guess she told you she used to have a real bad drug habit." He moistened his lips. "We both did."

He leaned backward, hanging on the fence like a kid. *Embarrassed. This six-foot-plus, cool-looking dude is embarrassed.*

Wayne picked up his story again, "Angel dust, LSD, crack— you name it. We got high together all the time, that's all we did. Well, soon as she found out she was pregnant, she just stopped, cold turkey. Even quit cigarettes, which is more than I can do. I saw her go through some real bad shit, but she refused to use anything to help her along. Said she wasn't going to take any chances with her baby. She talked a lot about what kind of mother she was going to be—how she'd never hit her kid, she'd always make time for her and everything." He pushed away from the fence. "Nah, she never hurt her baby."

As he ambled back toward the pickup, Cassidy had to clench her teeth to keep a manic voice from bubbling up: *Missed your gun? Wanna know who took it?*

ża ża ża

Zach called that night to tell her he'd scheduled an interview with the minister Dennis Halsey for Tuesday afternoon. Although the appointment wasn't until one, he picked her up more than an hour early. They drove west on the Eisenhower Expressway, then took a side trip into Villa Park, zigzagging through residential streets until satisfied no one was following.

Returning to the Eisenhower, Zach jogged from one interstate to another, moving generally southwest. He exited from I-55 onto a highway that angled southeast to Apple Creek. The Halseys' bungalow, located in a ramshackle section of town, was a few blocks off the main highway, which continued on to the church a couple of miles past Apple Creek.

Dennis Halsey, a jovial smile on his bearded face, opened the door wide. "You must be from the *Post*." He gestured them into a small living room overflowing with stacks of books, newspapers, sheet music, and bunches of dried flowers. Dennis' wife stood in front of a music stand in the far corner, her back to the door, a flute at her mouth. A silvery thread of music hung in the air, mingling with an aroma of home baked cookies so appetizing it set Cassidy's stomach juices to gurgling.

Dennis leaned in closer and said, half aloud, "She's ticked 'cause I agreed to talk to you." The minister left them standing just inside the door and stepped over behind his wife. "You're not going to stay where you are and play through the whole conversation, are you?"

Lowering the flute, she turned to face her husband. "*Interview,* Denny, not conversation. This man wants to quote you in the newspaper. Out of all the things you say, he'll pick the one comment that makes you sound the most flamingly liberal or wildly insane. Then our donors'll have yet another excuse to refuse to make their pledges."

Cassidy tried to remember the woman's name, but all she could come up with was Audrey Hepburn look-alike. Hepburn at her most irritated.

"C'mon." Dennis kissed her cheek. "You can stop me from saying anything outrageous."

"Me? When it comes to inserting lower extremity in facial orifice, I can top you any day. Which is why neither one of us should ever talk to reporters."

He pulled her around in front of him, grasped her upper arms, and marched her across the room. "This is my wife Annie, known far and wide for her ability to position herself at the center of every controversy."

"Don't take it personally," Annie said, mouth curving into an impish grin. "I just think it was stupid of Dennis to agree to an interview on Satanism. It's sure to stir up trouble." Cocking her head at Cassidy, she planted one hand on her hip, the tunic top and stirrup pants reinforcing the Hepburn look. "Haven't I met you before?"

"Cypress' baptism, over the punch bowl."

Annie and Dennis both registered shock.

"I see you've heard about the kidnapping," Cassidy said.

"We couldn't believe it." Brow furrowing, Annie shook her head. "That poor kid. Any news about Cypress? And Dana— how's she doing?"

"She's in pretty bad shape. But we're still hoping she'll get her daughter back," Cassidy replied.

"This seems sort of bizarre," Dennis said, a slight edge to his voice. "Meeting you at the baptism and then having you show up with this reporter."

"I'm confused." Annie looked up at her husband. "This is Dana's friend. He's a reporter. As in," she spoke with heavy emphasis, "writer of words that appear in the newspaper. What's the connection?"

Connection. Should've thought of it.

Zach extended his hand. "I'm Zach Moran and this is Cassidy McCabe. Reason she happens to be with me is, I've been investigating rumors of Satanic activity, and after Cass talked to you at the baptism, she mentioned that you two would be an excellent source of information. I brought her along 'cause you've at least met her once before, so I figured she'd boost my credibility. I know reporters are generally assumed to be vultures by trade, but contrary to popular opinion, my purpose here is not to make anybody look bad. If you don't want to be quoted, we can do the whole interview on background."

Dennis draped an arm across his wife's shoulder. "Like I said on the phone, I'll ramble about any subject under the sun—even unpopular ones." His fingers raked through his thick, reddish-brown hair, leaving mussed furrows in their wake. "But I always talk better with a glass in my hand, so

before we get started let's get ourselves something to drink."
Wearing tight jeans and a blousy cotton shirt, he stood just
under six-foot, his build that of a middle-aged athlete who'd
thickened through the middle but avoided flabbing out. "How
does chardonnay sound?"

Don't forget, clients tonight. "Well, okay. One glass."

Annie deposited her flute next to a half-finished flower
arrangement on the oak table at the far end of the room, then
followed Dennis into the kitchen. As soon as they were gone,
Zach took her arms and rotated her ninety degrees, pointing
her in the direction of a three-foot bronze satyr standing in
the corner. They moved in for a closer inspection. The slanted
eyes, upswept brows and rakish leer on the creature's face
exuded more lewdity per square inch than anything she'd seen
before in a work of art. Zach squatted to get a better view of
its nether regions. The goat legs were positioned to partially
obscure the groin, but when Cassidy bent down, she could
clearly discern a fat, sausage-shaped appendage protruding
straight out. Adorning the ever-alert projection was a wide
silver band of gumball-machine origin.

"I see you've met Tricky Dick." Dennis reappeared with a
bottle and four glasses on a tray.

"The ring was my idea," Annie explained. "To celebrate our
engagement. It was all we could afford at the time."

"This is fantastic!" The most enthusiasm she'd ever heard
from Zach. "What I wouldn't give to have Tricky Dick standing
at attention in my condo. You better lock your doors at night,
or you might wake up some morning and find him gone."

"Brainchild of the sixties, inspired by the pot and politics
of the day." Dennis' brown eyes sparkled. "Almost got me
thrown out of an art class back at Brewster, and he's haunted
me ever since. She," he tossed a look at Annie, who was setting
out snacks on the glass coffeetable, "won't let me get rid of
him. Insists we keep him on display, despite all the flak we

get in return. The fielding of which is no small task in a rural, semi-Bible-belt community such as this."

"How do you ever get away with it?" Cassidy asked.

Annie giggled. "A lot of our guests are too embarrassed to admit they notice."

"Some get on their high horse." Dennis rubbed fingers through the short beard along his jaw. "Then I go into my spiel about how God must have wanted man to have sex or he wouldn't have given him a penis, and I quote scripture at 'em."

The minister gestured toward the food. Cassidy sank into an overstuffed sofa and scooped up dip with a corn chip.

"Okay, shoot." Dropping into a recliner, Dennis picked up a book laying open across the arm and set it on the floor.

Zach sat forward on the sofa, his knees open wide. "What do you know about Satanic rituals in the forest preserves?"

"I don't *know* anything—but stories've been floating around forever." He dumped a handful of chips into a napkin and wiped his hand on his jeans. "I hear talk about fires at night. Once in awhile some brave soul tries to investigate, then afterward they never want to discuss it. People've told me about pets being stolen, spells being cast. When it comes to the curses and spells, I always suspect the poor sonovabitch screwed up all on his own and is looking for an excuse. But the main rumor—the really grisly one—is that years ago Satanists actually sacrificed a child every year on Halloween."

Cassidy's scalp tightened. "Do you believe it?"

Dennis glanced at his wife, who tipped up her glass, then gazed at a stack of phonograph records on the floor. "Hard not to." He cleared his throat. "We had kids disappear on a yearly basis, always a week or two before Halloween. But that was a long time ago, just after we started here."

Annie refilled her glass and popped a chip in her mouth. "This is ghoulish. I don't like talking about it." Her mouth twisted downward. "This interview was a mistake, Denny.

God knows, publicity like this isn't going to do Apple Creek any good."

He shrugged. "When have I ever done the sensible thing? Or you either, for that matter."

She thumbed her nose at him.

He topped off their glasses. "I think it was seven or eight kids altogether, children between the ages of zero and five. Then it stopped. It's been about twenty years since the last child disappeared."

Zach asked, "Any idea why they quit?"

"Nobody worried about why—we just thanked God it was over." Dennis stroked his beard. "Apparently the cult's still around, since reports of fires, missing pets, evidence of ritual activities keep coming in. A park supervisor got killed in a mysterious fire just a few days ago." He stuck a chip in the cheese, dropping a blob on the coffeetable.

"My guess is," Annie leaned over to wipe up the spill, "it got too hot for 'em. People were very jumpy. Everybody watching for the least suspicious move. Whoever it was, I think they decided it just wasn't worth the risk anymore."

Cassidy flattened a cocktail napkin on her plum-skirted knee, pressing out the wrinkles with her hand. "What do you think, Dennis? About Satanism. You think there's anything to it?"

His eyes glinted under the folded lids. "Ask me that question on a sunny afternoon like today, and I'll tell you it's all hogwash. Nothing more than a handful of severely damaged people banding together for a sense of belonging, plus the justification they get from their garbled doctrine. Misfits full of rage, looking for an excuse to vent their anger on small animals and children, the only beings more powerless than themselves." He pulled a pack of cigarettes out of his shirt pocket and stuck one in his mouth.

"But ask that same question in the middle of the night when I've just been out comforting the family of some poor schmuck who's died of AIDS and you might get a different answer." He patted several pockets without finding what he wanted.

Annie crossed to the cluttered oak table, located a matchbook, and tossed it to him.

"I keep trying to quit. It's embarrassing—nobody smokes anymore."

"Yeah, I know what you mean," Zach said. "It's been over a year since my last pack and I still carry around pistachios to stick in my mouth whenever those old oral urges get to me."

The minister lit up and took a deep drag.

Leaning back, Zach laced his hands behind his neck. "As we all know, Satanists sometimes set themselves up so they have access to children. What kind of groups existed for kids in the past twenty—twenty-five years?"

"Not much of anything," Annie replied. "Course we've always had Sunday School classes."

Cassidy remembered both Annie and Josie stating firmly that Dana had not attended Sunday School, so no point asking that question again.

Annie brushed crumbs off the coffeetable. "At one point some woman from Chicago volunteered to run the preschool group—seems like she was doing research for a grad school project or something. Aside from that, the only thing I can think of is Laurel's play group."

"Play group?" Dennis asked.

"Don't tell me you forgot?" Patting his arm, she sent Cassidy a men-are-such-simple-creatures look.

Zach asked, "How long did Laurel run the play group? Anybody else step in after she quit?"

Annie gave her head a slight shake. "Can't remember a thing beyond the fact that she started the group when Dana was fairly young, then had to drop it because of Ernie. It went on for a few years afterward but I can't tell you who took over."

"What about a daycare center?" Zach asked. "I've heard there was some kind of daycare or preschool in the area back then."

Dennis and Annie exchanged glances. Each seemed to be waiting for the other to speak.

What are they not saying?

"Not that I know of," Dennis replied finally. Padding over to the table, he searched under newspapers and books, finally uncovered an ashtray and carried it back to his chair.

"There's one more thing." Cassidy continued smoothing the napkin across her knee. "I feel a little strange asking this, but I'm going to throw it out anyway. As Dana's friend, I've puzzled over what could've happened to cause her life to get so messed up. And so I'm wondering if there's anything you can tell me about her, um, parents that might shed some light."

"I don't think we can—" Dennis started.

"I do remember one incident," Annie interrupted. "Back when Josie was in vacation Bible school. She came in one day all upset, needing to talk. Seems like she'd found this stray cat with a litter of kittens in the Voss backyard. She watched for hours—just fascinated. Well, she told the rest of the family and everybody else went out to look. Then Ernie said something like, 'there are too damn many cats in the world already,' and he picked those kittens up, one by one, and broke their necks."

ꝛ ꝛ ꝛ

On the drive back Cassidy said, "You were right. This isn't something we can ignore." He reached over and took her hand. "Now Cypress is missing and it's less than a month till Halloween."

"It's been twenty years. There's no reason to connect Cypress with those old kidnappings."

"Eight kids. Jesus." She felt weighed down by the misery of it. "I wonder if we could track down an Apple Creek cop from twenty-five years ago."

12

Woodworker

Ursula arrived promptly for her Wednesday morning session. She sank onto the vinyl sofa, laid a string bag down beside her, and smiled expectantly. Through the window behind Ursula's head, thin clouds spread across a bright blue sky like glaze on a cake.

"So nice bumping into you at Dominick's the other day," Ursula ventured. "I guess you're sort of an early riser, same as me."

Right. Up every day, noon at the latest. Cassidy took a sip from her purple mug and set it on the wicker table, nestling it under a coleus stem. "Do you remember discussing how it would be better if you'd bring something in to talk about?" *Last session, worked my butt off trying to find a focus.*

"Nothing, uh, comes to mind."

"Well then, why don't you start by telling me about the family you grew up in?"

"I'm not sure what there is to say." Ursula gazed upward, her deep-set eyes shuttling back and forth, searching for memories.

"I guess my family was kind of normal. Don't suppose we'd even qualify as dysfunctional." Her voice apologetic. "My father had himself a little gas station in Springfield. Made a decent living, came home every night." She twisted a strand of hair around her finger. "I seem to remember lots of hugs. And Mom—she was wonderful. Everything a mother should be." The frail voice trailed off, then picked up again. "We always did stuff together. Baked cookies, planted flowers. And stories. She read stories all the time. She was sort of like a friend, somebody I could talk to."

Shades of Norman Rockwell. "Any brothers or sisters?"

Ursula shook her head.

An only child herself, Cassidy remembered how empty the house had seemed with just Mom, Gran, and herself rattling around in it. "Ever lonely?"

"Mom was always there, and my very best friend, she lived next door. My girlfriend and me, we did things together all the time."

"Best friend next door?" Cassidy wondered how anybody's life could be so idyllic. *When it sounds too good to be true, it usually is.*

"Actually, Vicky's family was more interesting than mine. That is, she had a lot more, uh, problems." Her mouth twisted to one side. "Her dad used to . . . well, beat up on her mom. Then when she was thirteen, the worst thing happened." She paused, apparently for dramatic effect.

Cassidy had the impression she thoroughly relished recounting her friend's problems. *Is it possible Ursula's life is so boring she invents fantasies? Or is it the friend that's a fantasy and this 'worst thing' something that happened to her?*

"Her father actually killed her mother. We heard the gunshot ourselves, right in our own house. My whole family went into a wobble for most of a week. Course they put him in jail, but he got bailed out, and pretty soon he was right back in the house. Every time I saw him, I went into a wobble. Just didn't know what to say. But Vicky, she was really cool about it. She said he was still her father, and she wasn't going to leave him, wouldn't let anybody take her away, even if he did sort of, uh . . . ." Her voice took on a note of pride. "Vicky's the strongest person I ever met."

When the hour was over, Ursula handed her a check, then produced a foil-wrapped loaf from her string bag. "Zucchini bread. My garden's kind of going crazy. The zucchini just won't stop. Now I've baked so much zucchini bread I don't know what to do with it all." She handed the loaf to Cassidy.

Don't like clients bringing presents. Can't just refuse. Now I'll have to spend half the next session processing why she needs to push goodies on her therapist.

Around noon Cassidy placed a salad, glass of milk, and slice of cinnamon-scented zucchini bread on the dining room table. Starshine leapt onto the opposite end and started oozing toward the food.

Swallowing a mouthful of salad, Cassidy eyed the cat's rounded sides. "I wonder how many are in there? And when'll it be? You expecting midwifery?"

Starshine crept toward her milk. When she got within striking range, Cassidy covered the glass with her hand. "I've told you over and over—you have to wait till I'm finished."

Extending her pink nose toward the zucchini bread, Starshine sniffed, then jerked away. She retracted her whiskers, flattened her ears, twitched the tip of her tail.

"Lots of people won't touch anything with 'zucchini' in its name." Cassidy tried to stifle the uneasiness she'd felt when the cat pulled her nose away. "You're probably just put off because it's so organic and wholesome and you hate health food."

Cassidy cut a neat square and impaled it with her fork, taking more time than necessary to prepare the first bite. Starshine inched forward, her lips drawn up in a snarl, a guttural rrrr coming from deep in her throat.

Fork halfway to her mouth, Cassidy paused, her stomach threatening mutiny. *Don't be ridiculous. Starshine's got an overactive imagination. Can't take her seriously.* She shoved the bread into her mouth, but her throat refused to swallow. Something in the taste. Something bitter.

She spat it onto her plate, then took her plate to the sink and washed it down the disposal. Throwing the remainder into the garbage, she grabbed her bag of peanut butter cups and returned to the teak table, where Starshine was happily lapping milk from her glass.

"I feel like such an idiot." She unwrapped a Reese's and bit it in half. *Have to lie and say I loved it. Hate lying. If I lay it on too thick, she'll just bring more.*

Starshine curled a long, pink tongue over her nose. Her luminous green eyes regarded Cassidy warmly.

"I wish you'd stop looking so pleased with yourself." Cassidy unwrapped a second Reese's. "Do you realize my life's coming unglued while you're sitting there blissfully making babies? Dana won't talk to me. Mom hasn't called in weeks."

She plopped her elbows on the table. "Something's definitely up with Zach. And I'm mad at myself that I haven't had the nerve to confront it. He called last night to give me details about a meeting with some retired Apple Creek police chief. Then he was off the phone a minute later."

Starshine pawed at her hand, indicating she wanted to be held, so Cassidy dutifully leaned back in her chair. The cat stepped from the table to her chest as delicately as possible for a short, stubby, barrel-shaped animal. She curled up, face close to Cassidy's, and purred raucously.

Cassidy left the milk on the table and carried Starshine, squirming mightily to show her disapproval of anyone carrying her anywhere, upstairs. "I keep expecting Zach to dump me. And that makes me want to kick myself for getting into bed with him in the first place. Especially since I already knew about his track record with commitment. I should be locked up in a chastity belt for the rest of my life."

Cassidy dropped the cat on her satin comforter, which bore the marks of many claw-sharpenings, then sat at her desk. Hearing a raspy cough, she rotated her chair toward the bed. Starshine was flat on her belly, throat elongated, eyes bulging, gagging so hard it sounded as if her stomach were turning inside out. Cassidy jumped to her feet. The choking intensified into a strangulated death rattle. She took a step toward the bed, then froze in horror. The calico appeared to be gasping out her last breath. *Call nine-one-one? How'd you do a Heimlich on a pregnant cat?*

Starshine opened her mouth wide. A brown tubular glob issued forth onto the comforter. Hacking up the last of it, the cat thumped down from the bed and marched away, tail stiffly erect.

Pressing a hand to her stomach, Cassidy went to fetch the paper towels. *Must be my initiation into the famous hairball ceremony. One of the many joys of cat ownership, or so I've been told. Beyond my comprehension why there are so many cat–addicted people in the world.*

After cleaning up, she settled back into her desk chair. *If you're too chicken to put the question to Zach, at least you can tackle your mother.* She dialed and this time got a live voice on the other end.

"What? You actually answered? This is my mother, right? I've been calling for weeks, leaving messages on your machine. What the hell are you doing with a machine, anyway? You always said you hated them. I want to know what you're up to." *Can't believe I said that. I sound just like she does.*

"Well, dear, you remember I told you about this new friend of mine, this black girl Elaine? I think I mentioned we were going out together . . . . So you see, well, what we've been doing is . . . . As a matter of fact, you just can't imagine what happened." A girlish giggle came over the line.

"Do I have the right number?"

"I met somebody. His name's Roland. A real gentleman."
She giggled again. "And I've been wanting for you all to get
acquainted. So what I'd like to do is, I'd like to have Roland
and you and Gran over for dinner on Saturday night. And—oh
yes—you can bring that fellow you've been seeing—what's his
name? Zachary."

*Terrific. Zach's doing a Saturday night invisible-man rou-
tine, now Mom's having a dinner where we all play show and
tell.*

          ଡ଼ ଡ଼ ଡ଼

Friday morning Zach picked her up for the meeting with
the retired police chief, who lived in a remote area along the
Fox River. Checking the map, Cassidy discovered their desti-
nation to be much farther west than Apple Creek. Zach did
some evasive driving to shake off possible pursuit, then shot
fifty miles out I-80, turned south, and continued another
thirty miles along the river. They stopped at a mailbox beside
the road, then turned into a driveway that curved steeply
upward.

Zach parked the Datsun next to a glass and cedar A-frame
overlooking the Fox River. The area was thinly wooded, low
bushes and trees growing right up to the house. The sunlight
was pale; the air had a crisp feel to it. Cassidy noted streaks
of deep gold and russet in the trees, a thin layer of leaves on
the ground. *Autumn's landed, both feet down and running
fast. Halloween's gonna be here much too soon.*

A dirt path led around the A-frame's glass front to the
entrance on the opposite side. As they trooped past the glass
wall, they could see a tall man crossing the interior space. By
the time they reached the varnished cedar door, he already
had it open.

"Sam Berkus." He offered Zach a callused hand. His spare
body towered well over six feet, shoulders thin with a slight

droop, head fringed with white hair. He wore a blousy shirt in an earth-toned pattern with a Native American look to it.

The front portion of the house contained a large, open space with arrangements of furniture to designate different functions: living room area, dining area, and kitchen. Sam seated them on a moss green sofa that faced a free-standing fireplace, a small flame flickering in the grate.

"Let me brew up some coffee, then we can get into your questions." Sam headed toward the cluster of cabinets and appliances comprising the kitchen. In front of the sofa was a square coffeetable, an arrangement of polished wooden bowls and vases sitting on it, a stack of file folders off to the side.

Zach started browsing through the top folder. His face tightened as he read.

"One of the missing kids?" Cassidy lowered her voice, the sweeping architecture and open ceiling making her feel as if she were in church.

"File for each of 'em." Coming from behind her head, Sam's voice startled her. Setting a wooden tray on the coffeetable, he handed them each a mug, then settled in an armchair that right-angled the sofa. Cassidy added sugar and cream.

Zach replaced the folder and took a swallow of black coffee. "So, what can you tell us?"

Clasping hands behind his neck, Sam gazed through the glass wall above their heads. "When you called to set up this meeting, I almost said no. I'm still not sure it's a good idea."

"Why not?" Cassidy took a sip of rich, nut flavored coffee.

"Fact I never solved it still makes me feel like shit. There're a lot of personal memories attached here—most of 'em pretty unpleasant." His deep voice reminded her of a wide, slow—moving river.

"What happened?" Cassidy asked.

His hooded mahogany eyes shot her a skeptical look. "You sure you want to hear my sob story?"

"She always does this." Zach dropped a hand on her knee. "Wants to know all about everybody. But I put up with her."

Jerk! You want to put up with something, how'd you like to put up with cream in your coffee? She reached stealthily for the cream and poured a healthy glug into Zach's mug. His mouth twisted in disgust.

"Okay." Sam pretended not to notice the cream incident. "You asked for it, so here goes. Before those kids started disappearing, I was Apple Creek Chief of Police—big whoop-tidoo. Typical small town tough guy, married with a couple of kids, more interested in having myself a good time than being with the family. Drank too much, screwed around too much." He drummed his fingers on the chair arm. "Figured I was good enough at the job, meaning I could investigate burglaries, arrest drunks, and sometimes even stop guys from beating up their wives." He slugged down some coffee.

Cassidy's eyes swept the open space, searching for a wifely touch. A mint green robe, too feminine for Sam, was tossed across a chest in the corner.

Sam's somber voice picked up again. "Thirty years ago it was, just before Halloween. A three-year-old little boy, Marky Davis, showed up missing. The whole county turned out. We tramped the woods and fields but never found a shred of evidence—aside from this circle in the deepest part of the forest. We figured it to be the location of some kind of cult ritual because the remains of a fire and a boulder with animal blood on it were inside it. But we didn't come up with anything to link it to the missing boy."

Cassidy felt cold all over, thinking of the skull in the well. Couldn't be the same child. Dana wasn't even born yet.

"Can't tell you how much I hated having to talk to that mother and father. Day after day, their eyes pleading for some word, some news, anything. I did everything I could think of.

Didn't eat or sleep for days. Just couldn't let it go." He rubbed a hand over his face.

"Beyond my imagination, what it'd be like to go through something like that," Cassidy murmured. Zach reached for her hand.

"Next year it was a baby and a four-year-old. Year after that, a toddler. I felt like such a failure. For seven long years a child was taken every Halloween. During that period, my whole life fell apart. Wife left. Kids stopped speaking to me. Drinking got out of hand. I was barely able to hold down my job. Then the eighth year came, and nothing happened. Nobody disappeared, no report of a missing child. That was when I had my breakdown. Major depression, couldn't get out of bed. Three months in the hospital." He picked up one of the wooden vases and ran his finger over the smooth finish.

Zach waved broadly, indicating the contemporary house, wooded lot, river below. "You've obviously made a good recovery."

One corner of Sam's mouth turned downward in an ironic grimace. "Guess I finally learned my lesson, but it took me long enough to get here. I stopped drinking, took an early retirement." He rubbed his jaw. "Started running and woodworking. Found me a wonderful woman—math teacher at Fox Lake College—somebody looking for the same things in life I was. In a way, I'm glad it happened. But I never stopped feeling pissed off and guilty 'bout those kids."

"Woodworking?" Cassidy asked. "You didn't actually make these beautiful vases yourself?" She picked up an urn adorned with wooden strips of various shades.

"Got me a shop out back. There's a real sense of satisfaction, working with your hands. That piece you've got there— I'd like for you to have it. One of the things I like most is giving 'em to people who appreciate it."

She started to protest, saw the look of pleasure on his face, and thanked him instead.

"Case like this'd drive anybody nuts," Zach said. "But you must have some theories. What's your favorite?"

"I pretty much go along with the accepted version. Most everybody 'round Apple Creek thinks a Satanic cult grabbed 'em to sacrifice on Halloween."

Zach asked, "How'd you arrive at that conclusion?"

"That circle I mentioned? We came across two or three, every year located in a different section of the preserve. Hate to admit it, but whenever I had to investigate one of those circles, I got this creepy feeling. Had to force myself to step over that line they scratched around the outside. Anyway, one time we found human blood on some rocks. The kid who'd been taken that year had a rare blood type, and this blood matched, so we assumed it was the kid's."

Cassidy asked, "If you thought the kids were going to be sacrificed on Halloween, why couldn't you roust out hordes of people and comb the forest?"

Sam's mouth tightened briefly. "God knows we tried. We had a mob of folks out looking, helicopters flying overhead. But we bumped into an obstacle or two." His shoulders rose, then dropped. "First off, that forest preserve is huge, and also very dense. There are probably places way back there that nobody's seen in a hundred years. Another problem was, they stopped making fires so we didn't have any smoke to track 'em by. After that first year we never found any more fire remains. And the other thing was, most of the searchers didn't know the country, so they never got deep enough into it. I guess the Satanists were just thumbing their noses at us."

Zach said, "Once you guessed what was happening, I would've expected people to practically lock up their kids a month or so before Halloween."

Sam replied, "During the early years, they went after farm kids. Usually picked families with several children, crops to harvest, not enough adults to keep watch every minute. Then they switched to migrant workers who hadn't heard about it. Toward the end, we all had our guard up so high I figure they finally just quit or started bringing kids in from someplace else."

"What do you think about Satanism?" Cassidy asked. "You think there's any more to it than just a bunch of Manson-type crazies acting out their sadistic urges?"

He dropped his hands onto his knees. His hooded eyes squinted into the distance, his craggy face settling into deep grooves. "I'm convinced," he said slowly, "that both good and evil exist in the world, and that a struggle's been going on between the two forever. What really worries me is, the bad guys seem to be winning."

As they stood at the door to leave, Cassidy said, "One more question. I heard a daycare center existed in Apple Creek around twenty-three years ago. What can you tell us about it?"

He gave an apologetic half-shrug. "Wish I could help. But I was drinking pretty heavy back then and there're a lot of things I don't recall."

They took the wooden vase and stack of files with them when they left. As the car turned onto the main road, Zach said, "Remember when I was skimming through that top file?" The clipped quality of his voice signaled that something unpleasant was about to follow. "It starts off with a list of the missing kids, dates of abduction, and names of parents. I hate to tell you, but there are a couple of things on that list you need to know."

She hunched her shoulders. "What?"

"All the kids were male except for number two on the list, a four-month-old female baby. She was the daughter of Ernie and Laurel Voss, and her name was 'Cypress.'"

"Omigod! I can't believe it." Her mind reeled. The scenery outside the window blurred. She grabbed hold of the armrest and hung on tight until she was able to start thinking again. "I heard what you said but it threw me into such a wobble I can't begin to make sense of it."

"Wobble?"

"It's a word my new client says, and that's exactly how I feel. All wobbly. Anyway, I can't think straight right now, so tell me what you make of it."

"I think . . . ." He leaned forward, both hands gripping the wheel. "You're not gonna like this."

"Go ahead."

"I think Dana's crazier than a loon. I think she's living out some kind of fantasy, reenacting her mother's experience." He paused. "I think she killed her baby."

Cassidy turned her head, staring vacantly at the ribbon of green and brown unwinding outside the car window. *Maybe it's true. Oh shit. I can't stand it.* She remembered how Dana had looked before she had the flashback, the childlike quality in her face when she said she wanted Cassidy to play the same game her mother played.

Her left hand tightened into a fist, nails biting into her palm. "No, that isn't right. I just don't believe she did it."

13

Cuisine

She dialed the Voss' number then turned to face Zach, who stood on the other side of the kitchen.

"Hello?" Laurel, her voice tentative.

"This is Cassidy McCabe. We need to talk." She leaned against the doorframe, the wooden edge digging into her shoulder and hip.

"Dana's therapist? I don't understand. Why would you want to talk to me?" Starshine, less zoomy than she used to be, came swaying up to greet Zach.

Cassidy said, "This is for Dana. I need some additional information to determine the best treatment modality." *Listen to you. Little Miss Miracle Worker. You haven't a clue what to do for her.*

"I don't know . . . I thought she wasn't seeing you anymore."

"Right now she's angry, but she'll get over it and then she'll need to see me again. Just like she did with you. And when the time comes, it'll be important for me to have all the information. Can you meet me someplace this afternoon?"

"Oh, I couldn't do that. Ernie said not to talk to anybody. If we say the wrong thing, we could make it worse."

Zach picked Starshine up. She snuggled into his neck, sending Cassidy a smug look as if to say, *I've got him now.*

"When I called the morning after the kidnapping, Ernie wouldn't have wanted you to go, but you didn't let that stop you."

"I just don't know. It's so hard to tell what's right."

"If you let her down again, you may never get another chance. Dana's future—maybe even her sanity—is at stake here. You've got to talk to me."

A long pause. Cassidy shifted her weight from one foot to the other, her left shoe clinging to a sticky spot on the mottled linoleum.

Laurel said, "Ernie's out back now, but he'll be coming in any minute. I s'pose I could say I had to run out to the store. Could you maybe meet me at the Apple Dumpling Cafe, right in the middle of town, half an hour from now?"

Cassidy glanced at the clock above the window. Nearly three. "Make that forty-five minutes." *Zach'll have to drive like a maniac, but he won't mind.*

えか えか えか

As they hurried toward the entrance, Cassidy peered through the window into the brightly lit cafe. The restaurant was empty except for Laurel, seated in a red vinyl booth near the front. Zach held the door and Cassidy zipped inside, telling herself to slow down so the poor woman wouldn't feel pounced on. She stopped in front of the table, caught her breath, and said, "Hi."

Laurel's frightened brown eyes, the same color as Dana's, flitted back and forth between Cassidy and Zach.

They slid into the booth across from Laurel, who lowered her head and began busily realigning the place setting, water glass, and mug. The small room featured rosy-appled wallpaper above cream wainscoting, ceramic-apple sugar bowls, and apple-printed curtains that just missed matching the wallpaper. Cassidy groaned inwardly. *Least somebody tried. For all you know, the folks in Apple Creek love it.*

Laurel leaned across the table toward Cassidy. "You didn't say you were bringing someone," she whispered.

"This is Zach Moran from the *Post*." Resisting her therapist-urge to be reassuring, Cassidy maintained a carefully neutral tone. "He's been working on a story about Apple Creek, and he stumbled across something that relates to you. That's why we have to talk."

Laurel wrinkled her forehead in confusion and stared at Zach. "You're the one who called. But you lied. You didn't talk to the librarian—I checked."

Picturing Cypress' round face, sky blue eyes, and amber curls, Cassidy hardened herself. "Did Dana know she had an older sister who was kidnapped nearly two years before she was born?" *This is not fun. Feels like I'm nailing her to the wall.*

"Oh no, not that." Laurel's face drained. Moaning softly, she buried her head in her hands.

A teenaged waitress wearing a red dress, frilly apron, and cheerful smile approached from the kitchen in back. Laurel, her shoulders quivering, let out a long, choked sob. The waitress stopped halfway across the white-tiled floor, turned, and retreated.

The sounds gradually quieting, Laurel dropped her hands and looked at Zach. "If I talk, is it gonna turn up in your newspaper?"

"We're off the record here."

"I don't know." She moistened scaly lips. "I've been praying this wouldn't come up, but I guess it was bound to happen." She stopped to think, her watery eyes staring off blankly. "Where to start?" A heavy sigh. "Guess it's worth mentioning—my mother died when I was born, so I got handed around from one relative to another. Seemed like nobody ever wanted to be bothered."

"Not a good beginning," Cassidy murmured.

164

"Maybe that'll make it easier to understand why Ernie looked so good to me. When I first met up with him, I was only sixteen and he was a grown man, nearly twenty years older. But I just wanted somebody so bad. Somebody to love me and take care of me. And Ernie, he was just wild about me, right from the beginning."

The waitress reappeared and edged toward them, pad in hand.

"Course nobody much liked the idea of a young girl and a man over thirty getting together. So I got myself pregnant. I did it deliberately, you understand, so they'd let us get married."

The waitress sidled up to the booth. "Excuse me, but would you like to order?"

Zach said, "Coffee twice."

Where is it written I can't speak for myself? She turned back to Laurel. "The pregnancy—that was Cypress?"

Laurel nodded. "Reason I told you about my mother dying is so you'd see how, I don't know . . . how unprepared I was. I didn't have the slightest notion how hard it'd be. S'pose I thought it'd be like playing with dolls." She tried to pick up her water glass, but her hand shook so badly she had to put it back down. Clasping her hands on the table, she waited silently as the waitress moved toward their table with the coffee.

Sixteen years old, baby's abducted, probably thinks it's all her fault. Cassidy felt herself slipping from prosecuting attorney back to therapist. "This must be so hard to talk about."

After the waitress had clattered their mugs down on the Formica tabletop and disappeared into the back, Laurel cleared her throat and started up again. "I left her on a blanket in the backyard. Ernie worked in Oak Brook back then, so Cypress and me, we were the only ones home." Laurel hunched her shoulders, folded her arms on the table. "She was sleeping, I didn't want to wake her. So I left her there and went in to watch my TV show. When I came back out, she was gone."

Cassidy lay her hand on Laurel's arm. "You were so young. You never could have guessed something like that would happen."

Laurel's head drooped lower. "It was all so long ago. I hate even thinking about it." She looked up. "I was a mess afterward, and Ernie, he worried over me a lot. That's why he didn't want any more kids. He thought I wasn't up to it." She wiped a napkin along the lipstick smeared rim of her mug. "But I reacted just the opposite. Even though that first one'd been so much harder than I expected, I wanted another baby in the worst way. I needed to prove I could be a good mother. And I also needed a tiny, warm body to hold and cuddle and love. So I went ahead and got pregnant again, even though Ernie didn't want me to."

Cassidy asked, "That why Ernie never seemed to like Dana very much?"

Laurel tasted her coffee and made a face. "Cold. Oh well, I didn't really want it anyway. So . . . that's about all I can tell you, except that I tried my damnedest to do everything right. Read every book I could get my hands on. More than anything in the world, I wanted my daughter to have a good life for herself." An anguished expression came over her face.

Zach asked, "What did Dana know about her sister?"

"We never said a word. I s'pose it's possible she heard from somebody else, but why wouldn't she ever've mentioned it?"

Cassidy asked, "What reason would she have to name her daughter 'Cypress?' "

Laurel shook her head, face blank. "When Josie told me, I just about died. I've racked my brain trying to figure it out."

Zach asked, "What kind of preschool group was she in?"

"Preschool? What's that got to do with . . . ?" Laurel circled her mug with both hands. "It's so hard to remember. Nothing I can think of."

ða ða ða

When they left the cafe, Zach drove to a street near the edge of town where formerly prominent homes, once fashionable but now fallen on hard times, sat on large, double lots. Parking in front of an abandoned Victorian, he said, "This is where the daycare used to be. The one nobody ever heard of. Let's take a look."

A cracked cement walk led to a wide porch fronting a house with boarded-up door and windows. A broken sign hung above the entrance. As they approached the dilapidated wooden steps, Cassidy tried to fill in the missing letters. "Kiddie Korner," she said, finally figuring it out.

"Right." Zach stopped at the foot of the stairs and put a hand on her arm. "That porch doesn't look safe. Let's just walk around the outside." A steeply pitched roof rose above the three-story, clapboard building, a round tower jutting above one corner, a bay window protruding in front. The exterior had weathered to an overall streaked charcoal, the layers of gingerbread barely discernible now that the color was gone. Picking their way around to the side, they stepped over ancient newspapers, broken glass, and dog droppings.

Cassidy said, "I'm impressed, all right? So what's it gonna take to get an explanation? Shameless flattery? Debased groveling?"

"I always accept flattery, shameless or otherwise." He stood on tiptoe, peering into a broken window. "Whew! Don't get too close—the stink'll knock you over. Can't tell which is worse, cat spray or wino piss."

Taking her elbow, he guided her back toward the outer rim of the property. "Yesterday I drove out to Clearwater, a little town about fifteen miles from here. That's the closest office for the suburban *Sentinel*, which, thank God, dates back over twenty-five years." He nudged a wine bottle with his sneaker, turning it over so they could see the Thunderbird label. "When I put 'Apple Creek' and 'daycare' into their computer, up popped an interesting little puff piece. The house you see before you was bequeathed to Miss Marilyn Lockwood by her mother when she died. Whereupon, Miss Marilyn chucked her preschool director job in Atlanta and returned to the family homestead, which she promptly converted into Apple Creek's first daycare center."

"What year?"

"Nineteen seventy-one. Dana would've been around three. Anyway, the puffery included all kinds of congratulatory quotes: so wonderful to have Miss Marilyn back; how grand to be entering the twentieth century with Apple Creek's first daycare. Only thing that would've made a bigger splash is the first McDonald's opening in town."

Coming around to the rear, they discovered that the southwest corner of the house was scorched and burnt away.

"That's interesting," Zach observed. "Looks like a fire-bombing." His hand gripped her shoulder. "Something else interesting. After the original story, no further mention was made of anything remotely connected with daycare in Apple Creek. I tried 'Marilyn Lockwood,' 'Kiddie Korner,' everything I could think of. Nothing. Nada. Zip."

Cassidy's gaze swept the back of the house and the deep lot with coach house at the rear. Not much to see except yards and yards of litter covering what used to be a lawn.

They came full circle, got in the Datsun, and drove back toward Oak Park. "Dinner and a movie?" Zach suggested. "I'd just as soon get my mind off Satanism, missing kids, and other related grisly topics for a while. We can go back to your place afterward."

Slumping lower on her spine, Cassidy crossed her arms over her chest. "How come you've been staying at my house so much? I thought you hated sleeping anywhere except your waterbed."

"Hate's too strong. Staying at your place just seems simpler, that's all."

Simpler to get away. If we sleep at his Marina City condo, I might hang around too long in the morning. She stared fixedly out the side window. Just a few weeks earlier, the fields and bushes had been a deep, lush green. Now they were fading into dried yellows and browns.

Sleeps over Friday night, disappears Saturday morning. You've gotta find out what's up.

When a man starts avoiding Saturday nights, you don't need a polygraph to figure out that he's got another woman, he's letting you down gently, or both of the above.

Don't let him off. Make him go to Mom's dinner party Saturday night. Otherwise, your mother will have a date and you won't. Plus, you'll have to explain.

What's to explain? Mom said Zach was a jerk right from the start. Mother knows best.

ટ⁄   ટ⁄   ટ⁄

The next morning Cassidy was awakened by a raucous scree-scra-screee, loud as a jackhammer outside her window. The sudden screech brought up a memory, banging at her consciousness and setting off a sense of deep melancholy. A wiry, brown-uniformed man rocking on his feet, and overhead a black crow gliding down to settle in a tree.

She burrowed deeper under the blanket, but a damp nose prodded insistently at her uncovered hand. Moving her fingers, she scratched vaguely at a furry face. The nose poked down under the blanket, accompanied by a familiar rumble. Whiskers prickled her cheek.

Cassidy opened her eyes and hoisted herself into a sitting position. "Okay, you win." She plumped the pillow behind her back, gathered Starshine into her arms, and bestowed a proper face-scratch. Used tissues, junk mail, and crumpled paper were scattered across the carpet. Evidently Starshine had entertained herself with the contents of the wastebasket while waiting for Cassidy to awaken. The clock said eight-thirty. The other side of the bed was empty.

"Couple of months ago, when he was coming on strong, I never would've guessed he could disappear so fast on a Saturday morning."

She stumbled into the bathroom, where Zach had stationed her purple cat mug filled with coffee that was just the right color, a creamy tan. He knew her feelings about that first jolt of caffeine in the morning: the sooner the better, even if she had to drink it cold. She took a large swig and returned to bed, mug in hand. Sitting back against the pillow, she wiggled her toes under the blanket and Starshine obligingly attacked.

Your worst nightmare all over again. Remember Kevin? You knew there were other women but kept your mouth shut 'cause you didn't want to lose him. And then, of course, you lost him anyway.

Starshine sank her fangs into Cassidy's big toe. She yanked her foot away. "That hurt. If you're going to bite hard, I won't play."

The cat glared in disgust and marched out of the bedroom.

Remember how scared you were after Kevin left? Every little sniffle, thought you had AIDS. You've gotta find out where Zach's spending his Saturday nights. And who he's spending them with.

How? Hire a private detective? He can tell you anything he wants.

She had tried once before to check out the monogamy question. After three Saturday night sleepovers at Marina

City, she'd reached the point where not knowing who else might be in his life or his bed was driving her crazy, and so she made him talk about it. He'd said the right words but had been so difficult she was reluctant to tackle the question again.

🐦 🐦 🐦

That first discussion had occurred during their regular Saturday night date at Zach's condo. They were cuddling on his sofa, gazing at city lights through the sliding glass door to his balcony when she decided it was time for The Talk.

Cassidy refilled her wineglass, knowing she was slightly drunk already, pulled his arm around her, and fumbled for the words. "Since you said you wanted to work on commitment, I've been assuming you won't be sleeping with anyone else as long as we're together."

"Mmmmm." He nuzzled her neck.

"I want to talk."

"You're always talking. It gets in the way."

She pulled back from him and sat erect, her knees touching. "You make everything so hard. All right, if you won't let me ease into this, I'll just say it straight out. I need to know that this is an exclusive relationship. And I want us both to get tested."

"You really do know how to spoil a mood. Look, I told you already, I don't sleep around. You've got nothing to worry about on that score. But an AIDS test . . . I don't know."

Cassidy got a fluttery feeling in her chest. "Any reason you wouldn't want to?"

"No point to it. I'm not bisexual, I don't stick needles in my arm." He got up abruptly and went out to stand on the balcony, hands gripping the iron railing. She followed, leaning backward so she could see his face.

How many women had Kevin slept with over the years? "You may not be at risk, but I am."

171

"So you take it."

She tried to wait him out, her back teeth clenched, a hard knot of anger in her stomach. When he refused to talk, she finally said, "What is this about, really?"

Zach sighed. "I know what you're asking is sensible. No reason not to. I just don't like being backed into corners." He lay his hand on her shoulder. "I'll get the test."

🐾 🐾 🐾

He had followed through and they both came up negative. *Maybe he's still angry. Maybe he feels pressured. It's possible he told you the truth, he really is monogamous, and you're just overreacting because of Kevin.* Cassidy had met his mother Mildred, knew her to be a little Hitler. With a mother like that, he must be wary of controlling women, which she on occasion could be.

She heard familiar footsteps on the stairs. Here she was, once again assuming the worst, and Zach hadn't sneaked out early after all.

Wearing yesterday's wrinkled shirt and a morning stubble, he ambled into the bedroom, kicked off his sneakers, and sat beside her on the bed. "Starshine held me hostage in the kitchen till I fed her a second breakfast. When's she due anyway?"

"End of October—nearly a month away."

"Halloween kittens? When trick-or-treaters come around, you can tell them to hold out their bag, then drop a kitten in. Think how surprised the mothers would be."

"How come you're up so early?"

"Can't sleep on your lumpy mattress. I need my waterbed."

She bumped her head against his shoulder the way Starshine did. "What's that?" She sniffed his shirt. "You smell like grass."

"Nah, switched to booze. Grass took the edge off, blunted the old type-A drive I need to be a hotshot."

Cassidy picked a blade of grass off his jeans. "What've you been up to?"

"You know that Toro you swear at all the time?"

"I do not swear."

"Cleaned the spark plugs and she purred like Starshine."

"You didn't mow the grass." *God, you sound bitchy.*

Zach swung around to sit on the edge of the bed. "Don't start."

"What?"

"You're so damned prickly about letting me do anything. Your house is falling apart, but anytime I try to help, up goes your back, you spit and hiss like a cat."

Her jaw tightened. "Now you sound like my mother."

"What's wrong with saying 'thank-you' instead of chewing me out?"

She wrapped both hands around her mug, raised it to her mouth, and took a long swallow. *'Cause you don't let me into your life enough to even the score. 'Cause I hate feeling obligated. 'Cause I might get used to it, then I'd really be in trouble when you run out.*

Lowering her mug, she wiped the corners of her mouth with thumb and forefinger. He put on his sneakers and came around to plant a light kiss on the top of her head. "Call you next week."

Cassidy watched his large-shouldered body recede through the door. *You didn't say a word about Saturday nights. Or Mom's dinner. Still letting him jerk you around, appease his conscience by mowing your grass. You're so fucking scared he'll leave.*

૨ટ ૨ટ ૨ટ

When Zach was gone, she settled on the wicker couch to see what the *Oak Park Review* had to say about Dana. The weekly newspaper arrived on her porch every Saturday with its litany of village squabbles, organizations begging for vol-

173

unteers, citizen groups protesting each other. Cassidy found the local news much more to her taste than the scandal and violence served up routinely by the dailies.

Cypress' kidnapping had made the front page. Skimming through the article, she found only one piece of new information. "Police have verified that the child's father, Edward Salaski, was playing in a blues band at Del Ray's Chicken Basket from ten p.m. Saturday until two a.m. Sunday." *There goes my last hope she was telling the truth.*

જ જ જ

That night, seated at her mother's kitchen table, Cassidy tried to put aside envy and spite and appraise Roland Mertz, the paunchy man who sat across from her, on his own merits.

"So glad I finally got the chance to meet you," he said in a flat voice, nodding at Cassidy and Gran. "Helen brags about you all the time."

He looks like this when he's glad, I'd hate to see him when he's down. Roland had sparse hair combed over his crown, droopy lids above his hangdog eyes, a pinched mouth beneath his thin mustache.

"I hope you appreciate," Gran said to Helen, "that I restrained myself and wore my Marion the Librarian wig." She patted the mousy brown braid on top of her head. "I figured this was your show and it wouldn't be fair to steal it. Though now I see how you've blossomed out, I needn't have worried."

Helen, who'd previously appeared only in gray perms and sparrow-colored pant suits, had taken on a whole new image. She wore frosted hair and a red silk dress, draped and fringed around her plump body. She said, her voice turning shy, "Guess that means you like my new look."

Roland grasped her hand. "Anything'd look good on you, sweetheart."

"Aren't they revolting?" Gran cackled shrilly. "Course I'm just saying that 'cause I'm jealous. Here I've been fishing for

174

years and haven't caught anything worth bothering about, and Helen goes out once and snags a keeper."

Keeper? I guess, if you're not looking for any of the little extras—like cheerfulness, humor, excitement.

Gran's wizened hand lifted her wineglass. "Here's to true love—may they never find a cure!" She downed her wine, then hopped up from the table, her tiny body brimming with energy. "Speaking of fishing, I just got myself some new bait." She pulled the elastic top of her turquoise dress down over her shoulder, displaying a peacock tattoo above her left breast. "Isn't that sexy?" She chuckled gleefully. "Doesn't it just add heaps to my allure?"

"I love it!" Cassidy replied. "But this is Mom's night, remember? Just this once you were going to let her have the spotlight."

"Oh shoot." Gran plunked down in her chair. "I forgot. But she shouldn't mind. After all, she's got herself a real peach."

Helen beamed. "Roland's been divorced for years and this is his first relationship." She removed her hand from his and stood up. "Why don't you tell them about yourself while I bring out the main course. Cass, maybe you could pick up the salad bowls and pour some more wine."

"Sure thing, hon." Roland emptied his glass, patted his mouth with a paper napkin, and leaned back in his chair. "The wife and me, we had five kids. She didn't really want such a big family, but I refused to quit till we got ourselves a boy. Every man should have a son to follow in his footsteps, that's what I always figured. Even though I can't say my boy did all he could in that department." One corner of his mouth twisted down.

"Kids got their own personalities," Gran commented. "You gotta take 'em the way they come."

"Anyway, with five kids to look after, the wife had her hands full. Sometimes she talked about going to work, but I couldn't see it. I'm not a believer in farming your kids out for someone else to raise, and money was never a problem. The family business, it did okay." He laced his hands together on top of his stomach. "She'd complain sometimes about the hours I put in. But she never complained about spending the money." He snorted a brief laugh.

Cassidy collected the white bowls her mother had purchased through a special deal at the grocery store, then refilled their glasses with blush wine. Helen brought out a platter of brown-sauced chicken surrounded by mushrooms and placed it in the center of the Formica table.

"My God, Helen, what's that?" Gran asked in her boisterous voice.

"Coq au vin," Helen murmured.

Wine and French cuisine? My mother, the milk-and-lasagne queen?

"Go on with your story," Helen prompted as she served the chicken.

"Like I said, she'd complain about this or that, but I thought it was part of a wife's job, nagging her husband from time to time. Way I saw it, we were basically happy, not much of anything wrong." He stroked his droopy mustache. "Then one day she just up and left. Found me a note on the refrigerator with instructions on how to do the laundry."

Shaking her braided head, Gran waved a fork in the air. "You better watch out, Helen. He sounds like one of those men who insists on getting everything his own way." She turned to Roland. "I hope you don't expect my daughter to start washing your socks or doing up the dishes you leave piled in the sink."

"Not me. I'm not making the same mistake twice," he replied. "I've been looking for the right woman ever since my wife left. Now I've met Helen and I'm not taking any chances.

There's no way I'm gonna make her do anything she doesn't want."

He's the type who'll do everything right till she's hooked. Then his other side'll come out.

Don't be nasty. You're just mad 'cause your mother's got a guy who's willing and eager, and you don't.

"So, Cass, what do you think?" Gran asked. "Shall we give him our stamp of approval, long as he doesn't get sexist or domineering on us?" Gran clinked her glass against Roland's, then turned to Cassidy. "But I thought you had somebody to bring. Where's that fella you've been trying to reel in? Don't tell me you let him get away."

"Well, um . . . ." Under Gran's scrutiny, Cassidy failed to keep her expression as neutral as she would have liked.

"Oh shoot. I must've said the wrong thing." Gran patted her hand and leaned closer so Helen and Roland, who had their heads together on the other side of the table, wouldn't hear. "I been out there lookin' for ages, and there've been plenty of times I'd meet some gorgeous guy my heart said I had to have. But my head always answered: anybody makes you unhappy, you're better off without him."

Cassidy squeezed Gran's hand. *Lesson you need to learn.*

As soon as the dishes were washed, Cassidy herded Gran into the Toyota to drive her home.

Gran buckled her seat belt and said, "So, what do you make of this big transformation? Does Helen really love Roland or is she just getting carried away by all that red silk? Or the money maybe? And Roland—does he really love Helen or is he just looking for somebody to do his laundry? Tune in next month to see if Helen's still cooking coq au vin or if she's back to tuna casserole."

On the drive to Gran's bungalow in south Oak Park, they passed a gray stucco that resembled Josie's. Recalling her sense that the woman was keeping secrets, Cassidy got the idea of checking her out with Gran, who maintained her own villagewide web of information. Josie herself had lived in Oak Park only a few years and was therefore unlikely to be registered in her grandmother's database, but her husband's family had been around forever. Stopping in front of Gran's house, she said, "I've got a friend married to Howard Crandel. You happen to know anything about either of them you'd like to pass along?"

Gran gave a thumbs-up sign. "Swoosie Crandel and I go way back. I suppose you'd like to know about Howard. Well, according to Swoosie, who's just beside herself over the way her son turned out, Howard's one of those wandering types— keeps turning up in the wrong bed. She can't figure out why Josie puts up with him."

As Cassidy helped her out of the car, Gran added, "You know, I just love gossip. 'Specially about hometown folks. I can't understand why it's got such a bad name. Why should I care what Liz Taylor's up to? Give me a good, juicy story 'bout people I know any day."

14

Fantasies

"Detective Perez, please," Cassidy said to the officer behind the window. She stepped away from the wall separating the police department from the waiting area and scanned the austere, brick interior of the basement-level police station. She had not been surprised when she received the call earlier that day asking her to come down and talk to him. She only wished she had been able to figure out what to say.

Don't wanna do this.

Gotta cooperate. Gotta do everything you can to help find Cypress—and hope to God it's not too late.

The lock buzzed and Manny Perez swept through a door in the wall, his lithe figure sleekly and expensively outfitted in a dark blue suit, light blue shirt, and shiny black boots. Cassidy admired the ability of others to make an art form out of clothing their bodies but had no interest in doing so herself. He held out his hand. "Thanks for coming. Let's go inside where we can talk."

They proceeded to a long room lined with utilitarian wooden desks. The only other occupants were a gray haired man working at his computer and a man and woman conversing in back. Cassidy's stomach winced at the smell of burnt coffee. Perez placed a straight-backed chair in front of the second desk for her to sit in, then slid into his own swivel chair across from her. He laid his arms across the desktop, which was bare except for a computer and one small stack of papers.

"Can I get you some coffee?" His voice held the warmth of a cozy, low-burning fire.

"The coffee as bad as it smells?"

"Worse." His dark eyes sparkled.

He flirting? "I'll take a pass."

"Wise decision. Well . . . ." He jiggled a pen between thumb and forefinger. "I asked you down here to get some background on your client. You've been seeing Dana for around six months, so I expect you can give us some insight into her personality."

"Far as I know, she hasn't signed a release of information."

"We've got a situation here, child at risk." His voice conveyed concern without sounding pushy. Not at all what she'd expect from a cop. "As I'm sure you realize—"

The guy's good. Establishes rapport to overcome resistance. I know exactly what he's doing—it's still hard not to get sucked in.

Cassidy said, "I'm aware of the law. If there's a life at stake, I have to provide all necessary information." *But what does* necessary *mean?* "The article in the *Oak Park Review* said the father's got an alibi. Before I start handing out privileged material, I just want to make sure—is there any possibility it could've happened the way Dana said?"

The sparkle in his eyes flickered out. She looked into two bottomless, black wells. "Not a chance in hell." He took out a spiral notepad and flipped pages. "I can understand your loyalty to your client, but we really have no choice. So—will you talk to me?"

Cassidy nodded.

"You ever get any idea Dana might've abused her child? If not physically, maybe verbally or emotionally?"

"Not at all. She'd formed a strong bond with her daughter. Being a good mother was the most important thing in her life."

"What about the boyfriend? And the cousin—that woman in the flat below. They both babysat from time to time, didn't they?"

"Right. But they were extremely fond of Cypress. I never got the sense either one was abusive."

Perez tapped his pen against the pad. "How did Dana get along with her boyfriend and cousin? Any conflict or resentments?"

"Definitely not. They both had her best interest at heart."

His eyes narrowed. He scribbled a note. *What does he know that I don't?*

He glanced at his watch, not a Rolex but similar, then grimaced apologetically. "It's gotta feel like going to the dentist, talking about your client to a cop. An ordeal like this, kid missing so long, it's hard on everybody."

"I wish I had something to give you." Cassidy remembered how devastating it had been to Sam to have kidnappings he could never solve.

His black-coffee eyes smiled. "You're doing more than you realize. If we can cross the cousin and boyfriend off the list, it'll be easier to focus in."

Focus in? That means Dana.

Perez looked down at his notepad. "How would you describe your client's state of mind prior to the disappearance?"

Cassidy recounted Dana's anxiety about spending the weekend alone. She paused, remembering their last session: saw Dana hugging Cypress until the child cried out, heard her saying, "If we ever talked, Satan would know and we'd be punished."

Perez asked, "Is there anything else you can tell me? Anything at all, even if it seems unrelated?"

Previous psychotic break. Involvement with Satanism. Possibly programmed to harm her child. You've gotta tell him.

They're building a case against Dana already. The more you hand them, the less motivated they'll be to check out other leads.

Cassidy caught her lip between her teeth. "I can't believe Dana'd harm her child. I know it looks bad, but I'm convinced she didn't do it."

He shook his head slowly. "I hope you're right. My best case scenario is some crazy lady ran off with Cypress and is feeding her ice cream as we speak. But if that were true," he rubbed a manicured hand over glossy black curls, "why make up a story about the father? Why lie if there's nothing to hide?" He closed his pad. "You want to think the best of her, and that's as it should be. But we have to be objective."

Am I doing the same thing I did with Ryan? Seeing only what I want to see? She had made serious mistakes with a former client, Zach's brother, by failing to recognize how severely disturbed the man was.

Perez leaned back, automatically straightening his jacket so it hung smoothly. He made presenting an immaculate appearance look easy. She glanced down at the white cat fur spread generously across her garnet blouse. *What does it mean—an Oak Park detective wearing Italian silk suits and a knock-off Rolex?*

The humorous glint was back in his eyes. "Now that I've subjected you to this ruthless grilling, can I take you to lunch?"

She blinked. *Zach's starting to evaporate. Why not?* Pushing her chair back, she stood facing his desk. "Let me guess." An undercurrent of amusement in her voice. "Two ex-wives. Five kids. Heavy-duty support payments. Some form of lucrative extra income. And every woman who crosses your path, you hit on, using the ever popular, just-part-of-doing-business rationale."

A flash of white teeth in the tan face. He shoved his chair away from the desk and rocked backwards, raising the front legs off the floor. "You make me out twice as big as life. One ex, two kids, moderate child support, a few bucks on the side from real estate investments. And I don't *hit* on anyone, although I might, on occasion, ask a pretty girl to lunch."

Girl? She ought to be indignant but couldn't work herself up to it. "Well . . . ." *Go ahead—this'll make it easier when Zach breaks up with you.* She got hold of herself. "Thanks anyway. Maybe another time."

⁊⸙ ⁊⸙ ⁊⸙

Two days later a second and even more unexpected luncheon invitation came her way. The instant she heard Kevin's voice on the line she knew the word "yes" should not come out of her mouth, but curiosity got the best of her. She picked a small Italian place in Forest Park, a bar-ridden, blue-collar suburb adjoining the village, and told him she'd meet him at noon.

Kevin opened the door of the Trattoria d'Roma and she groped down three wooden steps, her eyes gradually adjusting from the glare outside to the dusky halflight of the restaurant's basement interior. The heavy marinara aroma kickstarted her stomach juices.

Kevin's rumbly voice whispered in her ear, "Not quite what I had in mind, darlin'."

Her glance took in the black vinyl booths, checkered plastic tablecloths, candle-dripping chianti bottles, tables and chairs crammed too close together in the small room. "What I wanted exactly," she told him. "Obscure. Off the beaten track. Kind of place nobody I know is likely to step foot in."

Chuckling, he placed his hand on the back of her neck, setting nerve endings atingle. "So, babe, why the hideaway? You after a little secret liaison here? I've always been a sucker for trysts."

183

Tell me something I don't know.

A waiter, hair slicked down, mouth pouty, seated them in the back corner. Cassidy faced the door so she could peer over Kevin's shoulder and check out whoever came in. It would be embarrassing to be caught having lunch with her ex, especially considering all the bad things she'd said about him. As soon as they were settled, she asked, "Now that you've conned me into this meeting, why am I here? Or perhaps I should put it another way: how much this time?"

"Did I ever happen to mention," he reached across to fondle a strand of her auburn hair, "that you suffer a wee bit from impatience?" She pushed his hand away. He continued blandly, "First we'll have ourselves a drop of wine, shall we?"

As he read the menu, she studied his face. In her imagination, he always radiated his own special light, glowing with the brightness and intensity of a glossy Kodak ad. But today he seemed like a dim photo of himself, the bronze in his dissheveled curls faded and washed-out, the mahogany of his deeply tanned face turned ashen. A shaggy new mustache stretched across his upper lip, and she wondered if its purpose might be to disguise the increased fleshiness of his face. A slight sag had developed in the lids above blue eyes that for the first time seemed less than sharp and clear.

The waiter sidled up and asked what they wanted, his voice bored. Kevin ordered a bottle of chianti and Caesar salad. Cassidy ordered carbonara.

"Salad?" She arched her brows. "Mustache?"

"You have to be flexible, you know. Takes change and new horizons to keep the old testosterone pumping." He delivered his high-voltage, lopsided grin. "God help me, love, should I ever get past the point that my blood stirs at the prospect of a new game 'round the bend."

Same old razzle-dazzle. "Isn't that the speech you used when you wanted my approval for your escapade with that little kewpie-doll, IQ of 20?"

Kevin plunked his arms on the table. "A man needs to be able to admit to his mistakes."

"Mistakes?" Her voice went shrill with surprise. "I've never heard you admit a mistake in your life."

"I should never have left my darlin' wife. Sweet, bonny Cass. You were the best thing ever happened to me. I'm here to say I want you back."

"Wait. Stop. Cease and desist. Not another word until I toss down at least one glass of wine."

He stroked his shaggy mustache, eyes gleaming with love the same way Starshine's did when Cassidy happened to put out food she liked. *What's the scam this time?*

Behind his head Cassidy glimpsed someone coming into the restaurant. A woman in a watermelon pink shirt with curled-under brown hair fumbled down the steps. *Oh shit— Josie.* The newcomer glanced around, but Kevin's large body blocked Cassidy from her view. Josie took a table up front, sitting with her face to the door.

The waiter brought the wine and Cassidy chugged her first glass. Folding her arms on the checkered tablecloth, she leaned forward. "Okay, I'm going to ask some questions. If you lie once—even the teeniest white lie—I'll be out of here like a rocket shooting past your head."

"Ah, Cassy." He shook his head reprovingly. "Whatever happened to that sweet, trusting girl I married?"

"*You* happened to her. Now, who is it that's just dumped you?"

" 'Dumped'—such a harsh word." He reached for her hand but she pulled it away. "The truth be known, I was keeping company with this wee slip of a girl. Only twenty, she was. Model, as it so happens. But the young are so ambitious, so eager to get on with their lives. They've no sense of what's really important. Ah, but no matter. We both knew from the start it was too bright not to burn out. She was never important to me. None of them were. You're the only one—only you out of all of them—that's ever meant anything to me."

"So you were dumped by a twenty-year-old. Beginning to feel old, by any chance?"

His head snapping up, he gave her a stern look. "You know I'm only forty-two."

"How're you currently supporting yourself?"

"I've got this great idea." His voice strained for enthusiasm. "Recruitment agency for personal services. Cleaning ladies, nannies, organizers. You know how hard it is for dual-career couples to find quality service. I've got this massive ad campaign mapped out—radio, magazines, television—"

"Soon as you find the right investor."

"Matter of fact—"

"So, what did you have in mind? You want to move back in? Get remarried? What?"

He ran his fingers down the side of her face, lingering on her cheekbone, tracing the outline of her lips. "You and I, we were so good together, babe. It's not too late. We can have all that again."

Her throat tightened to keep back the tears. *If only . . .* She gulped down more wine. *If those words had come out of his mouth any time during the first year after he left, I'd have jumped.*

She removed his hand and laid it on the table, then smoothed his new mustache. It was coarse, not springy like his hair. "Oh, Kevin, I'm so sorry."

The sullen waiter plopped their plates on the red checkered tablecloth. Kevin finished his second glass of wine and devoured his salad. She pushed carbonara around her plate. *Nothing changes. I still take everything harder than he does.*

For Kevin, life was one whim after another, including thoughts of reconciliation. If she were in his place, she'd be crushed. But Kevin possessed the enviable capacity to deflect rejection and give up easily. Had she said yes, he probably would have gotten distracted before he managed to return. Having received a no, he'd already moved on to something else.

Wanting to get away, she asked the waiter for the check, then laid down two tens. Kevin protested half-heartedly, but she ignored him and stood to leave. *Who cares if Josie sees me with my ex?* They headed for the door.

The air outside was bright but nippy. Kevin tucked her arm into his, preventing her from making her intended dash for the Toyota. The crackling of dry leaves underfoot reminded her of days flying by too fast. Too many days since Cypress had disappeared.

Kevin asked, "This because of your new boyfriend?"

She heard the screech of brakes, the slam of a car door. Her head swiveled. A red pickup had hauled up to the curb behind them.

"You in love with him?" The hint of uncertainty in Kevin's voice flagged her attention.

He feeling insecure? Can't be. Impossible. She searched his grayer-than-usual face, then parroted back, "In love?"

"That's the question."

"Don't ask me about love. I always get it wrong." Glancing back at the empty pick-up, she realized what had caught her eye. The words in curlicue letters on the passenger door: Class Act Painters.

15

News Story

Following her Friday afternoon appointment with Ursula, Cassidy jotted notes on a legal pad: "Session five, still don't know why she's here. Seems satisfied with therapy. Discussed old boyfriends." She knotted her forehead, tightened her lips. *Keep getting that dissonant feeling—way I feel when I work with personality disorders.* She tore off the page and dropped it into Ursula's folder in her office cabinet. Noticing that the leaves on her coleus were as limp as dead men hanging from a gallows, she headed into the kitchen for water.

As the watering can filled, she stared through her window into the Roberts' backyard two houses away. Dad was pushing a lawn mower similar to her recalcitrant Toro. His son followed with a toy mower, mimicking his father's movements precisely.

What is it with this family that I'm so fascinated? 'Cause they look too good to be true, especially compared to my clients? My own family, for that matter. Or some part of me still wishing for what they've got?

Cassidy dumped water on her plant, then returned to the sink as Starshine lumbered into the kitchen. The calico scowled at her food-encrusted bowl in the corner next to the fridge. The gray linoleum surrounding her dining area was littered with small brown lumps resembling dog turds.

"I've watched you deliberately spread pieces around the floor. Why do you do that?"

Starshine leapt on the counter to supervise as Cassidy scrubbed out the plastic dish. Cold amber eyes seemed to say: "I'm not sure what you're up to—but if that isn't filled soon, you'd better watch your back."

Cassidy hastily spooned out food and set it in front of Starshine. The cat's eyes softened as she buried her face in it.

"Count yourself lucky you don't have some gynecologist ordering you to keep it down to two ounces a month." She crossed her arms and leaned against the sink. "Hurry up. I've got urgent matters to discuss."

Leaving just enough food to glop up the bowl, Starshine attempted to clean up by pushing her dish over the edge of the counter, but Cassidy swooped down in time to grab it. The cat bestowed a benign, full-stomach gaze on her human, then lazily licked her mouth.

"Isn't it weird how things come in bunches? First Perez, then—the real kicker—Kevin. Now that I'm having semi-regular sex, I must be reeking with pheromones."

Purring ardently, Starshine stood and stretched her face for a nosekiss. Cassidy touched noses, then scratched under her chin. "Here's Manny Perez, a great dresser, at least five on the sensitivity scale. Not bad for a cop, albeit a tad on the make. Then there's Kevin, finally saying all the words I ever wanted to hear come out of his mouth. And what do I do with all this male attention? I mope around about Zach, the one man not asking me to lunch. The one man who is, in fact, slipping and sliding around, trying to find a way out of this relationship he worked so hard to get into."

Having had enough conversation, Starshine made a stab at washing the base of her tail, although twisting around to reach it was something of a challenge these days.

Cassidy fetched a whisk broom and dustpan out of the cabinet. "If I could get my head in control for once instead of my heart, I'd pick a guy like Roland Mertz, somebody who'd put me on a pedestal and adore me. Then I'd treat him like you treat me: keep him insecure and guessing, toss him the occasional crumb." She squatted on her heels and swept up chunks of dried cat food.

The back doorbell started ringing, one sharp ring after another, someone punching it hard. She dropped the whisk broom and scrambled to her feet, then hesitated. Maybe she shouldn't answer. The staccato rhythm continued. Whatever it was, she'd have to face it sooner or later. She brushed her lint-covered skirt, straightened her shoulders, and marched around the room divider into the waiting room.

A narrow face with bald crown, mottled cheeks, and straggly mustache glared through the window in the back door. Where had she seen that face before? The baptism. Ernie Voss—Dana's father.

Don't open it. She paused, hand on the knob, then pulled the door all the way back. Standing close to the screen, Ernie stooped down so that his head hovered just above hers.

"You're going to be sorry!" He bit the words off venomously, ending the sentence with a pronounced click of his teeth. Crossing her arms and spreading her legs, she planted herself squarely in front of the screen door. She would not be intimidated.

"You and your boyfriend both—you're going to regret what you've done to my daughter." He shoved a long finger into wire mesh that was coming loose from the door's metal frame. The finger's joints were knobby; the nail ridged and blackened at the base. "There may be bad blood between Dana and me, but that doesn't mean you can violate her rights and I won't do anything about it. I suppose you thought that just 'cause I don't like her much, I'd stand back and let you get away with your little exploitation. Well, let me tell you—I take care of my own. Doesn't matter how messed up she is." Ernie jammed his finger farther into the screen, apparently trying to break through and ram it in her face.

Cassidy reared back. "Stop yelling at me." Her voice came out too high-pitched and thin. She cleared her throat and tried again. "I don't know what you're talking about."

"Don't know?" He lowered his face, pushed it closer to the screen. Dark nose hairs infiltrated the wiry gray mustache. His horselike front teeth, long and yellow, snapped out words so fiercely she felt they would tear into her flesh without the screen as a barrier.

"Suppose you don't know your boyfriend wrote a story about Dana. Suppose you don't know the newspaper printed up all that confidential information you handed out to him. Another thing you probably don't know is, my wife spilled the beans 'bout how you two've been pumping her."

Oh shit. Never should've talked to Zach. I've way overstepped the boundaries here, and this guy knows it. Her stomach felt jumpy, as if she'd swallowed ice cubes.

Straightening to his full height, he shook a clenched fist in her face. "You think I'm some stupid bumpkin who doesn't know how to look up the social work code of ethics? Or how to file a grievance? If you had half a brain, lady, you wouldn't have underestimated me. 'Cause I'm going to get you for this." His flinty eyes bored into hers. "From here on out, you and that boyfriend of yours better stay the fuck away from my family."

As he turned to leave, thrusting his narrow shoulders in a belligerent sweep, she called after him, "Nobody's ever done more to hurt your family than you have, Ernie Voss."

She slammed the door, then leaned weakly against it. *What the hell's in that story? How could he do this to me?* Gran subscribed to the *Post* and regularly clipped cartoons and articles for her. Grabbing the phone off the kitchen wall, she asked her grandmother to look through recent issues for a story about Dana Voss. As Gran rummaged through the papers on her dining room table, Cassidy shifted from one foot to the other. Stretching the cord, she picked up the dust pan and whisk broom and put them away. She reread the cartoons on the fridge, noticing again how old and yellow they were. Ripping them off, she crushed them into tight balls and heaved them across the kitchen. She wanted to throw dishes but had a strong inhibitor that prevented her from crossing the line into anything that verged on actual violence.

She had removed all the cartoons from the top half of the fridge by the time Gran's perky voice came back on the line. "I found it. Yesterday's paper. Looks like your boyfriend wrote it."

"Read it to me."

"Just a minute now," Gran said. "Gotta put on my glasses for the small print." Cassidy drummed her fist against the wall next to the phone. "Okay, here goes. The headline says, 'In child's disappearance, Mother's story false.' "

Cassidy groaned.

"Now this is the part under the headline." Gran began to read in a monotone. "In an investigation into the October third disappearance of an Oak Park two-year-old, the one thing that's certain, according to Detective Manuel Perez, is that 'the mother's story does not check out.' " Next came a carefully worded statement by Perez implying that Dana was the chief suspect.

Gran stopped to comment. "When I hear stories 'bout mothers killing their own kids, it always gives me the creeps." She then said, "Okay, this part's the article again. 'Police have confirmed that Wayne Farelli, the mother's live-in boyfriend, served three years in Attica State Prison after a conviction of manslaughter in a reputedly mob-related slaying. Farelli moved to Chicago in 1990, breaking his parole with only one month left to serve. According to Perez, extradition is uncertain due to the short time remaining on his parole.' "

Mob-related? More to Wayne than meets the eye.

Gran's dry reading voice continued through another section, then a new topic exploded over the line, sending the blood pounding in Cassidy's ears. "Stop. Read that last part over, would you?"

" 'According to an informed source, Voss was hospitalized at Tinley Park following a psychotic break seven years ago. After release from the state psychiatric hospital, she lived with the child's father for four years, then moved into her current residence, a two-flat owned by her cousin, Josephine Crandel. According to the same source, her parents refused to allow their daughter to return to the family home, citing Voss' history of drug abuse and promiscuity as the reasons.' "

Informed source? That must be me.

When her grandmother reached the end, Cassidy thanked her and got off the line. She instantly dialed a second number.

"Moran here."

"We have to talk," she said through clenched teeth.

"I guess you've seen the story." His voice was flat with detachment, the device he used to avoid feelings. It drove her crazy when she was itching to fight and he just got more distant.

"You think I wouldn't find out?"

"I knew you'd hear about it."

"So why didn't you warn me?"

"We can talk about it tonight."

☙ ☙ ☙

Only three o'clock, hours and hours till 'around nine,' the time Zach said he'd arrive. No more clients, no way for her to turn off the imaginary conversations that played and replayed in her head. Six more hours and *she'd* have a psychotic break.

Despite the sharpness in the air, she bundled up, got out her bike, and pedaled as hard as she could, hoping to get mental relief through physical exhaustion.

She'd been cycling half an hour when she passed a house that pushed Zach and his story completely out of her mind. A dummy made of stuffed clothes hung from a large elm. The porch was webbed with silvery ropes. Two ghosts floated side by side from the roof.

As a kid, at the beginning of October she'd started looking forward to Halloween. This was the first time in her life she couldn't bear to think of All Hallow's Eve coming so soon.

16

Break Up

Exactly what you deserve, screamed the voice that pointed out her every fault. *Ryan told you Zach couldn't be trusted, but you wouldn't listen.* When Ryan was her client, he had often expressed frustration over his brother's disregard for their relationship.

She held up her watch, squinting to read the dial in the faint light filtering onto the porch from her living room. Quarter past ten. *What if he stands you up? What if he figures, now that he can't use you anymore, might as well blow you off?*

"You think he's going to weasel—just disappear and cheat me out of my right to yell at him?" She addressed Starshine, who lay on her back on the floor exposing a round white tummy dotted with prominent pink nipples.

The cat squirmed in response to Cassidy's question.

A chill wind whipped through the trees, clattering the chimes and shaking panes in the casement windows.

Cassidy poured a second glass from the jug of Carlo Rossi sitting next to the couch. She'd been holding off, aware that she would need all the control she could muster when Zach finally appeared. But he was taking too long. She couldn't go on waiting indefinitely, not knowing if or when he'd show, without another glass of wine. The alcohol in her system would keep her from cracking into tiny pieces and flying apart.

She forced herself to drink slowly, holding each sip a moment or two. Her glass was half empty when the Datsun wagon drew up at the end of her walk. As Zach moved toward the house, an image flashed into her mind of their first meeting. She had been sitting right where she was now and he'd approached through a rainstorm. Since she'd been receiving threatening calls at the time, her initial impulse was to run inside and lock the door. Now she was sorry she hadn't followed it.

Zach opened the screen and took his usual place on the wicker couch, bringing a joyful Starshine up from the floor to greet him. As he dropped heavily beside her, the smell of Jack Daniels hit her in the face.

He said, "Where's mine?"

"Haven't you had enough already?" Cassidy grudgingly filled the glass she'd brought out for him and handed it over.

"Sorry I took so long. I stopped off at Marina City after the commission meeting and had a couple of drinks while I thought about what I was going to say."

Needed booze to get up his courage. This is gonna be bad, I know it.

Curling into his lap, Starshine nipped his hand to show she wanted petting. He said, "But don't worry, I'm sober enough to get through this conversation. I just wanted to take the edge off is all."

The words came out slowly. She understood that his hesitancy was not from alcohol, but from having to talk about something he would prefer to avoid. *Least he's not getting remote on me, way he did on the phone. You have to give him credit for that.* She knew well enough the difficulty of owning up to behavior she didn't want to admit, even to herself. A wave of protectiveness washed over her, accompanied by an urge to let him off. Then she remembered what he had done and shut off all warm feelings. Empathy would be the death of her.

"Okay," she cranked up her anger. "So tell me—why did you use confidential information? 'Cause I wasn't smart enough to extract a promise the way Laurel did, or what?"

"The 'informed source' was a police guy, not you. The thing is, he wouldn't let me identify him that way. He's convinced they'll make him if I do."

"But everybody knows about us. They're all going to assume you got it from *me*." She pressed her fingertips to her temples. "The mere fact that your byline's on the story makes me look bad. Why didn't you get somebody else to write it?"

He took a large gulp of wine. "I've never ducked a story in my life. I like to think I can handle anything, just stash it all in separate boxes. Keep my personal and professional lives apart so they never overlap, never even touch. I convinced myself I could do the story without compromising you. Same as if I didn't have inside information."

"You expect yourself to function like a computer, everything in its own separate file? You have to be Superman? No wonder you can't let anybody get close."

He lay his arm behind her head and squeezed her shoulder. "Hey, look who's talking. The original, I-don't-need-anything-from-anybody, Ms. Independence. You and I are a matched set, lady. Wonder Woman and Superman."

Her body, which had been known to betray her in the past, relaxed against his. A dull ache started in the back of her head. What Zach had done was not okay and she couldn't let it go, but she also couldn't seem to think straight.

Starshine poked an insistent nose into the pocket of Zach's denim jacket. Taking out a pistachio, he tossed it to the floor and she dived clumsily after it.

Trees moaned in the wind. Starshine bapped the pistachio to the far end of the porch, then carried it back to drop in front of Zach. He reached down and she struck at his fingers. *She's pissed at him too.* He jerked his hand away, wiping blood on his jeans. Starshine grabbed the pistachio and trotted into the house.

Cats and men—just when you least expect it, they rip you off or rip up your heart. What's the matter with me, I keep falling for the same old game? Charlie Brown and the football.

Zach poured another glass of wine. He hunched forward, hands dangling between his knees. "There's something else I have to tell you. That's what I was going over at Marina City—whether or not to bring this up. I decided I had to."

Here it comes—the old I'm-feeling-pressured sayonara speech. Her mouth got desert-dry. She took a large slug of wine, holding it until the taste turned vinegary on her tongue.

"I set out to do the piece thinking I could keep your information out of it, that I could do it just like any other story. Then somewhere in the process the line got blurred. What I did—in spirit if not in fact—violated your confidentiality. But you need to understand, I never intended for that to happen. Sometimes when I'm chasing a story, I get so tunnel-visioned I lose track of the consequences. Or, if I think of them, I do some kind of internal rationalization to make them go away. I've gotten in trouble like this before."

Swallowing, she asked tightly, "What do you mean, 'violated my confidentiality?' "

"When I first started talking to the police, they didn't know about Dana's hospitalization. They would have uncovered it eventually, but they hadn't gotten to it yet. I didn't come out and tell them, you understand, but by asking the right questions I put them on to it."

She stopped breathing for several seconds, then sucked in air and said, "Anything else?"

"That's all." He looked up at her. She wished the light were stronger so she could read his face. *Don't crucify him,* said the voice that clung to something's-better-than-nothing as a golden rule of life. *God knows, you've gotten single minded and screwed up often enough yourself.*

Oh no you don't! yelled the other voice, the one that wanted her to stop being such a sucker. *You're just trying to give him the benefit of the doubt so you don't have to break up.*

A porch window blew open, the frame lashing backward to crash into the window next to it. Cold wind gusted across her skin, raising goosebumps on her arms.

Hugging herself against the chill, she said, "I realize that ultimately I'm responsible for this whole mess." Feeling very cold, colder even than the sharp wind whistling through the windows, she set her jaw against the shivers vibrating down her spine. "I brought it on myself by being stupid enough to tell you in the first place. By thinking you might put me ahead of your story for once. But even though this is primarily my own fault, what you did was still a betrayal."

He stared at the floor. She had no idea what he was thinking or if he was even listening. When he didn't respond she continued, "You betrayed my trust by using privileged information. You exploited our relationship by not telling me what you were up to. And you've broken your promise to work toward commitment by backing off and getting so erratic I can't begin to tell what's going on anymore. Were you hoping to push me over the edge with the story? Get me so pissed I'd break it off and save you the trouble?"

Sitting up straighter, he cocked his head quizzically. "What makes you think I want to break up?"

More words came from his mouth but the noise in her head drowned them out. She remembered Kevin looking her right in the eye, just as Zach was doing now, face so sincere, telling her he absolutely was not doing the very thing he was doing. Telling her black was white. *Remember how confused you got?*

How you started doubting your own sanity, believing Kevin's words instead of what your gut said was true?

She stood abruptly, bumping the bench in front of the couch and smashing her half-filled glass on the floor. *When Kevin left, you thought you'd shatter just like that glass. You didn't then, won't now.* "I'm not going to listen!" She put her hands over her ears. "I won't let you twist things. You *have* been backing away. You *did* betray my trust. This time I'm going to do it right. I'm going to do what I should have done before and kick you the hell out of my life."

≈ ≈ ≈

"How long since you told him to fuck off?" Maggie asked. Dressed in tan shirt and pants, no make up, with short brown hair curling around her face, Maggie was delicate and pretty in a no-nonsense kind of way.

Cassidy had taken her friend and fellow therapist to an upscale Chicago restaurant to celebrate Maggie's birthday. The cost of dinner at Gable's was way beyond her means—one glance at her wine-bottle savings told her that—but the what-the-hell, nothing-matters-anyway mood she was in made her want to splurge.

"Over a week now since the grand exit." Cassidy pushed pieces of lightly oiled romaine around a sleek white plate. *Chocolate. I want chocolate.*

"No calls either direction?" Maggie's voice was deep and gravelly, not up and down, all over the scale like hers; the kind of voice Cassidy would give a year of her life for—especially a bad year.

"My right hand keeps reaching for the phone but my left hand slaps it away."

"Even though Susie and I live together, we still break up all the time. But I can never go two days without talking." Maggie stuffed the last bite of salad into her mouth and chewed thoughtfully, causing her long silver earrings to quiver. She asked, "So, why not call? You really want it to be over?"

Cassidy glanced at the waiter with the upswept, moussed hair—"Hi-my- name-is-Tom"—who, in the half-empty restaurant, had taken up a post just behind her right shoulder, apparently having decided that Cassidy's love life was the most interesting topic under discussion in his sector of the room. She lowered her voice. "One part of me's dying to—"

"May I pour you ladies more wine?"

Cassidy nodded curtly. *Does this guy think hovering will increase his tip? Or that eavesdropping is a sincere form of flattery?*

As Tom stepped closer, his mouth settling into its practiced smile, Cassidy could feel his curious eyes glide across her face.

Maggie cocked her head, earrings shimmying, and raised one brow, the expression that appeared on her face whenever she was preparing to skewer someone. "May I offer a suggestion? You might not need to relieve your libidinal tension by listening in to other people's conversations if you had a sex life of your own."

His smile froze. Color rose in his cheeks as he poured the chardonnay, replaced the bottle in the ice bucket, and scuttled away.

Cassidy grinned in appreciation. "Wish I'd thought fast enough to say that—I might've relieved some tension of my own."

"We'll probably pay for it by waiting two hours for the main course."

"Anyway, I'm afraid if Zach did come back, his only reason would be to retaliate by dumping me. Long as I get to be the dum*por*, I can at least retain the small pleasure of not having been left this time."

"God, dating's awful. Irritated as I get at Susie, it's better than dating. Remember when you flaked out of my barbecue? I could tell by your voice back then you were miserable." She shook her softly curled head. "I should've made you talk, since I know by now you never tell me anything voluntarily. Here you are a therapist, and you won't even open up to your best friend about problems. Always acting like you have to have everything under control."

"That's 'cause I can't face how out of control things sometimes get."

Maggie pushed the bread basket in front of her. "C'mon, you've got to eat. I'll bet you've been starving yourself."

"I've been eating okay. Two full bags of peanut butter cups in the past week." Cassidy dutifully took a chunk of French bread. Chewing absently, she noticed a thin woman in a long black skirt and gauzy tunic drift toward the front door. *Ursula? What's she doing here? I see clients in Oak Park all the time—but not the same ones over and over. And not in Chicago.*

"Why so quiet?"

"I'm eating. You told me to eat so that's what I'm doing." Cassidy clinked her glass against Maggie's. "By the way, happy birthday. I'm in such a lousy mood, I almost forgot that's why we're here." She sipped her wine. "There's something else I wanted to ask. You ever had any experience with ritual abuse survivors?"

"Cult victims? One of the trendy types, like multiples and post traumatics? Nope, can't say that I have. Not sure I even believe it's for real."

"I've had a few doubts myself. Anyway, I've been researching Satanism this week—trying to get my mind off Zach. And it reads like a Stephen King novel. One woman claims she was used by the cult to breed babies for sacrifice." Cassidy shuddered. "She describes seeing her newborns skinned alive."

Maggie wrinkled her nose. "Why're you telling me this before dinner?"

"I can't seem to get it out of my head. You remember that subpersonalities method I told you about? I'm starting to think maybe everybody has an evil part, and there are a bunch of people running around with their evil parts in control." She drew her brows together. "The whole idea of a war between God and Satan could be simply an internal struggle between altruistic and destructive parts. I find this version a lot easier to swallow than the concept of a horned, cloven-footed bogeyman whose mission it is to seduce humans into selling their souls."

"I suggest you go back to Barbara D'Amato and Nancy Pickard and lay off that horror stuff."

"You talk about trendy—it seems like nowadays everybody is into spirituality, and most of what they say doesn't make sense to me. The word seems to mean different things to different people."

Resting her cheek on her hand, Maggie smiled benignly. "I shouldn't have shot off my mouth. We *are* going to have to wait two hours."

"To some, it's having Big Daddy in the Sky assume responsibility for keeping 'em on the straight and narrow—'Let go and let God.' To others, it's fantasizing that they'll be taken care of by some omnipotent being—'Please, God, give me the man of my dreams.' There's another bunch that sees it as a ticket out of all the normal unpleasantries of life. They want to go around being serene—or lobotomized—or something." She twisted her wineglass in a slow circle on the white tablecloth. "Another group thinks spirituality means having emissaries from the netherworld provide a preview of coming attractions—sort of like an insider tip on the stock market."

"What's it mean to you?"

"I don't claim to be spiritual. But if I did, I guess I'd think of it as doing whatever serves the greater good, not just what I want. Not running my air conditioner if it's going to make holes in the ozone. Not letting my cat have kittens if we're overrun with homeless cats already. And on both counts, I fail."

Maggie's eyes gleamed like sunlight on Lake Michigan. "Well, my girl, it's obvious you're still working out the bad karma from your previous life as a philandering, noncommital male."

17

Flowers

Cassidy returned home to find the red light on her answering machine blinking once. She felt the familiar surge—three parts hope, two parts anxiety—the feeling triggered by the phone ever since her fight with Zach. She quickly clamped down on her emotions.

Stop being so goddamned optimistic. He hasn't called by now, he's not going to. Besides, you had a very good reason for kicking his butt out, you just can't remember what it was right now. She pushed *play*.

"This is Wayne." His voice—slow, almost a monotone in the past—now had a jittery quality she hadn't heard before. "I don't want to scare you or nothin' but seems like Dana's getting worse. The deal is, she's not sleeping. Josie keeps giving her Xanax, which I'm not so sure about. Last night, even with a double dose, she didn't sleep hardly at all. And the way she was talking today didn't make much sense."

Beep.

Oh shit—headed for a break. She lands on a locked ward, it could really destroy her.

She dialed Dana's number and Wayne answered.

"This is Cassidy." Her therapist training clicked in, enabling her to sound calmer than she felt. "Has Dana seen the psychiatrist yet?"

"She gave us the slip." Frustration in his voice, and something else. Defensiveness?

"It's hard to get her to do anything if she doesn't want to," Cassidy said.

"Her mom made an appointment for yesterday afternoon, but when Josie went up to get her, she'd disappeared out the back. She came home around midnight . . . pretty much bombed."

"I know she hates the idea of going into the hospital, but it may be the only way to keep her safe. If she gets really agitated or delusional, you need to call me or take her into the emergency room."

"She's okay for tonight. She was all over the place when I phoned earlier, but she finally calmed down and got to sleep."

Cassidy offered to set up another appointment with the psychiatrist, urged Wayne to keep her posted, and rang off.

Later, as she sat up in bed, a bag of peanut butter cups, pile of candy wrappers, and unopened mystery in her lap, she saw Starshine come swaying out of the closet. "Sniffing out potential nests?" She unwrapped another Reese's. "Any way to persuade you not to give birth on whatever piece of clothing happens to be on my closet floor at the time? Ridiculous, to think I could talk you out of anything." The cat plopped onto the bed and rolled over on her side, looking relieved to take the load off. Cassidy could identify. With the weight of her pain over Zach, she felt as heavy and clumsy as the cat. She bit the Reese's in half and chewed slowly.

Her shoulders slumped, her eyes burned, her stomach harbored a continuous dull ache that not even chocolate could take away.

He was a jerk, a user. Why are you feeling so bad?

Cassidy heard a childlike voice in her head: *He went away. I'm all alone. Nobody loves me now.*

Can't you remember anything? You were the one who broke it off.

Suddenly the memory returned as clearly as the day it happened. She was in a mauve bedroom with limp lace curtains at the window. A flimsy brown suitcase lay open on a chenille bedspread. Her father, a large, broad-shouldered man with curly black hair, was throwing clothes into the suitcase.

Her two small hands grabbed his forearm just as he was swinging around. She whipped into the air, then flew off, banging her head against the wooden bed frame. Whimpering, she curled into a ball. Her father lifted her from the bed and hoisted her onto his chest. She wrapped her legs around his waist and her arms around his neck, attaching herself like Velcro.

"Sorry, Cassie." His large hand cradled her head. "I've gotta get outta here. I just can't take your mother no more."

Sobbing, she rubbed her dripping nose against his Old Spice-scented shirt. "Don't leave, please Daddy, don't go. If you go, there won't be nobody to love me anymore."

ટ‌ટ‌ ટ‌ટ‌ ટ‌ટ‌

"I didn't want to come today," Carla said, twisting the opal ring on her slender right hand. The curly golden head was lowered, the china blue eyes flat. "I come to therapy week after week and I don't get anywhere. Maybe I should just give up."

"Give up what?" Crossing her leg, Cassidy smoothed her flowered skirt over her knee. *Monday morning, always hard to concentrate. And today's worse than usual, what with worry over Dana on top of old memories.* The waiting room radio wailed in the background, "Lay your head upon my pillow. . ."

"Trying to break off with Jim," Carla said. "The first time he stood me up was way back in May, remember? He's disappeared three times since then, and here I am, still hanging in, hoping next time will be different."

Maybe she should *give up. Must love pain, the way she keeps throwing herself in the fire like a stupid moth.* Stifling her irritation, Cassidy asked, "How does it make you feel, taking him back?"

"I hate myself." Carla ran a pointed nail around the tape that covered a missing button. "Every time he pulls some stunt, I swear it's the end. Then he calls and I go running back."

Cassidy heard the faint sound of a doorbell coming from the front of the house. *Zach?* A flutter of hope. *No—he'd use his key. Which you, of course, conveniently forgot to take back.* The bell rang twice more, then stopped.

After Carla left, she went to the front door to find Starshine hunkered down, nose to the crack, a soft growl emanating from low in her throat. *No understanding cats.* Shaking her head, she proceeded onto the porch.

A tall basket of flowers, purple bow on the handle, sat on the bench in front of the couch. Excitement brought a flush of heat to her face, stirred up *maybes* and *what-ifs* in her mind. She found a folded card attached to the ribbon. *No envelope?* The florist's name was printed in tiny letters across the front. Inside, thick, black handwriting said, "Love, Zach."

Starshine's tail lashed her ankle. The cat's huge, dark eyes were fixed on the basket. The growl deepened.

"You think maybe I'll lose all common sense and take him back? You're probably afraid I'll end up as pathetic and lovesick as Carla."

Starshine nipped her knee. Cassidy pushed the cat aside and picked up the basket. Mums, zinnias, and dahlias. Her favorite colors, deep purple, lavender, and bright pink sparkled in the sunlight flooding through the porch windows. Maybe he wasn't all bad after all.

Starshine zipped into the house just as the door closed, no small feat considering her girth. "Moved a hair slower, you'd have gotten your abortion anyway." Setting the basket on the dining room table, Cassidy grabbed the phone from the kitchen wall intending to thank Zach.

Stop! her proper behavior voice commanded. *Don't be impulsive. You want to call right away 'cause you're afraid, if you give yourself time to think, you'll remember all the reasons not to.*

As she reluctantly withdrew her hand from the phone, it rang. *Must be Zach. ESP.* "Hello?"

"Ms. McCabe?" A thin, uncertain voice. "This is Laurel."

"Laurel?" Putting aside her disappointment, Cassidy quickly shifted gears. "Is it Dana? Something wrong?"

"We've got, I don't know, a new development here." Her voice was barely audible. "Something I need to talk to you about, but not over the phone."

"I called the psychiatrist this morning and he can squeeze her in tomorrow. Once she's on medication, she should start to improve."

"I'll do my best to get her in to that doctor of yours, but she can be awful slippery. Anyway, the reason I called is, I'm starting to get scared . . . real scared. I need your help. And there's something I gotta tell you. Only it's gotta be confidential."

Cassidy pictured Ernie's face hovering outside her screen door, his voice commanding, "Stay the fuck away from my family." She stiffened her back and said, "What would be a good time?"

"Not till Wednesday. I promised Wayne I'd stay with Dana all day tomorrow, and Ernie, he's watching my every move. But I could get to your place Wednesday around one, 'cause Josie'll be home and Ernie's got to drive into the city."

Where's my calendar? Oh hell—I'll reschedule a client if necessary. "One o'clock Wednesday it is."

She suddenly remembered seeing her calendar on the wicker table in her office. When she went to get it, she discovered a noon session coming up in an hour, a session she had lost track of in the flurry of flowers and Laurel's call.

She would grab a bite to eat, see her client, then think about phoning Zach. For the first time in a week, she actually felt hungry. She pulled out the nearly untouched remains of last night's dinner at Gable's.

The microwave was humming when a crash from the dining room startled her into dropping the carton of outdated milk she was dumping down the drain. *God save me from a clumsy, watermelon-bellied cat.* She marched into the dining room, ready to yell at Starshine. A blue pitcher, one of her grandmother's wedding gifts, lay in pieces at the foot of the credenza.

Starshine was in stalking mode on the opposite side of the teak table, round body low-slung and tense, tail puffed, fur standing upright along the ridge of her spine. Her nose pointed like an arrow toward the corner.

Cassidy tiptoed around the table, craning her neck to see what the cat was after. *Cockroach maybe, or a mouse.* She saw a flicker of movement. Vivid colors. Her breath caught. Panic flooded her. Jerking her head back, she averted her eyes from the creature she had just glimpsed. Very slowly she forced her gaze to return to the whiplash in the corner. A tiny snake, ringed in black, red, and yellow, the black head raised, tongue snicking in and out, a whispery "ssss" issuing from its mouth.

Starshine hunkered less than a foot from the coiled snake, ears pricked, muscles frozen, standing guard to keep the intruder from leaving its corner. The sleek head flashed forward, missing the cat by no more than an inch. The calico reared back on her haunches, sitting fully erect. Her right paw hovered above the snake's head.

Holy shit! Cassidy pressed a hand against her stomach. She was terrified of snakes. All snakes, even garter snakes. And this was no mere garter snake. This one—she knew it in every cell—dispensed poison through its fangs.

In one heart-stopping motion, the snake lowered its head and whipped around the cat, coming to rest between Cassidy and Starshine. The calico sprang toward it, then pulled back. The snake tried to coil itself again, but the cat zipped closer, forcing it into motion. It curled around, retreating slightly, then stopped a couple of feet from the wall, still positioned to cut off access to the cat.

Folding her arms tightly across her chest, she tried to fight off the panic. *Can't stand it. Can't do it alone. Have to call somebody.*

The bulging cat hopped a few inches nearer and feinted a strike. The snake coiled.

You don't get rid of that thing right now, Starshine's dead.

If I try to reach her from this side, the snake'll take off and she'll chase after it. If I go around the table, I could get her distracted and push her closer. Only thing to do is kill the snake.

She searched her mind for weapons. A broom? She could chase the snake with a broom but not kill it. *Can't let it get away.* A shovel? *Have to leave Starshine, go down to the basement.* A shovel was probably the only thing that would kill it, and she had to have it dead. She flew into the kitchen, down the stairs, across the cement floor. Fumbling through the garden tools, she snagged the shovel and raced back to the dining room.

The snake was still coiled, black head weaving, eyes locked on Starshine. The cat advanced slowly. Cassidy crept up from behind.

Oh God, oh please, don't let her get bitten.

She raised the heavy shovel, hands trembling, and slammed it down flat on the snake. The impact sent shock waves through her arms. Starshine ran under the table. When she lifted the shovel, the snake lay flat against the floor. Placing the implement's sharp edge behind the head, she bore down. The body began thrashing, scaring her so badly she nearly dropped the handle. She closed her eyes and pressed as hard as she could but was unable to cut through the muscular fiber. Nausea churned in her stomach. Opening her eyes, she gritted her teeth and hacked away until the snake was finally decapitated.

Grabbing Starshine, she squeezed the frantic cat against her chest, not even aware of the claws digging into her throat and arm. She deposited the cat in the basement, then shoveled the snake's head and body into a trash bag. Saving only the card, she threw the basket of flowers in the bag, stuffed everything into her alley garbage can, and jammed down the lid.

She opened the door to let a howling Starshine out of the basement. The cat zoomed past her, trundling as fast as her short legs would move, back to the dining room corner, where she took up guard duty for the rest of the day.

Cassidy washed thoroughly, wishing she had time for a shower and change of clothes before her session. At a minute past noon she dropped into her director's chair, thankful that her client was running late. She took a deep breath and performed the same internal separation Zach had described, putting the snake episode into its own box, closing the lid, and freeing her attention for her client.

Afterward she carried the florist's card upstairs, sat at her desk, and reached for the phone. She described the snake to a librarian who promised to look it up and get back to her. It crossed her mind to report the incident to Perez but the thought faded before she could act on it. She considered calling

Zach. *Glad I didn't offer up any gushy thank-yous. But it would be okay to let him know about the snake. As long as I keep it strictly business.* She tried his work number, then his home number, leaving the same message on both machines: "An urgent bulletin regarding the investigation. Call me."

He'll get back to me this evening. Unless, of course, my replacement's already on line and he's spending the night. In which case he'll call tomorrow. So if I don't hear from him today, at least I know where I stand: Out in the cold. Over and done with.

Gazing at the handwriting on the card, she wondered how she could have mistaken it for Zach's. She realized now that the envelope was missing because it bore the florist's return address, which the sender obviously didn't want her to see. *No address, but at least the name.* The word was printed in small letters on the front: *Rosebud.* She dialed directory assistance and the operator told her she could check only two regions per call. Punching up four-one-one over and over, she continued until she'd searched the entire metropolitan area, finishing with a total of three florists by that name. She spoke to managers at all three places, but they denied knowing anything about the basket she had received.

She called her grandmother. "Have you ever heard of a flower shop called 'Rosebud?' "

"Nothing comes to mind. But my friend Mable, she used to work for a florist—that little place on Marion and South Boulevard. She must've worked there, oh, more than twenty years. Flowers are all right once in a while, but I can't see how anybody could keep sticking 'em in vases all that time without going 'round the bend. I'll give her a call and see what she knows. And while I've got you on the line—this must be some kind of precedent, us talking twice in a week—I wanted to ask whether you think your mother'll be able to put up with that sad-sack Roland very long."

"Maybe." *Don't be a brat.* "They seem to have a similar outlook."

"Know what I think? I think they both want to play victim, and sooner or later they'll fall to squabbling over whose lot in life is worse."

ᨑ ᨑ ᨑ

She changed from therapist to around-the-house clothes, sat in her desk chair again, and took out a notepad. *What does the snake mean? Somebody trying to kill me? Or just frighten me—the way they tried to stop us when they burned out Korsac?* The snake had to have come from the Satanists, although not necessarily from the same individuals who murdered the child in the well. Anybody currently connected with the cult would have a reason to try to scare her off. She thought of all the people she had talked to: Josie and Wayne, the minister and his wife, Laurel and Ernie, the retired police chief. *Who signed up for Satan's team instead of God's?* It could be any or all of them, or someone else altogether.

Glancing at the pad, she realized she had covered the page with doodles resembling coiled snakes. *What if there are more of them?* Snapping to her feet, she sprinted downstairs to check on Starshine. The cat was under the teak table, crouched behind one of the legs. The calico apparently considered herself in hiding, seeming to think the pole-leg concealed her bulging body as she stalked the empty corner.

Does she know something I don't?

Cassidy suddenly felt a quite unfamiliar urge to scrub the hardwood floor, both dining room and living room. As she filled a bucket and took out a barely used string mop, she recalled cleaning days with Mom. During the years she and her mother lived with Gran, they had repaid her generosity by keeping the bungalow spotless.

Every Saturday Cassidy had been involuntarily recruited for all-day cleaning marathons. Now that she had a house of her own, she'd swung to the opposite extreme, maintaining a what-you-don't-see-won't-hurt-you attitude toward dirt, thus escaping the drudgery of her childhood cleaning frenzies.

But today, driven by the paranoid idea that the reptile she had killed was only the mother snake, she threw herself into the job. Swinging the wet strings furiously, she started with the snake's corner and moved across age-darkened boards, her gaze reverting frequently to the splintery hole she had dug in the wood when she decapitated the reptile. She pulled the credenza away from the dining room wall, shoved the mop under the living room shelves, rolled up the area rug and washed under it.

When she had scrubbed every inch except the space beneath the blue paisley sofa, she dropped into a small, upholstered chair. Wiping an arm across her forehead, she tried to stop her runaway thoughts. The sofa rested firmly on the floor. There was no room for anything underneath, not even dust. The idea of tiny ringed snakes burrowing deep into the crevices of her house was patently ridiculous. Why move the heavy sofa?

Gotten this far, you might as well finish. One thorough, no-holds-barred mop-job in ten years can't hurt. 'Sides, you don't wanna dream about snakes slithering out from under the sofa tonight, do you?

She shoved one end out a couple of feet and gazed down at the vee-shaped gap. Right in the middle was a heap of strange items stuffed into the four-inch space between the back of the sofa and the wall. She pushed the other end out, then crawled into the gap to investigate. It was a fur-clumped nest of champagne corks, bottle tops, lids, napkins, tissues, and other *objets d'trash*: Starshine's treasure trove.

So that's why the thievery's slowed down. She must have a helluva time cramming herself in here now.

An image drifted into her mind: Zach popping a champagne cork and Starshine zooming off with it. That was the night he'd said he wanted to "make this thing work." Cassidy had to fight an urge to run to the phone. She swallowed hard, reminding herself that he wasn't home, hadn't called, didn't care.

As she swept the debris into a dustpan, a shimmer of gold caught her eye. She picked a grubby article out of the pile and wiped it on her T-shirt. A gold and garnet earring, one of a pair Gran had passed down to her. She had snarled at Starshine for most of a week over the cat's jewelry heist.

She could hear her mother's I-told-you-so voice: *You would've found it a long time ago if you cleaned properly. See what happens when you don't do things right?*

Her own rebellious voice answered back: *Oh yeah? I avoided all that stupid cleaning, my cat's a well-adjusted cork collector, and now I've got my earring back anyway.*

ᶺᴥ ᶺᴥ ᶺᴥ

Cassidy was rinsing the mop when the phone rang. The caller identified herself as a reference librarian. "The snake you described is an Arizona coral, a smaller cousin of the eastern coral. As you probably know, all coral snakes are highly poisonous."

How would a person go about getting a poisonous snake from Arizona? *If I wanted to give someone a snake, I wouldn't have a clue how to do it. Fly out to Arizona and catch it? Buy it from a catalogue? Maybe my bouquet-sender keeps 'em as pets, has glass cages full of them all over the house.*

The phone did not ring again. As midnight approached, Cassidy gave up hoping Zach would call and prepared for bed. She did half an hour of yoga in an attempt to quiet the chatter in her mind, then turned off the light. But even with the yoga, she was plagued by her failure to call Perez. The idea had surfaced, then instantly slipped away.

She had a long history of refusing to ask for help, even when it was clearly insane not to. She thought she'd learned her lesson, yet here she was doing it again. *What's wrong with me, that I so hate calling in the cavalry? If I had the slimmest grasp of reality I'd know in a minute—there's no way I can handle this alone.*

≈≈ ≈≈ ≈≈

She was jammed into a child's sled, her hips bulging over the sides and Starshine snuggled in her lap. Her father's broad-shouldered back rose a few feet ahead of the sled as he pulled it behind him, trudging up a snowy mountainside. Dragging the sled onto a ledge, he dropped the rope, and then, without a backward glance, bounded into the black mouth of a cave. Starshine, thin and svelte as she used to be, leapt up and raced after him. With a growing sense of dread, Cassidy hoisted herself out of the sled and followed into the round, dark opening.

The cave turned into a tunnel, then emptied out into her foyer. She heard voices from her bedroom. Starshine zipped upstairs and Cassidy plodded behind. When she reached the top, Starshine was waiting for her, nose sniffing at the cracked door. The cat slipped through the narrow space and entered the bedroom, tail waving jauntily. Cassidy's brain told her to run away, but some other, more primitive part pulled her toward the voices. Heart pounding, she pushed the door wide.

Purple flowers sprinkled the satin comforter. Zach and Kevin were sprawled out naked, one on each side of a woman who stood in the center of the bed, her back to Cassidy. Tall and stately, she was robed in a gauzy black gown. Growing out of her large head, like wriggly lines around a cartoon sun, were hundreds of writhing, red and yellow snakes.

Starshine hunkered low to the ground, let out a deep growl, and launched herself at the woman.

18

Confession

The following night when all her sessions were over, Cassidy dragged across the bedroom and stared down at the steady red light confirming what she already knew: no calls had come in during the time she was in her office seeing clients. A day and a half now since she'd left the urgent-bulletin messages, and she had no other numbers to try. Even though he carried a beeper and a cell phone, he kept them exclusively for work and had never let her use them.

Starshine gazed up thoughtfully at the desktop, no doubt doing feline calculations as to the amount of liftoff necessary to propel her poundage from floor to surface. Pretending to lose interest, she rolled over on her back, showing a wide expanse of snowy tummy and giving her legs a rest.

Can't believe he didn't call. He's never not returned my calls.

Ryan—his own brother—said that when Zach got fed up, he just stopped getting back to him.

A cold breeze blew through the window beside her desk and she stepped over to close it. Too late in the season for open windows. She tried to think of the date but couldn't pin it down. *Know exactly how many days since you broke up with Zach but can't keep track of numbers on the calendar.*

Halloween decorations were popping up everywhere so it must be near the end of the month. But she resisted looking at the calendar. Every time she registered the date, it reminded her of the number of days since Dana's child had disappeared.

What's the connection, Cypress and the snake? Who sent those damn flowers? Why hasn't Zach called back—especially since it's about his precious investigation? And why, why, why are men never there when you need them?

She stepped over Starshine's stomach, stood in front of her desk, and lifted the heavy green bottle. Eyeballing the coins had convinced her they were insufficient to pay for Maggie's dinner, so she had left them where they were, a head start for next year, and taken the money from her mortgage fund instead. Right hand gripping the neck, she swung the bottle back and forth. Her stomach clenched, her arm tightened. *How would it feel to smash a window?* Some of her clients threw things, broke dishes, cracked walls with their fists. When she thought of pounding a wall, her first reaction was to feel the sting of bruised knuckles. But a wine bottle filled with coins. Now that would be different.

She allowed herself a brief fantasy of swinging her arm, hearing the crash, seeing the shattered, flying shards. But she'd never do it. On the other side of that one glittering moment, there was the mess, the clean-up, the dollars out, not to mention the anger at herself. No matter how tempting, it would never be worth it.

Was that it? The difference between her and people who were genuinely evil? Did evil stem from an urge to destroy—calculated, not impulsive—an urge that brought so much ecstasy they were willing to pay the price, no matter how high?

She plunked the bottle back on the desk and limped over to her chest of drawers on the other side of the room. *Why the hell do I torture myself with these pointy-toed pumps?* Sitting on the bed, she hurled one after the other into the far corner under her desk. Startled by low-flying objects, Starshine lumbered to her feet, her flattened ears and angry eyes indicating that she took serious offense at shoe throwing. Cassidy peeled off her violet dress and tossed it on the bed, not even caring that Starshine considered all cast-offs fair game.

She opened her sweater drawer, then couldn't decide what to wear because she couldn't decide what to do. *Gotta get out of the house. Zach's not calling and I can't stand waiting.*

Where to go, nine-thirty on a Tuesday night? She pictured herself climbing into Kevin's empty bed, imagined his walking into the bedroom, face alight with pleasure at seeing her there. She rewound the tape and played it again, but this time Kevin arrived with a woman on his arm and his face was definitely not alight. She tried to envision herself perching seductively in a miniskirt on Manny Perez's desk, but this last scenario was so absurd it made her laugh.

"Besides, I don't own a miniskirt," she said as Starshine climbed into the open drawer and began rooting in her sweaters, evidently considering the merits of lambswool and cotton as nesting materials. "No, please, not in my drawer."

She flopped down in her panties and bra on the satin comforter that, through the cat's vigorous claw-sharpenings, had come to resemble something a street person might carry around in a shopping cart. Hands behind her head, she stared at the cracks in her ceiling. Starshine settled on her chest, the cat's pink nose nearly touching her face.

"Something's wrong. I can't believe he'd simply disappear—not when I said it was urgent."

Starshine's scratchy tongue licked her chin.

"I know how it looks. It looks like Zach's decided to blow me off. It also looks like Dana killed her baby."

The cat nipped lightly, a reminder that Cassidy wasn't scratching her cheek the way she was supposed to.

"So what's wrong with this picture?" Her fingernails scraped fur in just the right place.

Her mother would call it stubbornness, a refusal to see the writing on the wall. The therapist in her head would call it denial. But her gut told her that appearances could be deceiving, that the way a picture looked was not necessarily the way it really was. And her gut could not be totally wrong because the snake proved that there was more to this picture than a mother harming her baby and a boyfriend taking off.

❧ ❧ ❧

Twelve-thirty Wednesday afternoon. Outside her bedroom window, a light rain dripped through the few remaining leaves on her maple. Cassidy stared blindly at the paper piled on her desk. The morning had been taken up with clients, but now she was faced with an empty half hour before Laurel was due to arrive.

Her hand went automatically to the phone. She punched up Zach's number at the *Post*, listened to his recorded message, then tried him again at home. *Why doesn't he answer?*

She pulled the phone book off the shelf above her desk and looked up Zach's sister-in-law Kristi. She and Kristi had gotten to know each other after Ryan's death.

"I need to get hold of Zach but he doesn't seem to be answering his phone. Have you heard anything?"

"Is something the matter between . . . . I mean, I guess there must be some kind of problem if you can't reach him." Kristi's bright, flutey voice softened. "Oh, I'm sorry. I always say the wrong thing."

"No, that's okay." Cassidy said, her throat tightening.

"You know how Zach is. He just sort of pops in and out. But if he's not returning . . . . He's such a jerk. It's a shame that you two . . . . I'd like to, you know, punch him out."

"Well, thanks anyway." *Too humiliating. Can't put myself through another call like that.*

221

Almost involuntarily her hand crept back to the phone book and turned to Zach's mother, Mildred Lawrence. *You can't call Mildred. She's hated you ever since Ryan died.*

"This is Cassidy McCabe. I'm calling because . . . ." *Don't say it. Hang up now!* "I wonder if you might know where Zach's keeping himself lately?"

"You sound like one of those Do-you-know-where-your-child-is-tonight? bumper stickers." A short, malicious laugh. "Does this mean your tawdry little affair's run aground? I take it my sneak-thief son's gone into hiding again. Well, good luck, my dear. I can't think of any two people who deserve each other more." Click.

Cassidy slammed down the phone. *What if he's hurt? What if he can't answer because . . . ?* Rubbing the chipped desk corner, she pictured Zach's Marina City condo, beige walls devoid of pictures, black leather furniture, a glass table and two chairs. What if something had happened and nobody knew? The way Zach lived, disconnected from everyone, it could take a long time before anyone noticed he was missing except Cassidy—and she, as his ex-girlfriend, had less credibility than the *National Inquirer*.

If only she had a key. *Damn, you* should *have a key.* She had given Zach hers a month after the relationship officially began, thirty days after he asked her to be patient while he tried, for the first time in his life, to develop a real, as in long-term and committed, relationship. Be patient, let him fumble around with it, but no promises, no guarantees.

She had insisted on celebrating their first-month, sort-of anniversary, so Zach arrived with groceries and took over the kitchen. Together they assembled almond-kiwi-mangoed chicken breasts—well beyond her tuna-salad, peanut-butter-sandwich range. They dined on a candlelit, linen-covered picnic bench, the light jangle of wind-chime music in the background.

She gave him a card that said, "You are so beautiful to me," significant because she had initially considered him rather ordinary in appearance, but now was able to see the strength and character in his face. Accompanying the card was a foil-wrapped box containing her key. Step one toward long-term.

He seemed genuinely pleased, but there were no cards, boxes or keys in return. That night after lovemaking—a quick, fierce going-at-each-other, unlike their usual lingering encounters—she rolled over and to her surprise felt hot tears streaming down her cheeks. After crying herself out, nose plugged and face gritty with salt, she had vowed never to mention his key. And if he didn't want her to have it, to hell with him.

⁊⹁ ⁊⹁ ⁊⹁

At twelve-forty the doorbell rang and she dashed downstairs to answer it. Laurel stood on the steps in a gray mist, head lowered so that all she could see were dark roots blending into blond poufs. Cassidy spoke a few words of greeting, then led her visitor across the porch and into the living room. Laurel's floral scent brought on a twinge of nausea, it reminded her so sharply of the night Cypress disappeared.

Laurel shrugged off a lightweight raincoat that seemed too summery for the day's raw weather. Perching on the edge of Cassidy's paisley sofa, she folded the coat across her lap. Cassidy moved around the glass coffeetable to face her, stepping softly so her heels didn't clatter on the hardwood floor. *Looks as if she'd fly off into little pieces if I so much as raised my voice.*

"Would you like something to drink?" *Coffee, tea or milk,* a hysterical voice mimicked in her head.

Laurel looked up vaguely. Tiny new lines had crimped her mouth and creased the ridge between her brows. "Just water, please."

223

Cassidy fetched ice water, then sank into the small arm-chair next to the sofa. Laurel's knees were locked, her pumps primly aligned. She wore a navy wool suit with high-necked blouse and long gold chain. Courage from overdressing. It reminded Cassidy of her mother's ritual of donning her one and only Marshall Field's dress when PTA meetings forced her to mingle with Doopers, the intact and monied families of Dear Old Oak Park.

"This must be very difficult." Cassidy folded an arm beneath her chest and rested her chin on her hand.

Laurel took a deep breath and started talking. "Ever since her baby disappeared, Dana's been a wreck, barely making it from day to day. Then, on Sunday night, Wayne told her 'bout him and Josie, and things got a whole lot worse. Guess he figured, what with the police knowing and all, Dana was bound to find out eventually. And it'd be better coming from him than somebody else."

Cassidy pictured a red pickup parked next to the restaurant where Josie waited. "Wayne and Josie—they were together?"

"Seems like the weekend Cypress disappeared, the two of 'em were holed up in a motel."

"How did Dana react?"

" 'Bout what you'd expect. She threw a fit, can't say as I blame her. Didn't want either of 'em around, so I've been staying over there all week. The things she was saying . . . . Maybe I'm wrong, hope I'm wrong. But the way she was talking, I got the idea that she's gonna . . . that something terrible's about to happen."

The daylight from the picture window behind the sofa grew steadily grayer. *Room's so gloomy, should've turned lights on ahead of time.* The clammy air and darkening sky made it difficult to fend off the waves of infectious anxiety emanating from Laurel. Cassidy asked, "What did she say?"

"She talked about . . . ." A pause. "I don't know—about not wanting to go on, not being able to face another day. She made a list . . ." Laurel moistened her lips, "of who should get her things."

"You think she's suicidal."

Laurel's faded eyes met hers. "She feels like everyone's betrayed her. First me, then Josie and Wayne. Even you."

Abandoned by her real mom, then her therapist-mom. "The only safe place is a hospital."

"It was so bad that first time. I don't know, I was hoping maybe you could talk to her, talk her out of it. So she didn't have to go back in."

Cassidy gazed downward. Her right hand was clenched around a fistful of fabric, the plum crepe skirt she liked so well. Forcing her hand to open, she smoothed the material against her leg but a circular pucker remained. "I thought she didn't want anything to do with me."

"I could get around her, get her to see you. Will you come? Make her understand that killing herself is no way out?"

Can't take chances with other people's lives. "I'm willing to give it a try. But if I can't change her mind, she needs to be in the hospital." Cassidy leaned forward, ready to rise. "Is this a good time? Would you like to go now?"

"Something else I've gotta tell you." Laurel's frail voice grew hoarse. "What I said before, 'bout my first baby Cypress. It wasn't entirely true." She lowered her head, talked into her lap. "My baby wasn't stolen. It was me. I did it myself."

19

Promises

The room got so quiet Cassidy could detect a whisper of rainslick oozing down the side windows. She asked, "What did you do?"

"I'm not exactly sure how it happened. Cypress'd been crying for hours. I'd done everything I could think of and she just kept on. Then it was like I suddenly woke up. I had my hands around her and she wasn't crying anymore. She was just limp with her head hanging loose, not making any noise at all. Then I remembered how I'd started shaking her . . . . I just couldn't stop." Laurel raised her head and blinked as if coming out of a dream.

Cassidy was aware that the damp chill in the room had gotten sharper. *Damn, why didn't I turn on the heat? Stupid to sit here and freeze just to save a few pennies.* She ought to say something. Laurel needed some kind of response. But the usual words of comfort would have sounded inadequate and trite.

Laurel's voice resumed, "I put her in the cradle and she just lay there, so quiet and still. I kept stroking her, kissing her, saying how sorry I was. I thought sure that any minute she'd come out of it. That she'd open those big brown eyes and give me a smile. But she never moved. So after waiting a long time, I called Ernie and he came home. Said we had to bury her in the garden and tell everyone that she'd been stolen—just like that little boy the year before. And never, ever let anybody know."

Neither spoke for a full minute. Sirens from Austin Boulevard grew louder, then faded away. The screech of a car alarm intruded violently on the house's silence.

Laurel's hands were tightly clasped, her thumb and forefinger rubbing together. "That's why he kept me so close, you see. Watched over me like he did and tried to keep me from overdoing. He thought I wasn't strong enough to handle everyday life. He was always so afraid I'd break down again, like I did that time when she died. When I killed her."

"Everyone thought it was the Satanists? I suppose it was just before Halloween."

Laurel sucked in one cheek. Her flat brown eyes, the same shade as Dana's but without the sparkle, rolled upward to focus on the ceiling. " 'Bout three months before. But we didn't let anybody know till near the end of October. After my baby died I couldn't get myself out of bed for several weeks, and Ernie, he had to get a leave of absence to take care of me. So we told folks I had a bad case of the flu, and Ernie just kept buying baby food on his regular shopping trip, same as if nothing'd happened." Her eyes filled. "Oh God." She lowered her head, raised a blue-veined hand to her forehead to shield them.

Cassidy felt tears sting the back of her own lids. "I can't even imagine what that must've been like."

"It was almost a year later I started wanting another baby. I kept thinking about how I'd do it different. If I could just try again, I knew I'd be a good mother, and that way I could make up for that one horrible mistake. I know this sounds crazy, but I had the idea I'd carry around this terrible curse forever unless I could do it over and get it right."

Leaning back in her chair, Cassidy rubbed her arms to warm them. "Doesn't sound crazy to me."

"Well, it sure did to Ernie. Dead set against it, he was, and I couldn't blame him. He was so scared it would happen again. But inside myself, I *knew* I could do it just perfect. So I went ahead and got pregnant. Jesus, Ernie was pissed—thought he'd never get over it."

Cassidy pictured his contorted face looming over her, the finger with the blackened nail jabbing into the screen. *She's a braver woman than I'll ever be. I'd never deliberately piss Ernie off.*

"After Dana was born, I forgot about naps and television and put my whole self into taking care of her. She was such a happy baby. Didn't cry like that first one. We were so close, sometimes we just melted into each other. I know this isn't true, but in my mind I pretended she was Cypress. Sometimes, when no one else was around, I'd rock her and whisper in her ear that she was my own Cypress come back to me."

Cassidy's head snapped up. "That's why she called her baby 'Cypress.' The name must've come back to her from those warm, early memories."

Laurel's forehead knotted. "I never thought of that."

Although it couldn't have been more than half an hour since Laurel had arrived, the gray light from the window lent a twilight cast to the room. Cassidy had an eerie, hollow feeling, as if they'd been sitting there for hours, off in a dimension of their own, and time had moved on without them. She ran her fingertips across the velvety nap of the chair arm. Clearing her throat, she said, "You've kept your secret so long. I can't help but wonder why you're telling me now."

Laurel sipped her water, then replaced the glass on the coffeetable, carefully setting it inside the same wet ring. She twisted the gold chain around her fingers. "When I was born, my mother died. I killed her, you see, by getting born. And then I killed my first baby. When Dana came along, I went all out to be a good mother, but she still turned bad on me, getting into drugs and sex, going crazy like she did. So you see, what I'm afraid of is . . . " She took another sip, "I'm afraid I've got some kind of bad seed in me that I've passed on to Dana."

Cassidy sat motionless, unbelieving. Gazing into Laurel's eyes, she recognized the flatness as despair. "You think Dana killed her baby."

The creases in her face deepened, lines running from her cheekbones to the corners of her mouth. But her eyes didn't waver.

Cassidy took a long, slow breath. "You wanted me to know because you're afraid Dana did the same thing you did. You're afraid that unless I know the whole story, I won't be able to stop Dana from killing herself."

So much misery. Misery in Laurel's life, misery she had passed on to Dana. Laurel wanted more than anything to rescue her child, but she was too ensnared in the family pattern. So she'd been forced to approach Cassidy, who represented the good mother neither Laurel nor Dana had known. How much had it cost her to come begging to the therapist who'd nearly stolen her place in her daughter's life?

Cassidy sat up straight, making herself return to the present. *Any loose ends, anything else I need to know?* "There's one more thing. What about daycare? Dana attended Miss Marilyn's Kiddie Korner, didn't she?"

Laurel's eyes flickered. "Huh?"

"Did Dana go to daycare or not?"

Laurel gave her head a quick, nervous shake. She looked away. "Ernie wouldn't have it."

What? Ernie never wanted Dana in the first place. Tried to protect Laurel from the stress of mothering. Why the hell wouldn't he want her in daycare?

ᔥ ᔥ ᔥ

Cassidy and Laurel drove together to Josie's two-flat. On the way Laurel said, "Dana doesn't know anything about this. So if you don't mind, I'd like to go up and talk to her myself first."

Pulling up to the curb, Cassidy remained behind the wheel while Laurel went upstairs. She leaned against the door, one arm along the back of the seat, the other looped around the steering wheel, and watched the gray stucco until she got bored. Her gaze bounced to the house next door, which was Oak Parkish to the max. A freshly painted tricolor Victorian, all the scrollwork neatly detailed. Every leaf removed from the well-trimmed grass. A row of orange jack-o'-lantern-faced leaf bags in front of the porch. Three carved pumpkins on the porch ledge, which, no doubt, were conscientiously lit every night.

How can anybody be so anal, so compulsive? Why would anybody want to rake the stupid leaves when a child's been missing twenty-five days?

Glancing back at Josie's porch, she wished she'd bought another bag of peanut butter cups. Her fingers were stiff with cold, her toes numb inside her boots. How long would it take? Of all the faults her mother ever accused her of, impatience topped the list.

She pictured Dana's face, the wounded-spaniel eyes filled with blame. As she began an imaginary conversation aimed at justifying her call to the police, one of the house's two side-by-side doors opened. Josie dashed out to the Toyota and hopped into the passenger seat.

"Laurel said you were here and I just had to come and talk." When they were teachers together, Cassidy had always envied Josie's smooth brown pageboy, so docile, so manageable that it remained neatly in place even when everything around her was in chaos. But today Josie was coming unglued, and it showed in every aspect of her appearance, including her hair. Brown tufts stuck out all over her head, as if she'd styled it with a blow torch.

"What's on your mind, Josie?"

"You know what this is about. I've got to . . . . Oh shit, I don't know why I feel like I have to explain myself, but I do." First time Cassidy had ever heard her swear. Josie pressed both hands against her cheeks, the gesture so clichéd it might have been comic were it not for her stricken expression. "Oh Lord, I've made such a mess of things. I don't know what to do." No chirpiness now. Her voice was hoarse, roughened from too much crying.

"We all make messes sometimes. God knows I do." Cassidy flexed her chilled fingers.

"I didn't. Not before this. I always had to be so damn perfect. Perfect and in control. That was all I had to hang onto when my life and marriage were falling apart." Josie raked her fingers through spiky hair. "I don't know why you even speak to me—I was such a bitch about your divorce. I'm so ashamed of the way I treated you after Kevin took off with that slut. You see, Howard'd been running around forever and that's why I couldn't stand hearing about your asshole husband—because he reminded me of mine."

"It can be pretty threatening to listen to somebody else's divorce when your own axe is about to fall."

"I knew about the other women, but I didn't really. The signs were all there but I was absolutely perfect at ignoring them."

Cassidy nodded. *Same thing you did, kiddo. First Kevin, then Zach.*

Josie squeezed her eyes shut, gave her head a little shake. "But that's not why I need to talk. What I have to tell you about is Wayne. You see, all this time Howard's been out in California, and there was Wayne, right upstairs. We'd sit around at night, drinking wine and discussing Dana. It must seem insane that I could even think about a guy who's twelve years younger than me, involved with my crazy cousin, and a house painter, for Godsake. But Dana'd stopped having sex right after the baby . . . . And I was feeling so lonely and cheated and mad."

"These things happen."

"There'd been this tension between us for a long time. We'd sit across the table at night, and sex was so thick in the air we could almost smell it. But we never said anything, and I felt so sure I could just be my perfect self and rise above it."

"What changed?"

"I was planning to spend the weekend out in Frisco, remember?" Her face crumpled. "A week before the flight, I got this letter from Howard. He said it might be better if I didn't come. He told me he was living with someone else." Her chin dropped; her voice got huskier. "That night, after Dana was asleep, I poured it all out to Wayne."

Talk about your inevitability. Dry forest waiting for a spark.

"He just held me and it felt so incredibly good. Seemed like we were on the verge of spontaneous combustion. Anyway, he suggested that since I was already planning to be gone, we could take that same weekend and spend it together. Guess we both rationalized we could do it just that one time—just once, to help me through the shock—and there'd be no repercussions." She laughed bitterly. "We almost backed out. God, I wish we had. When Wayne told Dana he had to fly home, she got this panic on her face, and Lord, I thought I'd die. But then she said she'd be okay, and I remembered you telling me she was stronger than I realized. And I wanted that weekend so badly."

Cassidy tapped two fingers against the back of the car seat. *Denied herself too long, then she backlashed. That's what happens.*

Josie continued, "It couldn't have been worse. We both felt so damn guilty. Disaster from start to finish."

Cassidy gave her a sisterly smile. "Disaster? You're talking about every relationship I ever had."

"But our misadventures at the romantic Hillside Holiday Inn are irrelevant. Dana's ordeal is the only thing that matters."

Ah, the rescuers of the world. Cassidy slowly shook her head, a dismal, repetitive motion. *Hellbent on solving everybody's problems but their own. And just look who's talking?* "Exactly which part of Dana's ordeal do you claim credit for?" Her voice had an edge to it.

Gray eyes startled, Josie lifted her chin. "I don't see anything to joke about." The teacherly disapproval was back in her voice. "Isn't it obvious? The kidnapping's the worst of it. If Wayne and I were where we were supposed to be, Cypress wouldn't have been taken. The other thing is, now Dana feels like we're all against her. She's almost ready to . . . I mean, it seems like she might . . . I'm so afraid that finding out about Wayne and me is pushing her over the edge."

"You're very greedy with the guilt, aren't you? You want it all for yourself—don't want to share with anybody. Not Laurel, Ernie, me—not even Dana herself."

Josie's eyes widened in confusion. She wiped a hand over her face. "You're trying to tell me something. What is it you're saying?"

Cassidy glanced past Josie's shoulder at the empty porch, suddenly feeling restless. "I still don't get it. Why explain all this to me?" The same question she'd asked Laurel.

Josie's naked face stared through the windshield. "I don't know. Maybe because you've managed to get through your own divorce and straighten out—"

The front door opened and Laurel stepped onto the porch. Cassidy's hand slammed down on the door handle.

❧ ❧ ❧

Laurel said, "She's not happy about it but she agreed to see you. I'll wait down here till you're done."

Cassidy mounted the stairs and knocked lightly on the door at the top. A long moment, then Dana's voice through the wooden panel: "Okay, you can come in."

She lounged on the threadbare sofa, back propped against the arm, knees bent, bare feet flat on the seat. As Cassidy entered the room, she flicked a disinterested look in her direction, then stared off toward the opposite end of the sofa. She wore a plush velour robe, loosely tied at the waist, the bottom hanging open to reveal her legs and panties. The playpen had been removed, the clutter picked up. Containing only the sofa, chair, end table, and television, the room seemed nearly empty. Thick floral air spray partially masked the acrid smell of smoke.

"Hi." Cassidy spoke to the side of her head.

Refusing to acknowledge her, Dana raised a cigarette, inhaled, then puffed out a stream of smoke. Remembering the pride Dana had taken in kicking both cigarettes and drugs, Cassidy sighed inwardly.

Dana tapped her cigarette against the heaping, toilet-bowl ashtray on the floor and said, "Well?"

The room offered two places to sit: the opposite end of the sofa, which put them face to face; or the armchair right-angling the sofa, which put her face to Dana's back. *You sit on the sofa, you'll be pursuing, she'll probably distance. You sit in the chair, she gets to decide.*

Cassidy eased into the armchair. "I'd like for us to talk. But obviously I can't force you. If you don't want me here, I'll leave."

Swinging her feet to the floor, Dana sat up. Her features had settled into a sullen expression but at least she'd moved into Cassidy's line of sight. She said, "This isn't going to do any good, okay?" Her voice held the same kind of flatness Cassidy had seen in Laurel's eyes.

"Then why agree to see me?"

Dana mimicked nastily, "One part of me hopes that it will."

"You've got every right to be angry."

Dana took a long pull on her cigarette, threw her head back onto the sofa rim, and blew a stream of smoke toward the ceiling. "Yeah, lot of good that does. Sure, I've got every right—right to be pissed. Pissed and fucked . . . ." Her vocabulary failed her. "But I'm not—that is, not really. What I mean is, I'm not even *angry* like you therapists always say. Well, only a little."

"What does that mean?"

Slowly straightening her head, she met Cassidy's gaze. Her eyes had shifted to dark chocolate, the milky lightness extinguished. But steady. Calm and resolved. Too calm.

Worse than I thought. Presuicide phase. Sense of relief people get when the decision's made, end's at hand.

"Are you planning to hurt yourself?" Cassidy asked matter of factly.

"Knew you'd ask that," she gloated. "The first question, it's always the same. 'Are you thinking about it?' The second, they always say, 'what's the plan?' And the third, what they say is, 'when and how?' You social workers—you must all've taken the same class, know what I mean?"

"So, what's the plan?"

Dana wiggled her toes against the mud-colored carpet, her toenails the same bright pink as the tips of her fingers. "I'm gonna fill the bathtub clear to the top, nice and hot. And I'm gonna—I mean, I'll pour in lots and lots of bubble bath." Her voice had regained its lilt. "Then I'll get myself a bottle of wine—bottle with a cork in it maybe, not that Gallo junk I usually drink." Taking a drag on her cigarette, Dana draped her left arm along the rim of the sofa.

Cassidy said, "You've got this down pat, haven't you?"

"Then I'm gonna climb in, just let the water splash on the floor, know what I mean? And I'll play all my favorite songs—I mean, the sad ones. And after I drink the wine and listen to the music, then I'm gonna slash my wrists, all right? And watch the water turn red. Or maybe pink. Pink bubbles, that'd be pretty, don't you think? But you're probably gonna say I'm being unrealistic again, hoping for pink when people've got so much blood in 'em, there's no way the water wouldn't go red. Maybe brown even, like dried blood."

She really wants to. Ripples of fear ran from the top of Cassidy's head down to her toes. "Why so eager?"

Dana shrugged, her face settling into deep grooves of pain. "You think I killed her, don't you?"

Cassidy searched inside, both mind and heart. At last she said, voice unequivocal, "No, I don't believe you'd ever harm Cypress."

Dana sat up straighter, a flicker of something—hope?—in her eyes.

Cassidy said, "I realize you've got good reason for wanting to give up. Your child's disappeared—the worst possible nightmare. Then you've got all those people out there thinking you did it. And on top of that, everybody you ever counted on has let you down. Me included."

Dana's face twisted into a fierce scowl. "I really trusted you, all right? When Mom gave up on me, when she—after the hospital, when she kicked me out, I could understand that. I mean, I sort of drove her to it, and besides, she never could, you know, stand up to Dad. But you were—I thought you were different. Always seemed like you were strong enough, you wouldn't let anybody push you around. You were—I thought you really cared." Her eyes filled; she swiped them with the back of her hand.

"Why do you think I called the police?"

"How should I know?"

Cassidy was silent.

"You called them—it was because you thought . . . ." Her hands fluttered vaguely. "You thought I killed Cypress. You never—I mean, you didn't really believe me. When I had that flashback, okay? You thought maybe I was going crazy again. And then, when I said I was gonna be punished, you thought I was being paranoid, didn't you? I know you felt sorry for me. Maybe you even—maybe you did care. But you didn't believe me."

A lead weight gathered in Cassidy's stomach. *Know how she feels. Same way I felt when Zach wrote that story. Why was I so hard on him? What I did to Dana—it was just as bad.* "I screwed up." Her mouth was dry. "I *thought* you wouldn't hurt Cypress. My gut said you wouldn't. But my gut's been wrong before. And since I wasn't a hundred percent sure, I broke my promise and called the police—to protect myself as much as anything. But I've had time to think it through, and now I *know* my instinct's right. You didn't harm Cypress. I was wrong to call the police. I wish I could've done better."

Dana fiddled with the belt on her robe. Thick lashes fluttering, she glanced up shyly, a painful reminder of Cypress. "Now that I've said it—all that stuff I was mad about—it doesn't seem so bad."

"God knows I've made mistakes, but that doesn't mean I don't care about you."

"Yeah, I guess I can understand that. 'Cause I did a lot of bad shit to Mom and that didn't—well, I still loved her, no matter what. It's just that, what with all these people thinking I killed my baby . . . Seems like there must be something wrong with me, like I'm bad or something. Nobody'd ever imagine you or Josie hurting anyone, know what I mean? But everybody thinks— they're all so sure I did it." She stared helplessly at Cassidy, her large doe-eyes running over.

"You really think you're bad?"

She lowered her chin. "Must be. Drove Mom almost crazy, didn't I? Fucked up taking care of Cypress. And now—now my baby's gone. She wouldn't be gone—nobody could've taken her—if I'd been a good enough mother, okay?"

"You playing that game again? You say something mean about yourself and your mother says you're the best little girl in the world?"

"You never play it right." Her childlike voice.

"You love Cypress?"

"With all my heart."

"If you love your daughter with all your heart—the way your mother loves you—could you really be so bad?"

"I don't know. It's all so confusing. Maybe not."

The door squeaked open and Laurel's shaggy blond head poked around it. "Am I interrupting anything?"

Cassidy tried to imagine what it must be like for Laurel to wait downstairs. Obviously, she hadn't been able to stand it and so had created an excuse to come up. Not being able to wait was something Cassidy could understand.

"I'll just be a minute." Laurel carried a tray with coffee and a plate of cookies into the room. "Just put this down and scoot on out of the way."

"Jeeze, Mom," Dana said.

Interesting triangle. Laurel, who thinks Dana killed her baby because that's what she did. Dana, who considers her mother a saint, herself a fuck-up. And you—the therapist who's supposed to be Mother Theresa and fix everything. What a set-up.

Laurel said, "I thought it'd be nicer if you girls had something to sip. More hospitable." She looked around blankly for a place to put the tray.

"I'll take care of it." Cassidy removed the tray from her hands and set it on the television.

"Guess I've got bad timing." Laurel retreated, closing the door behind her.

"Kind of hard, picking up where we left off." Cassidy sat back down.

Dana nodded.

"Seems like you just agreed that if you really do love Cypress so much you must not be all bad."

"I guess."

"Would you be willing to give up this idea of killing yourself?"

Dana dropped her face into her hands, her long, wavy hair sliding forward to shield her. "It hurts too much."

"Losing Cypress?"

"Uh huh."

"You want to tell me about it?"

Her muffled voice filtered through the thick curtain of hair. "Every day when I wake up, I wanna die. There's this huge, empty place right inside me—I mean, it's like a giant vacuum that just sucks, it sucks up everything. And my mind, it keeps going round and round. I never stop thinking 'bout her. Never stop wanting her back."

"What would it be like for your mother if you killed yourself?"

"I dunno . . . Never thought about it."

"She thinks about you every day. What would it be like for her?"

"Bad, I guess."

"What about Wayne and Josie? And me? How do you think I'd feel?"

Silence from behind the fawn-colored hair.

"You want to hear how I'd feel?"

Dana raised her head, pushed her hair behind her ears. "You're just trying to make me feel guilty," she said, irritation in her voice. "I always hate it when Mom does that."

"I'm trying to keep you from doing to others what was done to you. Losing a child is the worst pain in the world. But it doesn't give you the right to hurt other people or be so damn selfish."

"You mean, I've just gotta go on?" Her voice trembled. "I don't think I can stand it."

"Yes you can. You have to." Cassidy remembered how bad it had been when Kevin left, and bad again, now that Zach was gone. And knew that what she felt was nothing compared to the sorrow Dana experienced. *I can't say—"maybe the police will find her." Dana knows who took her. She wouldn't have made up that Curly story otherwise. Considering she knows more than I do, I can't pretend to offer hope.*

Cassidy tilted her head to one side. "You just have to keep on going, no matter how much it hurts. Because you're not a bad person. And you don't really want to hurt the people who love you—even though we've all hurt you."

Dana sighed deeply, but Cassidy could see a change in her face, a realignment in the direction of resignation and letting go.

Flexing her shoulders, Cassidy said, "Now, how about we shelve this pink bubble fantasy and get to work on the problem?" Dana pulled her knees up tight against her chest, wrapped her arms around them, and giggled. "I feel kind of silly wearing this robe in the middle of the day."

"Why don't you go find a T-shirt to put on?"

Dana hopped up and disappeared into the bedroom. While she was gone, Cassidy glanced around at the newly waxed end table, freshly scrubbed windows, tidily dusted photos on the shelf above the sofa. *Laurel trying to catch up on her mothering? Josie doing penance? Dana creating an orderly stage for her final appearance?* Not that it mattered. Regardless of whose handiwork, it had more the effect of sterility than sanitation. With the debris of daily life removed, the childless-ness of the room hit her full force.

Returning in jeans and an extra-large T, Dana plopped down on the sofa and folded her legs beneath her. "Okay, what's next?"

"Do I have a promise you won't do anything to hurt yourself?"

She grimaced. "Do I have to?"

Cassidy waited.

"I promise, okay?" Leaning her head back to gaze at the ceiling, she crossed her arms over her chest, hands resting on opposite shoulders. "But what've I got—I mean, what's there to live for without my baby?"

"Tell me what happened."

Straightening her head, she shot Cassidy a baleful look. "Now it's your turn, all right? You gotta promise. And this time, no weasling. This time, you gotta keep it."

"Not talk to the police?" *Who's got her so scared? One of those robes from the past? Somebody I know?*

"Not to anyone. I won't say a thing—not one word—unless you promise, I mean, *really* promise—not to tell."

You can't! We're talking a child's life here. You're legally, ethically bound. "But what if the police really need to know?"

Dana's face closed. "All right, just forget it, okay?"

She's shut herself completely off. I try to convince her, she'll just dig in deeper. Cassidy heard the clock tick on the wall behind her. Through narrow windows on either side of the television she saw a glimmer of afternoon sun penetrating the overcast sky. The sound of footsteps below reminded her that Josie and Laurel were waiting.

"If I promise, you'll tell me what happened?"

Dana crossed her arms and stared stubbornly at the blank television screen.

If I don't promise, I won't stand a chance in hell of finding Cypress.

If I do promise, I might be able to find her—but how can I possibly get her back all on my own?

20

Daycare

"I think leaving the police out is a big mistake." She looked at Dana's stony face again and sighed. "All right, I promise."

Dana's large, solemn eyes gazed into Cassidy's. "This is really—I mean, I'm really scared to tell you." Her voice, so tough and unyielding a moment before, sounded once again like a ten-year-old's. "Scared—scared you won't believe me. Scared you'll think I screwed up . . . just scared, okay?"

Cassidy touched her knee. "This time I'm going to try very hard not to let you down."

Dana took a deep breath. "It started off just like I said, all right? I got, well I got a little drunk—that's 'cause I was so nervous about being alone. Around midnight I was feeling—feeling woozy and figured I'd better, you know, stop. So I checked on Cypress like I always do. She was there, asleep in her crib, right where I put her. And then I just, I went to bed."

Dana scrounged in the sofa cushions for her cigarettes, then lit up. Closing her eyes, she pulled in a lungful of smoke, shuddered slightly, and blew it out through her nostrils. "Next thing I know, the phone's ringing. I picked it up and . . . Jesus, this is—it's hard to talk about. Anyway, what I heard was, there was this voice and it said . . . ." Her own voice dropped into a husky cadence. "We've taken Cypress. Whether she lives or dies is up to you. Tell anyone about this phone call, and she'll die, a virgin sacrifice, on Satan's altar. Keep your secret, tell no one, and she will be raised as Satan's hand-maiden. Just remember, Satan hears every word coming from your mouth, every thought passing through your mind. His darkness is om . . . om-something or other."

"Omigod!" Cassidy's hand clutched the base of her throat.

"When I saw . . . ." Dana's breath caught. "I mean, when I saw Cypress was really gone—they really had her—I sort of, I lost it, know what I mean? Just picked up the phone and dialed your number, wasn't even thinking. Then you said you were coming over, and I knew I had to—well, I had to get hold of myself. Had to keep my mouth shut. No matter what happened, I had to remember one thing—not to tell anybody about that phone call. So I said Curly took her." Pressing a fist against her cheek, Dana nibbled her little finger.

"All this time, you've had to keep your secret—even with people thinking you killed her. I don't know how you did it."

Dana squeezed her eyes shut, lashes beaded with tears. "That's one of the reasons I was gonna, well, you know. Take that bubble bath. I was afraid I couldn't go on just holding it in."

Cassidy replayed the whole scenario in her mind. "I wonder how they knew you'd be alone? Remember that time you called to tell me both Wayne and Josie were leaving for the weekend? Your voice sounded distant, like a bad connection. Maybe they bugged your phone, then removed the bug when they took Cypress."

"Maybe. A few days before that, somebody snatched my purse. They could've, you know, grabbed the key."

Cassidy stood abruptly, paced over to the window, and leaned both hands against the frame. A narrow band of light slanted through low gray clouds. "There has to be some way to find her." She turned toward Dana. "You do believe she's still alive, don't you?"

Dana's face drained. She wrapped the end of her T-shirt around one hand. "I think about it all the time. I see these flashes—what I see is, those guys in robes slashing that poor little puppy. Then I see Cypress, she's on that table instead, and the knife—it's slicing down. That's what—I know it's coming. But not yet. It hasn't happened yet. I can feel it. Feel it here." She pressed an open hand against her stomach. "If she were dead, I'd know."

"Then let's figure out how to stop it. What about the voice on the phone? Male or female? Anything distinctive?"

Dana looked at her helplessly. "Nothing. Just a voice, just a kind of whisper."

"Maybe we can track down how these people got to you way back when you were a kid. You had to be in some kind of group. There's a part of you that knows what that group was. Don't try to remember. Just sit quietly and allow the part to tell you."

Dana sat motionless, eyes closed, for more than a minute. When she finally opened them, her face was chalk white. "It's just . . . I can't get it. It's so close, know what I mean? But it won't come."

"What's close?"

"Well, they're—all I get are these flashes. Big guys in robes. This group of, you know, kids—always the same ones. Five or six of us. A large room. Table with—it's got this red cloth, and there's an upside down cross. And what they're doing . . . ." She paused, then resumed in a whisper. "They're making us do these, you know, these nasty things. And taking pictures." Her face puckered in disgust. "That's just about— that's all I come up with."

"Does the name 'Miss Marilyn's Kiddie Korner' mean anything?"

Dana focused intently. "I get some kind of bad feeling, but no actual memory."

"That's all right. Maybe later." Stepping in front of her, Cassidy lightly massaged her shoulders.

Wrapping her arms around Cassidy's waist, Dana buried her face in her bosom. "Oh, Cass, they're gonna kill her . . . and I can't—I just can't bear it."

Cassidy stroked Dana's hair. Reassuring words surfaced in her mind and she wanted very badly to say them—for herself as well as Dana. But to palm off easy lies would be a cheat, and they both would know it.

🙦 🙦 🙦

By the time Cassidy left, the sun had given up its struggle to break through and rain was trickling again. She let Laurel off at her car, then trudged up to her back stoop, where a cranky and corpulent cat huddled against the door. Too pre-occupied to conduct a paw check, she allowed Starshine to precede her into the house. The cat stepped daintily across the threshold and made straight for her post on the counter, leaving a wet, gloppy trail behind.

Cassidy grabbed but Starshine, bulky though she was, eluded her. The cat ran the length of the counter, picked her way across the stove, then lunged to the floor. Cassidy attempted a doorway tackle, but the calico squeaked through and sped across the hardwood floor toward the upstairs bed-room. After tracking her to her lair in the far corner under the desk, Cassidy got down on hands and knees and dragged her out. She clutched the drenched cat against her lambswool sweater, twisting her head to avoid the musty, wet-fur smell. Carrying her downstairs, Cassidy shut her in the basement. From behind the closed door came a piercing lament that, in pathos and volume, exceeded Madame Butterfly's swan song.

After changing clothes and mopping mud, she let the unrepentant but thoroughly washed cat out of prison. Returning to the bedroom, she checked the answering machine's one tantalizing blink.

"Cass, honey, it was just wonderful having you and Gran for dinner last Saturday—or was it two weeks ago?" Her mother's voice, which normally ranged from whiny to sharp, actually verged on bubbly. "I've been meaning to call but somehow the time just gets away. That's what you always used to say and I could never understand, and now I'm doing it. But the reason I called is to tell you about our Halloween party. Can you believe it? It's going to be at Roland's—just a week away. Everybody's wearing a costume. You and Gran just have to come. And Zach. I was so sorry he couldn't make it to our dinner, but now you can bring him to the party."

Beep.

You come as the Queen of Hearts, I'll be the Old Maid. God, I hate it that I'm so spiteful.

She stood and looked out the window. Only four-thirty, already the gray light was waning. A few yellow leaves still clung to the maple by the corner of her house but most had fallen. The Steins' and the Roberts' leaves were piled into huge mounds in the gutter awaiting village pick-up, but her yard was still thickly covered with a sodden layer of brown and gold, leprosy of the lawn.

Starshine has her blissful pregnancy. Mom, her madcap romance. Even Gran, her sexy tattoo. What've I got? A notorious jerk. Said he wanted to work on commitment, bullied me into investigating Satanism, now—just when I need him the most—he's pulled his famous disappearing act.

Her mind was recalcitrant. The harder she tried to focus on Cypress, the more she veered off onto Zach. By now he might have collected all kinds of leads that would help in her search if only she could talk to him. *Can't do this alone.* A few days ago, she'd berated herself for not getting help when she needed it. Now, she was desperate for help and couldn't get it.

She dialed Zach's condo and the machine clicked on. *Moved in with his new babe, or what?* She said to the recorder, "Something terrible has happened. I've got to talk to you. There's a life at stake here." Click.

She curled up on the bed, fully dressed, under a ragged comforter that smelled like cat.

      🐚 🐚 🐚

Awaking early the next morning, she looked out at bright sunlight streaming through her maple's sparse gold leaves. As if to make up for yesterday's gloom, the weather had turned warm, almost springlike again. She poured coffee and took it out on the porch. Lofty elms arched across the street, most of their leaves still attached. The keening wail of a siren picked up volume, then died away.

Her new neighbor Cal Roberts, attaché case in hand, strode north on the sidewalk in front of her house. He was headed toward the intersection, where a right turn on Briar would take him to an Austin Boulevard bus stop.

A chorus of children's voices, "Daddy, Daddy, Daddy," brought him to a stop and spun him around. Three children at stair-step heights and one fluffy dog rushed toward him.

Carrie, dressed in school clothes, handed him a paper bag. "You forgot your lunch," she said in a motherly voice.

Chip, wearing baseball cap and jammies, grabbed his father's hand. "Me too, take me too."

The smallest girl, also in pajamas, wrapped her arms around one leg.

Dad squatted, eye level with the middle child, and pulled them all into a bear hug. The white dog yapped and ran in circles. "Wish I could take you all to work." *Am I watching the Disney channel by mistake?* After removing arms and patting heads, he pulled the boy's cap down over his face and started off again. As he reached the corner, he turned to wave one more time. "Bye kids, see you tonight."

A dull ache in her chest, Cassidy dragged upstairs to her bedroom. *Where did I go wrong? Oh, right—I hooked up with Kevin and Zach.* She sat at her desk and called directory assistance, then jotted a number on the back of last month's unopened electric bill. Pushing heavily on the pen, she retraced the number several times. *Can't do this.* She stood, then forced herself down again, picked up the phone and dialed.

"John Hammersmith, please."

"I'm sorry, he's not at his desk."

"Could you page him? This is urgent."

"I'll see what I can do."

Three minutes later a male voice came on the line, "Hammersmith speaking."

"You're Zach Moran's editor, is that right?" Starshine took several moments to prepare, then launched herself at the desk. She made it to the top, but just barely.

"He's in my department, yes." Guarded.

"My name's Cassidy McCabe, a close friend of Zach's. I've been trying to reach him for nearly two weeks—something really important—and I can't get hold of him. Is he in the office now?" Starshine poked papers with her nose, perhaps wondering if a pile of bills might not provide her kittens an auspicious start in life.

"Let me give you his direct number."

"I've got his number. I've been leaving messages for days. This is really urgent. Just tell me, is he at work now? Has he been coming in regularly?"

"What did you say the nature of your business was?"

"Um, we're planning to be married soon. Now please—"

"I can't say if he's in at the moment or not. Your best bet would be to leave a message on his machine." Sitting erect and alert, Starshine snagged the phone cord in her teeth and chewed contentedly. The look in her eyes seemed to say, "Why do you do this to yourself?"

"Please, I'm afraid something may have happened. I have to know—has he been in the office this week?"

"I'm sorry, I really can't get involved in Zach's personal life. I'm sure there's nothing to worry about. We've seen him around. Whatever's going on between you two, when he gets ready, he'll give you a call."

She slammed down the phone. *What does that mean? That he's been out of the office for a couple of weeks but his boss isn't about to say so? Or that he's sitting at his desk and his editor's protecting him from a pushy ex-girlfriend?* Waves of embarrassment ran through her. Starshine's moist green eyes conveyed sympathy.

                          🐦 🐦 🐦

Standing on the sidewalk in front of the boarded-up daycare center, Cassidy raised a hand to shield her eyes from the sun as she gazed at the dilapidated Victorian. If only she could stare it down, the way she sometimes did clients, stare it into revealing its secrets. The yard surrounding the house was ankle-deep in trash, a patchy layer of dry leaves covering the debris.

It was one of those perfect fall days, the temperature almost balmy. She turned her back to the glare, raised her eyes, and focused off into a sapphire infinity. Straining to see farther, she felt as if she was looking directly into the eyes of God. *Sun's out, sky's blue, I start thinking God's so close I can almost touch Him. The idea of Satanic rituals, killing babies as remote and unbelievable as a Friday-the-Thirteenth movie. My reality—changeable as the weather.*

She glanced at her watch. One-thirty already. A waste of time standing in front of this poor, sad, wreck of a used-to-be painted lady. Next client at four. Less than two hours to find out what had happened in this house. So far everyone she had talked to denied knowing that the daycare even existed, and everyone was lying.

But someone will talk. All I have to do is keep asking till I find one person willing to speak up.

The Victorian was located on a street of elderly houses ranging in upkeep from knee-high grass to neat and trim. Nobody out raking leaves, no bikes or toys in the yards. Cassidy had a sense of secrecy and collusion, as if the other houses were pretending their disreputable neighbor didn't exist. A hedge surrounded the lawn of the colonial to the north. An ancient face peered down from the Georgian to the south. All had covered windows, their visages closed and unapproachable. They reminded her of what it had been like after moving out of Gran's bungalow. Her mother, who got an apartment for the two of them, had insisted on keeping the blinds shut so no one could see into their gloomy cave of a home.

Cassidy crunched through the trash, circling around behind the Victorian with the hope that the backside of the block would yield more activity than the front. *This is avoidance. Doesn't matter that you hate knocking on doors—just do it.*

A coach house stood at the rear of the Victorian's deep lot, its front facing the opposite direction. Behind the small house, a shriveled black woman balanced on a rickety stepladder to clean the gutter. *Begin with her? Catch her by surprise, the whole works might collapse. Last thing I want is to topple an old lady off her ladder.*

Cassidy continued full circle around the Victorian, then approached a neighboring house. During the next hour, she was talked to through one-inch cracks, shooed off porches, told to mind her own business, and threatened with the police. Finally she retraced her steps, plodding through layers of litter to get to the coach house, the possibility of precipitating an old woman's fall now seeming less of a worry than it had before.

The woman was no longer working in back, so Cassidy traipsed around the small garage to the front yard. Parked in the driveway was a shiny black Ford, fifties vintage. On the other side of the Ford the elderly woman stood in front of the house fussing with her ladder. *Thank God, at least her feet are on the ground. Not so far to fall.*

At a yard's distance, Cassidy halted and said, "Can I talk to you a minute?"

The woman folded the ladder's paint-bucket shelf, then pushed the braces up into a slightly bent position. She grasped the step-side with both hands and eased it backward, allowing it to fall against the house as it collapsed. Once it was propped solidly in place, she turned to study Cassidy through thick, wire-rimmed glasses that magnified her rheumy eyes.

Glad I dressed down. Her Kmart jeans, faded T, and discount sneakers were almost in the same league as the black woman's overalls, flannel shirt, and ragged tennis shoes, one of which had a hole so wide her big toe stuck out.

The woman asked in a creaky voice, "What you wanna talk about?"

"That house in front, didn't it used to be a daycare?"

She pulled back her frail shoulders and crossed her arms.

"Reason I'm asking, my sister went to that daycare. We only lived in town a little while but we both remember her going to Miss Marilyn's Kiddie Korner."

The bleary eyes squinted. "Daycare started, a lotta kids went there." Turning away, she planted her hands against the edges of the ladder and put her weight into a mighty shove. The stepladder slid sideways to the ground, crashing thunderously. Cassidy expected to see it sink into a pile of splintered wood, but amazingly, when the rattling stopped, it was still in one piece.

"I'm here because my sister needs help. She's been having these nightmares, you see. And they always take place at the daycare center." She folded her arms, pulled them up tight beneath her chest. "A few grown-ups are there, and five or six kids. Something terrible happens, then she wakes up screaming. But she never remembers exactly what it was. And I thought . . . ." *Life imitating soap operas.* "Well, what I wanted to ask is, why did the daycare close down? And Miss Marilyn, where'd she go? And the kids . . . you have any idea what might've happened to them?"

The tiny woman, so short the top of her kinky head was eye level, stepped closer and shoved her small, wrinkled face up into Cassidy's. "Nobody at that daycare ever did nuthin' to any of those kids," she snapped.

"Then you know something about the center?"

"Course I do. Know everything about it." With bone-aching slowness, she stooped to lay the ladder on its back, then pushed the rung side down flat against it.

"Can I give you a hand?"

"I can manage." Straightening, she rubbed the small of her back. "Thank the Lord, the gutters're done for one more year. The kids, they yell at me 'cause I don't get 'em over to help. But I figure, time comes I can't do it myself, that's time for me to feed the worms. No point taking up space if you can't be of any use."

Woman after my own heart. "Would you be willing to tell me about the center?"

"Why not? Those low-life white folks never shoulda got away with shutting it up in the first place." The woman bent over to pick up one end of the ladder, so stiff and wobbly Cassidy felt a sympathetic pang in her own back. She grabbed the other end, and they hauled it into the garage, then ambled out to stand in the drive.

"Well . . . ." The old woman rested her rear against the car's fender. "Reason I know all about it is, I was Miss Marilyn's nanny practically from the day she was born. My husband and me, we lived here in the coach house and I took care of Miss Marilyn—Miss Merrie, we called her, 'count of her sunny disposition. And my old man, he tended the garden. The missus, she treated us like part of the family. So when she passed on, this little ol' house got left to me."

Cassidy glanced around at the small white frame. The paint had a few chips, the lawn a few weeds, but the place was generally well kept. "Looks good. Better than mine."

The stern mouth softened. "Not so good as it used to, but I do what I can. Anyway, after her mama died, Miss Merrie come home to open her daycare, and this little ol' town just couldn't get enough of it. The highfalutin' folks, those that got theirselves a little money, they said Apple Creek gettin' its own daycare was gonna turn this place into a first rate town. And the mothers, they just plain needed somebody to take care of the kids. Miss Merrie and the town fathers had theirselves a good ol' honeymoon for 'bout six months. Then ol' Galen followed her up from Atlanta, and the whole thing come crashing down."

21

Rosebud

"Galen?" Cassidy moved around so she didn't have to squint into the sun and leaned against the Ford.

"Her boyfriend. Big as a football player, black as coal. Black man, lost an eye in 'Nam. Guess I should say African-American but I'm too damn old to keep changing the words. Anyway, the town just hated it, and I don't know what they hated worse—black man and white woman living in sin, Galen not working and letting his woman support him, or Galen sayin' out loud that pills and pot oughta be just as legal as beer and wine. Once Galen moved in, the town fathers wanted both of 'em out, fast as possible."

"Seems like it'd be easy to put a daycare center out of business. If the families took their kids out, Miss Marilyn couldn't keep going, could she?"

"A bunch of 'em yanked their kids out quicker 'n you could take a piss. But there were some mothers, 'specially the single ones, that needed a place for their kids, and they couldn't just quit. Enough kept comin' she was able to limp along."

What would a therapist say about Miss Marilyn? Codependent? Woman who loves too much?

"And Miss Merrie, she was stubborn from the day she was born. This is what she told me: 'We're not doing nuthin' wrong. We love each other and we got a right to live our lives the way we want. Galen never goes near those kids, and I'm a trained preschool teacher. Those ol' farts, they got nuthin' to complain about.' "

"But I guess that wasn't the end of it." Cassidy ran her hand across the Ford's sleek top, amazed that anybody could keep a car so clean. She'd never lean against the Toyota.

"One man in particular, name of Ernie Voss, took on a mission to get rid of 'em. Most purely spiteful person I ever knowed, black or white. Put together this white trash group and launched a campaign that woulda done the Klan proud. Spread rumors Miss Merrie was feeding the kids drugs. Threatening letters, rocks through windows. Even burned a cross. You see that corner over there? Firebombing, that was. Did everything they could to torture Miss Merrie and Galen into quitting, and they had both of 'em 'bout scared out of their wits."

"My God! How did she manage to hang on?"

"She just kept saying, 'I won't let 'em run me out of my own town.' Went to the minister of one of those whitebread churches—what's-his-name, Halsey, who's 'sposed to be so liberal. But he caved in to the V.I.P.s in his congregation. Police chief warn't no better. Mayor leaned on him so he just kind of left it alone."

A chill ran down Cassidy's spine as she stared at the scorched corner. *This is not a story with a happy ending.* "So," her words came out scratchy, "what happened?"

"Well, ol' Galen, he never was too stable, and I guess all the pressure just pushed him over the edge. One night he took his gun and shot her and him both. Miss Merrie crawled down from the upstairs bedroom 'most all the way to the door. That's where I found her the next day, on the floor in the front hall." Her voice grew hoarse. "Worst part is, I was right here and didn't know nuthin' about it. Loved that girl like my own, I did. Been happy to die for her."

After a moment of silence, Cassidy cleared her throat. "I've asked several people and they all act like they never heard of the daycare center."

"I think they're all just so ashamed of theirselves. First few days, everybody was buzzin'. I heard tell some of 'em were bragging 'bout what they got away with, but that didn't last too long. The mayor, he didn't want no outside investigation, so the word come down that folks should keep their mouths shut. Some ol' honcho even managed to keep it out of the papers. I guess they all convinced theirselves—if they acted like it never happened, they wouldn't have to feel guilty. One time I actually seen that low-life Ernie standing out front with a sick look on his face, so I guess even he didn't feel so good about it in the end."

Pushing away from the car, Cassidy examined the small, wizened face: skin weathered, nose broad and flat, dark eyes magnified through the lenses of her glasses. The old woman's expression struck her as peaceful, despite the terrible story she'd just told. "How could you stand it, that the town destroyed those two people and nothing was ever done about it?"

"First off, I couldn't." She straightened and started tottering in the direction of the front door. "S'cuse me, I gotta go pee." As she moved toward the porch, Cassidy inched along beside her. "Spent 'bout a year grinding my teeth, madder 'n I'd ever been before. Used to be, I couldn't understand those militant blacks. My white missus done okay by me. But after Miss Merrie died, I had feelings of hate inside me for the first time. Wanted to get myself a machine gun and shoot 'em all down—minister, mayor, police chief, 'specially that bastard Ernie. But after a lot of talkin' to my own pastor, lot of prayin', I finally figured it out." She climbed the steps of the small wooden porch and reached for the doorknob.

"Figured what out?"

"We all got a lot of meaness in us. Even Miss Merrie, when she went after bullies, she could be mean herself. So the way it goes is, different things bring out the meaness in different people. Take Ernie Voss. Made him wet his pants, it did, thinking 'bout that big black cock poking inside that white girl. Only real difference between folks is how they act when the meaness strikes 'em. Me, I never did buy that machine gun, so I guess I just think better of myself than ol' Ernie does."

She pushed the door open. Cassidy lay a hand on the washed-out flannel sleeve. "Wait a minute. Isn't it possible Galen could've gotten those kids off alone and—"

The watery eyes bestowed a look of pure disdain as the woman crept through the door and closed it behind her.

ð ð ð

When she arrived home at three-fifty, Carla was waiting in her car at the curb. Cassidy dashed upstairs to change and discovered the red light blinking once. *Gotta be Zach. He couldn't not call after I left that life and death message.*

"I tracked down that florist you asked about," Gran's voice boasted gleefully. "Don't you think I'd make a crackerjack detective? Next time you and your boyfriend take on a case, you'll have to let me be your official assistant. Anyway, that shop on the corner of Madison and East, it used to be *The Rosebud*. Only it changed owners a few years back and the new guy renamed it. You want more information, you can check out the old owner, Ursula Kronos. Last anybody heard, she had herself a condo in Forest Park. Mabel didn't know too much about her, except to say she's a little weird. So, aren't you proud of me? Oh, and by the way, I've got an envelope full of cartoons you can pick up next time you're over."

Well, isn't Ursula a busy little bee? Baking zucchini bread, stalking her therapist, arranging an occasional bouquet. Wonder if she might've stashed away a robe or two along with the cages of snakes in her condo?

৵ ৵ ৵

Later that night, when her last client was gone, Cassidy stood in front of the calendar hanging on the waiting room wall. She rubbed her arms against the cold air leaking in under her back door. *October twenty-ninth.* Starshine bumped her ankles and wriggled between her legs, begging for food, but she scarcely noticed.

All the kids sacrificed on Halloween. She pictured a clearing in the woods, cloth-covered table in the center, Cypress laid out on the table.

৵ ৵ ৵

At ten-thirty the next morning, Cassidy marched up to the door of number 6210 in the plushly carpeted hallway of the Gold Coast Regency. During the three years since her divorce, she had, up until now, refused to visit Kevin at any of his ten different addresses. Straightening her shoulders, she punched the bell.

He opened wide and pulled her into a bear hug. "Couldn't believe it when you called, darlin'. Never thought to see your bonny face at my door."

I can't believe it either. Can't believe I'm doing what I'm doing.

She snuggled into the thick blue velour of his Jovan-scented robe, allowing herself a moment to enjoy the solid comfort of his large body. Looking up into his sunny blue eyes, she caught a whiff of something else. Mouthwash or alcohol? *He taken to drinking beer for breakfast?*

"So, love, what's up? What could possibly have induced you to step foot in my abode, considering what a starchy spine you've always had."

"Me? Starchy? You had it your own way every time."

"Not after that steel-trap mind of yours snapped shut."

Only took me ten years too long to snap it. She pulled away from the blue-velour arms and headed toward what appeared to be a leather beanbag chair, Nieman-Marcus version. She sank into an amoeba-like blob that molded itself to her body as if intending to ingest her. Kevin sprawled on a kidney-shaped loveseat across from her. Wan light from an east facing window lent a cold cast to the black and white room. Making a quick appraisal, she noted that the lopsided smile seemed forced, the periwinkle eyes uneasy. He'd shaved off the mustache. *Must've recovered from his feeling-old spell.*

Cocking her head, she said brightly, "I've decided to take you up on your offer. You can move back any time."

His eyelid twitched. "Well, um . . . what do you know? I'd no idea you could be so . . . forgiving. But as the fates would have it, you and I seem forever destined to be star-crossed lovers, our timing always a wee bit off."

"Relax, it was only a test." She let out a sardonic chuckle. "Just making sure you aren't some alien creature who's taken over Kevin's body. Now I know it's the real you."

His mouth slipped into the old arrogant-adorable grin. "Okay, darlin', a point for your side." He chalked up an invisible score. "But I'm still in the lead and jumping ahead fast."

How does he manage to suppress every part that's got the least sense of responsibility? She glanced around at the mirrored wall, the window boasting a small slice of lake view, the dining room table encrusted with the remains of last night's dinner for two, the crumpled ball of red silk under the loveseat. *Wonder what he did with Red Silk? Sent her home early? Locked her in the bedroom?* A faint, noxious odor, like rotting food. *Never could get him to take out the garbage.*

Cassidy said, "Quite a place. Things looking up?"

He launched into an elaborate explanation of his newest venture, voice animated, eyes sparkling. But this renewal of enthusiasm failed to erase the increased fleshiness in his jowls, the sag in his eyelids. *He'll always bounce back, but never as high as he used to.*

"I need to borrow your gun," Cassidy said, cutting him off midsentence.

His mouth gaped.

She took a small, malicious pleasure in her ability to divert his attention from himself, to shake loose his complacency after all these years. *Me, the original antigun fanatic. Never thought he'd see the day. Come to think of it, neither did I.*

Kevin sat up, propping an ankle across his knee. His robe flopped open, displaying muscular legs covered with curly bronze hair, leopard-spotted bikini briefs. "This new boyfriend, what's-his-name, must've seriously pissed you off. There were times you'd get your dander up about some of my escapades, but you never came after me with a gun."

She smiled sweetly. "I'm on a mission for the CIA. Rush Limbaugh's coming in for therapy, and the feds recommend I keep a gun in my bra for protection."

"This is a joke, right? Real reason you're here is to beg me to come back."

"The real reason is to borrow your gun. Along with shooting lessons. I need you to show me how to use it."

"You know carrying's illegal?"

"I guess so."

"What happened to those excellent rants you used to deliver whenever I'd bend the rules a little?"

"I've seen the light." She struggled to sit forward, but the chair, which reminded her of the plant in the *The Little Shop of Horrors*, sucked her in.

"Cassy . . . ." His voice turned serious. "I know it doesn't show much, but I really do love you. I don't think this is a good idea at all."

"But you'll do it anyway. You owe me big time, and you know it. Lending me the gun is only a small down payment."

"Okay, you win." He stood and shrugged his shoulders. "But whatever you're up to, love, this seems like one of your dumber moments."

"When it comes to dumber moments, you're still well in the lead with a big jump on me."

"Hey babe." He pulled her up from the chair. "You look downright sexy in that sweater and jeans." He curved his hands around her butt. "You'd worn sweaters like that when we were married, I might never've left."

She pushed him away. "This is the sweater I was wearing the day I found that bimbette's letter in your sock drawer."

He brought his Beretta out of the bedroom and showed her how to insert the magazine, turn off the safety, and cock it for the first shot. Holding it in both hands, fending off the sense of revulsion guns always brought up, she compared her memory of Wayne's revolver with Kevin's Beretta. The Beretta was sleeker: with its fifteen-shot magazine, a far more efficient killing machine. The Beretta was what she needed.

She pointed the gun at Kevin's image in the mirrored wall, striking a pose intended to resemble a TV cop's. Checking her reflection, she decided her Cagney/Lacy routine needed work.

"Better get dressed, Kev. This gun-slinger's gonna take a lot of help."

He took her to a shooting range in back of a gun store and instructed her on target practice. At the end of an hour, she had acquired some ease in handling the gun. A few of her shots even hit the paper.

Afterward, she stowed the Beretta in her handbag and they returned to the parking garage under Kevin's building. He walked her to the visitor's slot where she'd left her Toyota, lay an arm across her shoulder, and said, "Don't get hurt. Fuck-up that I am, I still need to know you're out there. And okay."

She squeezed the large hand dangling over her shoulder. "Do me a favor?"

"You want more? What's with you, woman?"

"I know you think you're invincible. And I know you think I go way overboard on doing the right thing. But maybe it'd be a good idea to get an AIDS test. For me."

Pulling his hand out of hers, he ruffled her hair. "When you come back safe and sound, I'll let you know."

🖙 🖙 🖙

Returning home she picked up the *Oak Park Review* from the front porch and sat down to flip through it. A headline caught her eye:

DEAD MAN FOUND IN VAN

Berwyn police responded to a six a.m. call from a Fitzgerald's roadhouse employee who discovered a dead man sitting at the wheel of a van parked in Fitzgerald's lot. Edward 'Curly' Salaski, blues musician and alleged drug dealer, was killed by a single bullet through the temple in what police are calling 'an execution style' slaying.

Wayne? If he'd been the shooter, how did she feel about it? A small voice in her her head cheered, *Way to go, Wayne!*

🖙 🖙 🖙

This is worse than standing in line behind a heaping grocery cart, price checks on every item, customer pays with food stamps.

Impatience was a familiar theme in her mother's what's-wrong-with-you lectures. Maybe not the worst of her sins, but right up there with hard-headedness and a fuck-you attitude toward authority.

Resting her head against the back of the driver's seat, Cassidy pressed her fingertips against her eyelids to relieve the strain of staring at the exit to the parking garage beneath Ursula's building.

There must be a God—how else can you explain my being put to the test like this? Can't be mere coincidence. The most important challenge I've ever faced in my entire life—rescuing Cypress—requires dealing with my greatest weakness— impatience. Gotta hand it to Him, Her, or It, this is a God who's very clever at constructing tests. Possibly even devious or malevolent.

She glanced at her watch. Close to ten. She'd been sitting in Maggie's Volvo for nearly three hours. The trick-or-treaters had come and gone. *How long's it gonna take her to get her butt in gear? Maybe she's got a stomachache, skipping the party this year. Maybe she caught a ride with someone else, left me sitting here while the festivities proceed without me.*

Her chest constricted in cold fear at the thought of what would happen if she had made the least miscalculation. Sucking in air, she pushed the image of Cypress lying across an altar out of her mind.

Ever since linking Ursula to the snake-infested bouquet, she'd been developing her plan. The first step was acquiring Kevin's gun. The second, borrowing Maggie's Volvo. The Toyota, which Ursula obviously had been following, would be too recognizable. She had refrained from taking in liquids all day to minimize the needing-to-pee problem and also had stowed a just-in-case coffee can in the back seat. Before leaving she'd packed a tote with the Beretta, a flashlight, and a bag of peanut butter cups, now long gone.

As soon as she arrived, she scoped out the parking garage, relieved to find the GTSHED Cadillac in the same place she had seen it earlier that day. Her research had clarified the significance of the plate: goat's head, a Satanic symbol.

Rolling down her window, she inhaled cold air in an effort to fight off the drowsiness beginning to blur her mind. A hazy half moon emerged from behind a bank of clouds. Blowing out a stream of air, she watched the curling breath-fog fade into darkness. As each elongated second ticked by, the greatest danger was allowing her attention to wander, her eyes to close, her alertness to drift off into sleep.

Insane. An idiot to be tackling a whole Satanic cult on your own. What's important here? Saving a life or keeping a promise? Cypress is gonna die and it'll be your fault for not hauling in the cavalry.

If only she'd been smart enough to forget her promise and call in Manny Perez and a fleet of police cars like they did in the movies. Or to get Dr. Kramer, her cult expert, to spell out the exact right formula for fending off Satanists, the way vampire-busters used crucifixes and garlic to repel vampires.

Headlights appeared at the garage exit. A sedan rolled out, turned left, picked up speed. Although not certain it was Ursula's, Cassidy started the engine and went after it, lights off. When she had closed to about three car lengths, the letters on the plate became visible: GTSHED.

22

Sacrifice

Cassidy dropped back slightly, snapped on headlights, and continued tailing the Cadillac. The sedan drove west on I-290, south on Mannheim, across the Des Plaines River, and into the southwestern forest preserve. A route she knew well. *St. Paul's?*

Shortly after entering the preserve, Ursula turned left onto a two-lane road that meandered toward the heart of the forest, a different direction from any Cassidy had taken before. Evidently they were not headed toward the cemetery, which would at least have afforded the advantage of familiar territory. They were now the only two vehicles on the road. She cut her lights, nerves tightening as she peered into heavy darkness relieved only by a pale sheen from the moon. Easing up on the accelerator, she gave Ursula a longer lead. Miles passed with no break in the wall of trees. Then the Caddy's taillights slowed to a stop, hung a sharp right, and disappeared.

Where'd she go? Trees dense as a fortress. Cassidy sped up to the spot where, according to her best guess, Ursula had turned off. She parked and stepped outside, flashlight in hand. A sharp chill pricked the exposed skin of her face. Wind rattled the remaining leaves on branches overhead. The glimmer of moonlight blinked out as thick clouds closed off the last gap in the sky. From the forest came an occasional snap of branches and rustle of underbrush but no hint of an engine. The Caddy had vanished. *Satan more powerful than I thought?* Goosebumps rose on her arms.

She paced along the edge of the road, sweeping the ground with her flashlight. The highway shoulder ended in a three-foot dropoff, below which the forest began. Ten feet in front of the car she discovered a narrow dirt track leading off into the trees. She shone her light along the track as far as it would reach. Nothing. *Walk or drive? Could be too far to walk. Could be impossible to drive without lights.* If she used parking lights, would they see her coming? She shifted from one foot to the other, running through every possible scenario.

Finally she jumped into the Volvo, flicked on her parking lights, and bumped roughly down the nearly vertical slope. *What if I destroy Maggie's car? How'll I ever face her?* She crawled along about a block's distance, then got out, feet squishing deeply into a thick layer of vegetation. Closer to the city, an aura of peach-colored light maintained visibility from dusk to dawn. But in the middle of the forest preserve with a cloud cap on the sky, the blackness was impenetrable. She aimed her flashlight down the track, illuminating an empty, rutted road. She listened intently. Nothing but the wind in the trees, surging like waves against a rocky shore. She got in the car and drove another short block.

She had repeated this same scenario a dozen times when she stepped out of the car and saw a flicker of light accompanied by a low murmur that might be voices. *This must be it.* In preparation for a fast getaway, she jockeyed the Volvo around so the nose pointed toward the highway, no small feat on a track only a couple of yards wider than the car. She slung her tote over her shoulder and started off toward the glimmering light. The hum of sound that came from the same place as the light sometimes seemed distinct from the forest noises, sometimes merged with the rise and fall of the wind.

Dressed entirely in black from the knit cap covering her hair down to her tennis shoes, she was less worried about being seen than heard. Her feet crunched dry leaves at each step. Invisible twigs exploded underfoot, making it seem like a minefield. Prickly branches slapped her face, tore at her clothing, cracked off in her wake. The lights disappeared. The sound blended into the swoosh of trees, then separated, gradually becoming more audible as she sidled closer. *Voices, definitely voices. Singing or something.* She crept along with the speed and grace of a caterpillar. *Be lucky to get there before they pack up and leave.*

One step at a time, she edged nearer. The ghostly lights reappeared, multiplied, then became visible as a cluster of individual candle flames. Another few yards enabled her to detect a handful of black figures weaving around the candles. *Knew there'd be a party but didn't expect a scene from The X-Files.* Several more steps brought her right up to the bumper of Ursula's Cadillac, the last in a short string of cars parked along the dirt road. To the right of the Caddy about ten yards' distance from the track, the hooded figures shuffled around some structure on which the candles were arranged, moving within a circle of bare ground. The sound she'd been following was a chant.

She leaned against the car and tried to control her breathing, which had started accelerating much too rapidly. *Can't afford to hyperventilate.* Squeezing her eyes shut, she focused her entire attention on the shallow stream of air pumping in and out. *Take a deep breath.* After a minute or so, she was able to draw in enough air to fill her lungs and stop her heart from racing.

But even with her breathing back to normal, fear kept her from taking a single step forward. She heard a small voice screaming in the back of her head: *Look at how many. This is impossible. Just get the hell out while you can.*

She clenched her teeth and pushed the voice away. No matter how scared, she had to see this night through. Had to force herself to move closer. Close enough to see what else beside candles lay on the altar. Close enough to fire the gun and hit her targets if necessary.

The ten yards between road and clearing offered little cover, so she traveled in a wide arc, approaching the circle from a point where the trees grew right up next to it. She located a large log at the circle's edge and scrunched down behind it.

At the center of the clearing was a flat slab of limestone shaped like a long table, a panel running down the middle, purple velvet she guessed from her reading. The candles stood on the end farthest from the road. On the other end, the end closest to Cassidy's log, a smaller panel of red satin was draped over some object. A large dagger, silver bowl, and glass decanter filled with what Cassidy assumed to be wine were laid out in the middle. From where she knelt she could just glimpse the upside down crucifix attached to the purple velvet hanging down in front. *Where's Cypress? Oh shit, what if I guessed wrong?*

On the opposite side of the altar a black kettle rested on glowing coals, clouds of steamy incense rising from the kettle's mouth. Five hooded figures, larger than life in their long, black robes, shambled and swayed to the rhythm of the chant. Concentrating on the low-pitched, slurry sound, Cassidy was gradually able to distinguish the words: "All hail to the father Satan."

Figuring that the Satanists were too tranced-out to notice, she crunched leaves recklessly, arranging herself on the ground with arms crossed on top of the log. Minutes crawled by. Her chin dropped onto her arm. A strange feeling started to come over her, a feeling directed at her from the outside. As if by osmosis, it seeped through her skin and permeated her body. It was something that radiated outward from the center of the circle, a force she could no more keep out of herself than a sponge could avoid soaking up water.

As her mind blurred, words she had heard previously drifted into her consciousness, words spoken in someone else's voice: "oppressive, suffocating, evil." Roger Korsac's voice, the man burned to death by the swaying figures in front of her.

She struggled to her knees, lifted her head, and held it rigidly upright. Ridiculous. What was she thinking? Nothing more than a handful of lunatics, boosting their puny egos with make-believe magic. *Reaction to trance-inducing stimuli, that's all. The kind of mumbo jumbo that'd make anybody's imagination play tricks.*

But the feeling did not go away. It intensified, pulled at her. The altar had become the vortex of a whirlpool sucking her in toward the center. It was almost a physical tug, as if she were caught in an undertow, dragged under, drowning.

Darting flames, undulating figures, long, wavering shadows. Her head swayed, her lids drooped. Increasingly woozy from the incense, she could barely keep her eyes open. She tried to shake her head but could not break out of the rhythmic motion. The chanting grew louder, its murmury tones distorting and filling her mind, the words changing into her name: "Cass-i-dy, Come to me." *Am I hearing voices?* A twitch of panic in her stomach. Her whole body becoming heavier. She was not sure she could get to her feet, even if she wanted to. And she didn't, didn't want to move, didn't ever want to move again. She was drifting rapidly toward immobilization, as if some alien power had invaded her.

"Don't believe in Satan." She mumbled the words aloud, her mouth stiff. "He's got no power over me." A little clearer.

"I won't give in. He can't take control if I don't let him." The words started sounding more normal.

She blinked and gave her head a hard shake. Slipping the tote over her shoulder, she hauled herself to her feet. She wobbled, took a step backward, and grabbed a branch for support. Blundering two more steps back from the circle, she wrapped her arms around a large tree. She stiffened her spine and set her teeth, refusing to let her body respond to the chant in any way.

The robes arranged themselves in a semicircle facing the line of cars, which numbered six. The chant ended and the group called out in unison, "Prince of Darkness, send us your priest." A figure descended from the lead vehicle and walked with measured steps toward the altar. As he entered the light, Cassidy noted that the new arrival was slightly taller than the others and wore a scarlet cape over his robe, which Cassidy assumed to be a symbol of priesthood. *Must be chief honcho.* The caped figure took the dagger from the altar and, with arms extended, pointed to the north, intoning in a deep voice, "The father awaits his communion." He turned in a slow circle, stopping to point east, south and west, accompanying each gesture with the same words.

The priest beckoned to the nearest robe, who stepped up to the altar, grasped the silver bowl in his left hand, and stretched out his right wrist above it. The head honcho drew the dagger across the robe's wrist, then stood with head bowed as several drops of blood splashed into the bowl. *So that's why Ursula always wore long sleeves.* Each robe in turn contributed to the ritualistic blood drive, finishing with the caped honcho slicing a vein of his own. Setting aside the dagger, he added a generous glug from the decanter, lifted the bowl above his head, and muttered an incantation.

The robe standing next to the priest, evidently his number one Satanist, clasped a corner of the red satin coverlet and whipped it into the air, a flash of crimson. Underneath lay a small naked body, face upward, amber curls tumbled around her head. *Jesus!* Cassidy's legs buckled. Her hands turned to ice. "Oh God," she whispered aloud. "It's too late."

You saw the lump under the satin. Had to realize it was Cypress. How could you not have known?

Didn't let myself know. Couldn't bear to go near it in my mind. Still can't.

Sucking in air, she stepped away from the tree, pulled the tote off her shoulder, and held it in her left hand. Unconsciously her right hand moved down into it, fingers closing around the Beretta's handle. She released the tote, letting it slip to the ground. Slowly she raised the gun, flipped off the safety, got both hands around it the way Kevin had shown her. She placed her index finger on the trigger. *Can't hit a bullseye, but with fifteen bullets in the clip I can spray enough metal to mow them all down.*

Catching her lower lip between her teeth, she bit through the inner lining. The salty taste of blood brought her back to reality. She breathed in deeply.

"Satan is pleased." The caped honcho flung the contents of the bowl over Cypress. A hint of movement from the pale form. Was that a twitch? Had Cypress flinched? Cassidy couldn't be sure.

She's alive. Maybe she's alive. If she is, I can't risk hitting her. She lowered the gun.

"Go." The honcho thrust his arm toward the line of cars. "Bring forth the intruder."

Number-one robe and the robe standing next to him came forward, each holding a smaller version of the official dagger. Together they strode toward the cars, stopping at the vehicle just behind the priest's. They opened the rear door and dragged out an adult-sized figure. Squinting into the darkness, all Cassidy could see was a hunched form. But she knew instantly it was Zach.

Oh shit—what am I gonna do? Her left hand clutched a branch; her right arm hung at her side, fingers clasping the Beretta. Her brain went as blank as a dead computer screen.

The three figures returned to the circle. Zach, hands tied in front, stumbled along with a robe on either side to hold him up. *So drugged he can't even walk.* They positioned him in front of the altar, the two robes standing on guard. The caped figure raised the official dagger above Zach's head and chanted something that might have been the Lord's Prayer backward. Then he placed the handle in Zach's bound hands, his fingers encircling Zach's, and held the blade poised above Cypress' chest.

In her mind Cassidy knew she had to stop them, but her body failed to respond. She put forth a tremendous effort of will, struggling against a force intent on stopping her. Her muscles refused to move. No matter how many neurons her brain shot off, her arms and legs remained motionless. She concentrated harder, using every ounce of psychic energy, and at last broke loose from whatever it was that had her paralyzed. Moving in slow motion, she lifted the gun and pointed it above their heads.

A ringing voice, a voice she'd heard somewhere before, proclaimed, "You now belong to Satan."

She squeezed the trigger, recoiled backward, squeezed again.

The three figures standing farthest from Cypress skittered into the trees in a flurry of black robes. The other three moved in to surround Zach, who suddenly lunged sideways. He drove his shoulder into the robe on his right, knocking him to the ground. At the same time, he jerked his hands upward and sent the dagger flying to the other side of the altar. The head honcho dove after it as Cassidy, gun extended in both hands, stepped into the circle.

She moved toward Cypress, her attention fixed on the priest who was scrambling on the other side of the altar to retrieve the dagger. From the corner of her eye she saw Zach struggling to regain his balance. She spun in his direction just as the robe to his left jumped behind him. A black-sleeved arm snaked around his waist; a white-knuckled fist pressed a blade against his throat. Blood trickled down his neck and onto his black T-shirt.

A muffled voice came from behind Zach: "Drop the gun."

At a distance of ten feet, Zach locked eyes with her. His mouth moved. "Shoot!" Knees buckling, head slumping, he went straight down. The dagger sliced his throat and face. His body became a heap on the ground. Blood spurted; stains darkened the fabric of his shirt; leaves clotted his face and hair.

Cassidy's eyes snapped up to the hooded figure standing behind Zach. Up to the huge frightened eyes gaping at the gun Cassidy still held rigidly in front of her. The hood had slipped, revealing a gamine, Audrey-Hepburn face. *Oh no!* Annie, the woman who baked cookies and played the organ and wanted to spike the punch. The gun was pointed directly at her chest. Cassidy's finger, with a will of its own, tightened. The gun exploded. Annie's body jerked, then crumpled behind Zach's.

"Don't die," Cassidy screamed, stumbling toward them.

Raising his head slightly, face smeared with blood and dirt, Zach mouthed, "I'm okay. Get Cypress." He closed his eyes and eased back down.

Cassidy whirled toward the altar. The baby was gone. She saw a black shadow disappear into the trees on the far side of the clearing. The head honcho had taken her. Tightening her grip on the Beretta, Cassidy raced around the circle to the spot where the priest had vanished.

A barricade of tree trunks, branches, and spiny bushes rose in front of her. She lifted her left arm to shield her face, held the gun firmly against her chest, and crashed into the forest. *Hope I don't fall on my face, run headlong into a tree, or shoot myself.*

Brambles jerked the knit cap off her head. Twigs stabbed through her sweatshirt and into her skin. Branches grabbed at her hair, yanking her head back. As she thrust forward, she felt a handful of hair ripped from her scalp. She yelped with pain, then clenched her teeth to stop the cry. Her raised arm slammed into a tree trunk. She'd completely lost her bearings, had no idea where she was or where the robe who'd grabbed Cypress might be.

She tried to listen, tried to detect some sense of the Satanic chieftain's presence, but the wheeze of her own ragged breathing, the hammer of her own racing heart drowned out everything else. Cautiously she circumvented the tree she'd just run into. She stood still a moment, then continued slowly, waving one hand in front of her. As she moved forward, she strained all her senses for some indication of the other person who was out there with her. *You got this close to Cypress, now you've lost her.*

"Just keep going. You're on the right track."

Holy shit, I am hearing voices. She stopped dead. She'd come too far to allow herself a psychotic break. *This is not hallucinatory. Gotta be real.* It was just that the voice had sounded so disembodied and weird, coming out of the darkness as it did.

Raising the Beretta, she padded warily toward its source. She heard a soft whimper. Two pale blobs gradually became visible: one, an oval face about four feet off the ground, apparently belonging to a seated figure; the other, an elongated mound, Cypress stretched out on the figure's lap. The darkness was too thick to make out features on the face, but she could detect a slight, lethargic movement on the part of the baby. *How far? Two yards, maybe less.* She spread her feet, straightened her back, pointed the Beretta at the face. Setting her jaw, she determinedly shut out the thought of what might happen if she failed to do better at hitting faces than bullseyes.

"I've been waiting for you." A congenial tone. "I must say, you've exceeded my expectations. I was certain the father would be able to pull you into our circle, but you somehow managed to resist." The voice paused. "This time."

The tone was conversational, quite different from the ritualistic cadence Cassidy had heard earlier. "A woman. And your voice . . . I recognize it." Narrowing her eyes, she strained to bring the face into sharper focus. "Where've I heard you before?"

"My office. When you brought Dana in for consultation."

"Victoria Kramer. Ursula's friend Vicky. So that's how the cult found out Dana'd talked."

23

Final Sacrifice

"I'm glad you followed. I prefer having someone here to witness my final sacrifice. I realize, of course, that you're holding a gun, but I doubt you'd be so foolish as to fire. Considering that I've got the child."

"What do you mean, 'final sacrifice'?" *You* know *what she means.* Cassidy's palms were damp with sweat, making the gun feel slippery. She wanted to wipe at least one of them on her shirt but didn't dare break her aim.

"My final act, of course. Just before I die. I don't mind dying, you understand. Life has become tedious, and leaving it in this manner will ensure a permanent place at the father's side. After all, Satan appreciates his martyrs every bit as much as the other one does."

Cassidy steadied the gun, tightening her finger ever so slightly. "Wait—I don't understand. Why?" She noticed the robe shifting, a long, metallic object sliding out from a fold in the fabric. Her gaze returned to Kramer's face. She concentrated on her aim.

"I told you already." Dr. Kramer sounded annoyed, as if talking to a dull child. "You asked that same question the first time we met and I gave you the answer then."

A flash of movement accompanied by a shriek from Cypress.

Please God. She pulled the trigger. A sharp retort. Victoria Kramer went over backward, both she and the child disappearing into darkness.

Cassidy flew across the intervening space to the log where the psychologist had been sitting and peered down on the other side. Black fabric; black blood; splayed limbs. And coming from somewhere in the tangle, a baby's stifled cry. Bile rose in her throat. She swallowed hard. *Can't be sick now. Have to wait.* Dropping the gun, she stuck both hands down into the mess. She tore away the robe and grappled with body parts coated in warm ooze. Putting all her strength into one big push, she rolled the body over and uncovered the wailing child. *Keep crying, just keep crying.* Cypress, slick with blood, squirmed out of her grasp.

Cassidy groped around, finally managing to get both hands firmly planted inside Cypress' armpits. She lifted her out and laid her on the ground. Running her fingers over the child's flailing body, she discovered a long gash across her stomach. Cassidy ripped off her sweatshirt and wrapped it around the toddler, then grasped the child tightly to her chest, which was now uncovered except for her bra. Once Cypress was snuggled into her arms, she located her thumb and plugged it into her mouth.

Sagging against a tree, Cassidy caught her breath and tried to think. The gun was gone, lost somewhere in the weeds. No telling how long it would take to find it. But there were three robes who had disappeared into the trees, robes who might suddenly get their courage back if she were unarmed. Who might want to finish what they'd started, even without Victoria Kramer. *Need the gun. No, can't waste time—have to get Cypress and Zach to a doctor. Just have to chance it.*

Hauling the thirty-pound toddler, Cassidy moved as fast as possible, scuttling like a crab around bushes and under branches, back toward the pool of candlelight. As she neared the clearing, she was relieved to see that Zach had gotten himself off the ground. Squatting next to a heap of rags she knew to be Annie's body, he was wrapping a strip of black fabric around the wound on his neck.

Cassidy called to him from the woods. "I've got Cypress. She's hurt too."

Zach tossed the strip around his neck, leaving the loose end to dangle over his shoulder. Moving into the lighted circle, Cassidy got a better look at the still uncovered facial portion of the wound: a deep groove of raw flesh running diagonally across his left cheek.

Zach said, "I heard a shot."

"Victoria Kramer. She was starting to cut—"

"She dead?"

Cassidy nodded. "We've gotta get Cypress to the hospital right away. Can you walk?"

Pushing off with both hands, Zach got to his feet. "Course I can," he said faintly.

Cassidy juggled Cypress onto her left hip, the child grabbing hold with her legs. Using her left arm as a sling for the toddler, she succeeded in sliding her right arm around Zach's waist. Reflexively she turned her head away from the stench that rolled off him, a combination of blood, unwashed clothes, and other indistinguishable body fluids.

"You can't carry both of us," he said, trying to pull away. But his protest lacked muscle, either in voice or body, so she jockeyed in closer and grabbed a handful of T-shirt to keep him in place.

"Wait a minute." He still held back. "What happened to your shirt?"

"Cypress."

"You'll freeze. Let me hold the kid while you wrap up in what's left of that black stuff." He pointed his chin toward Annie's robe.

A shudder ran through her. "I'll take freezing any day. C'mon, let's get going."

Zach was shaky at first, but he gradually regained the hang of walking as they stumbled over uneven ground toward the dirt track where six cars had been parked earlier. Three were now gone, but the lead car, Kramer's, plus a couple of others, were still in place. *Annie and one other person. Somebody probably lost in the woods. Just keep moving.*

Ursula's Cadillac was among the missing. *Maybe she'll show for her Tuesday appointment,* her manicky voice shrilled. Reaching the road, they followed it back to the Volvo, where Zach settled into the passenger seat and took Cypress on his lap. Cassidy turned on the engine and drove toward the highway, pressing the pedal as hard as she dared considering the danger to Maggie's axle. They went over a bad bump. Cypress squawked once, then fell back asleep.

"She's too quiet," Cassidy said, fear gnawing at her.

"Just sleeping off the drugs."

Once they were back on concrete, Cassidy asked Zach to call on the car phone and locate the nearest hospital, then get hold of Laurel and tell her where they were headed. She wanted Dana to hear the news from her real mother.

Zach made the calls and said, "What's the matter? How come you're not grilling me?"

Her hands tightened on the wheel. "I'm too pissed."

"At me?"

"That's right." She pushed down on the accelerator. If a cop stopped them, so much the better. They could use a police escort.

"What'd I do?"

"Oh, nothing much." She clenched her teeth to hold back the words but they pushed through anyway. "Just betrayed my confidence. Set up a fight so I'd break up with you. Ignored my calls. Took off alone on our joint investigation and nearly got yourself killed, that's all."

He stared straight ahead for several moments, then said in a tight voice, "What the hell am I doing, dating a shrink? Why the shit would I want to put up with someone always analyzing my behavior, assuming she has everything figured out ahead of time. Since you've got all the answers, no reason for you to bother listening."

She opened her mouth to yell back at him, then snapped it shut, realizing she wasn't so much angry as worried sick and exhausted. "I'm sorry. Let's start over. Pretend I just asked nicely how you're doing with that knife wound."

"That's better." He readjusted Cypress, who was breathing heavily in sleep. "Didn't feel anything at first but it stings like the devil now." He ran a finger down the exposed part. "Don't worry, a facial scar will be fine. Women'll find it sexy, just you wait."

She grimaced. "Well, that's a relief."

"Getting sliced, that's not a problem. They'll sew me up good as new. What you just did—shooting two people—that's likely to be a whole lot worse. The sort of thing you can't just stick a bandage on."

"Right now, all I feel is numb." She pulled in her bottom lip. "Wonder when it'll hit me? I actually took a semi-automatic and blew away two people. But if anybody deserved . . . No, I don't want to do that. Who knows? Maybe I'll feel fine about it. Consider it a benevolent deed, a socially correct, righteous action." *You're babbling . . . must be hysteria setting in.* "While we're waiting to see what feeling I come up with shooting-wise, why don't you fill me in on all the stuff you just said I can't be bothered to listen to."

"You mean, how did I become the main event in a Satanic ritual after you told me to go fuck myself?"

"I didn't—"

"I figured, just because you were premenstrual was no reason to drop the investigation."

"I hate it when—"

"I know, 'premenstrual's' a sexist-pig word. Sorry—we've both been through a shitload of angst. It gets me irritable and mean, same as it does you. I'm sorry, really." He patted her knee. "I'll try to be nice. Okay, so here's the scoop. In all our poking around, we'd only been able to come up with three groups that existed in the right time frame—Laurel's play group, the mysterious daycare, and various Sunday School classes—particularly the class a grad student set up to do research. Remember that little tidbit Annie threw in near the end of our interview?"

"Vaguely." Starting to shiver, she boosted the heater to max. Now that her adrenalin level had dropped, every cell of exposed skin was sucking up cold air.

"Since everything else had run dry, I got myself a list of kids in Dana's kindergarten class, figuring some of them must have participated in one or the other of those three groups. Then I planted my ass in front of an Apple Creek phone book and called every matching last name."

Why didn't I think of that? Two conflicting feelings tugged at her: a pride in Zach's cleverness and irritation at having been outdone. She rubbed her shoulder and arm with her free hand, trying to warm herself.

"You *are* cold. Why don't I take off my shirt, wrap it around you?"

"No, that's all right." *Rather shiver than stink.* "Go on with your story."

"So I called all these people and enough of them were willing to talk that I was able to narrow it down. The first one I crossed off was the daycare. When I found out how determined Ernie was to close Miss Marilyn down, I figured there was no chance he'd ever let Dana go there. Next I crossed off

Laurel's play group. Nobody'd ever heard of it, and later I learned it was an invention Annie had devised on the spot in your first conversation with her. Evidently, your questions put her on guard right from the beginning."

"What a lot of nerve, making up something like that."

"Oh, Annie's got balls, all right. Anyway, eventually I hit the jackpot—the mother of a kid who'd participated in a Sunday School class run by a Vicky Adams. This mother remembered the Adams woman as a U. of C. grad student who'd arranged to have preschoolers sleep over at the church one night a month so she could study separation anxiety. She also remembered that the grad student teacher was a close friend of Annie's, and that Annie had gone all out persuading parents to sign up their kids. After that, I switched my attention from the phone book to Christ's Love Church."

Zach dabbed at his wound with the loose end of fabric hanging over his shoulder. He grunted quietly and she asked, "Still bleeding?"

"Not bad. Just a little gooey, that's all."

If only men would complain. Admit when something hurts instead of having to be so damn stoic. "Okay, tough guy, tell me how you got yourself overpowered by a gang of women."

"Where was I? Oh yeah, focusing on the church."

"Right. Weird, isn't it, that Annie voluntarily told us about the teacher doing research?"

"Not so weird when you understand her attraction to risk-taking. But I'm jumping ahead. Another reason for checking out the church is that Satanists get off on desecrating holy places. That's why they liked to schedule events at St. Paul's. Anyway, lucky for me—or maybe not so lucky, considering how close this came to being the ultimate story to die for—I found out the Halseys always take their vacation the last half of October. So, a couple of weeks ago, I embarked on a little midnight B and E."

"Why let a little thing like the law stop you?"

"Exactly. So, after putting more hours than I cared to into prowling—you'd be amazed how many nooks and crannies they can stuff into one little church—I discovered a locked trunk in the basement. The lock piqued my curiosity, so I pried it open with my trusty crowbar, and there it all was—a pile of black robes, velvet panel, satin coverlet, bowl, crucifix, daggers. Everything your hip, well-outfitted Satanist could ask for." He cranked the heat down a notch.

Cassidy said, "You know, I wish it hadn't been Annie. I really liked her."

"Anyway, I was just about to repack the works—this is the part I hate to admit, makes me look inept at burgling—when I got overconfident and stopped watching over my shoulder. That's how Annie was able to sneak up and clobber me. Next thing I knew, I woke up in this little closet of a storage room, leg-ironed to a steel pipe, just enough mobility to hobble to the bucket toilet."

"Locked in the church for two weeks?" She sped through a stop sign and barreled around a left turn, spinning out on the gravel shoulder. "You mean, Dennis and Annie pretended to go on vacation but were really holed up in the church all that time? You sure you're not suffering delusions from that bump on the head?"

"Slow down! This is not life or death here, unless you roll us off the road."

Reckless driving's only permitted when you're at the wheel. Women aren't allowed.

"Dennis Halsey doesn't know a thing about it. Years ago Annie set it up so they do separate vacations. She packs him off to commune with nature on Wolf Island, while she ostensibly goes on a woman's retreat with her dear friend Vicky Adams Kramer. Believe it or not, Annie's managed to keep her extracurricular activities a secret all this time. Course

Dennis wasn't particularly eager to find out. Amazing what denial can do, isn't it?"

"You really spent two weeks in that church with Annie?" She shook her head in disbelief. "Was Cypress there too? And what about Vicky?"

"Ursula had Cypress at her place, and both Vicky and Ursula came around fairly often. But mostly it was just Annie and me."

"So what went on with you and Annie?"

"Woman's addicted to adrenalin. Spent the whole time partying, having orgies with her pals. I have to hand it to her—she's very good at creative decadence. I got the impression she loved dancing right on the edge."

Cassidy slammed on the brakes as a small animal streaked across the highway. "Sorry 'bout that." Cypress whimpered and kicked, one small foot catching Cassidy in the ribs.

"Close your eyes, little sleepyhead," Zach crooned, rubbing her back.

"How'd you get all this lowdown on Annie if you were locked in a closet the whole time?"

"Do I detect a note of suspicion? Annie came in at least once a day to shoot me full of downers. Most days she was in and out several times, looking for someone to talk to. She was on a lot of drugs herself and more than willing to share."

"So the two of you were partying together?" Her voice crackled with anger.

"Life takes unexpected turns. When I was a kid, I lived to get high. Last couple of weeks, all I wanted was to get alert. Fortunately, by the time tonight's festivities rolled around, I'd built up enough immunity that my head was pretty clear. Annie'd laid out the plan, and I was fairly certain I could get away myself. The main thing I had to do was act like a zombie and keep them off guard. But the part I couldn't work out was how to take Cypress with me."

A traffic light appeared ahead, the first since they'd left the clearing. "That's Mannheim," Zach said. "Hang a left. Palos isn't too far."

Her shoulders tightened. "You want to drive?"

"Okay by me."

She slowed for the red light, glanced both ways, and zipped on through. Taillights a block ahead, headlights approaching. They weren't the only two people on the road at three a.m. after all. The trees beside the highway were thinner here, and an orange glow was visible to the east. Overhead, the clouds had blown off and a sprinkling of pinpoint lights showed in the sky.

Cassidy moistened her lips. "Annie try to seduce you?"

"How'd you guess? Her first choice was women but she swung both ways. Annie and Vicky were lovers back at good old Brewster where they went to school together, and Vicky brought Ursula into it. The rest were women who'd been sexually abused—same as Dr. Victoria herself—and had a lot of rage toward men. Women Kramer'd had as patients and been able to brainwash. Annie said they normally sacrificed only male children but tonight they'd make an exception."

Cassidy shook her head. "I hate having to accept that women can be as violent as men."

"The main appeal for Annie was the sense of corruption. She really did live a double life. Most of the year she was this nice minister's wife who worked her butt off being helpful. Then, on these certain occasions, she'd backlash to the opposite extreme."

"Having Annie come on to you must've been a lot more exciting than dating a shrink."

"She gave it her best shot. Evidently Satanists are as big on proselytizing as anybody else. Showed me her kiddie porn."

He ran a hand over his face. "Talk about disgusting. Made it with Ursula right in front of me—really got off on having me watch. Constantly pushed drugs. Tried every trick in the book to turn me on."

"She have any luck?"

"What do you think?"

ஐ ஐ ஐ

When they arrived at the hospital, Zach carried Cypress into the emergency room, then returned to the car a few minutes later with a green smock for Cassidy. Inside, the waiting room was harshly lit with fluorescents. Half a dozen people sat or sprawled on vinyl-covered chairs, two of them playing boomboxes tuned to different stations.

"Where's the take-a-number?" Zach muttered as he guided her to a seat. After a long wait, Dana and Laurel appeared through the double doors. The foursome stood together in a tight knot, shouting over the mix of rap and rock. After another long wait, a nurse came to collect Zach. Skillfully evading their questions about Cypress, she directed the others to the insurance desk.

Many long waits later, Zach rejoined the group, his neck and face bandaged. Finally a woman in doctor's greens carrying a fussy, white-gowned Cypress entered the room. Dana made a grab, tears streaming down her face, but the doctor held her off.

"She has a minor cut across the abdomen and she's recovering nicely from the barbituates."

"Mama!" Cypress reached for Dana and the doctor relented. The child wrapped her arms in a stranglehold around her mother's neck. Dana released a long, shuddering breath.

"Physically she'll be fine," the doctor continued. "As to the emotional repercussions . . . only time will tell."

Standing outside the hospital to say goodbye, Cassidy touched Laurel's arm. "There's one thing still bothering me. I hope I'm not putting you on the spot, but I have to ask. Why did you say Dana never went to Sunday School when she was in Vicky Adams' group?"

In the early dawn light, Cassidy could see Laurel was flustered. "I know this sounds crazy, but I actually got it all mixed up in my head and started thinking she never went to that group. The way it happened is, Ernie just laid down the law and said she couldn't go, but I thought it'd be really good for her, so I signed her up on the sly and then just made up some story for Ernie. And I told that story so often, I started believing it myself, and it got so I honestly didn't think she ever belonged to that group. I feel just terrible now that I realize how much trouble I caused by not remembering."

She "made up some story." Same thing Dana does. What Cypress'll probably do. If parents only knew how the little quirks they hand on to their children can screw the kids up.

24

Kittens

Sunday at last. Finally a chance to slow down and catch my breath. Pushing the covers down, she raised up on an elbow. The back of Zach's head rested on the pillow next to hers, his fine dark hair swirling outward from a pinpoint spot in the center. Starshine lay between them, triangle face alert, eyes huge and melting.

Cassidy rose, pulling Kevin's old Springsteen T-shirt over her head, then sat up in bed. She curled her legs into a round nest and Starshine stepped inside. Shifting to settle her large stomach, the cat left a trail of gooey splotches in her wake. *She's leaking from the backside—it must mean something.*

Cassidy wormed her fingers under the comforter and tickled Zach's neck. "It's time."

He rolled over and opened his eyes. The white bandage across his cheek still shocked her whenever she first saw it. He said, "She finally gonna do it?"

"I think she needs me to stay and hold her. Why don't you make coffee, then bring up her box?"

Zach disappeared downstairs, returning some time later to set a cardboard box lined with soft towels next to the bed. Starshine remained firmly planted in Cassidy's lap, the cat's enormous, scared eyes gazing into hers for reassurance. When the calico's stomach started visibly contracting, she jumped to the floor and began pacing and licking herself. With each new contraction, she let out a sharp yelp.

Cassidy frowned at the increasing number of wet spots on the carpet and worried over what to do. "I've never been a midwife before," she said to Zach, an onlooker from the desk chair. She got no response. His face had taken on its detached look, indicating that he'd retreated from this essentially female ritual into his characteristic remoteness.

"I think she ought to stay in her box," Cassidy said, making one more bid for assistance from the other side of the room. She placed the cat on the towel lining, then sat on the floor next to her, petting and soothing.

A long, gurgling howl from Starshine announced the first birth as a mouse-sized kitten encased in a silvery membrane slid out onto the towel. Biting off the cord, the cat began licking the kitten for all she was worth, accompanying the wash-down with an ecstatic purr: *I love you, I want you, you're mine.*

Cassidy knelt over the box, enchanted by the cat's fierce display of love. It was the kind of love Dana had shown consistently for Cypress, Laurel had shown in snatches for Dana. "Isn't this amazing?" She looked up at Zach, who was leaning forward now, unable to hold out against the irresistable tug of Starshine's big moment. "I kept saying she had to wait till Sunday so I wouldn't miss out. First time she's ever followed orders."

"She probably wanted an audience." Zach scooted the chair closer, his face relaxed, eyes softer than usual.

Propping her back against the bed's sideboard, Cassidy asked, "You feel like talking now?" Five days had passed since Halloween, and during the interim he'd said he had something to discuss with her but needed time to work it out. Waiting was making her crazy.

He touched the bandage on his cheek. "It's never easy admitting you've screwed up, but I might as well get it over with. When you said I was backing off, you were right. I just didn't see it at the time."

Her whole body tensed. *Here it comes—the you're-a-nice-person-but speech.*

"You accused me of trying to dump you, but that wasn't it." He scratched his jaw. "Truth is, I was making excuses to avoid you, but I never thought of it as wanting out."

Unable to wait one second longer, she blurted, "So which is it? You breaking up with me or not?"

He leaned back, hands behind his head, legs stretched out in front. "While I was drifting in and out on that stinking cot, this little voice in my head started saying—the only reason for avoiding you was, I was scared shitless. Scared I'd open my mouth and some spirit from the netherworld, channeling through my brain, would say, 'Let's move in together.' "

"What?" Her stomach lurched. *Easy to say I wanted him to do it, long as I thought he never would.* She bit down hard on her bottom lip. "Spirit from the netherworld? I suppose then you could get out of it by saying the devil made you do it."

"Well, obviously, we both know I'd never say anything like that in my right mind."

A yowl from the box interrupted them. Spreading her legs, Starshine licked furiously and another silvery little mouse popped out. The first kitten, its black fur shiny and wet, snuffled against Starshine's stomach in search of a nipple.

When the second birth was finished, Cassidy returned her gaze to Zach. Although he'd never admit it, she could tell by his face he was nearly as fascinated as she. "So, one part of you thinks you might want to move in with me, the other part's going berserk."

"The weird thing is, I might've succeeded in deep-sixing the whole works if I hadn't been unconscious most of the time. As long as I was up and moving, I could keep my feelings cut off. But getting shot full of drugs seemed to knock out the old defenses." He pressed a thumb and forefinger to his forehead, then forced himself to meet her eyes. She saw something in the smoky depths—guilt? regret?—something he'd never let her see before. "The other thing I have to tell you is, you may've been right when you talked about sabotage. Looking back, I can see how messing up that story could've been an attempt to get you to break up."

Cassidy sent him a warm smile, appreciating how difficult this must be. *Imagine—a man who can admit when he's wrong. More than I can do.* Lowering her eyes, she gazed dreamily at Starshine, who had rolled over and extended her stomach so the blind newborns could find a faucet. She reached out a tentative finger to stroke the second kitten, its wet fur having washed up to solid orange. "Well, that all sounds very nice, but what does it mean? Will you have to regress and become a dopehead again for us to live together?"

He laughed. "Hope not. All I can say is, I'm ready to move in now, and if I start drugging afterward, you'll just have to send me to treatment."

Starshine reared up, knocking the kittens out of the way, and started licking herself again. She screeched as her stomach contracted and another kitten popped out.

Cassidy pulled her knees up tight against her chest. "What were you up to all those Saturday nights?"

"Hanging out in bars—all my old haunts. You wanted me to be predictable and responsible. Expected me to show up every Saturday like clockwork. And I didn't like the idea of being accountable. Or controlled."

"I wasn't trying to control you."

"Sure you were. Women always control men. Anyway, I rationalized by telling myself I was under a lot of pressure, needed time alone." He leaned forward, hands dangling between his knees, to watch the kittens. "Since you always scowl when I take a second drink, I figured I'd keep my extracurricular boozing to myself. Now that I'm seeing things differently, I'd have to say I was avoiding the seditious urge to bring up the topic of living together."

She paused a long moment before the next question. "Any chance you might have a problem with alcohol?"

He grinned. "Nah—I just drink too much."

As the third kitten underwent a vigorous licking, a miniature version of Mom was revealed. Cassidy blinked back sudden moisture, surprised at the stab of pleasure she experienced in seeing this tiny recreation of her own Starshine.

Neither spoke for several minutes as they watched mother cat bliss out with her babes, Cassidy wallowing in a remarkably contentment-filled, second-hand experience of feline joy.

Finally she rose, standing behind Zach's chair to massage his neck. "You know what bothers me?"

"The shootings starting to get to you?"

"This is something else, something that's been on my mind since I first showed up at the clearing. I'm almost afraid to tell you—you always get that skeptical look on your face."

"But you're going to anyway."

She rubbed the back of her hand across his stubbly cheek. "I could hold off awhile if you'd like to say more about moving in."

He wrapped his arm around her neck, tugging her head down to nibble an earlobe. As she pulled away, he said, "There're a couple of other things I wanted to tell you. I had a long talk with Dennis Halsey and the guy's going through a real crisis of faith. Annie was the center of his life. Finding out about her has blown his world apart." He reached for her hand. "You're not going to turn devil-woman on me, are you? Once I give up the fight and move you into that central position."

Cassidy said, "You never did say what happened when you talked to the police. Perez was not at all pleased with my solo performance, but I guess he's not going to charge me with anything. Did they beat it out of you that I blabbed confidential information?"

"The cops didn't push me to name my source. They were more interested in leaning on me for not reporting the skull in the first place. But at this point—now that we've busted a cult—they're not going to do anything."

Kneeling beside the chair, Cassidy rested her cheek against his leg. "I saw Dana yesterday, and she's doing remarkably well. This whole godawful experience may've given her some kind of validation, since it turned out she was right after all."

"The other thing you need to know is, they found Ursula in her car in a remote area outside Springfield. She'd shot herself in the head, been there for days."

"Just like Curly, only he had help getting dead."

"Since you refuse to read the newspaper, you probably didn't hear that they picked up the shooter who did Curly. A black guy who figured Curly didn't do right by him in a drug deal."

Not Wayne? She felt a wave of relief. "What about the other cult members?"

"Three of 'em got away, and with Ursula dead, there's not much chance they'll ever be caught. Although they probably won't get into much trouble with the leaders dead."

"Well . . . I still haven't said what I wanted to tell you. It was this thing that happened while I was watching the Satanists. This may sound dumb . . . I'm embarrassed even saying it . . . . But I had the sense I was fighting off some evil force—a force trying to get possession of my soul. Pretty ridiculous, huh? 'Specially since I've never much believed in people having souls anyway."

"Power of suggestion."

She studied his face. "You feel anything like that? When they brought you into the clearing, I mean?"

His eyes clouded briefly. "Don't know what I felt. Too preoccupied with acting zoned out."

Cassidy scratched Starshine's snowy chin. Curled around the newborns, each tiny kitten latched-on and kneading, the calico lay with her head upside down, luminous green eyes radiating motherly pride.

She said, "I asked Victoria Kramer why anyone would torture children and she said some people are simply born evil. I can't stand that idea. It violates everything I believe in as a therapist."

"Look," Zach said briskly. "Annie told me Kramer's father sexually abused her from early childhood. At the age of thirteen she murdered her mother so she could have Dad all to herself. Don't you think that constitutes sufficient motivation? I don't see any need to go digging around for any additional religious or metaphysical explanations."

Cassidy did an instant replay of her final encounter with Victoria. "Religious or metaphysical. Reminds me of something I heard once. The church says that God is omnipotent, God is good, and evil exists. But only two out of those three statements can be true, so we have to throw out one of them. Now we know for certain that evil not only exists, it abounds. So which of the other two do we get rid of?"

"You dispense with the idea of God, the problem goes away."

Cassidy held the calico kitten in her palm. Its eyes were sealed, its ears rounded flaps. The lion-shaped head, too heavy for the tiny body to support, snuffled her hand. "Just look at this kitten. Every cell in my body wants to believe that all newborns arrive in a state of total innocence, and evil exists only because some people get so beaten up and brutalized they develop an endless supply of rage. But as I got deeper and deeper into this case, I started thinking that maybe we don't start off so innocent after all. Maybe we all have an evil part—a kind of little Satan inside our heads. A part we have to constantly fight off in order to be decent human beings. Sort of like the concept of original sin."

"Bullshit."

"Yeah, I guess you're right. I certainly like the modern, psychological, everyone-starts-with-a-clean-slate version better."

The kitten squawked, emitting more decibels than seemed possible for so small a creature. Starshine rose out of her box, dark eyes peering anxiously, to sniff at it.

"So why can't I make it go away?"

"What?"

"Victoria Kramer's voice telling me—some people are born evil."

Did you miss the first
Cassidy McCabe mystery?

It's every therapist's worst nightmare!
When a client apparently commits suicide
and blames his therapy as the reason, Cass must work to clear
her name and find the killer.

"Cass McCabe is an empathic and believable addition to
the crime scene." — *Sara Paretsky*

FREE subscription to our mystery catalog
Fill out the coupon below or call
1-800-99-MYSTERY. Act now! Don't miss out
on your favorite mystery series.
And, log on to our web site to get FREE sample
chapters, author signing schedules, and more.
http://www.intriguepress.com/mystery

Intrigue Press

Bringing you the finest in Mystery, Suspense, and Adventure fiction.

If your favorite bookstore doesn't carry Intrigue Press titles, ask them to order for you.

Most stores can place special orders through their wholesalers or directly with us. So, don't go without your favorite books — order today!

And if you liked this book, recommend it to your friends!